MOLLY'S MILESTONE

Marlys Beider

Molly's Milestone

Copyright © 2024 Marlys Beider. All rights reserved. No part of this book may be reproduced or retransmitted in any form or by any means without the written permission of the publisher.

Published by Wheatmark®
2030 East Speedway Boulevard, Suite 106
Tucson, Arizona 85719 USA
www.wheatmark.com

ISBN: 979-8-88747-171-6 (paperback)
ISBN: 979-8-88747-172-3 (hardcover)
ISBN: 979-8-88747-173-0 (ebook)
LCCN: 2024904315

Bulk ordering discounts are available through Wheatmark, Inc. For more information, email orders@wheatmark.com or call 1-888-934-0888.

This is a work of fiction. Unless otherwise indicated, all the names, characters, businesses, places, events and incidents in this book are either the product of the author's imagination or used in a fictitious manner. Any resemblance to actual persons, living or dead, or actual events is purely coincidental.

Other books by Marlys Beider

Fateful Parallels
Continuum
I Am Here

To Fran—
—and to all worthy of love and trust

Some stories are true that never happened.

—Elie Wiesel

ACKNOWLEDGMENTS

Great thanks to everyone on the Wheatmark team! Special thanks to Daniel Beider, Aimee Carbone, Frances Epsen, Olivia Geyelin, Jerry Spivack, and to Susan Wenger for your professional knowledge, inspiration, patience, and many valuable contributions.

My heartfelt gratitude goes to the readers for breathing life into these pages and for bringing joy into my journey.

PROLOGUE

"Molara!"

I look up from the pretty flowers I'm drawing for Mamá. A huge man who looks like the unfriendly giant in "Jack and the Beanstalk" is staring down at me.

"Vámonos!" The grisly-looking man bends closer. Why is he sweating so much?

"Your papi and your abuelo sent me. They're waiting outside with a big surprise for you." His voice is dark.

"No." I shake my head. "I don't know you."

He points to his uniform. "I'm with airport security; you can trust me! We must hurry or your surprise will be gone."

"No!" I don't like his creepy smile, and why is he blinking so fast? "Go away!"

"Tranquila," he grumbles and yanks me off the floor. My flower picture falls out of my hand and flutters down, next to Mamá's overnight bag.

"Let go of me!"

He jams my head against his shoulder.

Stop. I want to yell, but my mouth is pressed against his body.

With one eye I peek over the giant's shoulder. A man with a big red scar across his cheek is pulling Marisol. He also wears a uniform, but I recognize him; he's one of abuelo's bodyguards. Did abuelo tell the giant and red-scar man to disguise themselves? Are they the seekers in the game we are playing? Then why are they so grim and mean? And why does Marisol look so scared?

I press my hands against the giant's chest to free my mouth. "I don't know you! Let me go," I shout and bang my fists against his arm. He shoves my head hard against his shoulder. "Ow! You're hurting me. Let go of me, you bad monster!"

"Be quiet," he growls. With his huge hand he pushes my face into his stinky, sweaty neck.

I kick my shoes against his fat tummy. "Stop! Please stop!" I cry into the giant's smelly skin.

Abuelo's bodyguard and Marisol are still behind us. She's punching him; he's dragging her.

I twist my head to the side so I can breathe. "Let me down! Please!"

A man is trying to block the giant; he speaks in a language I don't understand.

The monster says a bad word in Spanish and starts to run.

A woman yells, "¡Ayuda!"

More people are shouting.

When I scream, the monster presses his huge hand over my mouth. That's when I bite him in his fat finger.

He says that bad swear word again and whacks me on the head. *Ow!*

He's running through a door. We're outside now.

I hear him huff and puff.

"Let go of me!" I kick my shoes against the monster's belly. "¡Quiero a mi mamá!"

"Cállate," he grunts and says another really, really, really bad word.

I bang my fists against his chin, his nose, his eye. I dig my fingernails into his face and scrape down his skin as hard as I can.

"Tu putita de mierda," he grunts and shoves my head into his stinky, sweaty neck again.

I bite into his skin. It tastes very bad, but I keep biting. Harder. Deeper.

He lets out a yelp and whacks me with his big hand.

"OW!"

I keep punching and kicking, and like the slimy earthworms in Mamá's flower garden, I wiggle and twist until I slip through his sweaty arms and drop onto the sidewalk. The monster's hands reach for me, but I jump to my feet and run into the wide road.

A blue car speeds past me. "Amelia?" I chase after it. So many cars; they all honk at me. Where is the blue one now? I stop and turn and look. More cars are honking. I run forward, then stop and spin around. Looking. Searching.

"Mamá! Miggy! Marisol!"

What if Mamá and Miggy are still in the shop looking for a stuffed animal? I must hurry back inside the airport, warn them about the ugly, horrible giant and the red-scar man.

"Molly! No!"

Marisol? I turn and run towards the familiar voice, and a loud car horn frightens me. "Stop!" I scream at the huge black car rushing towards me. "NO!"

ONE

Mateo, March 2019
Mira, Wisconsin

Mateo Miraldo fumbled for the remote and turned off the television. The late-night shows, the repetitious news, even the old movies had failed to catch his attention. Vacantly he looked at the now silent and dark fifty-five-inch Samsung screen in the middle of his baroque entertainment center.

Damn Ambien! Why wasn't it working? He rubbed his burning, tired eyes.

He thought of the vital years on his vast estates in Mexico, where daily dares thrilled him and nightly passion rewarded him with hours of peaceful sleep. How he missed the beauty of the country and its culture, longed to sing ranchera music again and listen to mariachi bands. How he thirsted for his abundant adventures.

All gone now. Why had he failed to anticipate the chicanery of those he trusted? How dare Manoel, his flesh and blood, betray him? Mateo gazed into the absence of light for answers. But instead of solace, unpleasant scenes continued to twirl through his head.

And what was wrong with Pelón? Was he in hiding?

"I did what needed to be done," the bald bodyguard had said. Did that mean Pelón had killed the old man? "Do not call me! I'll know how and when to get in touch with you" was all he'd said before disconnecting the call.

Mateo squeezed his eyes shut, struggling to recall any gratifying memory, but as soon as he managed to retrieve a well-defined, attractive image, it got crushed by more upsetting reflections.

By now it had been over two weeks since Pelón told him to destroy the burner phone and wait. With so much at stake, how much longer should Mateo wait, especially after paying the bodyguard an enormous amount of money? More intrusive thoughts triggered Mateo's anxiety. He felt weird; his heart was pounding.

Cursing into the darkness, Mateo realized that his yesterdays were by now far more numerous than what was left of his tomorrows. Even if he still had time to make all the wrongs right, how would he do it? He groaned as he envisioned his own footprints in the graveyard of unresolved desires.

How many decades had passed since he'd asked Marta to move out of their bedroom? As he counted backwards, flashes from the past became alive again behind his heavy lids.

Booming music stung his senses when he opened the doors to her studio. Marta was standing several feet away from her easel, loudly singing along with whoever that foreign pop group was. Her right hand held the brush in midair, ready to put new strokes on her newest creation. Her reddish-brown hair trailed to the middle of her back, glistening like polished mahogany. Under a kimono, flowing with wild abstract print, she wore only a purple bra and tight matching shorts. Her motley attire mirrored her newest creation, like she wanted to morph into her work.

She stopped singing and, without turning around, asked, "Mateo Miraldo! What brings me the honor?"

"I can't hear myself think," he shouted. "Turn it off!"

Giving him a challenging look, she lifted the tonearm off the record to replace it on its resting spot. "Bet you never even heard of the Beatles," she grinned. After cleaning off her brush, she wiped her hands on the colorful kimono. "Well, why are you here?" Mateo swallowed. Even in her bizarre outfit, Marta managed to look exotic. Striking. Despite having had two children and being a lover of food, there wasn't an ounce of fat on her body; her skin was smooth like alabaster, her face almost free of wrinkles. Even though Mateo had long ago fallen out of love with his wife, pangs of jealousy returned whenever he thought of the stream of accolades Marta received from people; admiration and applause that should have been his. To this day, Mateo envied her sparkling spirit and zest for life. Those attributes had not only had a magnetic effect on him the first time he'd laid eyes on her, but her striking features and bubbly personality still magnetized everyone she met. Fucking Marta, he thought, so stunning, yet cunning.

He cleared his throat. "I'm sorry you were diagnosed with catathrenia, Marta, but that's the reason why I'm here." He cleared his throat again. "It will benefit both of us not to share quarters anymore. The sounds you emit with every single expiration of breath keep me up all night." Hoping to look weary, he rubbed his eyes. "You are my wife and I respect you, but without seven hours of sleep, I simply can't function." Trying to camouflage his boredom, Mateo hoped he sounded empathetic. But he really was tired of her and the monotony, fed up with the lack of variety and the night-and-day-sameness of it all.

Marta shrugged and nonchalantly said, "Who are you trying to fool, Mateo? It's your international exploits that keep you out of our bedroom, not my mild form of catathrenia." With a dismissive grin, she lifted each finger as she counted his paramours. "Let's see—first there was Yolanda, then Lisette and Norma, followed by Kate, Maria, and Francesca."

Mateo felt his face redden, more in anger than surprise. "As usual, you don't know what you're talking about."

"As a matter of fact, I trust the sources that keep me informed. Not just about your appetite for women and flattery—it's all the other dishonest things you've gotten up to."

"Your sources?" To this day, Marta still baffled him; he loathed the way she wielded her sharp wits like a weapon. Mateo threw his head back, forcing a laugh. "Are you referring to the stories your father kept fabricating about me? That man never liked me, never gave me credit for being a self-made man."

"Self-made?" Marta plopped herself down onto the small sofa under the skylight. "Did you forget that my father was instrumental in starting your business? Not only did he finance you, but he also introduced you to the most influential people in Mexico."

Mateo stared at her when she spread her arms across the backrest of the sofa, and for a second the kimono opened, exposing some of her body. His eyes narrowed when she pulled the fabric over what he still considered to be his property. Though he had no proof, he suspected she had a secret lover. But the few times he'd instructed his moles to dig up dirt, they'd returned with empty hands. He squared himself in front of her. "So what? It's not my fault your father died before I could pay him back. But since I afforded his daughter to live the life of a queen in majestic homes all over Mexico, travel on private yachts and planes, and stay in the presidential suites of the finest hotels while being adorned with jewelry, I think I repaid . . ."

"Mateo! Stop!" Marta pulled the kimono even tighter around her slender body. "You may still manage to trick your global goddesses with your good looks, your wealth, and your promises, but your attempts to pacify me stopped working long ago."

"What the heck are you talking about?"

"The only blessing that came out of our marriage is our two sons. I love Marco and Manoel unconditionally and have an unbreakable bond with them. One day they will understand why I refuse to interfere with the relationship they individually still need to form with you."

"Marta, I came here in good faith to discuss something simple. Why do I have to listen to all this gobbledygook? What the heck are you trying to tell me?"

"I'm done with you and demand a legal separation immediately. But until Marco and Manoel are old enough to understand the severity of what's going on, I insist on living in one of the guest houses on the estate; I already hired an architect to draw up plans for the addition."

Baffled, Mateo watched Marta cross the room. "I don't give a damn where you live, but what do you mean by . . . until Marco and Manoel are old enough to understand the severity of . . ." He threw his hands into the air. ". . . of fucking what?"

"The truth!" Marta opened the door and motioned him to leave. "The truth is about to surface, and when it does, it will be the death of all your joy, Mateo Miraldo."

"*Thetruththetruththetruth* . . ."

Her voice echoed in his head so clearly, it ripped his eyes open. As Mateo groped for his water glass, he glanced at the digital clock, realizing he had slept for less than an hour. "That dream was so damn realistic, like it was yesterday," he whispered and stared at the dark shadows, expecting a reply. "Nobody ever appreciated when, after the separation, I continued to be more than generous with Marta. I never questioned her comings and goings. For many years I let her live in the most lavish of the guest houses on my estate," he mumbled, hoping the ghosts of the past would understand and finally leave him alone. But . . .

A month before Marta turned fifty years of age, she began to vanish in the labyrinth of early-onset Alzheimer's. Under the watchful eyes of Marco and Manoel, Mateo promised his sons their mother would always be properly cared for in her ample quarters. But as time went on, Manoel was the only one who spent time with his mother, whereas Marco's fleeting visits became less and less frequent.

On the rare occasions of Mateo's own compulsory drop-ins, he found Marta smiling and singing while painting demonic creatures on endless canvases. Trapped in the prison of her abandoned mind, she was unaware of her own beauty and the great talent that had made her a celebrated artist. She did not remember that the Galeria de Arte Moderno had several of her paintings on permanent exhibition and that most of her creations were sold to private collectors.

Manoel was devastated when Marta failed to recognize him and his brother, addressing her sons by various god names from Aztec mythology. And he immediately fired two caretakers who referred to Marta as the *compassionate cuckoo* behind the family's back.

For years Marta caused no problems to others, but as soon as it was brought to Mateo's attention that his estranged wife had begun painting the canvases with her own bodily waste, he had no choice but to admit her into a private and very expensive memory care facility. Complications with the decline in her brain function led to her early death at age fifty-nine.

Mateo sighed and turned on his back again, desperate in his need to forget past miseries. When was the last time he'd felt a warm body next to his? He reached for his groin and groaned. Why was it so difficult to zero in on the rapture of countless nights of pleasure, when he'd showered his paramours with promises that were meant to be broken? Now the nights had become his enemies. Watching television kept him awake. Reading a book only helped on rare occasions.

What he truly hungered and thirsted for was one exceptional woman, the one his heart painfully ached for.

"Ula-Ula," he whispered. "My Ula! It's only been you I've wanted!" How he longed for lust and passion to return, to experience the exquisite exhaustion and the deep, dreamless sleep afterwards.

He rolled from his left side to his right and then onto his back again, scrutinizing his life, scanning himself.

Wasn't he still in good shape for his age? His diet had always been relatively healthy. To this day, a personal trainer put Mateo through a methodical workout four times a week. He very much enjoyed hearing from others how handsome, hale, and hearty he looked at eighty-two.

Still, his body had started to play tricks on him. Shortly after his eightieth birthday, his physician had told him he had elderly-onset rheumatoid arthritis and hypertension.

Mateo kicked the damask sheet and brocade duvet cover aside. *Fucking old age.* He lay still for a while, letting his mind go as dark as the hours of night.

Suddenly he felt a chill and fumbled to retrieve the sheet again. With another groan, he pulled it all the way over his shoulders, up to his chin. He rolled onto his right side and clasped the long body bolster tightly to his chest and abdomen, like he was spooning another body. He closed his eyes and pressed his lips to the soft pillow.

When he woke, it was still dark and he felt confused. Where had she gone? Hadn't she just been here? Next to him in his bed? He still tasted her magnificent body, distinctly heard her fruity voice.

"You're right, she's more than magnificent," he told Robert Graf when the banker introduced his daughter Ursula in Switzerland. She soon became his Aphrodite, and he plotted a scheme, a ruse that would backfire years later in the worst way imaginable.

But back then, the Miraldo-Graf arrangement worked as planned. The moment his son Marco, hand-in-hand with Ursula, walked into the foyer of the grand old hacienda in Mexico, Mateo promised himself he'd be patient. There was no need to hurry; according to Mateo's formula, this gorgeous young woman—this magnificent creature that took his breath away—would one day be his alone.

There she was, in that lilac silk organza dress, its transparent fabric silhouetting long legs, narrow hips, and firm, developed breasts. A few strands of her wavy honey-blond hair had escaped from her loose ponytail, brushing against her golden-tanned skin. And when she held out her hand, Mateo took it into both of his. He cradled her fingers for too long; he simply had no desire to let go. Her green eyes, her straight-edged nose, the dimple in her right cheek, and those plump rosy lips kept him hypnotized from that very moment.

"My Ula," Mateo whispered as these recollections echoed into the now. "Why did you leave me when everything was so perfect?"

He felt dizzy, suddenly nauseous, exposed. He gasped for air, yearning to retrieve the moments when nights were filled with delicious scents. He gasped again. What was happening? He touched his forehead, then his chest. He felt peculiar.

Mateo tried to focus. And suddenly, in the absence of light, he saw a shadow. He lifted his head. A silent storm grabbed hold of his emotions.

"¡Mi cielito! Don't go! Come back here!" When he stood up, he felt the room tilt and reached for the nightstand. With a sigh, he sank onto the edge of the bed again. "Come here," he pleaded and strained his eyes against the darkness. He sniffed. There it was. The delicious fragrance of pheromones, mixed with the scent of her fresh hair and young body; it made him feel lightheaded.

Trembling, his hand searched for the remote control to turn on the lights. He cursed when he heard it drop on the floor. The darkness remained. His chest felt tight, his throat was dry. He hesitantly sucked in air, not wanting to remember the taboo, the criminal and verboten—the unforgivable.

There was a rustle. Was that her shadow?

"Ula? Where are you going? Don't leave!" He stood up and stumbled forward. There! He knew it. It was her. So beautiful, so young. He chuckled hesitantly, and then, with overwhelming happiness, he laughed out loud. "Ula, ¡mi cielito!" Determinedly, he took another step closer and leaned forward. "Ula-Ula, mi amor," he breathed and giddily reached out to touch her.

TWO

Ursula, June 1992
Coyoacán, Mexico

When she arrived with her twins at the annual Fiesta Miraldo, she didn't see the colorful spectacle, nor did she hear the loud chatter of guests competing with amplified pop music by Vida Viva, the voguish and highly in-demand Latin band.

Would Ursula be punished by a higher power for her risky plan? Would she be damned?

She repeated Thucydides's words to herself: *The secret to happiness is freedom . . . and the secret to freedom is courage.* If ever there was an opportunity, today would be it. Courage!

Earlier in the day, she'd told Marco she didn't feel well enough to attend the event. "Let me stay home with the children," she'd pleaded in a feeble voice. "It would be better for Miguel anyway; you know he has trouble with big crowds."

But her scheme had slammed into a wall of ice.

"¿Estas loca? My Portuguese grandfather started this tradition in 1902," Marco yelled, wagging his index finger. "Nobody—*nobody*—ever misses it!"

She tried again, feigning migraine and nausea—she so needed the extra hours to execute her plan—but he threw several bottles of prescription meds at her. "Pick one," he challenged. "Or better, take them all. The combo will numb your malaise."

You should know. She pushed the bottles off the bed and turned away from him. But he yanked the sheet off her, lifted her body as if she were a lifeless doll, and planted her feet solidly on the bedside rug. He grabbed her by the shoulders, his face a few inches from hers. "You will take a shower and fix yourself up!" He thrust his face even closer and tightened his grip. "I'm going to tell you something now and you better listen. You will *not* embarrass me. If you do, I will hurt you in ways you've never dreamed of. Do you hear me?"

She nodded hastily.

"Good. ¡Estoy harta de tu locura! I'm going to watch you like a hawk."

She nodded again, even more hurriedly than before.

"Stop bobbing your head—you look like a marionette." Still muttering insults, he went into her closet and pulled out a Pierre Cardin haute couture red silk strapless cocktail dress and a pair of high-heeled sandals. He laid them on the bed. "There! Get ready!"

"Okay, Marco," she said, looking him in the eyes and willing her face to relax. "The children and I will make you proud." With a sphinxlike smile, she kept nodding until he was out of the room.

Through damp lashes, Ursula eyed the exquisite dress, with its dramatic red silk flower smack in the middle of the wide black waistband. Though the dress and uncomfortable stiletto sandals wouldn't have been her choice, she knew to keep any further objections to herself.

Marco must believe he's in charge, especially today. She resolved to behave in accordance with all the absurd Miraldo rules, hopefully for the last time.

She picked up the dress and pressed it against her body, pitying her reflection in the mirror. What had become of her vigor, her ambition? She let go of the red gown and watched it puddle around her feet like a shallow pool of blood, then lifted her chin and pointed at her image. "The secret to happiness is freedom . . . and the secret to freedom is courage."

But her determination melted away as soon as she saw the crowd of people. Despite the pleasant summer warmth, Ursula's whole body felt cold. The chills were symptoms of her anxiety; like unwanted boarders, she couldn't get rid of them. Holding Molara on her left and Miguel on her right, she clasped their warm little hands tightly, seeking strength from their purity and innocence.

Her husband, already several meters ahead, excitedly embraced friends and other guests. His deep voice resonated like a tuba in this orchestra of human inflections. He laughed loudly, and Ursula shivered.

The secret to happiness is freedom . . . and the secret to freedom is courage. Those words played like a refrain in her head, accompanied by a heartbeat as fast as a galloping horse. She had trouble concentrating. As if programmed, she walked a few steps behind Marco, oblivious to heads turning and gazes fixing on her.

"It's too hot here. Too many people," Miguel wailed, tugging on his dress shirt, about to shrug out of it.

Ursula bent down. "We won't stay long, Miggy, I promise," she said gently. "As soon as we get home, we'll play a surprise game. Molly and you will have fun."

"Yes!" Molly leaned forward, nodding encouragement at her brother. "We love surprises."

"I want to leave right now," Miggy insisted.

"Get this kid under control," Marco hissed into Ursula's ear while pretending to kiss her. Behind him stood a stylishly dressed couple.

"Meet Ula, my magnificent wife. Tomás and Lucia Gonzalo." He made the introduction with his usual winsome smile. "And these are my twins, Molara and Miguel."

"Indeed!" Tomás said to Ursula. "Your husband isn't exaggerating; you're beautiful. Where are you from? Sweden?"

Before Ursula could answer, Marco put his arm around her shoulders and pulled her closer to him, away from the children. "Before we got married, my Ula was a fashion model and more—a contestant for Miss Switzerland."

"Oh, that explains it," Tomás Gonzalo said, nodding mischievously. "Then, *you* must be the reason for the big plus in the Swiss flag!" Without taking his eyes off Ursula, he gave Marco a thumbs-up.

"Molara and Miguel." Lucia Gonzalo bent down to the children, touching their cheeks. "You're twins? You don't look alike. How old are you?"

"They're four," Marco answered, distractedly tapping the top of his children's heads.

"Papi! The lady asked me. I can tell her myself," Molly protested. She lifted her chin and looked Lucia in the eye. "We turned four years old a week ago, on the first of June. And the reason we don't look alike is because we're fraternal twins. We don't have the same DNA. Miggy has the XY chromosomes, and I have the XX chromosomes."

"Oh my!" Lucia straightened. "What a bright little girl you are. You know more than I do. Are you sure you're only four years old?"

"Too many people here!" Miguel wailed louder. "It's hot. I want to go home."

"Ehm." Marco abruptly released Ursula from his embrace and turned his back on her and the children. He put his right arm around Tomás's shoulder and hooked his left with Lucia's arm. "Allow me to show you my family's latest art acquisition—you of all people will appreciate it." He glanced back and gave his wife a brief side nod, indicating that she needed to control Miguel. "I'm ready for a cocktail. How about you?" he asked the stylish couple.

Molly's eyes narrowed as she watched her father disappear in the crowd, and she pulled on her mother's hand.

"Mamá, we're thirsty, too! Can we get limonada?"

Ursula looked around. No waitstaff was nearby. She led the children to an empty table, shaded by an old Mexican fan palm.

"You two stay here in the cool shade. I'll get limonada," she said.

Miguel tugged on his shirt again and threw himself on the ground, pressing his face into the grass.

"I know you're warm, sweet boy." Ursula quickly lifted her son onto the chair. "Would you like your sister to tell you the story about the hippo and the bee?" She fastened the two buttons on his shirt again. "Please leave it on. You know Papi doesn't like when—"

"But it's too hot. Too many people," Miguel said, squirming to slide off the chair.

"Watch this, Miguelito." Molara removed a small palm leaf from the elaborate centerpiece and waved it up and down in front of her brother's face. "It's a fan, just like the one over your bed."

Ursula rewarded her daughter with a grateful smile. "I'll be right back."

But she was wrong. Before she could find a server, she was constantly stopped by members of the Miraldo clan and their international guests.

"Ula! So good to see you. Feeling better?" Danilo Costas said, nodding approvingly while looking her up and down.

"Yes, we heard you'd been under the weather for some time," Lola Costas said. "But you certainly look well now."

What were they talking about? Had Marco found excuses when he showed up without her at some event? Before Ursula could answer, she was being pulled into the arms of Mireille Bardot.

"Pierre and I have not seen you in forever. Where have you been hiding? We miss you, chérie."

"Can I catch up with you later? I need to fetch some lemonade for my children, they're—" But when she turned, Pedro Castro, one of Marco's shadier friends, was blocking her path.

"¡Mi amor! Como siempre, te ves divina."

"Nice to see you, Pedro." Ursula stepped back before he could hug and kiss her.

"Will you attend the José Luis Cuevas Museum opening? I'd like you and Marco to be my guests at the gala afterwards."

She nodded hastily. "Thank you, something to look forward to." She excused herself.

"¿Cuándo vendrás a visitarnos en Cuernavaca?"

Good grief, she had no idea who this couple was.

"Love your dress, Ursula," said the woman. "Has got to be Cardin couture. Am I right?"

"Leave it to Marco," said the man. "He knows what looks good on his ladies."

In a trancelike state, Ursula kept shaking hands, tolerated hugs—some almost too intimate—and waited for the right moment to free herself from the smothering jet set.

"There she is! My magnificent daughter-in-law," Mateo bellowed. The patriarch and host of Fiesta Miraldo separated the crowd with an outstretched arm, briskly walking towards Ursula. As the guests dutifully moved out of his path, a friendly voice shouted, "Ay Mateo, you look like Moses parting the Red Sea—all you need is a staff." Cheers and laughter followed.

Mateo stopped in front of Ursula. "¡Magnifico!" His eyes lingered on her before he pulled her into a tight embrace. "I missed you," he breathed into her ear.

"I said it before and I say it again," he announced loudly. "The first time Ula entered this house, she was the most exquisite gift Marco brought to the family." Mateo stretched his neck, as if to look over the gathering. "Where is that lucky son of mine?"

Despite her unease, Ursula forced herself to make small talk with people she didn't care about and guests she'd never met before; if everything went according to plan, she would never have to see any of them again. Her mind buzzing with activity, she thought of the next few hours.

"Please excuse me," she said and stepped away from the group to stop a server carrying an empty tray.

"Can you bring two glasses of limonada to my children, please?" She turned to indicate the table under the Mexican fan palm and saw that a small crowd had formed there. A chill ran down her spine when she heard her son's high-pitched shriek.

"Excuse me," she said again and slithered away from Mateo, who was about to introduce her to another one of his illustrious guests.

Molly stood by the table, looking flushed, wiping tears away.

"He's crazy, Mamá," she sobbed. "I couldn't stop him." She pointed under the table.

Part of the white cloth had been flipped over the tabletop, covering a portion of the floral centerpiece. Miggy's shirt, pants, and shoes lay scattered on the grass.

"No!" Ursula called, but it was too late. Her son had already pulled off his underwear, throwing it next to his shoe.

An elderly couple gasped and shook their heads. "Something is wrong with that boy," said the woman.

"Where on earth are the parents?" said the man. They turned and walked away.

Ursula crouched down, blocking her son's nudity from the bystanders' stares.

"Miggy, let's put your clothes back on."

"No!" He drew his knees to his chin. "Don't want to."

Ursula felt perspiration form under her thick hair; slowly it trickled down her spine. Every second under the table became increasingly claustrophobic, as if she were being held captive in yet another prison.

Don't abandon the plan!

"Go away," she heard Molly say to the onlookers. "Stop staring at my brother. He's not feeling well."

The lump in Ursula's throat was getting thicker, and she barely had control over her shaking hands. She had to stay calm.

With her index finger she lifted Miggy's face. "Remember how scared the little bee was, sitting all by herself because her wings were broken, and she couldn't fly across the river? Just like you, she felt too warm in the sun; she was very thirsty and wanted to return to her hive."

Miggy remained in a tight knot of arms, legs, and chin; the knuckles of his locked fingers were white, his eyelids clenched.

"Can you tell me who came to her rescue?" Ursula said, fumbling for her son's clothes.

Without looking up, the little boy nodded. "The hippo."

"Okay, if you pretend to be the tiny bee, then I'll be the big hippo." Ursula pulled the underpants and dark-blue slacks over Miggy's legs and hips. "As soon as the bee hops on the hippo's nose, the hippo takes her across the water to her hive, her sanctuary." She fastened the buttons of Miggy's shirt. "Just like the hippo, I'll take you home, where you'll be safe."

Her son looked up. "Talk like the bee," he said with a pale smile.

While tying the laces on his shoes, she made her voice high and tiny. "My wings may be broken, but I am still strong. I will make it home to where I belong." She winked at her little boy. "Now, can you tell me what the hippo says?"

Miggy shook his head. "You do! And talk like the hippo."

And in the lowest voice she could manage, she recited, "I too like your home 'cause there's plenty to eat. A lot of thick grasses and flowers so sweet. I may look scary and huge like a brute. But rather than meat, I eat grasses and fruit."

Ursula pulled her son from under the table and in one fluid move stood up, holding on to him tightly. She heard his soft whimper when he faced the onlookers.

"Miggy, put your head on my shoulder and close your eyes until we get home."

She looked between the remaining few spectators for Molly, trying to avoid their glances.

A middle-aged woman, wearing a royal blue organza hat as big as a wheel, shook her head. "Your boy was naked," she said sharply in an unmistakably British accent. "Outrageous." The man next to her stiffly agreed.

Ursula pretended to be unperturbed. She spotted her little daughter standing behind the palm tree, sticking her tongue out at the woman and the man.

"Here you are!" Ursula heard Marco's booming voice before she saw him coming towards her in his brand-new, off-white suit. "What happened?"

"Miggy isn't feeling well. I'm taking the children home."

"How many times do I have to tell you to stop calling them by those baby names? They're Miguel and Molara. And. You. Are. Not. Leaving," he hissed into her ear. "Benito will take the children home and Marisol can—"

As Marco attempted to pry his son's hands from Ursula's neck and shoulders, Miggy shrieked and attached himself even more tightly.

It was then that Molly planted herself between her father and mother. "No, Papi! Mamá needs to go home with us. She didn't even want to come. She felt sick, but you didn't care."

Marco let out a half-suppressed laugh, glancing at the people watching the scene, some of them his good friends. "My feisty little Molara," he said with a sheepish laugh. He bent down to pick her up, but she stepped aside. He stumbled and collided with his wife.

Carrying Miggy, Ursula lost her balance, and as if in slow motion, the three of them fell against the table, overturning it.

Two nearby servants set down their trays and, together with a couple of partygoers, rushed over to help.

"Excuse me! Excuse me!" Mateo pushed his way forward and stared at the chaos on the grass. "What the hell is going on here?" He pulled his son off Ursula and told his grandson to stop crying. He bent down to her and whispered, "Did Marco hit you? Did he push you?"

"No, it was an accident," Ursula said, quickly drawing the red dress over her exposed thighs. Mateo offered his hand to pull her off the grass, but she shook her head and, in a swift move, stood up by herself. Miggy attached himself to her leg and buried his face in the fabric of her dress.

"I'm going to take the children home now," she declared without looking at her husband or father-in-law. "Once Miggy calms down, Marisol will take over and I'll join the party again."

As Ursula walked away from the scene with her twins, she felt Mateo's commanding eyes on her, as if he was trying to pull her back to him. *The secret to freedom is courage.* She quickened her step, hoping her absence wouldn't be missed until long after her escape.

THREE

Ursula, thirty minutes later

How long had she waited for this day? When Marco forced her to attend the annual event, she'd feared her one-time chance to get away was being sucked down the drain. Luckily, the long-awaited golden opportunity had received the kiss of life from Miggy. His conduct, his problems with social interactions, had reopened Ursula's window to freedom.

"Really? Papi will play escondidas with us?" Molly looked surprised. "He never likes playing any game."

"Abuelo's played escondidas," Miggy said. "But he thinks it's stupid."

Ursula hoped the twins wouldn't see her flushed face or notice her shaking hands as she helped them change into jeans, T-shirts, and sneakers. "We have to hurry before they start looking for us," she said. "Where are your baseball hats?"

"Papi won't get mad if I wear my Superman hat?"

Ursula shook her head. "Not this time, Miggy."

Molly opened a drawer and removed a Pac-Man hat. "This one will hide my face," she said and pulled the visor below her eyebrows.

"Yay. Disguise." Miggy clapped his hands and mimicked his sister.

"Quick. Quick." Ursula handed each of them their backpacks. "Remember, we have to be v-e-r-y careful, so we won't be seen."

Molly put her index finger over her lips. "And v-e-r-y quiet so we won't be heard, right?"

Miggy's eyes widened. "Like an adventure." He ran to his toy chest. "Can Julio play hide-and-seek with us, Mamá?" He pressed his small gray stuffed elephant tightly to his chest.

"Can Rosi?" Molly waved her favorite baby doll.

"Yes, yes."

"And Marisol? Will she come with us to play the game?"

"Definitely!"

Ursula exchanged her Pierre Cardin attire for a pair of jeans, a nondescript shirt, and comfortable shoes. She wiped the lipstick off her lips, removed the mascara, and braided her hair into a thick single braid, which she tucked under a dark-gray baseball cap.

"¡Vamos con prisa!" Ursula motioned Marisol to follow her to the storage area. Several weeks ago they had packed their most essential personal effects into two suitcases that hadn't been used in years and hidden them behind the newer, pricier pieces of luggage in the storage room. They removed these two old cases from the back, then Marisol rearranged the remaining luggage and pulled the plastic over it to make it look as it had before.

Ursula turned to the opposite wall; stacked vinyl boxes were neatly lined up on racks.

"One, two, three, four," she counted, tapping the top of each box to make sure she didn't waste precious minutes. The fourth stack contained no-longer-needed baby clothes. Quickly she pulled out Molly's rainbow-colored sleeper, zipped it open, and removed three passports, four airline tickets, and two credit cards. From the fold of a baby blanket she extracted a pouch filled with US currency.

She turned to Marisol. "Where's your passport?"

The other woman opened two buttons on her blouse and pointed to the pouch hanging on her chest. "It's been here since I received it."

Making sure everything looked orderly again, Ursula turned off the lights and closed the storage room door. She checked her watch. "We have to leave right now."

*

"Why are we using Marisol's car?" Miggy asked.

"Sh-sh-sh. Talk quiet, Miggy," Molly whispered. "Papi and abuelo are the seekers; they won't be looking for us in Marisol's car. Right, Mamá?"

"That's the plan," Ursula said, suddenly overcome by ambivalence. Was she doing the right thing, taking her children far away from everything familiar? She nodded, accepting her inner reply. "That's the hide-and-seek plan, Molly," she said more resolutely, but her hands trembled when she buckled the children into their car seats. "Do we have everything? Passports? Money? Credit cards?"

"Yes. Please stay calm," Marisol whispered back. "You're not alone in this. I'll be with you all the way!" She squeezed Ursula's hand. "I've long been praying for this day. For you, for the children, and for me." She made the sign of the cross and turned the key to ignite the engine.

Ursula was grateful for Marisol's forewarning not to use the main driveway or the servants' road that led to the hacienda. Too many cars would be blocking their way, and many of Mateo's wealthy guests had arrived with their personal bodyguards.

Ursula shivered as she thought of the Miraldo bodyguards. Hidden behind their sunglasses, they would be on constant alert, stretching their necks, turning their heads, making sure their wealthy employer was safe. What if Mateo or Marco had gotten suspicious already? What if they ordered one of their guards to check on her and the children? And what about the other protectors, the ones stationed in the watchtower? As soon as Marisol made a U-turn, Ursula glanced in the direction of the chapel; to her relief, the tall Montezuma cypress blocked the view from the chapel's steeple. She put both of her hands under her thighs to stop them from shaking but couldn't control her rapid heartbeat, still galloping like a racehorse. Her mouth was dry; fear made her squint behind her sunglasses.

"I'm going slow, so I don't draw anyone's attention," Marisol said as she pulled away from the back of the main house, then drove past the three guest houses. "Gracias y adiós, beautiful flower garden," Marisol whispered.

Ursula briefly let her eyes linger on thousands of colorful blossoms, on grounds she and Marisol had cultivated with love. *Goodbye, my only place of refuge. Goodbye, my blooming friends in my sanctuary.*

The car stopped in front of the massive wall that surrounded the vast acreage of the hacienda. Behind the tall iron gate lay a narrow dirt road, used only by workmen who arrived with heavy equipment.

"Duck!" Molly said.

"Why?" Miggy asked.

"Because we're playing hide-and-seek, Miggy. We don't want to be seen."

"Okay."

Ursula held her breath as Marisol punched in the numbers to open the heavy automated gate. What if they'd changed the combination, as they did at random times? It would take too long to use the key. *Please, please, please.* Not until she felt the car move again and heard the loud clank of closure behind her did Ursula dare to gasp for air. Her fast pulse ping-ponged from ear to ear, as though her racing heart had jumped from her chest to her head.

It being Sunday, the dirt road was empty, and as soon as Marisol increased their speed, a thick cloud of dust kicked up, almost as if to shield the car from anyone guarding the grounds of Hacienda Miraldo.

"¿Todavía tenemos que escondernos ahora, Mamá?" Miggy whispered.

"No, mi amor. You can sit up again."

The moment the tires rolled onto paved roads, Ursula stared straight ahead, embracing every new meter ahead that would separate her from the hellhole Mateo said could be hers one day.

Thank you, my Mamá Marta. Ursula wiped her eyes as she thought of her beloved mother-in-law.

Before her illness, and unbeknownst to her sons and estranged husband, Marta had established an account at Banco Salina Suisse for Ursula—wisely under a pseudonym. "The day will come when you need this," Marta had told her. "One never knows where your path of life will take you. Even a bad road can lead you to a better destination."

Ursula swallowed and blinked away a new tear. She turned around and looked at her children; they had fallen asleep. The twins' heads had fallen to the side, and their plump, rosy cheeks almost touched. They were holding hands. *I will protect your sweet innocence as long as I can. Only when you are old enough will I tell you the truth.*

"I miss Mamá Marta so much—without her, none of this would be possible," she said to Marisol.

"Sssh, the children."

"They're sound asleep."

"Did I ever mention I lied about my age when I started to work for the Miraldo family?" Marisol asked in a low voice.

"You didn't."

"I wasn't even sixteen years old but knew nobody under eighteen would be hired. So I put sand into my Chukka boots to make me look taller, stuffed my bras with tissue paper, and wore two skirts under my dress to plump up in all the right places." Marisol glanced at Ursula and winked. "¡Niña! You're smiling. I can't remember the last time I saw that."

"Please Marisol, tell me more. Even if I've heard some of it before, it'll take my mind off everything else."

"First I was hired as part of the staff to keep the immense U-shaped hacienda in impeccable condition. I must've proved myself capable because within a year I got promoted to oversee the household help."

"Mamá Marta said your honesty, competence, and reliability earned everybody's trust, especially hers."

Marisol nodded. "She and I soon formed a deep friendship; I became her confidante."

"You barely were older than Marco and Manoel. How did that go?"

"Manoel and I got along famously. He was just like his mother:

kind and humble, trustworthy and loving, always showing great compassion and generosity towards other people." Marisol paused, shaking her head. "Strange how Manoel's gentle demeanor stood in sharp contrast to the complete indifference and shameful side of his father and brother."

Ursula sighed. "That's why Manoel moved his family away from the hacienda. I wasn't allowed to visit them, and on those rare occasions he and Claudia stopped by with their kids, Mateo or Marco watched me like a hawk. They never left me alone with them. Why?"

"They didn't want you to learn of their dark secrets, like their two-timing tendencies and unprincipled footsteps."

"Mamá Marta said she desperately tried to reset her older son's course."

"And each time it broke her heart when she failed. Marco even intensified his playboy adventures. He was oblivious to his controversial associations and practically rubbed his extravagant and obscene lifestyle in his mother's face." Marisol looked in the rearview mirror and whispered, "I can't tell—are they still sleeping?"

Ursula nodded. "Please go on."

"That's why it took Marta and me by surprise when Mateo announced Marco's engagement to you, a lovely eighteen-year-old girl from Switzerland. But whereas Mateo was jubilant, Marco acted defiant. Soon, Marta and I suspected something fishy had to be behind that whole arrangement."

Ursula inhaled sharply and closed her eyes. "Worse than fishy," she muttered.

"And when Marta got to know you, she hoped your beauty, your pure soul, and your unsoiled character would somehow have an impact on Marco but—"

"On our wedding night he broke my heart when he told me I meant nothing to him. Then, less than a month after a spectacle of a wedding, Marco started to spend days and nights away from me. I was a stranger on foreign soil with no one to turn to." Ursula wiped her cheek. "I had no money and was clueless where Marco had hidden my passport. Sinister-looking men watched me all the time—I felt completely abandoned." She laid her hand on Marisol's arm. "I'll never forget the day when I sat by the fountain, unable to stop the flow of tears. And then an angel embraced me." Ursula looked at Marisol. "You offered solace and advice and eventually led me to my surrogate mom. I don't know how I would have survived those problematic years without you and Mamá Marta."

Marisol pulled a handkerchief from her shirt pocket and handed it to Ursula. "The day Marta and I were prepared to let you in on our suspicions, you suddenly withdrew from us. Marta always had a sixth sense; she feared something worse than Marco's infidelities was troubling you, a torment you were too embarrassed to share."

Ursula sniffled and wiped her nose. "You're right. I was horrified and so scared."

"And then, five years into your loveless marriage, Marco announced your pregnancy. Marta became hopeful again, especially six months later when, for the first time, she held her precious grandbabies in her arms."

Ursula closed her eyes, remembering the day Mamá Marta commented how Molara had inherited much of her looks from her Latin ancestry. Her inquisitive, sparkling hazel eyes and thick brown hair were identical to Marco and Mateo's, yet her character traits differed greatly. At three months old, she'd already showed a laissez-faire attitude, taking the craziness of the world around her in stride.

Miguel, with his wavy blond hair, clearly resembled his mother. But unlike his twin's even-tempered, inquisitive disposition, he had the tendency to jump whenever loud noises startled him. The little boy was sensitive, always averting his eyes from a stranger's gaze.

Ursula turned to look at her children. They had not moved, breathing in unison.

"Did you ever wonder about the bizarre Miraldo tradition that each offspring's name has to start with the letter *M* and that only the father can choose the name?" Marisol's voice suddenly sounded very unlike her.

"I once questioned Marco, but instead of an answer, he physically abused me." Ursula shuddered. "Do you know the reason behind the naming tradition?"

"I don't, but I know Marta planned on telling you. Unfortunately, her bouts of confusion and forgetfulness took over."

Both women turned silent.

Ursula looked up through the windshield. Was it her imagination, or did she see the shape of an angel in that fluffy white cloud? She sighed, thinking of the day her beloved mother-in-law returned from a visit to the doctors, who had confirmed Marta's worst fears. Adamant about not wanting to share her illness with her sons, estranged husband, or household help at the time, she'd pulled Marisol and Ursula into her arms. "As long as possible, let this be our secret. I still need time to bring all my affairs in order."

And without Ursula's knowledge, Marta had regularly arranged for additional money transfers into Ursula's pseudonymous account. "Once I can't handle my affairs anymore, you must turn to Bruno Rossi," Mamá Marta had said. "Aside from being my investment banker, he's my trusted friend. Bruno is well-informed about everything and sworn to secrecy. Whenever you decide to break away from here, Bruno will be there for you; he'll help you with anything you need."

When Marta's illness had become apparent to everybody, Bruno Rossi secretly contacted Ursula via Marisol. Not only did Ursula find out that Marta's generosity had made her a wealthy woman, but she also learned about highly confidential matters involving Marco and Mateo's unlawful business proceedings. "Always remember," Bruno had said, "this knowledge can threaten the Miraldo enterprises—but more importantly, it will ensure your and your children's safety."

Ursula watched the angel-like cloud slowly disappear. *Thank you. Without your love, my children and I would forever have to live in confinement.*

When they arrived at Mexico City International Airport, she leaned over to Marisol. "Stay in the car with the children," she said. "Unless there's a long line, I'll be back shortly."

"Where are you going, Mamá?" Molly said in a sleepy voice.

"Ssssh—remember we're playing hide-and-seek." Ursula held her index finger over her lips. "I'll be right back."

"Mamá!" Miguel wailed when he saw his mother walk away from the car with the luggage.

"Don't worry, Miguelito," Marisol said. "It's part of the game."

"Too many strangers out there," Miggy whined, pointing at travelers scurrying by. "If the seekers find us, they'll take us away from Mamá." He tried to open his seat buckle.

"Let's hide from the strangers," Molly whispered. She reached for her brother's light-blue security blanket and pulled it over both their heads. "See, no more people. Just Molly and Miggy."

"My blankie will keep us safe?"

"Yes." Molly took her brother's hand into hers. "You and I will always be safe together."

FOUR

Molly, April 2019
Mira, Wisconsin

It's been three weeks since the phone call woke me at 5:15 in the morning. Yoli, Pops's longtime housekeeper, was completely hysterical. She said she heard him yelp from his bedroom, followed by a loud thud. When she ran upstairs, she found Pops on the floor.

I watch him cursing someone in a low voice from his hospital bed. Carlos de La Fuente? *Have I heard that name before? Is Pops hallucinating again?*

I lean closer to his bed and take his hand. "It's okay. I'm here—the only one in the room." I talk calm and slow. His doctors advised me to speak to him in English; since his stroke, Pops has only talked in Spanish.

His expression changes from angry to surprised. "¿En serio?" He smiles at me and closes his eyes. Fifteen minutes later, he gesticulates and rambles again. He's damning a Benito and a León; he's putting the evil eye on someone by the name of Robert. Who are these people? Why does he look so angry and yet worried at the same time?

Yesterday, when I expressed my concerns to his physician, Dr. Mundt explained that confusion and memory loss are often the worst during the first month or so after a stroke. But I don't believe Pops's babble is just confusion. While I can't explain it, some of the weird stuff he says rings vaguely familiar.

I finally manage to calm him down. He is quiet now, staring at the ceiling. Suddenly he smiles and whispers something. I lean closer.

"Mi amor," he breathes. "You look magnificent in your silk organza dress. The way the light shines through it, I see your long legs, your breasts." His arms reach forward; he's moving his fingers. "Let me untie your ponytail."

"Pops?"

He turns his head towards me and his smile fades. "Molara? When did you get here?"

I caress his arm and lean closer. "I've been here like every morning before work."

He looks around the room. "Am I still in the rehab center?" He shakes his head. "Was I hallucinating again?" He suddenly seems concerned. "What did I say?"

"Nothing that made sense."

"Whatever it was, ignore it," he says, sounding relieved. "All that damn medicine gives me bad dreams."

"Don't worry. Both Dr. Mundt and Dr. Brandström say you're making great progress."

He's staring at the ceiling again. What is he thinking? I suppress a yawn and lean back into the chair. These past three weeks have been grueling. Ever since my father left town, I've been overloaded with work. And since Pops's illness, I haven't had a decent night of sleep. Last night was another unsettling one. I tried listening to guided sleep meditation with soothing background music, but the app's calming voices did nothing for me. It must have been close to four o'clock in the morning when I finally dozed off, only for Alexa to wake me up two hours later. I stumbled out of bed, and my little toe caught on the bedpost. It hurt like hell, but the pain woke me up!

Murphy's Law remained in effect throughout the day. At breakfast I grabbed a charred bagel from the toaster and burned my fingers. When I let go of the scalding thing, I knocked over my coffee mug and watched the very-much-needed brew spill from the shiny granite counter onto my white ash hardwood floor. By the time I cleaned up the mess, it was too late to make another cup. With no caffeine, I don't think clearly. That probably explains why I took the black-and-white Chanel dress with the Peter Pan collar off the hanger. Having to cut off the price tags should've made me realize I'd dislike this outfit—a present from my father when he came back from Paris. I have a hunch he intended to give the pricey haute couture dress to Ava—wife number four. But either the dress was too small on her or she also didn't like it.

As I raced out of the house, I caught a glimpse of my image in the mirror. Yikes! It was like a thirty-year-old version of Hermione Jean Granger from Hogwarts School of Witchcraft and Wizardry was staring back at me. Unfortunately, by then it was too late to change my outfit.

"Are you ready for me, Mr. Miraldo?" Gertie, the occupational therapist, is standing on the other side of Pops's bed. *Good grief, is it nine o'clock already?* I have a meeting at ten in downtown Milwaukee, and I'll be hitting rush-hour traffic. I assure Pops that I'll come back later this afternoon.

While the meeting at the law firm of Schuster, Driebold, and Fahey drags, the lack of ventilation in their crowded meeting room causes me to overheat in my long-sleeve dress. My sprained little toe throbs in the tight confinement of my low-heeled leather ankle boot. And the discussion goes nowhere. Nobody can agree on matters that matter, and months of previous negotiations are falling apart like overstuffed tacos.

It's not even noon yet when I drive back to Mira, and I don't look forward to the hours still ahead at MiraCo. I wish the day were over so I could get out of this dress and kick off these boots. I finish the last of the Starbucks Nitro Cold Brew with an extra shot of espresso, but not even this caffeine monster can give me the boost I need. These past three weeks, with atypical happenings piling on top of unexpected developments, have exhausted me.

My heavy lids rip open when a lightning bolt zigs and zags through the dark clouds, followed by a crash of thunder. I read once that lightning is a metaphor for human emotions and can ignite our deeper selves. Maybe the universe is trying to send me a hint, like *Hey Molly! Get away from it all. You deserve a nice long break!*

"Hi, Judy. Morning, Mike." I manage to smile when I wave at the receptionists at MiraCo Global Enterprises. Normally I take the staircase, but since my toe is throbbing in my boot, I head straight for the elevator.

Cliff. Heather. Maddie. I nod at staff and hobble past them in my Hogwarts-like uniform.

I give Attila a thumbs-up. "Excellent presentation yesterday."

"Morning, Carol. How's your daughter? Better?" I force another smile.

Finally I step into my office. Its recently refurbished glass-and-steel scheme feels like a needed icy compress on my face. Automatically, my elbow touches the sensor, and as soon as the heavy door closes, I lean my back against it. Cold. Nice. Numbing. I lower my lids, then open my eyes again and blink away the gloom. In this momentary absence of movement and sound, I enjoy the solitude. I reach out with my hand, as if to catch and hold on to the stillness, when the office intercom intrudes.

I limp towards the Onda C desk and drop my heavy leather tote onto its mirror-finish top. As soon as I hear Maxwell's voice, the room seems to brighten. "Please tell me your meeting was more productive than mine; I need some good news," I say.

"It went better than well. I think you'll be pleased. Give me another hour to finalize the plans, then I'll stop by and brief you on everything."

I relax into the chair. Maxwell Walsh has been saving my sanity since practically the day I met him as a new volunteer at the Mother Mary Shelter. He'd been giving his time to the shelter since he was nineteen, and I took an immediate liking to him. After he showed me the ropes on my first day, we got an early dinner together at Owen's, Milwaukee's oldest pub, and fell into an easy get-to-know-you conversation that served as the foundation for years of best-friendship.

"I was five when my mother passed away, and my alcohol-addicted, abusive stepfather showed no interest in raising me," Maxwell told me when I asked him how he'd gotten interested in working with the homeless. "After my stepfather was arrested for violent offenses, I went through seven different foster homes and attended five high schools." He wiped his mouth and pushed the empty plate away. "Being moved around wasn't easy, especially for a someone like me."

"Someone like you?"

"Well, yeah," he said. "How would you describe me?"

"Even-tempered. Thoughtful. Levelheaded. You strike me as the type who can adapt to changes better than most, although it couldn't have been easy when you were that young."

"Okay, but what do you see when you look at me?"

"A really handsome guy around my age."

Maxwell grinned. "More specific . . ."

"Um, golden-tan pigment, dark curly hair, blue eyes."

"There you go. My mother was African American, my biological dad was white. I grew up in a tough neighborhood; not everyone there was accepting of a mixed-race kid," Maxwell said. "And my whole, shall we say, demeanor didn't gel with a lot of people either. When I was fourteen, one of my teachers pulled me aside and asked me about the bruises on my face and arms. Mrs. Brown was an angel, didn't stop working on my behalf until she saw me placed in foster care with Martin and Spencer." Maxwell finished the rest of his Hefeweizen. "Amazing guys. They taught me to be proud of my identity and how to deal with homophobia as well as any other type of discrimination."

"How long did you stay with them?"

"Until I was eighteen. Then I aged out of the system. If it hadn't been for Martin and Spencer, I probably would've ended up on the streets with no money and nowhere to go. But they wanted a better life for me. With their connections and my good grades, I was able to take advantage of extensive support programs, like scholarships and year-round housing." Maxwell grinned, softly adding, "I actually graduated from college with honors."

"That's amazing. So how'd you end up here?"

"I took a job at a commercial real estate firm in Milwaukee and enrolled in night school at the university, aiming for a degree in law."

"Good-looking *and* a success," I teased. "You must be quite the catch."

"I wish. Whenever I try dating someone, I end up in a vulnerable position." He smiled shyly. "But I don't mind being alone—maybe one day I'll meet the right guy."

I nodded. "That sounds familiar; I haven't been lucky either."

"Tell me."

I put my fork and knife on the plate and folded my napkin. "Let's see. During my senior year of high school I dated hunky Hunter, quarterback and every girl's heartthrob. Hunter truly believed I was clueless about his countless extracurricular activities with his female fan club. He completely fell apart when I ended things and actually blamed me for getting kicked off the team."

"Jeez." Maxwell made a funny face. We both laughed.

"Then there was brainy Buddy, a fellow law student at Northwestern. That lasted for just a few months. I know Buddy was well aware of MiraCo's worth because he developed a sudden interest in trust funds and kept insisting I introduce him to my grandfather and father. Big mistake! My grandfather didn't even allow him to come in the house. He called Buddy a con artist and slammed the door in his face."

"Whoa."

"The third relationship was the most genuine . . ." My smile faded. "I met Carlton at a real estate convention in January 2016. I never introduced him to my grandfather or father; they would've found ways to ruin things."

"What happened with Carlton?"

"We went heli-skiing in Canada after our three-month anniversary. On the last morning of our trip, I stayed behind in the hotel to prepare for a MiraCo meeting. Carlton went on one last heli-ski run with a guide and five other skiers. On their run down, an avalanche was triggered, and all of them were caught in it. Two skiers were able to extract themselves from the snow. Carlton wasn't one of them."

Covering his mouth, Maxwell whispered behind his hand, "I'm so sorry."

"Yeah. Well." I felt like an intense need to lighten the mood. "Being single can't be all that bad when my oh-so-glamorous career occupies most of my time."

The office intercom buzzes again. "It must be ESP—I was just thinking of the day we met."

"Most blessed day of my life," says Maxwell. "Second only to finding out I got this job."

I grin, remembering how thrilled I was after Maxwell accepted the entry-level investment analyst position I'd urged him to apply for. "Do you remember how we celebrated your new employment at Owen's that day?"

"How can I forget! The next day we suffered from a severe case of the beer flu," Maxwell says. "We both were so sick and acted like zombies." He snickers. "Speaking of which . . . your father is on his way. Thought you'd want to know."

"That's weird. His plane only landed an hour ago. I thought he'd go straight from the airport to the hospital."

"Perhaps your grandfather was in no mood to see him."

"That could very well be the case."

"I'll tell the front desk to let you know when he comes into the building."

~

I wonder what frame of mind Dad will be in. He wasn't due to return for another month from his meticulously planned-out honeymoon. Even after learning his old man had suffered a stroke, my father kept cruising on a private chartered yacht through the Aegean Sea with Ava. His first excuse was Ava had contracted a stomach virus, and then he blamed the European WLAN network for being incommunicado. All blatant lies—Ava kept posting new photos and video clips on Instagram, and in every single one she was all smiles, showing off her deepening tan in revealing couture dresses. A few days ago she posted about her displeasure with the French crew of the luxury yacht and gave the chef a thumbs-down. "Chef Lucien uses way too much butter and heavy cream in every meal; I'm holding him responsible for my weight gain" was Ava's caption for a photo that showed her slim and tanned body in a barely-there bikini.

I sigh when I look at the heavy workload on my desk. Now that my father is back in town, he, at least, needs to deal with the stuff he dumped on me. I organize his folders and put them in a neat pile on the left side of my desk. I wonder what his reaction will be when he hears that a couple of his new projects might fall apart because of his own strict demands and stipulations. If he tells me to resurrect the deals, I'll have to turn him down. Is it Schadenfreude that causes me to grin? I'm still not quite used to this feeling of defiance that managed to mature during these past few weeks.

My cell phone vibrates again; I've been ignoring it since this morning. I look at the screen and press Decline when I don't recognize the number. I check the previous missed calls—all from the same number but no voicemails. Without conscious thought, I turn my head. Thick raindrops stick like glue to the floor-to-ceiling windowpanes, and for a fraction of a second, a huge fork of atmospheric electricity flashes through the storm clouds, followed by a new round of deep, rumbling thunder coming from somewhere in the sinister sky.

The office intercom jangles like a pronouncement.

"Maxwell? Please don't tell me my father is here already."

"Nope," he says. "Just letting you know that I just took a call from Ray Conlee; he canceled our 1:30 meeting because his flight is delayed due to weather. He's scheduled to arrive at 3:45 this afternoon and hopes we'll both be available around 5:00. Better, he wants to know if he can discuss the deal with you alone over dinner later tonight."

"No way! Please let him know I already have plans. My father can meet him; they started this monster of a deal together."

I puff out air. Dinner with this self-obsessed, egocentric maniac would be about as much fun as listening to Kanye West's claims of being the next Messiah. Hopefully Conlee's flight will be delayed even further. The idea of my father and Conlee dueling again lifts my spirits: two self-absorbed individuals with the unwavering belief they are superior to everyone else.

For the next three hours I dive into my projects, the acquisition of land and the construction of two new resorts and hotels. Between phone calls, research on zoning, and the systematic investigation of sources for the best financing options, I lose track of time, barely noticing Maxwell when he places a chopped Cobb salad, a mug of matcha tea, and two chocolate chip cookies on my desk. How did he know I was in the mood for exactly all of that?

I'm enjoying my second chocolate chip cookie when my phone rings. My father has entered the building. The delicious cookie instantly loses its flavor.

"Molara, ¡mi amor!" My slick, suave father stands in the door with his arms wide open. He probably would love for me to tell him that he remotely reminds me of a salt-and-pepper Pierce Brosnan in a James Bondesque way, but I keep my mouth shut. When the door closes behind him, his big smile weakens, his arms drop.

He looks at the Aviator blueberry-blue sofa against the wall opposite my desk, then back at me. "Don't act so eager to see me." He opens his arms again, not nearly as wide as before. "How about a hug?"

"Sorry you had to cut your honeymoon short," I say and limply walk into his embrace.

He takes a step back, leaving his hands on my shoulders, and looks me up and down. "This dress looks like a uniform on you."

I chuckle. "You brought it back from Paris last fall. Thought you'd be thrilled to see me in it. It's the first time I've worn it." *And will never wear it again.* I make a full turn and pose like a fashion model. "Well?"

"Mmm." A crease forms between his eyebrows when he stares at my midriff. "Have you put on a few pounds? And why are you limping?"

I knew it. The man could've made a career as a professional nitpicker; no imperfection ever escapes his eyes. And he always insists on having the last word on everybody's wardrobe.

I recall when Annie, my second stepmother, went from a size six to a size eight and flat-out rejected her husband's ridiculous diet-and-fashion regimen. Of course, that wasn't the reason why the marriage had fallen apart. Annie's grounds for wanting out were many. Many marital indiscretions, that is. She had balls, though. She put him in his place when he tried to put the blame on her. I used to sneak out of my bedroom to listen to their vicious fights and inwardly cheered my stepmother on when her voice overpowered his and when she got the last word. That was years ago. Annie now lives with Dwight Dawson—a supercool guy—in Idaho, where they own and operate a ranch. To this day, Dad and Pops insist I stay away from Annie and Dwight; they have no idea we keep in touch.

I know Dad sees me rolling my eyes when he goes on about my two-pound weight gain. I ignore his criticism and decide to use reverse psychology. It's my turn to look him up and down.

"Wow, Papi"—he loves when I call him Papi—"you look amazingly fit and so well-rested." I smile and hope my eyes don't betray my agenda. I give him two thumbs-up. "Ava's obviously been good for you." I nod to punctuate my remark, then walk behind my desk to assemble all of his files and folders, plus the paraphernalia related to the MiraCo-Conlee project. "Take a look, Papi," I say cheerfully. "You'll be proud of me! I did a lot of work on your projects, and thanks to my negotiation, the Vancouver Hotel deal looks promising again." My father remains rooted in the same spot, looking flummoxed. "What's wrong, Papi?"

"I'm exhausted." He blinks and eyes the sofa again. "Jet lag."

"Really? But you flew on the company plane and usually sleep like a bear."

"Well," he says, reddening under his tan, "not on this trip. I was too worried about your grandfather."

Unbelievable. I want to tell him what I know, but I shake my head, trying to look sympathetic. "Yeah, it's too bad you couldn't rush to his bedside because of Ava's bad stomach and sprained ankle, plus all the other stuff you had to deal with." My fingers drum against the glass top of my desk. "Well, I'm glad you finally made it home. Ava can finish remodeling, and I'm sure you're eager to take charge of MiraCo and spend a lot of time with Pops while I'm gone."

"What do you mean?"

"It's been a rough three weeks, handling everything on my own. During the first few days and nights of Pops's hospitalization, I never left his bedside." I talk fast, not allowing my father to interrupt. "On top of that, you were incommunicado for more than a week—I was forced to make decisions on my own." I take a breath before turning into motormouth again. "I need to recharge. That's why I booked myself into the Five Elements Retreat. I'm leaving tonight."

"No way! You can't take off now, Molly!"

Molly, not Molara. Usually that means asking for sympathy or favors.

"Why not?"

"I, uh, well, theoretically I should not even be back yet—my honeymoon still isn't over. And you're my right arm in our organization."

I try to look baffled while suppressing a laugh. "Our organization? You never miss a chance to let me know who's in control of MiraCo," I say. "With Pops currently out of commission, don't you love that you are *it*?" Before I grab my leather tote, I hand my father three thick folders and a USB drive. "Maxwell's sent you an extensive file; it contains every detail you need to know for your meeting tomorrow morning at nine thirty."

"Wait! What meeting?"

I give him my extraspecial surprised look. "The meeting with Ray Conlee, Papi," I say sweetly. "Didn't you read the text I sent an hour ago?"

"Molara! Under the current circumstances, I must insist you finish what—"

"Finish what *you* started with Conlee, Dad? I'm sorry, I can't do that. This venture is *your* creation; you deserve to be proud of it." I peck the air close to my father's cheek and walk towards the door. "See you in ten days."

FIVE

Mateo, June 1992
Coyoacán, Mexico

After an enormous spread of hors d'oeuvres during the extended cocktail hour, Fiesta Miraldo presented a sumptuous plated dinner while the musical entertainment resumed in full swing. None of the guests seemed eager to leave; everybody was waiting for the night's grand finale, an impressive fifteen-minute fireworks display that was known to climax with a sensational bang.

Mateo, feeling on edge, kept walking from table to table, chit-chatting with guests he hadn't had a chance to greet. He normally took great pleasure in the flattering remarks about his generosity and good looks, but his merriment was subdued. Where was Ula? Why hadn't she returned? When he spotted Marco at the Bird-of-Paradise table—each table had been given a different tropical flower name, with harmonizing centerpieces and place cards—Mateo's already bad mood turned from sour to pungent. Sitting next to his son was the woman Mateo abhorred.

Carla de La Fuente had entered Marco's life at the University of California in Berkeley. Her family was an archetypal example of old Mexican fortune. Carlos de La Fuente, Carla's father, never stopped expanding his business across Latin America. His conglomerate successfully operated twelve major companies.

After college, Carla had worked in one of her father's enterprises, but less than a year later, she publicly announced her retirement at the age of twenty-four. From that point on, Carla's extravagant lifestyle garnered international headlines. Light-skinned and reasonably attractive, she was known to hunt desirable men during her escapades, like a collector chasing after rare antiques. Three of her spontaneous marriages were short-lived. Whenever she was done globe-trotting and partying with the rich and famous, she left a bleeding heart behind somewhere in the world. Yet routinely she found her way back to Marco.

"Hola, Mateo." Carla winked at him. "Te ves muy guapo." Without getting up, she moved her head right, left, right, kissing the air. "Muy, muy guapo," she repeated with a tight-lipped smile.

"How generous of you to return to Mexico, Carla," Mateo said, swallowing another backhanded compliment. He quickly turned his attention to other guests at the table before pressing his right hand on his son's shoulder. "May I steal Marco away for a moment?"

"¿Te has vuelto loco?" Mateo hissed, his face inches away from his son's. "Where is your wife? It's been two hours and she still hasn't come back." He camouflaged his anger with a dull smile. "Go find Ula now! And when you do, both of you will sit at *my* table!" He scoffed in Carla's direction. "I still can't believe you seated yourself next to that, eh, that . . ."

"That what?"

"Dammit. You know how I feel about the de La Fuentes. How dare you invite her behind my back?" Out of the corner of his eye, Mateo noticed two well-dressed men approaching. He turned his back on Marco and, with outstretched arms, walked towards his friends. "Fernando! Adrian! Where have you been?"

Twenty minutes later, Mateo spotted his older son weaving his way through the tables. From the grim expression on Marco's face, Mateo sensed trouble. His laughter caught in his throat when Marco, out of breath, leaned close.

"She's not there, Papá," he whispered. "Neither are the children."

"¿Qué?"

"They're not in our wing, or anywhere else in the hacienda. I looked everywhere, even asked some of the guards if they had seen her or the children. Nada."

"Will you excuse us for a moment, please," Mateo said, addressing the people at the table. "My son and I need to make sure the fireworks will start on time." He pretended to glance at his Patek Philippe watch.

"You seem worried," said Fernando Vasquez.

"Let us know if we can be of help," said Adrian Mars.

"Just some routine host responsibilities," Mateo said too quickly. "Keep enjoying yourselves, my friends. We'll return shortly."

With his stomach in knots, Mateo pulled Marco away. "You had quite a bit to drink—are you sure you looked everywhere?"

"Give me a break! I checked the entire house," Marco scoffed. "I even looked in the garages; all the cars are there."

"Benito! León!" Mateo motioned to his bodyguards. "You two go with Marco and wait for me. ¡Prisa!"

Trying to hide his agitation, Mateo worked his way through the tables, relieved that his guests were busy socializing. The volume of their voices, competing with the amplified music, suddenly felt head-splitting. Mateo pulled the party planner, Paolo, aside. "My son Manoel and his family. Where are they sitting?"

"At the Hibiscus table," Paolo said, pointing discreetly.

"Go, tell him I need to see him immediately. Be unobtrusive!"

Minutes later, his younger son arrived with all four of his children in tow. *Dammit, why is he bringing the kids?*

"Abuelo, when are the fireworks starting?" ten-year-old Carlos wanted to know.

"Why did Molara and Miguel leave so early?" asked eight-year-old Ana.

"Did Miggy really take his clothes off under the table?" asked six-year-old Consuela.

"Abuelo, abuelo, abuelo." Trying to get attention, four-year-old Ricardo kept tugging at Mateo's coat sleeve.

Mateo's pencil-thin mustache hitched ever so slightly with his annoyed smile. "¡Niños! I want you to go back to your table now. The fireworks will start soon." He signaled the kids to hurry away.

"Listen carefully," he said to Manoel. "You need to take over for me. If anyone wonders where I am, find an excuse."

"What? You're leaving? Why?"

Mateo gave a nod towards the east wing of the U-shaped hacienda. "Ula and the children have disappeared. Your brother can't find them anywhere."

"Really? Maybe she's finally had it with her two-timing husband." Manoel grinned smugly.

"¡Cállate!" Mateo's face twisted. "How dare you!"

"Just saying, Papá." Manoel waved his hand. "Go, do what you need to do. I'll take care of everything. Don't I always come to the rescue when there's a problem?"

Mateo was out of breath when he arrived at Marco's residence. "What's missing? Anything? Clothes? Suitcases? Jewelry?"

Marco shook his head. "First thing I checked was her jewelry; it's all in the safe. None of the closets or dressers look disturbed. Nothing seems to be missing." He looked thoughtful. "I haven't checked the storage room yet."

The four men sprinted down the long hallway. Benito and León pulled the protective cover from the three rows of suitcases.

Marco shook his head. "Looks like all the Vuittons are here." He looked at the second row of Samsonite luggage and hanging bags. "Looks in order."

"What's that in the third row?" asked Benito.

"No idea. Old pieces. Never used them."

"Old, new, what's the difference," Benito grumbled. "There are four of those. Were there more?"

"Are you deaf?" Marco glared at the bodyguard in annoyance. "I just said I've never used those hand-me-downs."

Mateo eyed the old luggage. "I think these are your mother's; she bought them decades ago! What the hell are they doing in *your* storage area?"

Marco shrugged.

"Anything of value in there?" León pointed to rows and rows of vinyl cases.

"Just toys, plus clothes the kids outgrew. My wife insists on hanging on to this shit." With a deprecatory gesture, Marco turned away. "Nothing in there worth looking at."

As soon as the four men returned to the living quarters, Mateo stopped in front of a large oil painting, one of Marta's early works. A pale, unclothed girl floating in space, below her a fierce-looking hyena spewing up into a tiger's mouth. Mateo hated that painting. He shivered and blinked himself back into the current situation. Behind the surrealistic painting in its heavy frame was a built-in safe. Had Marco checked it? He stared at his son, nodding at the painting.

Marco leaned his head close, speaking too quietly for the bodyguards to hear. "I already told you that all the valuables and passports are still here."

"Where's Ula's phone?"

Marco slapped his forehead. "Forgot about it because she hardly uses it. Must be in one of her handbags."

They found the two-year-old Motorola MicroTAC and one credit card in a purple straw bag.

"Smart bitch knew what to leave behind," Marco mumbled. "Phones and cards can be traced."

The four men searched other purses, even turned the pockets of pants, dresses, and jackets inside out.

"¡Puta mierda!" Mateo wiped his brow. "What about cash?"

"You know I never give her any. What for?" Marco chewed on his inner lip and scratched his shoulder. "So, without credit cards, cash, or passports, where can she possibly go?"

"If nothing is missing and your cars are in the garage, how did she disappear with the twins? Did they get swallowed by a sinkhole?" Mateo turned to Benito and León. "Come on, chicos. You're the experts. Think!"

"Wasn't Marisol supposed to be with the children?" Benito said, scratching the long red scar on his face.

"Marisol!" Marco jumped up.

The four men rushed to Marisol's room, ripped the door open. Like the rest of the house, the room showed no signs of disarray.

"Damn!" Mateo grumbled.

León raised his eyebrows. "Marisol has a car. Where is it?"

"Of course!" Marco rolled his eyes, slapping his forehead again. "She parks that beaten-up Ford Escort under one of the carports."

The men hurried down the stairwell and ran outside.

"It's gone!" Mateo yelled, glowering at his son and the bodyguards. "None of you noticed?"

"Stop glaring at us like we're vultures!" Marco shouted. "We all know this whole thing is a catastrofuck!"

"Okay, okay." Mateo raised his hand and looked at Benito. "What do you know about Marisol? Does she have family? Friends?"

Benito frowned. "If she does, they'd probably be in Venezuela. Her older brother Santiago fled that country and came to Mexico in the mid-seventies. I met him after he became a bodyguard for Juan Estrada."

"Where is he now? Spit it out."

"Got killed a couple of years ago by the cartel." Benito made a gurgling sound and moved his index finger across his throat. "Marisol was heartbroken, told some of the staff the Miraldos were the only family she had left."

"Family? Ridiculous. She was an employee, that's all. Unfortunately, she found a way to attach herself to my ex—eh—my wife."

"¡Sí! And after we moved Mamá to the Casa Namaste facility, Marisol managed to latch on to Ula." With narrowed eyes Marco snarled, "Puta."

Mateo stopped chewing on his inner lip and squared himself in front of the two bodyguards. "Okay. You guys split up and interview everybody. Someone must have seen a Ford Escort leave the grounds. Check all the guest houses." He scratched his head. "Be discreet. I don't want any rumors to start circulating. Come back here as soon as you're done. Understood?"

The bodyguards nodded in unison and took off.

"Listen, Marco. Even though nothing seems to be missing, I suggest you call the credit card company and see if there's been activity during the past several hours," Mateo said.

"Before I do that, shouldn't I notify the police?" Marco pounded his fist on the desk, then reached for the phone. "They need to know that my children were kidnapped by my fucking wife."

"Are you crazy?" Mateo ripped the phone away from his son. "Do I need to remind you that Ula has knowledge of your misconduct?"

"Mine alone?" Marco laughed shrilly and reached for the phone again. "You have no right to—"

"Shut up!" Mateo slammed the receiver into the cradle. "We need to find Ula and the children ourselves, you hear me? If she blows the whistle, we might be in worse trouble than she."

"She doesn't know shit, Papá. Aside from us, nobody has a clue about our involvement in Belize and Guatemala."

"Don't be an idiot, Marco! Your mother knew *a lot!* And she loved Ula. What if she told her you stole millions from the company in Guatemala, forged your brother's signature, and embezzled funds?"

Marco snorted. "After finding a copy of Mamá's will, wasn't I entitled to do what I did? She bequeathed her fortune to Manoel and all those stupid charities and left *nothing* to me!" He paced around the room and kicked a chair out of the way. "I only took from Manoel what he'll be taking from me when she dies."

"But your mother's will is a perfectly legit document, while your forgeries and theft are illicit. Let's not forget what she knows about Robert Graf and—"

"Okay, okay," Marco acquiesced. "Let's find Ula and teach her a lesson."

※

"We know how they got away!" Benito shouted when he and León returned. "Elva was cleaning one of the casitas when she saw Marisol's car drive by slowly. She thinks there could've been another person in the passenger seat but won't swear to it, and she wasn't sure if anyone was in the back seats." The bodyguard scratched his bright red scar. "Anyway, she said Marisol was heading towards the back gate."

"I have a contact in the Policía Federal Preventiva," León said. "If either of you know Marisol's license plate, I can—"

"Yes!" Marco hurried to his desk, fumbled for some keys, and opened a drawer. "When Marisol became the children's nanny, I took a photo of her driver's license and her car," he said proudly and handed the pictures to León. "Call your contact immediately; tell him there'll be an extra reward for speed."

"It would also be helpful if we had images of your wife and the twins," said Benito. He walked around the living room, picking up a beautiful headshot of Ursula and another of the children. "Can I take these from their frames?"

Marco nodded absentmindedly—he was busy writing.

"Be careful with these photos." Mateo took them from Benito. He looked at the one of Ursula and sighed. "Let me put them in a padded envelope."

"What are you doing?" Mateo glanced over his son's shoulder. "Why are you writing a letter now?"

"None of your business." Marco folded the paper in half and sealed it in an envelope. "While we're still waiting for León's friend to call back, I need to drop this off with someone."

I bet it's for that mujer fatale, Mateo thought but stopped himself from blurting it out; no need for the bodyguards to be alerted to another Miraldo conflict. "Hurry back," he grumbled.

"¡Espere!" Benito stepped in Marco's path. "Before you go, do you have a photo of Marisol?"

"There's one in Molara's room. My father will show you where," Marco said and shoved the bodyguard out of the way.

Mateo swallowed when he opened the door to Molara's colorful room. The little girl loved rainbows and unicorns. Ula had insisted on painting the rainbow that curved from the baseboard of one wall across the ceiling down to the baseboard on the opposite wall by herself. She'd also hand-painted unicorns of different sizes and colors and filled the in-between spaces with hundreds of glittering stars. It had taken her over two months to finish the project.

My little Molara, Mateo thought. *Where are you and where is your beautiful mama?*

On one of the shelves sat framed photos. Mateo's favorite was of Ula and the twins on a beach. He swallowed when he saw another photo of himself holding the babies shortly after Ula had given birth to them. There was one of the children with Snow White at Disneyland and another of Miguel embracing Dumbo. Mateo stared at a headshot of Ula from her modeling days. *Why did you leave me,* he silently asked the beauty in the photo. *What happened? Didn't you know that all I ever wanted was to take care of you?*

"This will do." Benito's loud voice interrupted Mateo's thoughts. The bodyguard handed him a photo of Marisol with the twins. "Put these in the envelope with the others."

Just before they left the room, Mateo noticed the unicorn backpack he'd recently custom-made for Molara. He took it off the chair, randomly picked a doll and two animals from the cluster of toys, and put them into the backpack.

I must convince Marco to let me handle the situation once we find Ula and the children. Realizing that things were getting more and more complicated, he swore under his breath. *Damn!*

"Jefe? You coming?"

"Sí." Mateo grabbed the backpack, then turned off the light.

SIX

Molly, April 2019
Milwaukee, Wisconsin

I hold the umbrella in front of me and push against the wind and rain while sprinting across the parking lot. My sneakers are sopping wet. As soon as I hop into the car, I take them off and, together with the dripping umbrella, put them on the floor. Another brilliant flash of lightning zigzags through black clouds, followed by a crash of thunder. All day there have been intermittent thunderstorms. I decide to wait out this latest one before I drive the fifty miles to the Five Elements Retreat. It's past rush hour already, so it shouldn't take more than an hour to get to Lake Geneva. Meanwhile, the sound of rain drums against the roof of my car; its regular rhythm is hypnotizing. I envision alternatives for my future, but when I blink, the options immediately drain away with the rain in the parking lot's sewer.

So weird how Pops metamorphosed into a different character after his stroke. Whenever I was with him at the Ascension Medical Center, this powerful, self-assured, extroverted man was filled with emotional instability, anxiety, and negative emotions. Obviously, the loss of peripheral vision on his right side, the balancing issues, and the severe headaches were reason enough to be depressed, but his irritability and outbreaks towards the hospital staff were tough to watch.

After one week, Pops was transferred to the advanced treatment and rehabilitation center, where his off-the-chart lack of agreeability intensified. I've been told that only my visits each day before and after work seem to cool his hot temper.

Meanwhile, an intense regimen of physical and occupational therapy has resulted in remarkable improvement given his age; Dr. Brenda Brandström and other caregivers at the rehab center are impressed. And hey, don't I know that Pops loves nothing more than admiration and applause? Though he continues to curse everybody, the staff's praises and encouragement make him work harder.

Amazing how fast he regained the tracking in his right eye and stopped needing the walker. During my second visit today, he insisted on showing me how well he could climb a short flight of stairs. Though thrilled about his progress, I'm confused about his weird infatuation with me. Granted, Pops has always treated me special and keeps telling me that I'm the favorite of his five grandchildren. Meanwhile, he hasn't been in touch with my four cousins in Mexico in over twenty years and never talks about them. But every day when I'm with him, he abruptly tears up, expresses a feeling of sadness, and keeps holding my hand. And when I ask what's wrong or if there's anything he'd like to share with me, he shakes his head and shrugs in defeat.

"I'm afraid," he said ten minutes ago when I told him I had to leave.

"Afraid of what, Pops?"

Misty-eyed, he shook his head again, staring at me, keeping silent.

What is he hiding? I sense it somehow involves me. But if he won't tell me, who will?

There's another lightning bolt. I count to fifteen before I hear the thunder. My car windows are completely fogged up, and I wipe part of the windshield with my hand to peek at the stubborn thick clouds, steadily releasing sheets of rain. Deciding to wait in the parking lot for another ten minutes, hoping the storm will move on, I lean against the headrest and close my eyes. Immediately I think about the last day of January.

I was invited to be one of the speakers during the ALIS Conference in Los Angeles, where I talked about the ingredients to MiraCo's success and how we pride ourselves on employing the top talented hospitality professionals in the business. At the end of the conference, MiraCo was given the Deal of the Year Award.

Feeling exhilarated and enterprising, I was overcome by an overwhelming urge to learn something about the many components amiss from my life. Who else could tell me what my mind kept a rein on? Of course! I had relatives in Mexico. Via the web, I traced the contact information for my uncle Manoel in Coyoacán. He was surprised and overjoyed to hear from me—after all, the last time he'd seen me was when I was four years old. I immediately booked an impromptu, very secret two-day trip to Mexico City, and I'll never forget the emotional embrace with my frail uncle. I was shocked to learn that he was in the terminal end stage of chronic pulmonary heart disease.

A thumping noise makes me jump. I look for Uncle Manoel; I want him to finish his last sentence. I rub my eyes and realize I'm in my car in a parking lot in Milwaukee.

There's the noise again. It's a knock on the window. Behind the damp pane I see Denis's face. He's one of the patrol guys who escorts me to my car whenever I leave the rehab center at a late hour. I lower the window.

"Is everything okay?" he asks, looking worried. "You've been sitting in your car for a while with the engine idling."

"Omigod. I'm sorry, Denis. I wanted to wait out the storm and lost track of time; too much is going on in my head."

"Are you on your way to see your grandfather, or are you on your way home?"

"I'm on my way to Lake Geneva for a few days. I need some time off."

As always in weather like this, the highway is a mess. In this stop-and-go, stop-and-go traffic, I can let my thoughts wander back to the trip to Mexico.

I still hear my uncle's voice. How I wish he could've finished his last sentence before he collapsed in front of me.

In the panic that followed, and after the ambulance rushed Uncle Manoel to the nearest hospital, I returned to the fan palm and sat on the grass, looking at the hacienda where I was born. I was hoping for memories to return, but instead I felt abandoned once again.

Before my return flight to the States took off, I called the hospital. My dear uncle had passed away.

SEVEN

Molly, January 2019
Coyoacán, Mexico

My uncle Manoel's driver takes us through the beautiful neighborhood of Coyoacán, and we stop at the Hacienda Serenidad, an exclusive hotel that is tucked away within extensive grounds and hidden from the hustle and bustle of Mexico City. "You don't remember living here?"

I shake my head.

"This once belonged to my father," Uncle Manoel says and gazes at the large U-shaped structure. "Does the name Carlos de La Fuente mean anything to you?"

"De La Fuente? I've heard that name before," I say. "But who is he?"

"A dear, dear older friend who acquired all this two decades ago and remodeled the ex-Miraldo Hacienda into this luxury hotel. There are twelve lavishly appointed suites here; every one of them is reserved more than a year ahead of time." Uncle Manoel points to the left wing of the building. "Miguel and you were born in that wing and raised there for four years."

"Really?"

"After your accident in Miami, my father and brother brought you back to the hacienda, and you lived here until Mateo, Marco, and I ended accords. I stayed in Mexico, but they moved with you to the States." Uncle Manoel's voice is strained; he leans heavily on his cane. "I haven't spoken to either my father or brother since then."

"Why? Nobody's ever given me a reasonable explanation."

Uncle Manoel groans when he attempts to shift his weight. "The court's ruling barred us from competing across our business interests and from interfering in—" He stops midsentence. "Sorry, I really shouldn't talk about any of this." He looks wary. "Isn't there anything you remember?"

"Nothing. Not even the accident. I only know what Pops and my father told me, namely that I was badly injured, had surgeries, and was hospitalized in Miami for a week before Pops brought me back to Mexico. He said it was a miracle I survived."

"Correct," Uncle Manoel says. "You refused to talk for months. Your aunt Claudia and I were very worried about you and kept asking to see you. But we were rarely given permission to visit. And only on few occasions were your cousins allowed to play with you."

"How come? Didn't you also live at the hacienda?"

"No! I didn't want my wife and children to be subjected to any of the unpleasantries around here." Again, he shakes his head reprovingly. "Shortly before I wed Claudia, I bought a lovely home twenty kilometers away from the hacienda where our children could grow up in a peaceful setting, surrounded by love. Your mother was never given permission to bring you and your brother to our home."

Condemning my lack of memory, I swallow my disappointment. "You said my four cousins are married now. Where do they live?"

"We all live near one another. Due to my illness, they run all my business operations and are doing a wonderful job."

"I'd love to see them."

"Regrettably, your cousins, Claudia, and I are legally blocked from having contact with you; I'm already taking a big risk meeting with you today."

"Legally blocked? Why? I don't understand."

He looks at me with pity in his eyes. "A few things I dare share," he says weakly. "After your accident—when they brought you back from Miami—Mateo and Marco forbade everybody from showing you photos or other memorabilia of your mother and twin brother; nobody was allowed to mention their names." Uncle Manoel sighs and grimaces. "I have to sit down." With difficulty, he walks to one of the shaded benches nearby. "My heart problem and the medication for it suck all the energy out of me."

I look at the old ex-hacienda again and take my uncle's hand into mine. "The first seven years of my life have been completely erased, but everything is crystal clear from the moment we moved to the States."

"To Wavetown."

"Wavetown!" I roll my eyes. "Maybe you heard that Pops found ways to change that name; he managed to incorporate the town into the Village of Mira."

"Of course. It's always been my father's fetish to see the Miraldo name everywhere, even if only in abbreviation." With a half-smile on his lips, my uncle leans back. "Perhaps it's for the best that you can't remember your early childhood."

I am thunderstruck. "Please don't say that. Pops and Dad claim I've been told everything there is, but I know they keep all their skeletons locked up." I scoot closer to my uncle. "Please help me fill in the empty holes."

Uncle Manoel shifts uncomfortably, then slowly gets to his feet and hooks his left arm into my right. "Let's walk through the gardens," he says.

"Are we allowed to do that? We're not registered hotel guests here."

He snickers. "When my father purchased this hacienda, he practically stole it from Carlos de La Fuente because he was envious of Carlos's wealth. Mateo hated him." Uncle Manoel's breaths come labored. "But Claudia, my children, and I loved Carlos; he considered us his family."

"Considered? Did he pass away?"

"Yes." Uncle Manoel lets his gaze wander over the beautifully landscaped gardens. "When he died, it felt as if I was losing the father I never had. We miss him every day."

"Did he not have a family of his own?"

"His only daughter also passed away." Uncle Manoel stops walking. "Since you can't remember anything, my sweet girl, this is all I dare tell you."

Overcome by great sadness, I quietly continue to walk arm in arm with my uncle. I sense a peculiar clash between the serenity of the manicured grounds and the trembling shadows of a forgotten past.

Even though I expect Uncle Manoel to deny me the answers, I ask, "Why did my mother abandon me in 1992? Why did she take Miguel and not me? What made her want to separate her twins?"

"Let's go over there." My uncle points across the lawn.

We walk to a table, shaded by a beautiful old Mexican fan palm.

As soon as we take our seats, a young woman, dressed in the hotel's trendy server's uniform, appears.

"Es bueno verte de nuevo, Señor Miraldo," she says. "¿Qué te puedo traer?"

"What would you like?" my uncle asks.

"Fresh lemonade, if they have it."

"Dos limonadas, por favor."

Uncle Manoel looks up into the canopy of the Mexican fan palm. "You, your brother, and my four children used to play in the shade of this old palm." He swallows. "Many times your mother prepared a picnic here; her basket always held delicious surprises. All you children loved her homemade chocolate almond cookies. She shaped them like stars and called them by their Swiss name, Basler Brunsli. They were delicious, but her limonada was even better." He smiles at me through misty eyes. "And here you are so many years later, sitting under the same tree, ordering lemonade. I was hoping my bringing you here would stir a memory in you."

I shake my head and lean across the table to reach for my uncle's hand again. "Why did she take my brother and leave me behind? What really happened, Uncle Manoel?"

"Molara, my beautiful girl," he says with a quiver in his voice, "I cannot tell you."

"Please." I feel his trembling hand in mine.

"Mateo, Marco, and I signed confidentiality agreements—same as your nondisclosure agreements in the States—when we parted company." He takes two small sips of the lemonade and with a shaky hand puts the glass back on the table. "Just as Mateo and Marco aren't allowed to reveal any of my trade secrets or manufacturing processes or my very personal reasons behind our estrangement, I am legally forbidden from disclosing information about anything that took place during those years."

I look at Uncle Manoel in disbelief. "But it's been so long—are these agreements still valid?"

"Unfortunately, or fortunately, they are!"

"Fortunately?"

"Look," he says tentatively, "there are a few things that I'm not proud of." He hesitates briefly. "Your aunt Claudia and I enjoyed a long, happy marriage. In these last weeks or days I have left, I don't want to besmirch all the decent acts I accomplished during my life." He takes another sip of the lemonade and looks at me through tired eyes. "Even though my father, brother, and I are forbidden from talking about the circumstances that led to the breakup, you deserve to know what was done to your mother and where you and your brother came from."

"What do you mean?"

"Countless unlawful acts were performed. Mateo and Marco assumed they were above the law. They were cocky and believed nobody would get in their way." Uncle Manoel scowls and wipes his eyes impatiently. "But I dare say now that they are *not* who you think they are."

"Please, Uncle Manoel." I look at him pleadingly. "Tell me more. You are the only one who can help me understand."

My uncle grimaces in pain. "Dear God," he whimpers and looks up to the sky. "How I feared this moment." He clutches his chest, and his eyes find mine. "Molara Miraldo," he says, barely audible, "even I'm not who you think I am. You call me uncle but . . ." His words fade as he collapses.

EIGHT

Ursula, June 1992
Mexico City and Miami

Ga-gong-ga-gong-ga-gong. Throughout the seemingly endless ten minutes at the ticket counter, Ursula believed the agent could hear her pounding heart. She held her breath while the middle-aged man behind the counter checked the four passports and processed the flight itinerary on the computer. But not until the barcoded tags were affixed to each piece of luggage and sent down the conveyor, and not until the passports and tickets were in Ursula's hand again, did she dare to breathe.

"You still have a lot of time," said the agent.

"I know." Ursula quickly returned the smile. "We'll be having dinner with friends nearby."

"Qué lindo. Remember, you and the rest of your party need to show your passports again when you go through security."

"Yes, of course." Ursula forced another frail smile.

Ga-gong-ga-gong-ga-gong. She pulled the stiff brim of her cap down over her face and readjusted her sunglasses as she hurried towards the exit, increasing her speed with every step. Her heartbeat didn't slow down until she spotted Marisol's car outside.

"¿Todo bien?"

Ursula nodded. "The children? Okay?"

Marisol pointed to the backseat. "Hiding," she whispered.

Ursula willed herself not to think about the precariousness of their situation.

"What happened to my Molly, my Miggy? Please tell me the seekers didn't find them!"

There was movement under Miggy's blanket on the back seat, followed by a double giggle.

"No lo creo," Marisol said as she drove the car away from the terminal. "The children told me they discovered a secret hiding place. I haven't seen them since."

"Well, we must stop the car right now and find Molly and Miggy. Wherever they are, I want to hide in their secret space with them. Don't you?"

"¡Si!"

Another fit of giggles came from under the blanket.

"Did you hear something, Marisol?"

"Sí."

"Boo!" Both Molly and Miggy threw the blanket away and broke into sidesplitting laughter.

"You scared me!" Ursula clutched her chest, almost feeling relieved to openly feign her actual panic. "What a great hiding place." She gave her twins a thumbs-up. "When we get to the hotel, can we all hide under Miggy's blankie?"

"Why are we going to a hotel now?" Molly asked. "I thought we're taking a plane to hide in another city."

"First to the hotel. Who's hungry?"

"Me!" Miguel cheered. "Can we get quesadillas?"

"And pizza?"

A half hour later Marisol pulled up in front of the Majestic Hotel de México.

"This is too elegant," Marisol muttered when she saw the porters and valets in their royal red-and-black livery rushing to open the doors of her old Ford Escort.

Ga-gong-ga-gong-ga-gong. There it was again. Ursula had no control over it.

"Any more luggage or just these?" The porter pointed to the two old pieces in the trunk.

"Just those, please."

"Once you've checked in, they'll be brought to your room."

"Thank you." Ursula took the ticket from the valet. "We won't need the car during our stay here."

Ga-gong-ga-gong-ga-gong. Holding on to her children, she never noticed the beautiful Art Nouveau architecture or the stunning Louis XV chandelier in the entrance. Like a robot she followed the instructions Bruno Rossi had drilled into her.

"You are booked into an expensive hotel because neither your husband nor father-in-law expect you to have any funds," Bruno had said. "As soon as you get your luggage, unpack a few items, but don't stay too long in the room and leave a bit of a mess. Ask the concierge to make a reservation for four at the Cocina Central Ristorante-Pizzeria; that's within walking distance from the hotel. But don't go there! Grab a taxi and head to La Cocina de Mamá; a reservation's been made there in your name. You don't have to rush through dinner, but be sure to allow enough time to get back to the airport. By then, someone at the hacienda will have started searching for you. Always be on the alert, but behave as normal and relax as much as possible."

Through the open car window, Ursula stared at the firmament as the taxi pulled away. The days had become lighter and longer; the dark-blue twilight dusk of evenings had not lost its vitality.

"Mamá, why can't we eat at that restaurant?" Miggy's high-pitched voice ripped her from her brief stupor. In protest, the little boy kept pointing at the blinking Cocina Central Ristorante-Pizzeria sign that quickly disappeared in the distance. "I'm so hungry."

"We're trying to trick the seekers," said Molly. "Right, Mamá?"

"Exactly! We're on our way to a different restaurant. You'll love the food where we're going."

※

La Cocina de Mamá was crowded, and they were led to an outside table in the far corner. Ursula noticed that her hands were trembling again when she put a slice of pizza next to the quesadilla on each of the children's plates. She already knew her own order of chili rellenos would remain untouched. While trying to keep Miggy calm—he kept whining about too many noisy people—she was barely able to control her own apprehension. Was she imagining it or had several other guests looked at her table? There! Two robust middle-aged men, three tables over, were stealing glances in her direction. *Ga-gong-ga-gong-ga-gong.* Yes! Both men were looking at her again. Why were they grinning? But as soon as their heaping plates of food arrived, they stopped staring and Ursula forced herself to blink away the haze of terror. *This is all such lunacy.*

"Tranquilo," Marisol said and wiped Miguel's mouth. "No comas tan rápido."

As if in suspended animation, Ursula watched Molly pull the tray towards her.

No, Ursula wanted to say, but it was too late—the tray with the last two slices of pizza had already collided with the floor.

Molly slid off her chair to pick up the mess. "Who cares," she said, laughing. "My tummy is full already."

"My pizza! I still want it," Miggy whined, fighting to pull the tray with sullied pizza away from his sister.

For another moment Ursula remained indifferent, frozen. She felt as if she were under a bell jar while lunacy unfolded all around her. She vacantly looked at the perfectly prepared chili rellenos on her plate; it made her feel sick, like all the countless horrible happenings during the past nine years.

Lunacy had been the arranged marriage to Marco, a man who'd mentally abused her and cheated on her. Lunacy were his threats to declare her an unfit mother, then take the children away from her. Lunacy were the years of isolation at the accursed hacienda, where she'd been drugged and sexually assaulted. Lunacy was her fate: a life worse than death when she'd realized what had been done to her.

"My pizza!" Miggy's wail pierced like a knife through her anguish.

"You can't eat it anymore." Molly tried to pull the tray away from her brother. "It fell on the floor—it's dirty!"

Ursula would have preferred to stay numb under the bell jar, but life forced its way into her again. Reflexively she pulled the messy tray away from Molly and, with a loud clatter, hurled it onto the table. "Enough!"

For a moment the children sat as rigid as statues. They looked at her, wide-eyed; they'd never seen their mother react this way.

"It's been a long day for all of us," Marisol said and leaned between the children and their mother, cleaning up the mess on the table. When she bent down to pick up a fork and napkin off the floor, she whispered to Ursula, "The passports. Their new names. The children need to know."

Omigod! "I am so sorry!" Ursula said, reaching out to her children. "Nothing is your fault." A snail-like wave of reassurance flooded through her but immediately ebbed away when she rummaged through her tote bag. What had happened to the passports? The tickets? She rifled through the inside pockets and the bottom of the bag. *I had the documents at the airport; what did I do with them? Ga-gong-ga-gong-ga-gong.* She kept searching, but not until she'd combed through everything a second time did she remember the exterior zippered pocket. There! She breathed a sigh of relief.

"Look what I have for you," she said with a shaky voice, quickly glancing at the other tables. Everybody was busy eating, drinking, chatting—including the two robust middle-aged men. She held up three passports. "These are our new IDs. Since we're playing a very long game of hide-and-seek, I changed our last name to confuse the seekers."

"Really?" Molly's eyes widened. "What's my name now?"

"I want my new name to be Superman," Miggy said.

Ursula opened one passport.

"That's me!" said Molly when she saw her picture.

"Can you read your name?"

"M-o-l-l-y! But I can't read the rest. What does it say?" The little girl pointed to the surname.

"Burgli. That's quite different from Miraldo, right?"

Molly nodded. "So my new name is Molly Burgli to confuse the seekers?"

Ursula forced herself to nod. She so resented telling her children lies, yet she was beyond grateful to Bruno Rossi for his ideas and help, arranging for the passports while keeping all their first names as familiar as possible. He'd suggested Burgli, for Ursula's maternal grandparents, Rosi and Anton Burgli.

"Mamá, let me see the book with my picture and new name." Miggy knelt on his chair, leaning over the table. He laughed when he saw his image. "What does my name say?"

"Michael Burgli." Ursula pulled her son onto her lap. "Michael is the English name for Miguel; your nickname can still be Miggy. Do you like that?"

"No. I want you to change it to Superman. Can you?"

"Not for this hide-and-seek game. Maybe next time."

Molly's eyes were glued to her and her brother's photos. "Who made these passports with new names, Mamá?"

"A very good friend."

The occasional rattling and creaking, the thumps and whooshing noises, the dings, beeps, and whirring sounds, and the fact that she sat in a floating seat of what was basically a huge tin can would have been extremely frightening even under normal circumstances. But considering her current situation, Ursula almost felt safe and secure, at least for the remaining three hours of their flight to Miami. She looked across the aisle. Marisol sat straight like a candle. Her eyes were closed and her lips moved in silent prayer. Molly's head rested against Marisol's arm; the little girl had fallen asleep before the plane reached its cruising altitude.

Ursula pushed the buttons on Miggy's seat next to hers, reclining the backrest. He was sucking his right thumb, clasping his silky blue security blanket. She picked the Superman coloring book and crayons off the floor, then covered him with a lightweight comforter, supplied by the airline.

She reclined her own seat and leaned back. No way would she allow herself to doze off. Not even for a minute—she had to stay alert. She thought of her phone conversation with Bruno Rossi prior to takeoff in Mexico City.

"Ursula? Why are you calling? I hope everything is going according to plan so far." He sounded alarmed.

"Yes! I just want to thank you, Bruno."

"Only thank me when you're really out of danger and when I know my job was well done."

She told him of her emotional chaos, the fears concerning her past, present, and future that she couldn't shake. "I never thought I'd feel so lost. The only reason I can hold it together is the children."

"We have faith in you, Ursula," Bruno Rossi replied. "You've shown heroic strength for years. You were promised a paradise but instead were forced to teeter at the edge of Miraldo's abyss." He cleared his throat. "I once mentioned that Marta had a devoted friend. He made a promise to Marta before she took ill. He is my superior, and his instructions are that I help you."

"Please tell me who this benefactor is that makes all this possible. You spoke of a powerful person in Mexico, but how can I express my gratitude to a phantom?"

"Patience, Ursula," Bruno said. "Focus on the present challenge. There'll be rough waters before you reach the harbor. For the next phases you'll need eyes in the back of your head."

I need eyes in the back of my head. Automatically she turned and looked at the other passengers in the first-class cabin; some were sleeping, others were reading.

Everybody was at peace. How she envied them. *Dear God, why did I allow all of this to happen? Ga-gong-ga-gong-ga-gong.* Ursula pressed her face into the palms of her hands. No longer able to control herself, she started to sob.

"Act relaxed. Assume every person you encounter is an officer." Those had been Bruno Rossi's instructions.

Ursula had no idea how they managed to clear passport control or how they made it through US Customs in Miami. Every single person had looked suspiciously official to her, with or without uniforms. She was convinced that a whole army of them kept circling around her with choreographed movements.

"I know God heard and answered my prayers," Marisol whispered when they walked through the exit doors.

Given the hour—it was past midnight—the line for the taxis was relatively short.

"Please take us to 561 Southwest Fourth Street," Ursula said, reading the address off a piece of paper Marisol had given her. "It's in Little Havana."

"I know," said the driver. "I live close by."

"Mamá, my head hurts," whimpered Miggy.

"Come here, sweet boy." Ursula pulled her son onto her lap. "You always get a headache when you're tired," she said, gently massaging his temples. "This will make the pain go away." She hoped he would fall asleep.

"Where are we going now?" Molly pressed her face against the window.

Outside, flickering lights swirled like a rapid river into the darkness of a Florida night.

"To a friend of Marisol's. Her name is Amelia."

Santiago Rodriguez—Marisol's brother—and Amelia Rubio had met in Mexico City in 1976. Two years after their wedding, Santiago was killed. Amelia, unaware of her husband's involvement with illegal activities, was warned of ripple effects from the cartel. She fled across the border and moved in with an old aunt in Little Havana. Amelia never remarried and considered Marisol her only living relative after her aunt died.

The taxi driver dropped them off. Right after he pulled away, a short, full-figured woman in her midforties rushed out of the house on Fourth Street.

"Por fin estas aquí." She flung her arms around Marisol. "How I missed you."

Ursula, carrying her sleeping son, felt a tug on her shirt. "Are we hiding in that little house with the red roof and the green door?" Molly whispered, pointing to the small building. "Doesn't it look like one of Miggy's Smurf houses?"

"Please meet Ursula and Molly and Miggy," said Marisol after Amelia released her.

"Welcome, welcome!" Amelia said in low voice. "I don't want to wake the little guy. Please come inside."

The kind-faced woman apologized for the tight quarters. "I know you're used to a big estate, but maybe this will do for a few days," she said. "It's only a two-bedroom home. Marisol and I will share one, and the three of you can sleep here." She opened the door to a clean, fresh-smelling room with two twin beds. She apologized again.

"Please, Amelia," said Ursula, "you have no idea how grateful we are. I can't thank you enough."

Less than fifteen minutes later, after she removed Miggy's shoes and made sure his little elephant and blankie were in his arms, she covered him with the colorful printed sheet and thin blanket.

Molly, in her pink pajamas, had turned to the wall. Her small shoulders bounced rhythmically, heaving out suppressed sobs.

"Sweetie, what's wrong?" Ursula sat at the edge of the twin bed and pulled her daughter onto her lap.

"Rosi," Molly sobbed. "I don't know where I left her. She's all alone somewhere."

Ursula kissed the tears off her daughter's cheeks. "Perhaps you left her at the hotel in Mexico? If Rosi is there, I'll make sure the hotel staff sends her to us," she said, hating herself for having to lie to her daughter.

"But my little baby doll is lonesome now." Molly wiped new tears away. "She misses me, and I miss her more."

"I know, my love. I would feel the same if you weren't with me." Ursula hugged Molly closer, curling up under the sheet and blanket. "Let's try and get some sleep now." She pressed her lips into her daughter's hair.

"I love playing hide-and-seek, but why do we have to hide so far away, Mamá?"

For a second Ursula thought of being honest; with difficulty she swallowed her sincerity. "It's complicated to explain, my love. We're both tired now. Can I give you my answer tomorrow?"

"Uh-huh." The little girl yawned. "I don't want Papi to get angry and be mean to you again. It always makes Miggy and me sad," she said drowsily. "If abuelo finds us first, he will want you to—" Her sleepy voice faded.

NINE

Molly, May 2019
Lake Geneva, Wisconsin

It's the first of May, and after just five days of being at the retreat, I've had a breakthrough.

What countless sessions of therapy during my teenage years failed to achieve, Dr. Shanti—a spiritual counselor—accomplished here in a few days.

I learned it's okay to admit that I'm angry and anxious, frustrated and confused! For too long I've refused to allow certain emotions to enter my consciousness, clearly failing to break through the wall of my defense mechanism. Enough! I'm done living in denial! From now on I want to acknowledge whatever unacceptable truth lurks in the shadows, and I will deal with whatever painful feeling comes along with it. I'm willing to lower my protective shield. I am now ready to actively search for the roots of my unexplained angst and sadness. I'm on my way to making peace with my inner rage and skepticism.

I stop writing, amazed that more than half the pages in my brand-new journal are already filled. I leaf through the pages of my journal—or should I call it a diary? What if I gave it a name?

I keep turning the pages. Crazy! Emotional mayhem looks back at me from every sheet. I scoff in disbelief. How the heck can more than one hundred billion neurons in my brain produce mostly pandemonium? I think of the underlying principle of chaos—isn't it called the butterfly effect? Like when a butterfly flaps its wings in China, it supposedly can cause a tornado in Texas? I know it might just be a metaphor, but what I've learned here at Five Elements somehow has stirred a tornado within me. Though my inner storm wasn't caused by flapping butterfly wings thousands of miles away, too many unanswered questions keep thrashing around within me. Dr. Shanti's guidance encourages me to remedy the chaos myself.

Relax. Reboot. Recharge. That's the motto at the Five Elements Retreat. I'm already more aware of how to use positive thinking and calming mental imagery to diffuse accumulated tension and stress. Instead of agonizing about unresolved matters, family, work, and miscellaneous daily stimuli, I've learned how to appreciate spending time by myself and happily embrace my temporary self-imposed exile.

I intentionally left my iPad and MacBook Air at home; my phone, for the most part, is turned off. I make sure to call Pops once a day to get an update on his progress, but I've learned how to cut him off the moment he starts griping about MiraCo or urges me to come back. This morning I actually told him that I simply needed to be away from everyone and everything in Mira to recoup my depleted energy. Being able to say that to Pops is a huge leap for me.

If someone had suggested the "Early Riser Meditation" to me a week ago, I would've laughed. But it totally surprised me how meditation calms me down, rewards me with a sense of joy and tranquility.

After the morning stretch, followed by a ninety-minute yoga class, I usually just grab a green tea—they don't serve coffee at Five Elements—and then plop down in one of the comfy chairs in the solarium to write. Here, under this glass dome where nobody bothers me, time seems to stand still. In fact, I haven't noticed many guests. Maybe the lousy spring weather—for the past two weeks it's rained every day—has kept them at home. Thick dark clouds, like scratchy old blankets, still covered the blue skies early this morning, but for the first time since I got here, the sun came through just thirty minutes ago.

> Hey, hey, hey
> The first of May
> Pushed every cloud away!

I chuckle at my impromptu limerick and close my eyes. The warm sunrays, filtering through the huge translucent enclosure, feel like kisses on my face and arms.

My growling stomach wakes me up—I must've dozed off for a few minutes. It's time to get lunch.

"Are you a writer?"

I turn my head towards the voice of a balding, pencil-thin man who looks like a gust of wind could blow him over. I've seen him before in the dining room, noticed him reading here in the solarium; just like me, he's always by himself.

"Nope, definitely not a writer. Just journaling." I grab my stuff and stand up. "If you want this chair, I'm leaving." I smile politely. "Lunchtime for me."

"Mind if I join you?"

I surprise myself when I give him a nod.

"Lovely," he says. "Felipe Flores from Chicago."

He has a Hispanic name but no accent. I glance at him quickly. "Molara Miraldo from Milwaukee."

⁓

There are only five other guests in the café adjacent to the solarium. We take a seat across from each other at a small square table.

"Really? Molara Miraldo? ¿Una compatriota?"

"Long story. My ancestry is Portuguese and Swiss, but I was born in Mexico and lived there for the first few years of my life." I fish the ice cubes from the glass of water and take a swallow, but it's still too cold. "Anyway"—I make eye contact with Felipe Flores—"I have no recollection of ever living in Mexico. You're looking at an all-American girl. Please call me Molly."

The server comes, and I ask for a glass of water without ice and a hot kombucha tea.

"I lived in Mexico City for the first thirty-five years of my life," Felipe Flores says and compliments the server for the speedy delivery of my water, kombucha, and his iced passion fruit tea. He keeps silent while he stirs three packets of brown sugar into his iced tea; the only sound in the café is the ringing of the spoon in the glass. He takes a sip, then looks at me.

"Like you, I love being a United States citizen but still hold dual citizenship." He smiles. "Please, call me Phil."

Five Elements is an all-plant-based retreat. For me it's a new experience, but the vegan menu has been surprisingly good.

Phil and I laugh when we simultaneously order the portobello mushroom burger. He places a second order of jackfruit pizza with almond ricotta.

"I can consume an enormous amount of food and never gain weight," he says. "Try the pizza—you won't believe how good it is."

"So, Phil," I say between bites of my mushroom burger, "what brings you to Five Elements? Are you still working? Do you have family?"

He chuckles. "Three questions in one breath." He wipes his mouth. "It's my first time at Five Elements. Good place to get away from the fast-spinning world." He looks at me through smiling eyes. "In Mexico I worked in the legal department of Banco Salina Suisse and transferred to the branch in Chicago when I was in my thirties." He offers me a slice of his jackfruit pizza, but I politely decline. "The Windy City has been my home since then," he says and takes another bite.

I wonder how old he is. Hard to tell. Despite his gauntness, he looks rather fit. His face is a bit weathered, and the receding hairline most likely makes him look older than he is. I guess him to be in his early seventies.

"I'm sixty-eight." He winks at me.

Oh gosh, did he read my mind? I'm blushing. Trying to save the situation, I simulate a laugh and give a thumbs-up. "I'll turn thirty this year."

"Could've fooled me, Molly. You look younger." Phil gestures at the last few slices of the pizza. "I'll give you one more chance to try before it's gone."

He has kind eyes—they twinkle even when he doesn't smile. I also like his low-pitched, rich, modulated voice. For whatever crazy reason, Phil makes me feel at ease.

Turns out we are both slow eaters, and throughout the meal we keep generating new conversation topics. Neither of us seems to worry about what to say—it's like we stopped filtering ourselves. I so enjoy his occasional clever jokes and love when he compliments me on my witty comebacks.

"Hey, you like dessert? They make a killer raspberry cheesecake and brownie protein bar here. You'd never know it's all vegan."

I laugh and decline the offer. "I don't know where you put it all."

"To answer the last of your three-part question," he says as he scrapes the final cookie crumbs off his plate, "I lived with a wonderful woman for twenty years, but we never married and had no children. My Linda passed away two years ago." He folds his napkin and gives me a quizzical look. "I can tell you have something else on your mind. What might that be?"

"Earlier you mentioned you stopped working for Banco Salina Suisse, but that it wasn't the end of the road for you. You called it the beginning of an open highway. Where has that highway led you to?"

"You'd never guess." He chuckles. "Long before I took early retirement, I wanted to make a distant dream a reality. And, drumroll"—he drums his long fingers on the table—"my lifelong weakness for detective and mystery novels inspired me to become a private investigator."

"Really!"

"Since I already had a law degree and a financial background, I only needed some online classes in computer forensics, surveillance, and psychology." His brown eyes sparkle. "Mission accomplished."

"That's impressive." I wonder how busy a private investigator is and who his clients are.

Again, he seems to read my mind. "I mostly work for attorneys, insurance companies, and private businesses. I rarely take individual clients with personal matters," he says. "Believe it or not, even my old boss, Banco Salina Suisse, has become a client."

It's almost three o'clock, and the sun is still shining. I suggest a walk before my massage appointment.

"Feel like sharing some more of your life with me?" Phil asks as we approach the path that will take us around parts of the lake.

Usually when someone asks about my life, I take large mental steps back, then close the gate to my personal information highway. During my adolescent years I barely allowed the shrinks to peek into my guarded inner sanctum.

How strange that walking next to this balding, pencil-thin older man, whom I only met a few hours ago, I feel comfortable enough to provide select bits and pieces of my complicated set of circumstances.

"They called it post-traumatic amnesia when I lost my memory at the age of four. From what I've been told, my mother and father were separating. That alone would be a blow to any kid, but I was also rejected by my mother. She vanished with my twin brother and left me behind."

My God, how easily had those words rolled over my lips? I actually feel relief. Nobody has passed us on the trail—it's like we're the only ones trusting the rain will not return. The rhythmic crunch of gravel mixed with the squelch of still-damp sand under our hiking boots is like an accompaniment to the other musical chords of nature.

"May I ask what happened?" Phil glances at me. "Of course, I understand if you don't want to—"

"You sure you're ready?" I wink at him. "Please stop me when something doesn't make sense."

And then I tell him that, according to my father, the accident happened outside the Miami airport. Apparently, I tore away from him after he told me about the separation. Why did I run? Who knows. Maybe I was looking for my mother and brother. Anyway, a car hit me and I suffered injuries to my head and neck, along with several bone fractures. The ambulance rushed me to the nearest hospital for emergency surgeries. Less than a week later, my grandfather arranged for a medical transport back to Mexico.

When I was old enough to understand, Pops told me being in a coma helped my brain stop swelling and healed the internal bleeding. And when I woke up again, I was unable to remember anything or recognize anyone. I also refused to talk. Pops said my psychogenic mutism was not only the result of the accident but more likely due to the trauma of my mother and twin brother abandoning me. Therapists and physicians got involved, but for almost a year I didn't talk at all. Obviously, my selective mutism didn't last, and as soon as I started to speak again, I wouldn't shut up.

"Just like I can't shut up right now," I add and elbow Phil. "Tell me if you'd had enough."

"Not at all. Listening to you is like reading a book. I'm ready to turn the page if you'll let me."

"I'm so frustrated that I can't recall the accident or anything that took place before or after that day in Miami. My first memories are those of our move from Mexico to the United States; it was springtime, right before my eighth birthday. That's when I began to lay the foundation for a new life."

Phil apologizes for interrupting. "May I ask why your grandfather and father moved from Mexico to the States? Didn't you mention earlier they had a very successful business in Mexico?"

I nod. "This is where it becomes complicated. Give me a moment to best explain the succession of things." When I stop walking, he looks at me—almost as if he knows what I'm about to ask.

"Before I go on, can we shake hands that all of this stays between us?"

"Just like attorneys have attorney-client privilege and doctors with their patients, I also have a strict confidential relationship between me and my clients." The sincerity in his eyes is genuine. He shakes my hand. "You're not a client," he adds, "you're a friend, and I certainly won't divulge any information you share with me."

"Well then—"

We start walking again, and I tell Phil about Pops's claims that his father, Manuel Miraldo, was the illegitimate son of Carlos I of Portugal. Really? Royal ancestry? I cringe whenever I hear about it, but Pops's stories never, ever varied. Still, wealth and clout had to have been available to my blue-blooded great-grandfather Manuel, supposedly a clever bigwig. Although he didn't inherit any of the alleged royal family's fortune, he did receive some start-up funds and was made head of a small Portuguese company that some years later became MiraCorp. According to Pops's tales, Manuel was granted the monopoly of a hotel chain. He also acquired some radio stations and, with his entrepreneurial skills, later expanded into the lucrative telephone markets of yesteryear.

Being Manuel Miraldo's only child, Pops—at a fairly young age—took his own big ideas abroad, settled in Mexico, and founded Grupo Miraldo. He gradually diversified his business and to this day proudly refers to his fortune as brilliantly self-made. Of course, he takes pride in and never misses the occasion to elaborate on his royal Portuguese ancestry.

During Pops's heydays in Mexico, Grupo Miraldo's economic interests kept growing; the real estate companies, shopping centers, and hotels flourished, not only in Mexico but also in Belize and Guatemala. It's no surprise that too much was never enough for Pops. His next goal was to branch out into the United States, and so he did.

When my father, Marco, and his brother Manoel (named after the *royal* Manuel) came of age, they worked under the strict supervision and guidelines of their father, but, as in many other wealthy families, the long-standing rivalry between the two brothers with clashing personalities kept escalating. Their fierce power struggle should have been apparent from the beginning, but since it was ignored, it became unfixable. The tensions between the brothers reached a boiling point when my uncle Manoel insisted on severing family ties.

"Pops and Dad told me these stories ad nauseam, but an impromptu encounter with my uncle Manoel in Mexico caused me to dig deeper." I stop talking and wonder if the needed mental break might be counterintuitive to all that is left to tell.

Phil suggests a water break. Neither of us speak. The lake is like a mirror and reflects everything around it. Suddenly a fish leaps for a swarm of flies; the motion upsets the smooth silvery surface.

"That was a largemouth bass," Phil says dryly. "My dear Linda introduced me to sportfishing. We spent many summers at Mille Lacs Lake in Minnesota." He returns the water bottle to his waist pack. "I'm ready to hear more if you still want to talk. But I do understand if—"

I turn my gaze away from the lake. "They fed me ugly tales about my uncle Manoel. None ever made sense. That's why after the secret meeting with my uncle, I tried to get to the bottom of the dark, murky family tank. But the more I plumbed its depths, the more I ran into iron walls. The Mexican court records were as classified as CIA top secrets. The only relevant piece I found was via a couple of Mexican tabloids from December 1988. One of them headlined it with 'The Most Money-Grubbing, Accusatory, and Bitter Blood-Relation Rift.' The other called the Miraldo split 'The Biggest, Meanest, Most Amoral Family Feud Ever.' But none of the tabloid writers provided meaningful substance to their accusations. It was all speculation."

"Wow," Phil mutters. "I mentioned earlier I worked for a bank in Mexico during the 1980s, and I vaguely remember hearing and reading about this."

"Are you serious?" I stop walking and square myself in front of him.

Phil shrugs. "I left Mexico in 1989, and from what I recall, wasn't there a settlement in the Mexican courts?"

"Yes. My grandfather and father sold their shares of Grupo Miraldo to Uncle Manoel, and in return they took one-hundred-percent ownership of the sister company in the United States." With great expectation I look at Phil. "Anything else you remember?"

"Sorry, Molly." Phil shrugs again.

I'm disappointed. For just a moment I believed meeting Phil had become my eye-opening destiny. *Maybe it still is.*

"Look at the bright side," he says. "Perhaps we met for a reason; perhaps one day in the future I can be of assistance to you."

"Who knows. In that case, you may want to hear more."

"Absolutely. You definitely piqued my interest."

So I tell Phil that whereas my father immediately embraced the American way of life and cherished his status as president of the company, it took my grandfather more time and effort to blend into America's culture. He kept lamenting how much he missed everything Mexican, repeatedly saying, "I founded Grupo Miraldo, I grew it, I made everybody filthy rich only for my empire to be cut in half. Damn the entitlements! Damn the legal tussles! Damn everything!" Regardless of his woes, Pops managed to reinvent himself again.

I explain that in the late 1980s, the headquarters of Grupo Miraldo USA were established in Wavetown, Wisconsin, a small village with a population of less than a thousand. After the ugly father-son-brother feud in Mexico, Pops, my father, and I moved to Wavetown, where the company's name was immediately changed from Miraldo USA to MiraCo. It's a privately held company that owns entities all over the US, Canada, and the Caribbean. Several years ago, MiraCo slowly began branching out into European and Asian markets. MiraCo's holdings are in hotels, resorts, and golf courses, as well as in large office and residential real estate.

Prior to our move, Pops had been in negotiations with the governing body of the municipality about long-range planning. And whenever Pops wants something badly enough, he usually gets his way. Thus, he got them to rename Wavetown by incorporating it into what is now the Village of Mira.

Pops's first project as CEO of the company was the noted Mira-Co Club Resort, close to our headquarters. He spared nothing to realize another of his American dreams. The result was a magnificent 298-room hotel with several ballrooms, meeting rooms, and conference centers, a spa and fitness facility, and an eighteen-hole championship golf course.

Whereas Pops has been the mover and shaker, my father contributes grandiose ideas; the few that materialize surprisingly turn into profitable venues.

Mira's population today is around 1,400, and many of the townspeople are employees of MiraCo. It's crazy, but wherever I look in Mira today, the name Miraldo pokes me in the eye.

The conceit and self-adulation have always bugged me. It's just not my thing, and it was reason enough for me to move to Milwaukee, where I can walk around incognito and rarely see the name Miraldo. I even created my own separate trusts and put my apartment in one of the trust's names. No mail gets delivered to my Milwaukee home, and due to my crazy work schedule, I rarely run into nosy neighbors. Meanwhile, Pops likes that my official residence remains listed as his address on Bayside Drive in Mira.

My walking partner doesn't interrupt; he just listens. I shoot him a sideways glance when I'm done with my adapted curriculum vitae. *Man, this guy has long legs.* For one of his steps I take two, and we're walking at a fast clip. He's in good shape.

For a while neither of us talk.

"We're almost at the end of the trail," I say. "I jogged this route yesterday in the rain."

"Time to turn around then." After another few minutes of silence, Phil speaks again. "Molly, your tell-all has been quite thought-provoking," he says. "I do have a few questions, if you don't mind."

"Depends on what they are."

"After you graduated from Northwestern School of Law, I assume you started working at MiraCo."

"What do you think?" I don't know if he notices my half-smile. Without going into my extracurricular achievements during college and law school, I tell Phil that it was Pops who prepped, primed, and groomed me for his empire.

"I'm MiraCo's general counsel, and I advise on management and other business issues."

"That doesn't surprise me." Phil excuses himself to retie his shoelaces. When he straightens, he winces. "My knee." He gives me a deadpan look. "Forgive me for being blunt," he says. "Are you married? Engaged? In a relationship?"

I roll my eyes.

"If I've failed to observe the limits of what is appropriate, please don't kick my ready-for-replacement knee."

I grin and make a mock attempt to strike him with my foot.

I see no point in sharing my few and always short-lived affairs with Phil. There's no need to tell him that Pops and Dad always find a way to drive away any guy that comes into my life.

"I'm married to my career; my dates are with projects, tasks, and deals," I say. "Lasting love hasn't been a priority. Maybe it's because neither my father nor grandfather have set the best examples. They made me rather cautious when it comes to affairs of the heart."

Right when I say it, some uncomfortable theory echoes through me. Without thought, I pick up a black stone and toss it towards the lake. I watch it skip only once over the surface before it sinks.

"Since they're so successful, I assume the personal and business relationship between your father and grandfather is quite good."

"Not necessarily. They often clash with each other, but physically they're carbon copies." I stop walking. "Do you want to know what they look like?"

Phil raises his eyebrows, looks at me quizzically.

I point to my face. "The third carbon copy but a female body."

"What do you know," Phil says, still gazing at me. "Then those gentlemen must be rather handsome because you, young lady, are quite beautiful."

"Strong genes, but thank God no royal resemblance to Carlos I of Portugal."

Phil grins. "If your good looks come from your paternal side, maybe you got your wit, charm, and intelligence from your mother."

I immediately clam up.

"You okay? Did I say something wrong?"

I shake my head. "I don't remember my mother or my twin brother; they passed away."

We walk the rest of the way in silence, and I appreciate Phil's backing off in the face of my discomfort.

When we arrive at Five Elements, he reaches out with both arms. "May I?" I nod and he embraces me.

"I hope our paths will cross again, Molly. You know where to find me."

TEN

Mateo, June 1992
Mexico City, Mexico

The forty-five minutes' ride into the city felt painfully endless, especially since Mateo and Marco had been at each other's throats the entire time. Luckily, they were alone in the Mercedes G-Wagon; Benito and León followed in an identical vehicle. Mateo had purchased three of these off-road luxury cars recently because he admired the outrageous power of their big engines and liked the fact that they were built like military utility vehicles. Safeguarding himself and his assets was his highest priority, and these expensive light-armored transports promised protection.

"You've been dishonest in every aspect of life," Mateo grumbled. "If it wasn't for your philandering, double-dealing, and thievery, we wouldn't be in this pathetic position." He glared at his son, whose smirk infuriated him even more. "Everything always revolves around you!"

Marco turned to his father and rolled his eyes. "I learned from the best."

"Watch out!" Without thinking, Mateo reached for the steering wheel, yanking their G-Wagon to the right, missing a van by a hair's breadth.

"¡Dios mío, Marco! What are you doing? You drive as recklessly as you live."

"As I said, I learned from the best. So stop trying to manipulate me and stay out of my affairs," Marco hissed. "Despite your constant criticism, I've made great contributions to the company and to our family, and I'm more than capable of handling shit on my own." He slapped the palm of his right hand against the steering wheel—twice. "I've had it with your fucking disapproval and ridicule. Being with you is like playing leapfrog with a unicorn."

Mateo realized that arguing wouldn't improve the situation they'd been thrown into, but he had to have the last word. "Am I in the wrong movie?" he grunted. "Do I need to remind you of your recent failures? We could've lost seventy-five percent of our advertising had I not come to your rescue again!" He pulled a Kleenex from the box and noisily spat into it. "Your pathetic never-ending display of cockiness makes me want to puke blood." He spat again and threw the ball of Kleenex out the window.

When had everything gone so wrong? Mateo wasn't a saint—far from it—but hadn't he built his empire all by himself? Hadn't he sacrificed and cared for his family? Hadn't he been fair and respectful to every single one of his employees? Wasn't he the one who could make allies out of competitors? Wasn't he known for his prowess as a fair negotiator? And had he not tried to instill these skills into both of his sons? Strangely enough, it was usually Manoel who showed the greater potential and produced better results, due to his principled determination. Manoel was also the one who consistently brought deals to a satisfactory conclusion whereas Marco, the idea man, had turned into a cunning overreacher.

He remembered when Marta held Marco in her arms for the first time. "You are a mirror image of your father," she'd said to the infant. Mateo had been unable to see the similarities then—to him all babies looked the same—but still, Marco was special. Wherever they went, people stopped and swooned over the boy, and photos of him soon appeared in newspapers and magazines with captions describing him as the most photogenic toddler in Mexico. Scouts called and companies tried to put Marco's face on their products. Mateo saw an opportunity. But Marta wouldn't have any of it.

Manoel, a year younger than Marco, was more like Marta. The little guy had a sunny disposition and never hesitated to ask questions that would help him grasp the complexities of the big world around him. His eagerness to learn new things was commendable, his enthusiasm and laughter contagious. Mateo's pride always swelled when people commented that Manoel was a pure joy to be with.

Too quickly the boys grew into young men. Why had Mateo allowed himself to miss so much of their childhood, when they were still malleable? These days, Mateo rarely saw eye to eye with his younger son. Manoel was dependable, intuitive, and trustworthy, but he lacked the guts to take risks, always needed to play it safe.

But Marco was the adventurer, the stuntman, the risk-taker, a replica of Mateo. Working so closely together was in turns an exciting profitable experience or a frustrating ordeal.

Hadn't it been the same with his own father back in Portugal? Mateo had never forgotten the devastation he'd felt when his father told him, "I've tolerated your nonsense far too long. Heed my warning that you are walking on thin ice. I don't give a damn that you've bankrupted your own code of honor, but I won't allow you to ruin the empire I've built!"

To this day his father's closing statement wounded him deeply. "I give you a choice: you can either go back to the bottom of the pecking order or you can leave and build your own kingdom somewhere else—but if you do, make sure it's far away from mine."

And that's exactly what Mateo did. He took what belonged to him and made a fresh start for himself in Mexico, far away from his father. But to this day, Manuel Miraldo's physical and mental abuse, his unfair conduct, deeply pained Mateo.

I shouldn't allow history to repeat itself, he thought, glancing at his son, who stoically stared at the road ahead. *Marco needs me, and I need Marco. Too much is at stake.*

He lightly touched Marco's arm. "Lo siento, hijo."

"I'm sorry, too. I should know to keep my mouth shut when I'm in deep water."

"Water under the bridge." Mateo pointed ahead. "Make a right turn on 16 de Septiembre. We're almost there."

Whenever Mateo came into the city for a night or two, he

resided at the Majestic Hotel de México, always in the same suite. He normally looked forward to these short stays, but instead of bliss, only misery would be waiting for him this time. Hopefully León's contact at the Policía Federal Preventiva had some leads on Marisol's car.

"Keep our two vehicles parked nearby," Marco told the valet. "We may need them again shortly."

When the two bodyguards exited their G-Wagon, Benito froze and muttered, "No lo creo." He slowly walked up to the valet and gave him a slap on the back. "Arturo! Since when do you work here?"

The valet whipped around, glanced briefly in all directions, and whispered, "¿Qué estás haciendo aquí, Benito?" He gave a small smile. "I'm trying to establish a new life. Nobody here knows of my previous employment." Nervously he looked behind himself again.

"Lips sealed already, cabrón." Benito laughed. "But it's good to see you again. Let's catch up later."

"How do you know him?" Mateo asked.

"Old friend—we grew up together."

"Find out if he knows other valets in the industry; if so, it wouldn't hurt to give him Marisol's license plate."

Benito nodded. "Good idea, señor. Consider it done."

"What's taking so long?" Mateo asked when he walked up to his son, still standing by the reception desk. "Problems?"

"We didn't make a reservation. The clerk is seeing if he can release the presidential suite."

"Ridiculous," Mateo said. "Get the manager."

"Señor Miraldo!" With outstretched arms the hotel manager strode towards Mateo and leaned closer. "My clerk is fairly new here," he said, handing Mateo the key cards. "Anything you need, I'm here, always at your service."

Once they were finally settled in the elegant, spacious suite, Marco poured himself a drink. "Can I make you one?" he asked without turning around.

"Make it a double," Mateo said, then instructed León to use one of the suite's phones to make the necessary inquiries.

As Mateo welcomed the relaxing effects of the alcohol, he watched his son pace back and forth like a caged animal.

"Gotta make a call," Marco said and walked into one of the three bedrooms, pulling the heavy door shut behind him.

Mateo instinctively knew who that call would be made to. What the hell did Marco see in Carla de La Fuente? There was no comparison between that perra de mujer and beautiful, sweet Ula.

His thoughts were interrupted when Benito bolted through the door.

"You won't believe this, señor." Benito wiped his forehead with the back of his hand. "They're staying in this hotel! It was my friend who parked Marisol's car a few hours ago."

Mateo jumped to his feet, ignoring the drink spilling onto his pants. "¿Qué estás diciendo?" He slammed the wet glass on the vintage Mexican marble side table.

"Patrón, there's more," Benito said, holding up a plastic bag. Like a magician pulling a rabbit from a hat, the bodyguard removed a doll from the bag, holding it upside down by a leg.

"That's Molara's!"

Benito grinned victoriously. "I found it on the floor of Marisol's car."

"Where are they?"

"Room 309, but they're not there. The concierge told me he made a reservation for them for seven o'clock at Cocina Central Ristorante-Pizzeria, practically right around the corner."

Mateo looked at his Rolex Daytona wristwatch. "That was hours ago."

He knocked loudly against the closed bedroom door. "Marco," he called at the top of his voice. "We found them."

"What? Where?" Marco stood in the doorframe, holding the phone pressed to his chest.

"Right here, in this hotel."

"Gotta go, mi amor, the . . ." Mateo couldn't understand the rest of Marco's sentence, nor did he give a damn.

"What's everyone waiting for? Let's get them now," Marco said, his face still flushed. "What room are they in?" He darted towards the door, but Mateo blocked his way.

"They had a reservation at a restaurant. You and I will stay here in case they return. The manager alerted the staff to be on the lookout." Mateo felt perspiration form on his forehead, but his fingers felt like icicles. "We need to handle this very carefully; we absolutely can't cause a scene in public."

Once the bodyguards had left neither father nor son was able to sit down. With new drinks in their hands, they kept traversing through the presidential suite.

"The manager said their room was prepaid in cash. By whom?" Mateo's voice was dark. "Ula has no money. She didn't steal anything. Nothing was missing."

"It had to be Marisol then," Marco replied, glowering at the empty glass in his hand. He poured himself another drink, this time filling the glass to the rim. "Who the fuck did that bitch rip off?"

⁓

Forty-five minutes later, the two bodyguards returned, looking crestfallen.

"Your group never showed up for their reservation." León's head dropped like a rotten apple. "We checked other restaurants in the plaza, but nobody saw two women with two children; we showed their pictures."

Benito nodded. "We looked everywhere, and given the hour on a Sunday night, there wasn't a lot going on."

"I just called the manager again. They didn't return to their room either." Mateo allowed himself to collapse into one of the sofas. "Where could they have gone with two young children at this hour?"

"Maybe the bitches left us a false trail," Marco said grimly.

"That makes sense, patrón," León said. "Earlier I made some other inquiries, and if you don't mind, I'd like to involve someone else. The guy once worked as a bodyguard and was a friend of Santiago's."

"Santiago? Marisol's brother?"

"Si. His name is Sergio, but he goes by El Gordo." León explained that El Gordo had information on Santiago but refused to share what he knew unless he was paid.

Mateo felt like jumping to his feet but instead only felt himself sinking deeper into the sofa. "Of course. Get this El Gordo over here as soon as possible. I'll make sure he's adequately compensated."

"He can meet us first thing tomorrow morning, if that's okay."

Mateo sighed. "I hate to wait, but it might be too late to accomplish anything at this hour." As soon as the words left his mouth, he was overcome by physical exhaustion, suddenly feeling the effect of all the alcohol he'd consumed. When he pushed himself out of the soft sofa cushions, his legs felt like al dente spaghetti. Hoping nobody noticed, he held on to the back of the chaise to steady himself. "I'm going to rest," he muttered. "Wake me if anything comes up. Otherwise I'll see you as soon as El Gordo gets here."

ELEVEN

Ursula, June 1992
Miami, Florida

For a moment Ursula believed she'd been divided in two. One part of her was sitting on a small kitchen chair in Amelia's tidy kitchen, saying her new name over and over again while practicing her unfamiliar signature as Ursula Burgli on a wrinkled piece of paper. The other part of her was trying to deal with the constant flow of questions racing through her, topics that moved around and around in her head as if they were printed on a rotating banner.

When the sound of joyous squeals tugged her into the present, she wished for the moment in time to linger. She crumpled the piece of paper into a ball and tossed it into the garbage pail, then walked to the window and gingerly parted the sheer white drapery with one finger to look outside.

Dusk slowly flowed into the daylight, giving the translucent haze an almost coral and lilac hue. The sun, not quite set, allowed a few of its already weakened golden rays to filter through the cracked slats of wooden fence that surrounded Amelia's small backyard.

Ursula raised her heels and put all her weight on the balls of her feet. She stretched her neck, trying to look above the fence, wanting to hold on to the light of day. Melancholy would arrive with dusk again; it would be followed by long hours of darkness and abandonment, anxiety and loneliness.

Vacantly she looked at the activity outside. Her twins, together with two other children, were trying to dodge the boy holding the water hose, but they seemed to be moving in slow motion.

"Ursula! Snap out of it!" Hearing her own sharp voice was like a slap to the face. "Snap out of it," she said again, this time softer.

She parted the curtain wider. Marisol and Amelia sat on two folding chairs in the corner of the yard, watching the children, undoubtedly still catching up on each other's lives.

For the past two days Ursula's twins had played with Amelia's Cuban neighbors' children. An involuntary smile spread over Ursula's face when she looked at Miggy. Her normally shy and suspicious little son was laughing and romping around in the small yard with five-year-old Maritsa and three-year-old Joel. Molly, on the other hand, had taken an instant liking to eight-year-old Alejandro. Though almost four years older than Molly, the boy with violet blue eyes never left her side. *Amazing*, Ursula thought, *these two share so many of the same interests; they can't stop challenging each other in games and dialogue.*

Then her smile froze. Little did her children know that in the morning they would have to say goodbye to their new friends and in all likelihood would never see them again.

She felt such gratitude for the temporary protection this hospitable, tight-knit neighborhood had extended to Marisol, herself, and the children.

While making the escape plans with Bruno Rossi in Mexico, Marisol had mentioned Amelia's dependency on welfare, and Bruno immediately had made financial arrangements to ease her financial struggle. But Amelia's acts of kindness could never be repaid in kind.

Ursula held up her hand, wiggling her fingers at both Amelia and Marisol. They both smiled and waved back. Earlier the two women had urged Ursula to rest, but she couldn't. Instead, she'd called Bruno Rossi.

"It was a good idea for you to stay three nights in Miami," Bruno had said. "By creating a triangle of tracks and scents, we've hopefully not only confused any possible bloodhounds but also tired them out. They don't have one clue as to where to begin looking for you."

"If only I could think that way," said Ursula. "I can't rid myself of the gloom that's hovering over me. It's so ominous, like the worst is yet to come."

"Nothing in the next phase should go wrong, Ula. By using different airlines and scheduling your layover in Miami, we've created a diversion."

As Bruno went over every detail again—their flight to Chicago tomorrow, switching to another airline before connecting to Zurich—Ursula listened with closed eyes while wrapping her fingers around both of her thumbs, making a tight fist, a gesture for good luck in her native country.

"I know I'm repeating myself," she said, "but allow me to tell you again that your time, effort, and generosity are beyond legendary."

"You are a brave young woman. Stick with the plan. Once you're safely in Switzerland, you'll be able to confront the future head-on. Meanwhile, in Marta's honor, Señor X and I remain completely committed to helping you."

Ursula's lids were leaden with fatigue. She let go of the kitchen curtains, refilled her glass with water, and walked to the room she shared with her twins. She closed the door and lay down. The sudden silence unsettled her. If only she could fall asleep, not have to think, not have to worry. But as soon as she closed her eyes, brooding thoughts were waiting for her in the prison of her mind. The harder she tried to get rid of them, the more controlling they became, always challenging her to admit her powerlessness. She wanted to focus on good times ahead, but so much of her past had been impacted by dramatic changes and trauma that it was impossible to get off the emotional roller coaster.

"Mamá?"

Ursula bolted into a sitting position and quickly wiped her cheeks when she saw Molly and Miggy standing by the side of the bed.

"Did we wake you?" Miggy asked, climbing onto the mattress next to her.

"Were you crying?" Molly, wide-eyed, leaned into her mother's face.

"No, no, just resting." Ursula feigned a yawn and rubbed her eyes, hoping to eliminate the remaining evidence. "You're already in your pj's, and you smell so clean and yummy." She pulled her children closer and kissed them. "Molly and Miggy, my sweet, delicious M&Ms. Did you have a good time today?"

"I don't want to leave here," said Miggy, snuggling into her arms. "Can you call Papi and abuelo and tell them I don't want to play hide-and-seek anymore?"

"Not yet. One more day and then the game can be over."

There was a knock on the door and Marisol stuck her head into the room.

"Are you okay?"

Ursula nodded. "Thanks for letting me rest," she said quietly and scratched a nonexistent itch on her nose, hoping Marisol wouldn't detect the gloom in her eyes. "Everything ready for tomorrow?"

"Todo bien. The children are tired from all that fresh air and playing in the sun." She blew a kiss. "Good night. See you in the morning."

Ursula transferred Miggy, already asleep in her arms, to the other bed and covered his warm body with a sheet. She kissed the long blond curl on his suntanned forehead. His cheeks reminded her of glazed caramel apples.

"I don't want to leave here either," said Molly when Ursula curled up next to her.

"I know it's hard, especially when you had so much fun."

"You know why I like Alejandro so much?"

"Tell me."

"He understands me. He makes me laugh." Molly looked at the ceiling and smiled. "Did you see his eyes? They remind me of flowers on trees. So beautiful."

"You're right, Alejandro's eyes are violet, like the petals on the jacaranda trees." Ursula pressed her lips to her daughter's forehead.

"Tell me the story of when you were a little girl and went skiing in the mountains," Molly said in a tiny voice. She yawned and laid her head on her mother's chest.

"You mean when I lived with my grandparents in Grindelwald?"

"Uh-huh." Molly yawned again.

Before Ursula had finished her second sentence, Molly's regular, relaxed breaths indicated she had fallen asleep.

When Ursula gently lifted her daughter off her chest, Molly's eyes opened, her long dark lashes fluttering for a fraction of a second. "Mamá," she whispered. Then she smiled and fell asleep again.

Ursula brushed strands of thick, wavy dark hair off Molly's deeply tanned face. A Miraldo face, she thought, focusing on her daughter's finely shaped nose and full lips. Even the attractive cleft in the chin and the defined cheekbones were so much like—

She shuddered, recalling the fateful day of her conception.

As soon as she switched off the lamp, a sliver of moonlight spilled through the small window into the room, illuminating its sparse furnishings. The infinite night sky was freckled with stars, and Ursula wished one would be her lucky one.

"Mamá Marta," Ursula cried into her damp pillow. "I hope you are at peace in that unknown world you entered." Her whimper faded into a sigh. She rolled onto her right side, letting her tears be dried by her daughter's honeyed breaths.

Ursula closed her eyes, hoping to join Molly and Miggy in that sphere where sweet dreams became a reality, but behind closed lids, her twins' sweet faces faded away and were replaced by haunting images of the past.

TWELVE

Ursula, years earlier

Her mother, Emma, had died in childbirth, and had it not been for Rosi and Anton Burgli, Ursula wouldn't even have had the vaguest impression of her mom. Her maternal grandparents made her mother come alive by telling enchanting anecdotes and matching all their stories with photos in thick albums.

"Our Emma's last beautiful gift to us was bringing you into the world," Rosi told Ursula.

"When one angel leaves this world, another one enters," Anton added.

But her father, Robert Graf, blamed Ursula for his wife's death. "Every time I look at you, I see her," he'd say. "I'll never love you the way I loved her." And whenever he'd had too much to drink, he slapped his only daughter's face and screamed, "You should've died instead."

Then Robert Graf decided to remarry. Bertha had no use for five-year-old Ursula and convinced her new husband to hand the child over to Rosi and Anton.

Residing with her grandparents in Grindelwald, a postcard-perfect village in the Swiss Bernese Alps, Ursula saw her life immediately improve. She hiked with family and friends during the summer, and at the onset of every winter season, her grandparents provided her with a new set of skiing gear, proud of the granddaughter who'd mastered even the most difficult pistes in the vast mountain terrain.

Ursula never considered herself a top student, but learning came easy to her. Growing up in a country with four official languages, she was fluent in German, French, and Italian. She also chose to learn English during her fifth year of primary school, and at the age of thirteen, she told her grandparents she wanted to become a teacher.

Burgli's Alpenhaus was a popular restaurant in Grindelwald, and when Ursula turned sixteen, her grandparents occasionally allowed her to assist, serving specialties of the house to the loyal clientele. Adjacent to the restaurant was Burgli's Après-Ski Bar, the in place to grab a drink before dinner, to be seen and make new friends.

That winter, a talent scout for a Swiss modeling agency discovered Ursula when she served him a steaming plate of Zürcher Geschnetzeltes with rösti.

"Your granddaughter," the scout told the Burglis, "is exactly what we're looking for, a fresh new face! With her natural beauty, Ursula will barely have to wear makeup. On top of that, she's the ideal height and has a terrific personality."

"Did you see this?" asked Bertha and pointed to an article in the local newspaper. Graf, just having returned from work, was in a foul mood. Reading the article about his daughter's opportunity put a grin on his face. The following morning he drove to Grindelwald and knocked on the Burglis' door.

"But it's a grown-up industry with grown-up pressures." Rosi and Anton tried to reason with him. "She hasn't even finished twelfth grade yet."

"I'll let her finish school, but she'll only attend university after she's outgrown her looks," he told his former in-laws.

"You can't take me away from here," Ursula protested. "I don't care about the stupid modeling, and I really don't want to live with you and Bertha in Zurich." She begged her grandparents to interfere.

Graf laughed into the Burglis' faces. "You have no rights whatsoever! I'm her father and legal guardian, and she'll do what I tell her to," he yelled.

Ursula kicked and screamed when Graf yanked her from the Burgli house, shoving her and her two suitcases into his brand-new midnight-blue Mercedes-Benz.

Soon after, he declared himself his daughter's manager and insisted on investing her quickly rising earnings while keeping her on a tight financial leash.

It didn't take long before Ursula noticed the discrepancies between her earnings and the modest bank deposit her father occasionally showed her.

Soon after her seventeenth birthday, Elke Schott, another runway model and Ursula's best friend, pulled her aside. "See that lady in the first row, the one that looks like Joan Collins?" Elke pointed to a woman with a big hairdo and heavy makeup. "She's a scout for Elite Model Management. She wants to talk to you."

Behind her father's back and encouraged by her grandparents, Ursula decided to accept the offer from the US model agency and move to Los Angeles.

Just when she thought her life was heading in the right direction, her nosy, manipulative stepmother searched Ursula's room and found correspondence from Elite—envelopes Ursula believed she'd safely hidden in books on shelves and between folded sweaters in drawers.

"What are these?" Graf screamed when Ursula returned home from school. "You planned on signing a contract behind my back?" One after the other he tore up the letters and tossed the paper shreds into the fireplace.

"Did she really think she could escape to Los Angeles without our knowledge?" he asked Bertha. They both snickered. "You're not going anywhere! Let me tell you that I have much bigger and more financially rewarding plans for you"—he elbowed Bertha—"as well as for us."

Ursula was completely caught off guard when, soon afterwards, her father insisted on a union between her and Marco Miraldo, the heir apparent to a Mexican conglomerate.

Panicking, she called her grandparents in Grindelwald.

"He wants to ship me off to Mexico to get married," she cried.

"What? He can't do that! Who is the man?"

"I have no idea. Supposedly, a few months ago he introduced me to a Mateo Miraldo, the father of the man I'm supposed to marry. But I couldn't pick that man out of a lineup of all the other wealthy guys my father has tried to hook me up with."

"Dear God." Ursula's grandmother sighed. "Graf's involvements always smell fishy. We'll have to find a way to stop him."

"Knowing your father, he made a cash deal for himself by selling you off to strangers in a faraway land. I won't allow him to ruin your life," added her grandfather. "We'll be in Zurich tomorrow to talk to him. Meanwhile, can you contact the US talent agency again? It might not be too late to get you out of the country."

But when Rosi and Anton expressed their strong disapproval to Robert Graf, he threw them out of his house and threatened to cut off all future contact with Ursula.

Aware time was running out, Ursula confided in Elke Schott, who immediately contacted the scout from Elite on her friend's behalf. But before Ursula could implement the new plan, Robert Graf arranged a dinner soirée at Zurich's Grand Hotel in honor of his Mexican guests, Mateo Miraldo and his son Marco.

"I'm not going!" Ursula squared herself in front of her father. "And you can't force me to get married," she protested. "Especially not to a complete stranger—someone you picked for your financial benefit."

Robert Graf grabbed her by the shoulders and shoved her hard against the wall. "How many times do I have to remind you that you'll do what I tell you? If I hear one more complaint coming out of your mouth, I'll ruin your life in ways you can't imagine possible." His breath was hot, his bloodshot red eyes glowed devilish.

"You may not remember, but we've met once before," said Mateo, drawing Ursula tightly into his muscular arms. She wriggled out of the confining embrace. Although her father's threats still rang in her ear, she concealed her contempt by rewarding the Mexican men with her most neutral expression.

"My God, you look ravishing," Mateo exclaimed over and over again, still holding Ursula's hand. He turned to his son. "Doesn't she?"

Marco nodded. "Yes. Very nice." He stared into his empty glass and conspicuously avoided eye contact.

Ursula interpreted the younger Miraldo's behavior as shy and humble, most likely owing to the powerful presence of his father. But as the evening progressed, she was unprepared for her reaction to him. Young, with relatively little experience on the dating scene, Ursula found herself glancing at Marco. His handsome tan face, brilliant hazel eyes, and long dark lashes had a magnetizing effect on her.

During the following two days, Ursula showed him the city, and by the time they'd strolled along the Limmat River and reached their last destination, she had told Marco most everything about her life. But had he been as honest with her? She wasn't sure.

All doubt ebbed away when he pulled her into his arms and his demanding lips parted hers. The intense mix of helplessness and bliss erased all her uncertainties. She held on to him tightly, as if he was the only dependable and trustworthy individual left in her world. Was it love that made her tremble? Was it hope that caused her nerves to tingle? Bathing in this warm pool of happiness, she let go of all inhibition and returned his kiss.

On their last evening together, Marco whirled her expertly across the dance floor, showing her new steps. Suddenly he stopped, pulled her close. His warm breath filled her ear when he whispered, "Marry me. You seem to have the power to free me from my father's chains." Giddy and innocent, Ursula believed she'd found her life's love and purpose.

Before she left for Mexico, she asked her father for her earnings and investments, but Robert Graf pointedly refused. "What for?" he sneered. "You'll never need another cent from me. Don't you realize you're marrying the heir to a Mexican fortune?"

Things thereafter accelerated, and Ursula felt as if she was on a runaway train. Her father had said he'd purchased airline tickets for himself, his wife, and Rosi and Anton. "All four of us will arrive in Mexico City three days before the best day of your life," he'd said. But when none of her family arrived, she knew she had been deceived again.

Heartbroken, she placed another call to her beloved grandparents. They too had been tricked by Robert Graf's treacherous cock-and-bull stories. He'd told his former in-laws the wedding had been postponed and that a new date was yet to be announced. By the time Ursula had grasped the deceit, it was too late for her grandparents to book a flight in time for the wedding.

Unable to stop crying, she sought solace from Marco, but he shrugged. "Get over it," he said. "Didn't you tell me you never liked your father or stepmother? So what's the big deal?" He excused himself and left her alone with her tears.

What should she do? She had fallen in love with a man who was suddenly treating her indifferently. What would the marriage, her whole future, be like in this foreign country? Maybe she could still get out of it, but where would she go? She had no money. In her despair she turned to Mateo.

"I don't understand what's happening," she said. "I feel as if there's been a conspiracy and I'm being manipulated by everybody."

"Mi amor," the older Miraldo said and took her in his arms. "It's a simple misunderstanding." He kissed her hair. "Give it time. I'll see to it that you love your life here." He kept kissing the top of her head, to the point it made her uncomfortable and she pushed him away.

"These are words I want to hear from my husband, not from my father-in-law."

Mateo swallowed. "Let me talk to Marco."

"I don't recognize your son," she said. "In Switzerland he promised me heaven on earth and showered me with love and attention, but since I arrived in Mexico he's become brash and brazen and rarely shows interest in me." Was that a fake or real smile on Mateo's face? Ursula couldn't tell. She knew so little about this man.

"Marco also promised to promote my modeling and acting career and bragged about his close ties to Mexico's best talent agencies. But once I arrived at the hacienda, he told me to forget about my dreams of a career. He even said I'm not fit to be a model or actor in Mexico. Instead, I should concentrate on being a *model* to the servants and learn how to *act* like mistress of the house." Ursula angrily wiped a tear off her cheek.

"Mi amor," Mateo said again, this time softer. "Give him time. Give me time. Everything will work out." He took her hand and kissed it.

But every day before the wedding, things only got worse. Ursula felt like an animal on a leash as she was forced to follow commands and orders. Even her wedding dress was chosen by Marco. And though she looked stunning in a beautiful ballgown designed by Alfonso Herrera, Mexico's top couturier, Ursula could barely breathe when the designer laced her upper body inside a tight corset, forcing her breasts close together.

"I don't like being exposed like Anne of Austria in the seventeenth century," Ursula protested. "I hate the way it makes me look!" Marco laughed and left the room, but Mateo, always present, took her aside, assuring her she would be the most magnificent bride in all of Mexico. He fastened a pearl and diamond necklace around her neck; its huge pendant, like a focal point, lay cold and heavy on Ursula's painfully enhanced cleavage.

It had been her dream to walk down the aisle flanked by her beloved grandparents. Instead, she felt Mateo's fingers tightly interlacing hers as he shepherded her towards the altar. She vaguely remembered the four flower girls in ballerina-like dresses sprinkling rose petals onto the chapel's old stone floors. One of the little girls tripped, fell, and had to be removed from the ceremony because she wouldn't stop screaming. The young ring bearer dropped Ursula's ring and took a long time to retrieve it.

During the seemingly endless ceremony, a heavy fog settled on Ursula's brain. Though it was difficult for her to understand the ceremony in a language she had only recently begun to learn, she'd delivered her rehearsed vows delicately and spoke slowly, whereas Marco recited them at lightning speed, as if he was losing a race against time. Later, when more than four hundred guests—all strangers to Ursula—applauded the union and complimented Marco on his bride's beauty, she choked back tears. She feared the many mishaps during the ceremony foreshadowed disastrous consequences yet to come.

How could she have been so blind and brainless? The times Marco paid attention to her and showed any kindness after the wedding were few and far between. She only felt desired when he introduced her to his wealthy, fashionable, influential friends, gloating over the compliments he received about his wife's beauty and sunny personality. She soon realized that Marco needed the excessive adulation to get turned on—the more accolades, the greater his amatory exploits. But how long do friends express their admiration? The moment the flattery fizzled away, Marco trailed off as well. Sometimes he wouldn't come home for days, and when he did, he usually was in a foul mood, tranquilizing his temper with tequila. And as soon as the desired effect kicked in, he demanded bizarre sexual acts from his wife.

Ursula wanted so much to please him, but the more she gave in to his desires, the more he asked of her. Her shyness and inexperience often caused him to physically abuse her, especially when she failed to fulfill his fantasies, which ranged from sadistic bondage to humiliating exhibitionism. At the climax of one of these long, perverse exploitations, he screamed out, "Yes, Carla! I'm all yours!"

"Who is Carla?" Ursula asked for an explanation.

Marco ripped off the chains that had tied her to the bedposts. "You want an answer?" He threw the metal bondage on her nude body. "The only reason you're in my life is to give me an heir, and so far you've even failed that simple task!"

Clearly, her marriage had been an unforgivable mistake. Though she lived on a luxurious, lush estate, the Miraldo hacienda felt like a barren, desolate wasteland.

Ursula had no desire to be impregnated by a brute of a man; all she could think of was getting a divorce and returning to Switzerland. But how? Her passport had been taken away from her, and someone was always watching her. Now that she'd married into the Catholic faith in Mexico, and with no money of her own, would she ever be able to break through the invisible bars of the opulent prison that held her captive?

She so badly wanted to talk to her grandparents, tell them about her misery and ask for help, but was afraid she might endanger their lives. Her father had cold-bloodedly sold her—why would he hesitate to rid himself of Rosi and Anton?

In total despair she turned to Mateo for help, but little did she know that her debonair father-in-law was practically waiting to take advantage of her vulnerabilities. Slyly, he finagled her trust and tricked her into believing in him. Since she was desperate for a friend, she convinced herself she had found one in Mateo.

Ursula counted it a blessed day when he allowed her to build a flower garden and introduced her to Marisol, the head housekeeper of the hacienda. With the help of other hacienda staff, Ursula and Marisol designed the plot, chose trellises, and selected varieties of flowers. Working so closely together, Ursula learned to trust Marisol and began confiding in her. And on a particularly beautiful spring day, Marisol introduced her young mistress to Marta, Mateo's estranged wife.

Ursula always had wanted to meet her mother-in-law, who, for unexplainable reasons, had attended the wedding ceremony but disappeared like a ghost immediately after, as if she were a figment of Ursula's imagination.

"I suggest you stay away from Marta," said Mateo matter-of-factly when Ursula told him of the introduction.

"What? Why?"

"Becoming a well-known artist turned Marta into an eccentric, nasty recluse, and other than her two sons, nobody visits her home. Though I allow her to live in the largest casita on *my* estate, I never go near her."

Mateo leaned closer. "She's not a nice person," he whispered. "That's why I haven't lived with her for many years."

Ursula pulled away. "Why didn't you divorce her?"

Mateo blinked rapidly. "I'm a man of great faith. I cannot break my vows." Lowering his voice, he added, "For personal reasons I *forbid* you to see Marta."

Marco was furious after being told Ursula had spent an afternoon in Marta's studio. "Didn't my father warn you? How dare you see my mother again!"

"I don't care! She invited me and wanted—"

"Didn't you hear me the first time?" He slapped Ursula hard across the face. "You stay away from her."

Since that day, more watchful eyes were on Ursula, and she didn't dare go near Marta's house again. Noticing Ursula's increasing depression, Marisol came to the rescue. At first she only carried messages back and forth, but slowly Ursula built up the courage to meet with her mother-in-law whenever both Miraldo men were away from the hacienda for either business or social reasons.

"You don't need to worry anymore," Marta said at one of their get-togethers, as they watered the plants in the terrarium. "Since money never fails to buy complete loyalty in Mexico, I paid off the staff they asked to watch you." Noticing how frail Ursula had become, Marta hugged her gently. "My heart breaks that my son is treating you so badly."

"I still have not given up hope," Ursula said on a rainy day when she sat in Marta's studio, watching her mother-in-law put the final brushstrokes on *Adiós a la Ira*, a contemporary triptych. "I wish Marco knew I'd do anything for him to love me."

Marta cleaned the brush and sat across from Ursula. "My sweet, innocent girl, you are my daughter, and I'm working on a plan to help you. In the meantime, you shouldn't believe much of anything either Mateo or Marco tells you, nor can you let them know about our close bond." Marta's eyes were dark with worry. "There's so much you don't know. In due time I'll fill you in. Meanwhile, I must make sure you're safe."

THIRTEEN

Molly, May 2019
Mira, Wisconsin

On this late afternoon, I squint into the saffron-yellow sun that already hangs low above the lake, almost as if it wants to dip into the mirrorlike water. I certainly will miss the spa grounds and tranquility here. *Five Elements, I'll come back,* I promise before I get into the car.

My return to reality won't be smooth. I expect the lynch mob to be waiting for me. At least this evening I'll be able to enjoy a few more peaceful hours in my apartment before entering the blistering core of planet MiraCo tomorrow.

Should I call Pops? Nah, he's okay; I talked to him this morning. A few days ago, he returned to his house on Bayside Drive. The advance treatment and rehab center released him early because he wouldn't stop bitching about his confinement there. Hopefully the visiting physical therapists and whoever else he hired will have an easier time with him in the comfort of his home.

I lied earlier when he asked me to stop by on my way home.
"Sorry, Pops, I have plans."
"With whom? Man? Woman?"
"Both."
Now I feel guilty.
Shit, what's going on? I stretch my neck. A slowpoke in a Honda

Civic is driving about forty miles per hour in the left lane of the expressway. Traffic behind is building up.

Why do I still have trouble telling Pops to back off whenever he treats me like a teenager? Like when he says "Who are you going out with tonight?" or "Make sure you don't get home too late" or "Who are you on the phone with?"

It's so annoying. I'm almost thirty years old, yet I never have the guts to say "Back off!" I think it's because for every part of my life I remember, my family consisted of Pops. My father was mostly unavailable, I had no mother, no siblings, aunts, uncles, cousins. He was the one who was there for me when I woke up in the morning and who said good night to me. He basically was the only one who showed me love and affection.

Oh good! There's an opening in the middle lane. Quick! As I pass the Honda, I manage a glimpse at the slowpoke and see a little white-haired lady, barely able to see over the steering wheel.

Immediately I think of Pops. Didn't he get his license renewed earlier this year? I shudder at the thought of him driving again after his stroke.

Ding. There's a message from my father on the screen. *Are you home yet? I need to see you tonight. It's of great importance.*

Shit. What could be of great importance? Maybe something wrong with Pops?

"Dial Dad," I command. It doesn't even ring twice before he answers.

"Molara, are you home?"

Typical. No hello, no how are you, no I missed you.

"Nice to hear your voice, Daddy," I say sweetly. "Are you and Ava still honeymooning on this lovely May evening?"

"That's what I want to talk to you about, Molara."

He sounds agitated.

"Hmm. Talk."

"Not over the phone. I can meet you at your place in forty-five minutes."

Darn it. Do I really have to invent another cock-and-bull story? "Sorry, Dad. I'm on my way to see friends for a birthday dinner," I say in a tight voice. "Is Pops okay?"

"Of course. He's like a round-bottomed tilting toy. Not even a stroke can keep him down; he miraculously pops right up again."

I think I detect hostility in his voice. "Then what's the urgency?"

There's a pause.

"Dad?"

"Never mind, Molara," he says, sounding wounded. "If you're too busy for me, I'll figure things out myself."

"C'mon, Dad." I hesitate before I say what I don't want to say. "If it's such an urgent matter, I'll cancel my plans. Otherwise, tell me now."

Another pause. A clearing of the throat. "It's Ava," he says hoarsely. "She's left me."

"What?" I pretend to sound shocked, but I'm not really. Ava is only three years older than me, and my dad is, well, my dad. If his trophy wife left him, he'll need to lament wife number four. First my mother, then Carla de La Fuente, then Annie, now Ava. I'm glad I'm not sitting across from my father right now; my grin wouldn't improve his already rotten mood.

"She's not answering my calls or texts, and I don't know where she is." His voice pierces through the speakers like a serrated knife. "It's a curse, déjà vu."

"Sorry, Dad. Why do you think I can help?"

"I want you to call her from your phone. She might pick up when she sees it's you—she admires you. She'll agree to meet you. And when it comes to negotiations, you're a pro."

"You want me to negotiate your relationship? I don't even know what the issues are between you two."

"That's why I have to see you tonight. I need to explain everything about Ava. She fools people with her naïveté and sweetness, but she's sly like a fox."

I roll my eyes. I saw through Ava the first time we met. She gave a lovey-dovey performance, but her acting wasn't even mediocre. I saw dollar signs dancing in her huge pupils the whole time.

I hear him sigh for the second time but don't feel sorry for him. I feel bad for myself. Once again, he's involving me in his warped affairs of the heart. Knowing my father's history, whatever happened is at least half his fault. Still, now isn't the time to grill him about the part he's played in fiasco number four.

"Molara? Are you there?"

"You want my advice, Dad?" I'm right around the corner from my apartment building now. "Stop calling or texting Ava. Have a couple of drinks and sleep on this whole thing. Your head will be clearer tomorrow." Afraid to lose the signal, I park in front of my garage. "Tomorrow, on my way to work, I'll stop by your house for coffee."

"Well, this isn't how I envisioned my evening. I can't believe other people are more important to you. Why do you—"

"Sorry, Dad!" I interrupt. "I'm at my friends' house. I'll see you in the morning."

I disconnect the call and, with a sigh, pull into my parking spot, hoping I dodged the bullet—at least for tonight.

I love my apartment. When it came on the market a few years ago, I immediately made an offer because it had amazing eastern and western exposure. On clear mornings, I watch the sun rise over Lake Michigan, and if I'm home before dusk, I love to watch the sun retreat behind the city.

I lean against the window frame, look at the horizon while taking a sip of my favorite Beaux Frères Pinot Noir from Oregon. I slowly count out loud: "Eight, seven, six, five, four, three, two, one . . ." And with that, the fiery red orb sinks from view, signaling twilight to beckon the stars.

The dryer buzzes; it's letting me know my final load of laundry—mostly fitness gear—is ready to be folded and put away.

While refilling my wine glass, I debate whether I should check emails and phone calls from last week. I only took my private phone to Five Elements, purposely avoiding all business matters on the other devices. Ah, what the heck. Why not get ahead of the game. I power on my work phone and my Mac; I'll survey some stuff now, then face the rest tomorrow.

After reading some important material and answering several emails, I forward a bunch of stuff to Maxwell, my go-between, my buffer against all unwanted stress—my very best friend.

I lean back in the chair and look at my empty wine glass. Should I have another refill? I realize I haven't eaten since the vegan lunch at Five Elements when I ordered the jackfruit pizza with almond ricotta, the one Phil Flores introduced me to. I smile, thinking of this older man who was so comfortable to talk to. Next time I'm in Chicago, I'll give him advance notice; maybe he'll be available to meet for coffee.

It's almost nine o'clock and I'm hungry. Yawning emptiness greets me when I open the fridge. No problem. In the freezer is a full assortment of Daily Harvest. I grab a flatbread loaded with sweet potatoes, brussels sprouts, tomatillo, and whatever-other healthy toppings. I sip my wine while the flatbread heats up, then carry everything to my desk.

Just as I sit down, a text message pops up from Maxwell.

Welcome home. Miss you. Saw you answered a few emails already. Tomorrow I'll clue you in on the good, a few bad, and some unavoidable ugly you'll have to deal with. Also, a Spanish-speaking woman kept calling on the main business line again and again, asking for you. They finally forwarded her call to me. Her English wasn't good. She pronounced your name in a strange way and kept saying something about you being unaware of the truth. Then she switched to Spanish, and the only word I understood was importante. She only left her number, no name. Anyway, enjoy a peaceful evening. Can't wait to see you tomorrow. —Me

I put the rest of flatbread on the plate and wipe my mouth with the napkin while my eyes remain on Maxwell's message. What unknown truth? Who is this woman? Maybe someone from the years I don't remember? *Wow!*

Maxwell didn't give me her contact information. I text him back. Within seconds there's an apologetic message with a phone number.

Area code 224. I stare at it. What if she's some sick crackpot? But curiosity is getting the upper hand. Didn't Einstein say something like curiosity has its own reason for existing? I stand up, and then, without another thought, I retrieve my business phone and dial the number.

"Sí."

"Me llamo Molara Miraldo—"

The woman's wail catches me off guard.

"Lo siento," she whimpers between sobs.

I continue in Spanish. "You left a message at my office. Who are you?"

"My name is Amelia Rubio," the woman says in a nasal voice. "I met you in Miami in 1992. Perhaps you don't remember me; you were just four years old."

I don't remember, of course, but see no need to share that with her.

"You stayed in my house in Miami with your beautiful mama, your twin, and Marisol."

I suck in some air, then exhale and dare ask her who Marisol is.

"You don't remember?" she says. "I was the one who drove all of you to the airport, but I'd already left when the accident happened. I didn't learn of it until later when Marisol phoned me; she, your mama, and brother were in hiding. It broke my heart listening to her."

I want to bombard her with questions but force myself to hold back. This Amelia could be a con artist; maybe she read about the airport accident in the papers, put the pieces together, and now sees an opportunity to get her hands on some easy money, especially if she knows about the Miraldo conglomerate. I must be careful.

When the woman talks again, I can't hear what she's saying. Quickly I raise the volume on my phone.

". . . and that's why it's so difficult to tell you." Her voice quivers. "Marisol was your and your brother's nanny. She was your mother's close friend and confidante."

My nanny? I swallow.

"Marisol wanted to know if you ever received the letters your mother wrote you."

"I never got any letters!" I hope this strange woman detects my annoyance.

"But your mama sent them—first to Mexico and later to your home on Bayside Drive in Mira, Wisconsin."

Whose house on Bayside Drive? My father's or Pops's? Of course, I don't say any of this out loud. I'm reluctant to believe this woman.

"Whoever Marisol is, why isn't she calling me instead of you?"

"Oh Dios mío," she whimpers. "I am so sorry, *Mull-ly*."

Something rattles a memory; it's the way she pronounces my name, *Mull-ly*. I reach for the chair behind me, pull it closer and fall into it. My heart pounds and my nerve ends begin to sting as if they're trying to pierce through my skin.

"Marisol begged me—" The woman clears her throat between sniffles. "To tell you when . . ." Her voice now sounds feeble and far away.

"I can't hear you!"

"She was so very sick but came to see you one more time . . ."

A grinding noise on the other end swallows parts of the woman's sentences.

". . . begged me to contact you, tell you that your mother and brother are waiting."

Her sobs are getting to me. I muster up my strength, press my hands against the edge of the desk, and forcefully speak into my phone as if I were addressing an audience.

"Enough!" I say. "My mother and twin brother are dead! They passed away in 1995! Are you and this Marisol shamans? Mediums who can communicate with the dead?"

"Mull-ly, no. Please listen to me before you might hear from the wrong people, maybe law enforcement."

Law enforcement? *Who is this crazed woman?* My chest tightens.

"Stop it," I say with less conviction behind my words. Part of me wants to suppress my urge to hear more, but I swallow my resistance. "What is it that you want me to know?"

"Mull-ly, please trust me. Your father and grandfather fabricated everything; they've been lying to you—"

"Stop! You don't know what you're talking about."

There's a loud crackle on the line, and the stranger's words keep getting swallowed up by static.

"Hello?" I say, raising my voice, suddenly afraid of losing the connection, of not learning more. "Hello! Speak up, I can't hear you."

". . . and was frightened to contact you again."

Another loud crackle. Dammit.

". . . Mateo's bodyguard threatened her, dragged her into . . ."

I strain, barely comprehending what she's saying. Am I really hearing fragments, or is my brain trying to block the incoming data?

"What are you trying to tell me, Amelia?" Omigod. Something strange lurks around the edge of my subconscious when I say her name. "Please stop."

"They lied to you, Mull-ly!"

There's more static now. I can't hear what she's saying.

". . . worries if you really wanted it or were forced to write your letter . . ." Loud, long crackle. ". . . you never want to see her again." Static.

I shake my phone as if that'll make the reception better. "I can't hear you!" I press the phone hard against my ear. "What letter? And who the heck did I never want to see again?"

"Your mama." The voice is now weak, as if from far, far away. ". . . scared something will happen to . . ." Static. ". . . but you must be very careful when . . ." Crackle. ". . . DNA test results . . ."

What is this crazy woman saying now? I feel paralyzed, at a loss for words. My head is spinning.

"Mull-ly? You still there?"

The static hurts my ear. "Stop harassing me, Amelia. You don't know what you're saying."

"I speak the truth, Mull-ly." Crackle. "Try to find the letters." Static. "Your mama and brother want you to know that—"

"They're both dead. Why are you telling me these lies?"

"I don't lie, Mull-ly. They are alive."

FOURTEEN

Mateo, June 1992
Mexico City, Mexico

Through narrowed eyes, Mateo watched El Gordo. The man had consumed an entire plate of pan dulce, followed by huevos rancheros and chilaquiles, downing the feast with sweet, creamy coffee.

This guy looks like the bleached version of the Incredible Hulk, Mateo thought grimly, holding his breath when the chair creaked under the hefty man's weight.

Annoyed with the whole situation, Mateo scratched his neck in irritation. Under normal circumstances he would never share the details of his current cursed circumstances with a stranger. All new employees, especially bodyguards, were thoroughly vetted before they were allowed to set foot into the inner sanctum of the Miraldo empire. But Mateo was basically clueless about this guy's background and connections.

Still squinting at El Gordo, Mateo reluctantly willed himself to swallow his skepticism and suspicion. What other choice did he have?

For an hour already, El Gordo had supplied Mateo with a steady drumbeat of information. He'd learned why Santiago Rodriguez had been killed by the cartel and why his widow Amelia had fled across the border, seeking refuge with family and friends in Little Havana.

"For reasons of safety, Amelia took her maiden name again but didn't have to," El Gordo said. "Once the cartel realized they'd killed the wrong guy, they had no interest in his wife or any of Santiago's connections."

Mateo looked at his watch: nine o'clock. He wished room service would pick up the mess of leftover items from breakfast. He hadn't touched any of his food, even had trouble looking at it due to the stress and the previous night's drinking. Plus, he had barely slept. Earlier he'd downed a large glass of AlkaSeltzer, but it took three cups of black coffee before he felt better.

"Is everybody done eating?" Mateo said, gesturing at the untidiness on the table. "What's the next step?"

Instead of an answer, the hulk emitted a loud belch. "Perdóname," he said and burped again. "Let me make another call." He walked over to the desk and picked up the phone. "I can't get a line," he grunted.

Mateo frowned. Marco had sequestered himself behind closed doors for forty minutes; no doubt he was still talking to the she-devil. Tight-lipped, he walked into his son's bedroom. "Marco! The new guy has to make a call! Get off the damn phone!"

"One minute," Marco mouthed to his father, then turned away, quietly speaking into the receiver. He gave a half-suppressed laugh and whispered again before releasing the phone into the cradle.

"Are we ready to go?" Marco asked, looking like a dog who just had consumed delicious forbidden food.

"I don't understand you, son. Don't you comprehend the crisis we face?" Mateo shook his head. "I really don't get it," he said, wondering if he looked as miserable as he felt.

"C'mon, Papá. You sound like you're dying; I can almost hear the death rattle from across the room." Marco laughed while buttoning his shirt and zipping up his pants. He glanced in the mirror and patted down a few strands of hair. "Okay, I'm ready. What's the plan?"

Mateo turned his back on Marco and walked through the door.

"The line is open now."

"Forget it. I used my burner phone." El Gordo shot Mateo and Marco an angry look. "Had you guys been here, I wouldn't have to fucking repeat myself now."

Mateo glared back at the hulk. "If you want me to pay your inflated fee, don't tell me where I should be or what I should do." He squared himself in front of El Gordo, looking up into his ugly pockmarked face. "Do you or don't you want to be on my team?"

Startled, El Gordo took a step back and apologized. "Jefe," he said in a softer voice, "you may not like what I just learned." The hulk cleared his throat and fidgeted with the collar of his floral Hawaiian shirt. "My contact found out that the party you're looking for left Mexico late last night. They're already in Miami."

"Those bitches took my children out of the country?" Marco kicked the nearest chair. "What. The. Fuck?" He swept a stack of magazines off the sideboard. "What the fuck are we going to do now?"

Overcome by lightheadedness, Mateo slumped into the swan chaise lounge. How had Ula pulled this off when their passports were still in the safe in the hacienda? Who had helped her plan this complicated getaway? If Marta were still healthy, Mateo would have bet on her. But she'd been locked up in a memory care facility for the past four years, didn't even know her own name anymore. He stared at his feet.

"Patrón, you okay?"

"I'm thinking." Struggling to regain his composure, Mateo straightened his back and looked at the hulk. "Call your informant immediately. Find out where this damn Amelia lives. If Marisol contacted her, then—" Mateo quickly weighed his options. "We have no other choice. We need to fly to Miami."

"¿Qué?" El Gordo's voice cut through the deadly silence in the room.

"You heard me! We will leave this hotel immediately. We'll get our passports and pack a change of clothes." The hulk attempted to interrupt, but Mateo paid no attention. "I'll make arrangements for us to leave at four this afternoon from the executive airport near Coyoacán."

"Wait!" El Gordo's voice sounded like a strained foghorn. "I don't like flying, especially not in small planes."

"Seriously?" Marco laughed.

The hulk glared at him.

Marco smiled smugly. "Don't worry, there's a tiny pill for big guys like you. Taken with a few shots of tequila, it's the perfect antidote for nervous flyers."

El Gordo looked down his nose at the younger Miraldo, grumbled an obscenity, then turned his attention to Mateo. "My fee didn't include flying out of Mexico!"

"What's the difference?"

"More safeguarding. Additional steps to avoid possible dangers," the hulk huffed. "For this scenario, we need manpower in the US, and of course, the new guys will want to get paid. So our deal is off unless you come up with additional—"

"You want more money from us? You want my kidney, too?" Marco said.

Glowering, El Gordo stepped towards Marco. "I promised myself I'd act pleasant, but now I wish I was born with a few more middle fingers."

"Quiet!" Mateo motioned El Gordo into the other room to negotiate the additional sum. When the two men reentered the suite's living room, Mateo told his son the hulk had lost his fear of flying.

Later that afternoon, while gazing through the window of his Cessna Citation into the endless skies, Mateo felt as if he were locked in an otherworldly cocoon, racing head-to-head with the unknown. Most of his life he'd been proud of his ability to muscle his way through risk and uncertainties, but this situation left him feeling strangely emasculated. His mastery of wheeling and dealing, his ability to maneuver a rival into submission, might be useless now.

Loud chatter yanked him out of his ruminations. Were Marco and El Gordo at each other's throats again? Mateo turned his head and to his surprise found his son and the three bodyguards engaged in a lively discussion. Whatever Marco was saying caused all four men to break into violent laughter.

Mateo knew how sharp-witted and entertaining Marco could be. When was the last time he'd praised his son for his shrewdness and practical knowledge? He couldn't remember.

The four men laughed again. Incredible how jovial they were when they were about to engage in a kidnapping on foreign soil. Earlier, through further phone calls, El Gordo had learned that his Miami connections already had wormed their way into Amelia's neighborhood, dug up information, and discovered that Amelia had houseguests—two women and two children.

Mateo loathed the hulk's constant half-suppressed giggles; the big man's tiny yellowed teeth kept reminding him of a row of dried-up corn kernels. Irritated, he looked at his watch. One more hour before they'd touch down at Opa-Locka, the airport used for mostly private jets, only eight miles north of Miami's International Airport.

They had a reservation for four rooms at a hotel in between the two airports, and a rented Chevy G30 surveillance van would be waiting for them.

Mateo got out of his seat, stretched, and turned to the four men, still engaged in a spirited conversation. "Have you been able to reach your contacts with the plane's phone?"

"Indeed!" El Gordo said between bites of a thick roast beef sandwich, dripping with juices. The hulk wiped his mouth and chin with the back of his hand. "I got Amelia Rubio's address. My contacts are watching her house."

"Do they have the number of the cell phone I gave you?"

"Si. My guys will be in touch with me." El Gordo belched loudly.

"Patrón," Benito cut in. "Why do we have to wait? If we have her address in Little Havana, why can't we go there tonight and do what we came for? We could be home by morning if all goes well."

"Whoa whoa whoa! Not so hasty, cabrón," El Gordo scolded. "The streets of Little Havana are filled with gangs, drugs, and violence. It's also a tight-knit, protective community where everybody watches out for one another. Certain folks there don't react kindly to intruders. And I'm not going to risk my reputation or lose my valuable Miami connections because of your imaginary blunders and your need for haste." He burped again and with downturned lips looked at his empty plate. "That sandwich didn't agree with me. Anyone have AlkaSeltzer?"

"Fuck it! I think Benito's idea is excellent," Marco chimed in. "I say we head to Little Havana immediately! I want to go after the bitches who kidnapped my children."

"No! We. Will. Not. Do. That!" El Gordo exclaimed, watching two tablets fizz in a tall glass of water. "I repeat: my guys are on top of everything; they will watch the house from a distance, and whenever Amelia Rubio and your party get moving, my guys will inform me." He gulped down the contents of the glass. "We're not going to make our move in Little Havana. We'll wait until they get dropped off at the airport." He belched again. "My guys are professionals. They'll have security uniforms for us to wear and will brief us on how to proceed step-by-step so we can accomplish the task." He faced Marco and Mateo. "Don't worry. Tomorrow, all you have to do is wait in the van until Benito, León, and I return with your family." He poured himself another glass of water and drank it quickly. "I've done maneuvers like this before." He wiped his forehead with the napkin. "But this will only work if we follow instructions and stick to the plan."

Around eleven o'clock the following morning, El Gordo received the anticipated call.

"Time to go," the hulk said. "Your party is just leaving Little Havana now; they're less than five miles from the airport. It'll take them about ten minutes to get there." He handed Benito and León each a black hat and black vinyl jacket with SECURITY across them in bright yellow letters. "Put these on," he grumbled as he squeezed his body into one of the jackets himself; even the hat looked small on his big head.

Marco was driving the van. When he pulled into the American

Airlines departure terminal, El Gordo, who had been on the phone the entire time, suddenly hit Marco on the shoulder. "Pull over to the left right now! Park and stop the engine."

"I can't park here," Marco protested. "It's a tow zone."

"Do I what I tell you," El Gordo hissed. "I'm following my guys' instructions. You follow mine."

A short, stocky man wearing an orange airport security vest appeared out of nowhere, knocked on the passenger-side window, and handed El Gordo a parking permit. He then pointed to a dark-gray Cadillac Fleetwood that was parked in front of their rental van before wordlessly disappearing.

"What's going on?" Marco asked. "Who's in that car?"

El Gordo, his ear still glued to the phone, whispered, "My guys."

A minute later, the hulk elbowed Benito and León. "Make sure you have your phones. Time to go!"

The hulk shot one more warning look at Mateo and Marco. "You two stay right here until we come back with the goods," he urged. "Do not leave the van!"

Despite his heavy build, the hulk moved surprisingly quickly and nimbly past the Cadillac in front of them. Like chimps trailing their alpha male, Benito and León obediently followed El Gordo.

Never before had Mateo been directly exposed to danger; he'd always had others do the dirty work for him while he was far away. Feeling faint and unable to calm his racing pulse, he stared through the windshield at the airport activity. It still wasn't clear to him how the hulk's contacts had obtained a special permit, allowing the rental van to park in the outer lane of the terminal. Every time a security guard walked by, or a police car slowed down, the officers peeked into the Chevy surveillance van, and as soon as they spotted the permit in the windshield, they nodded and moved on.

Twenty minutes had passed already, and with every new second Mateo's chest felt more compressed. Neither he nor Marco had uttered a word. They both stared straight ahead through the windshield. Waiting.

Suddenly, Mateo gasped and leaned forward. "Querido Dios,"

he whispered. "There they are." A blue Mazda Navajo SUV had pulled to a stop in the drop-off lane. Marisol Rodriguez and a short, full-figured woman emerged. Mateo suppressed the urge to jump from the van and sprint towards them.

"That must be Amelia Rubio," he said, watching the two women take small pieces of luggage from the trunk. "But where is Ula? The children?" Without conscious thought, Mateo opened the door. He was ready to move, but Marco yanked him back.

"What are you doing? Did you forget? We're to stay in the car until the guys return with them." Marco stopped and leaned across the steering wheel, his head almost touching the windshield, and pointed to the SUV. "There's fucking Ula!" He pounded the steering wheel with his fists.

Mateo was unable to swallow; his dry throat felt as though a swarm of stinging insects had forced their way into the back of his mouth, infesting his esophagus. He clutched his chest. Ula. There she was. Despite her nondescript clothing and the floppy hat hiding her face, he saw her beauty, imagined her voice, even detected her fragrance.

"What the fuck is taking so long?" Marco shifted nervously in the driver's seat, drumming his fingers against the dashboard.

"We were told it could take a while before the guys find an opportunity to grab them inside the terminal." Mateo's breaths were shallow, his right hand lay on his chest, as if to protect his heart from a deadly weapon.

"I don't think I'll be able to control myself once they're here," Marco grunted. "Man, I really hate the bitch!" He mumbled something else, making low, guttural sounds.

"Speak up; I can't hear you."

"This may not be the best time to tell you this, but I'm planning to divorce her immediately. I'll keep the children and get them a new nanny." Marco made another inarticulate sound. "For all I care, fucking Ula can rot in the streets. The whore needs to suffer for what she's put me through."

With his throat still on fire, Mateo dry-swallowed. "You'll do nothing of the sort," he said, hearing his own voice crack and creak like the rusty mechanism of an old iron gate. "Think about the children and our reputation." Without looking at his son, Mateo rested his left hand on Marco's thigh. "Once we're back in Mexico, we'll decide what's best for you and for Ula." He removed his hand. "As far as Marisol is concerned, she's a goner."

After a moment of silence, Marco said, "You know I never loved Ula and have no clue why you're so infatuated with her." He shifted around in the seat. "Maybe you'll want to—"

"Look!" Mateo pointed to the exit door on their right.

There was Benito, hauling a struggling Marisol. And right in front of the scar-faced bodyguard was El Gordo, carrying Molara; the little girl was pounding on the hulk's shoulder and kicking him.

"What the fuck?" Marco stretched his neck forward again. "This does not look like a smooth operation. Where's León with Miguel? Who's got fucking Ula?"

Two middle-aged men in black clothing came running to the Cadillac that was parked in front of Mateo's rental van. As soon as they jumped in, the vehicle shot away.

Holy Mother. Mateo watched Molara wiggle from the hulk's arms and fall to the pavement. El Gordo bent down to reach for her, but Molara slid away and started to run between the rows of moving vehicles.

Forgetting the hulk's instructions, Mateo opened the van's door and jumped out. Between honking horns and screeching brakes, he heard a woman scream, "Molly! No!"

FIFTEEN

Ursula, June 1992
Miami, Florida

She didn't get out of the car right away. Instead she looked in all directions at the hubbub of the departure terminal. She couldn't rid herself of the nagging thought that someone had been watching, following them. But all she noticed on her right were people hustling into the terminal with their luggage, some with children, a few others with dogs. In the lanes to her left, cars kept rushing by; no one seemed to pay attention to Amelia's borrowed Mazda.

While Marisol got the twins from the car and adjusted their backpacks, Ursula quickly pulled Amelia into a tight embrace. "Thank you for everything," she said. "Your hospitality and encouraging spirit meant the world to us."

"Thank you," whispered the small woman, giving Ursula an extra squeeze. "Your unexpected financial generosity will make my dream come true."

"You decided to move to New Jersey?"

Amelia nodded. "My aunt's two stepsisters will be my new family. Because of you, I won't have to depend on them supporting me. I'm exchanging Little Havana for Havana on the Hudson."

"Marisol has your new address. We'll be in touch once we are safe."

Even though they were to stay in Chicago before flying to Zurich, Bruno had arranged for their suitcases to be checked through from Miami to Zurich. Traveling with only two pieces of hand luggage that contained a change of clothes and other necessities would make the trip safer and easier.

Walking the long concourse to the boarding gate, Ursula couldn't stop herself from scrutinizing every passerby. In a state of nerves, she kept turning her head as if to assure herself they weren't being followed.

"Please calm down," Marisol said softly. "The children are sensing your fear."

Judging by the number of people already at the gate, the flight to Chicago would be completely full. Boarding wasn't for another forty minutes, so they found two available seats opposite one of the large windows. Straightaway, Molly plopped herself on the floor, took a coloring book from her backpack, and started to draw.

"Mamá, where is my Julio?" Miggy whimpered while searching his backpack. "I can't find him." The corners of his mouth started to twitch.

"You were holding him when you woke up." Ursula probed through Miggy's belongings. "Your blankie is here but"—she turned to Molly—"can you please check your backpack?"

"He's not in mine," Molly said.

"Julio." Miggy buried his face in his hands.

"Don't cry. I lost my Rosi, too." Molly knelt and hugged her brother.

"But Amelia gave you a new baby doll yesterday," Miggy said in a small voice.

"We still have time." Ursula pulled her son to his feet. "Let's find a small new friend for you in the gift shop. I'm sure Amelia will find Julio and send him to us."

"There's a shop right over there." Marisol pointed. "I see shelves with books and racks with stuffed animals."

"You two wait here for us," Ursula said. "We'll be right back."

While Miggy decided which of the stuffed animals he wanted—he was touching and squeezing every single one—Ursula pulled her floppy hat closer to her face and nervously eyed every new person entering the shop.

A dark-haired man she guessed to be in his midsixties pushed an empty umbrella stroller in her direction. He stopped when he saw Miggy sitting on the floor, surrounded by plush toys.

Ursula stiffened. Who was he? Why was he looking at her son?

"Hey, little man," the stranger said. "You're surrounded by so many animals. Are you the zookeeper?" He grinned and winked at Ursula.

She stared at the empty umbrella stroller. Where was the child?

The man pointed to the stroller. "It was for my granddaughter; she and her parents just left for London."

Ursula nodded and watched as he turned his attention to the books on the shelves.

Miggy held up two dolphins. "They look the same, but one is bigger than the other."

"Sweetie, we need to hurry." She crouched down to collect the other stuffed animals, returning them to the rack. "Do you want both dolphins?"

"Can I?" Miggy's eyes lit up. "Twins, like me and Molly." Ursula paid the cashier and put her wallet back into her tote bag, reassuring herself again that their passports and the envelopes with currency and credit cards were still in the side pocket. She tightly closed the zipper.

Somebody shrieked and Ursula instinctively stepped behind one of the racks and told Miggy to crouch down with her.

"Was that Marisol's voice?" Wide-eyed, Miggy pulled on Ursula's shirt. "If the seekers found her and Molly, is the game over?"

"No."

When Ursula peeked above the rack, it felt as if the floor had disappeared from under her feet. A tall, heavyset man was speeding by the shop, carrying Molly. He was followed by Benito, who was tightly gripping a struggling Marisol. Both men wore jackets and caps imprinted with SECURITY.

Ursula couldn't think; her brain wouldn't function. Her body remained rigid.

Oh no! There was León. He was talking on a cell phone while zigzagging between travelers, frantically turning his head as if on a hunt. He stopped right in front of the shop.

Ursula cowered in terror, pressing her right hand over Miggy's mouth. The man with the empty stroller turned away from the bookshelves and looked at her. She laid her left index finger over her mouth, hoping he would get the hint.

"Hey," León shouted into the shop, "anyone seen a tall blonde woman with a little boy?"

"Yeah." The man with the stroller took a few steps towards León. "I saw them! They left a few minutes ago. They were in a hurry, said their flight was boarding."

MollyMollyMolly! Ga-gong-ga-gong-ga-gong. Run! Rescue Molly! Ga-gong-ga-gong-ga-gong. Miggy can't run fast, he's too little. Through the chaos of her thoughts, Bruno Rossi's voice echoed through her. He'd told her to call him from the airport hotel if anything went wrong in Miami. He'd made an emergency reservation under her new name. Where was the hotel? How could she get there without being discovered?

"Mamá, I can't breathe."

Dear God. Miggy. She took her hand off his mouth. "Please stay quiet, I'll explain later—"

She saw two large sturdy brown shoes next to her and felt a menacing presence. Her eyes slowly moved upward. The shoes belonged to the man with the empty stroller.

"Don't worry, he's gone," he said. "He watched people board the Chicago flight, then ran towards the exit." He offered his hand to help Ursula up. "Are you okay?"

"I have to . . . find my daughter," she stammered.

"That guy didn't act like a security guard; something is fishy.

But whatever you're involved in seems serious," he said. "Can I escort you to the airport security office so you can—"

"I can't." Ursula kept shaking her head. "You wouldn't understand." When she tried to lift Miggy, she almost lost her balance.

"Here. Please take the stroller for your little guy. You'll be able to move faster."

Did she thank the man? She couldn't remember. *MollyMollyMolly* was the only thought that raced through her panic-stricken mind. Panting for breath, she glanced at Miggy in the stroller. He had pulled his blue blankie over his head and was clinging to the backpack on his lap. "Game is over, game is lost," he cried.

She was outside. Frantically she looked left and right. Where was the big man? Where was her baby? Where was Benito with Marisol? León was surely still looking for her and Miggy. Without thinking, she ripped off her floppy hat and threw it in the garbage bin behind her; she did the same with the tan sweater she wore over her white T-shirt. From her tote, she pulled out an aqua-and-green Miami Dolphins baseball hat—a farewell gift from Amelia—tucked her hair under it and pulled the bill deep into her face. Then she pushed the stroller behind a group of young musicians with instrument cases, her eyes constantly searching in every direction.

It all happened at once. A voice screamed, "Molly! No!" There were screeching brakes, then a dull thud. People shouted, some rushing towards the crash.

"Jeez, did someone just get hit?" one of the musicians said. He laid his instrument case on the ground and sprinted away. Another musician followed.

Paralyzed with fear, Ursula watched as they bent over someone on the ground. She spotted Mateo and Marco pushing their way through the pandemonium and yelling, heard their voices.

"Molara, mi bebé. Mi ángel."

"Mi hija. Is there a doctor?"

Molly! My Molly! Ursula wanted to run, protect her child, keep her from harm, but she couldn't feel her face, her legs, her arms. She just stood there, frozen in place.

She caught sight of Benito and León; they quickly backed away from the scene. She heard sirens screaming close and watched Mateo gesticulate wildly for drivers in their cars to make room for the arriving ambulance.

The two musicians returned.

"It was a little girl; she's unconscious," one of them said. "They're taking her to Melamed Medical Center."

Still jabbering, the musicians collected their instrument cases and left.

"Mamá."

In a hypnotic state, Ursula looked at her knuckles; they were white from clenching the handlebars of the stroller. Her knees buckled and she sank down next to him. Weakly, she lifted Miggy's sky-blue blankie.

"Mamá, I heard what the people said." He leaned close to her face and whispered, "The little girl that got hit—was it Molly?"

"Miss?"

Ursula barely heard the woman's voice over the wailing sirens.

They're taking her away. I have to go with her, tell her everything is my fault. She got hurt because I made a terrible mistake.

Miggy had both hands over his ears; he was crying and so was she.

"Miss?"

When she felt fingers tap on her back, her whole body deflated like a balloon. Nothing mattered anymore. The bloodhounds had found her, and she deserved what was coming.

"Before you punish me, please take me to the hospital," she pleaded in a hollow voice. "Let me be with Molly. Let me bring Miggy to her."

"Sorry, miss. I don't speak Spanish."

Ursula looked up. A teenager with heavy eye makeup, dark-plum lipstick, and Raggedy Ann red hair was looking down at her.

"I don't wanna get involved in shit, but there's an emotional woman in the bathroom over there." She pointed to the restroom signage in the departure area. "She told me to give you a message."

If the teenager hadn't caught her, Ursula would have lost her balance when she tried to stand up. "I don't understand," she mumbled in English.

"I don't either. Just go there. The woman said to let you know that Mary, ehm, Mary-something is waiting for you."

"Marisol?"

"Yeah. That sounds right." The teenager looked quizzical, then shrugged. "I gotta catch a flight. Good luck."

Could it really be Marisol, or was it a maneuver to lure her into a quieter space where she could be apprehended? Resigned to whatever her fate might be and too enervated to resist what lay ahead, she pushed the stroller into the departure terminal and entered the opening under the restroom sign.

"Marisol!"

Though in a fog, Ursula heard Miggy cry out the name as he scrambled from the stroller and into a woman's arms. She couldn't blink away the blur, the hazy shapes around her refused to come into focus. Where was she? Were the shadow people coming and going? Why should she care? Did anything really matter anymore?

—

The bright light was like a magnet, pulling her towards the window. Vacantly she looked into the blinding sky, searching for answers. Its infinite expanse offered no reply.

The door to the hotel room closed, evicting voices and other noises, yet the sudden silence in the room pierced through her like a scream; the absence of Molly was everywhere and unendurable.

Not until Ursula felt warm arms around her and heard the familiar, gentle voice did she perceive the complete horror, the unforgivable catastrophe.

"Lo siento muchisimo," murmured Marisol into her ear. "I fought Benito with all my strength, tried to get away to save Molly. I scratched him bloody, even lacerated his scar." Marisol's voice cracked when she pointed to the bruises on her face and body. "But only when Molly got hit did he let go of me. I'm so sorry. I tried." She tightened her arms around Ursula, as if begging for redemption.

Miggy tugged on Marisol's blood-spattered shirt. "Where did the ambulance take Molly? Will she be okay?"

"What shall I tell him?" Marisol asked, barely audible.

"The truth," Ursula whispered. "We tell him the truth he can comprehend." She wiped her eyes and knelt in front of her son, pulling him close.

"When I decided to play a hide-and-seek game," she said haltingly, looking into Miggy's wide eyes, "I believed it was the right thing to do for you, for Molly, and for myself." Ursula swallowed. "But my plan failed; I made a terrible mistake." She choked back her tears. "Ask me any question. I'll do my best to give you an answer."

"Will Molly be okay?"

"I'm sure the doctors are taking very good care of her."

"But why are you not in the hospital with her? Is it because Papi will hurt you? Will abuelo be angry with you, too?"

Her young son's clear intuition startled her. "I'm certain they're very upset with me because I took you and Molly away," Ursula admitted. "If you want to be with Papi and abuelo, please tell me and I will take you to the hospital. I'm sure they're there with Molly."

Miggy shook his head. "No, Mamá, I need to stay with you." He turned, searched through his backpack, and put on the Superman cape Amelia had given him. "I'm powerful now and can protect you. I won't let Papi hurt you anymore."

"My sweet boy." She pulled his head to hers, trying to smother her emotions. "I'll figure out what to do next."

*

Flee or fight? Flee or fight? The words bombarded her shredded mind like the stream of water that pelted against her skin as she stood motionless under the showerhead. Despite the warm water, she felt cold. How long had she been in the stall? Shakily she turned the knob and reached for the white terry cloth robe with the gold-stitched hotel emblem.

The outlines of unfamiliar furniture looked nebulous in the semidarkness of the impersonal hotel room; even the dim light coming through the cracked door of the adjoining bedroom didn't ease her persistent feeling of uncertainty.

Miggy. Her heart cramped. Was he okay?

"He just fell asleep," Marisol whispered as she tiptoed from the connecting room. She too had donned the hotel's robe. Earlier they'd given their only clothing to the valet to be laundered overnight.

"I need new ice," Marisol said and refilled the plastic bag.

"Let me see," Ursula said, inspecting Marisol's swollen eyes and cheeks. "It looks worse. If only we could get a doctor."

"No, the ice will do. I took aspirin; it'll help the swelling. I can hide the discoloration with a scarf and sunglasses if needed." Marisol held the new ice bag over the right side of her badly bruised face. "Have you reached Señor Rossi yet?"

Ursula shook her head. "I'll keep trying. I'm afraid to leave the phone number and our room number with strangers in his office." She walked to the window and stared into the evening sky. "What if he's out of town on a business trip? If I can't reach him, I don't know what to do." She sniffled and dabbed her face with the terry cloth sleeve. "I can't think clearly anymore, and I'm afraid I'll make another bad decision. Only Bruno can tell me what to do next." She looked at the clock on the nightstand. "He's an hour behind. I'll try him again." Her hand trembled when she reached for the phone.

"Ula? You're supposed to be on the Chicago flight." Bruno Rossi said. "Are you delayed? What happened?"

Between sobs, she gave an account of what had taken place, her voice tiny, like fragile falling snowflakes.

"Dios mío." Clearly emotional, Bruno Rossi cleared his throat on the other end of the line. "I'll fly to Miami first thing in the morning. Please don't leave the hotel. You're safe there for now; nobody knows your pseudonym."

"But I have to be near Molly—she'll believe I abandoned her."

"Ula, we don't know what Mateo and Marco have told the police. If you're arrested for kidnapping in the United States, you won't see either of your children again. On the other hand, your father-in-law and husband will do anything to protect themselves. They can't afford stirring up curiosity in American officials."

"Bruno," she said, her voice a bit stronger, "even if you come to Miami tomorrow, how can you possibly help us?"

"I need time to think. We have colleagues in the Florida banking industry as well as government connections in Miami. I will figure something out."

SIXTEEN

Molly, May 2019
Milwaukee, Wisconsin

My eyes are glued to the screen of my Mac as I feverishly type and scroll, type more and scroll again, mining the internet's vast treasury of resources.

LinkedIn, True People Search, TruthFinder, and Facebook turn up dozens of Amelia Rubios all over the country, but none of them seem likely to be the woman on the phone. But then, just like that, an Amelia Rubio in Miami's Little Havana at 561 SW 4th Street pops up. *Whoopee! Good job!* Excitedly I type in that address. The photo of a small house with a green door and red roof pops up. Below it: *Currently not for sale. 2 Beds, 2 Baths, 1,400 Sq. ft. house. Last sold July 1992.*

Omigod. That was a month after my accident. "They're alive" were Amelia's last words, and while I stare at the picture, that tiny sentence continues to hammer in my head. How could it be possible? I've seen my mother's and brother's death certificates. My father showed them to me right around my thirteenth birthday. As always, he lacked any kind of sensitivity when he slapped the documents on the table and said, "Look at them."

"I can't read what it says." I stared at the foreign words.

"It's German and it says they drowned."

"How?"

"In a boating accident in the Rhine River near Basel." Without another word, he shoved the documents back into an envelope and walked away with them.

I didn't really feel anything about it in that moment. It seemed easier to banish them from my thoughts and bury them in my mind since I had no recollection of my mother and twin.

Sure, there were times when painful emotions came up, but I never dared to share them with Pops or Dad.

I haven't felt abandoned in many years, but that all fell apart when I received this rather unsettling call from a stranger. If my mother and twin are still alive, why haven't they ever tried to contact me? And why would Pops and my father lie to me? Why did Amelia Rubio warn me to be careful of them?

I want to doubt her, but the way she pronounced my name, *Mull-ly*, stirred some strange recognition. And when she talked about a Marisol, I thought I sensed a faint echo.

I've always been angry that I can't remember my early childhood, but now I'm really, really frustrated. If wind and water can break down rocks, then why can't I break through whatever obstacles are blocking memories from my consciousness?

After staring at the bright screen for I don't know how long, I type in a new name: Ursula Miraldo.

Endless results with the name Miraldo pop up but none for an Ursula. It's like she never existed.

I start racking my brain to retrieve any morsel of memory but have nothing to go by. I've never seen a photo of my mother or of my twin, and neither Pops or Dad have ever volunteered any information. They've always claimed they want to shield me from unnecessary pain. "It's for your own protection," they say.

They don't know, though, that after we moved to Mira, I often sat in the dark at the top of the stairwell whenever they argued loudly below.

Think, Molly, think!

Dimly, something flickers. I must've been ten or eleven years old, and Pops and my father kept yelling at each other. They mentioned names.

What was it? *Concentrate!*

Out of nowhere the memory hits me like Zeus's lightning bolt.

"*Have you lost your mind, Marco? We can't get rid of Robert. He promised to get us out of the mess in Guatemala.*"

"*Really? The fucking asshole got us into it in the first place. And that was your fault, Papá. You allowed the bastard way too much freedom with our money.*"

"*Shut up! He bloodied his hands for us. Where the fuck would we be without his ruthlessness?*"

"*I don't give a shit. He's a rotten thief, and we'd be better off without him.*"

"*Did you forget what he did for you? Like when he finagled the needed documents from the Swiss civil registrar's office so you could marry again?*"

"*Yeah? And did you forget I never wanted to marry Ula in the first place? You and fucking Robert Graf set me up for this shitshow.*"

I gasp. Robert Graf! Could he have been my mother's father? If so, I now have her maiden name.

Afraid of being disappointed again, I decide to take a break. I lean back in my chair and look at the time. It's 3:48 in the morning. I get up to refill my glass, and after quenching my thirst, I wait for the Keurig to finish brewing. I return to my desk with a steaming mug of coffee.

I type in my mother's first name and potential maiden name and immediately zero in on a result from 1981: *Swiss beauty Ursula Graf engaged to heir of Mexican tycoon.*

Omigod! After agonizing over it for a few seconds, I click on the link with the date from almost four decades ago.

Shivers run down my spine and goosebumps form all over my arms; my heart palpitates as I gape at a young blonde beauty standing next to a much younger version of my father.

The article is in German, so I copy the text and paste it into Google Translate.

Swiss banker Robert Graf and his wife Bertha hosted a celebrity-studded engagement party last Saturday for their daughter Ursula (18) and fiancé Marco Miraldo (23), son of Mexican business tycoon Mateo Miraldo, at Zurich's Grand Hotel. The young pair was honored by thirty guests during an intimate dinner ahead of the party, before celebrating into the early hours with many more prominent business associates and friends. Stunning Ursula Graf, a highly in-demand Swiss model, caught dashing Marco Miraldo's eye during his previous visit to Switzerland. According to the father of the bride-to-be, the striking young couple will tie the knot in a fit-for-royalty wedding in Mexico. The date is being kept secret.

I calculate quickly; if my mother was eighteen years old in 1981, then she was born in 1963. That would make her fifty-six today.

And my father's age checks out perfectly. Even though he always pretends to be younger, we celebrated his sixty-first birthday this past January.

I go back to the article from 1981 to look at more photos of my mother and father with other people, but none of their names mean anything to me.

I also find pictures of Robert and Bertha Graf, supposedly my maternal grandparents. But then, in another brief mention, I see that Robert Graf's first wife, Emma, died in childbirth. Based on the dates, I realize Emma was my biological grandmother.

I'm on a roll now and can't stop. Ideas keep popping into my head, new approaches that will grant me access to additional lines of inquiry and courses of action. Is it possible that after all these years I can uncover what they hid from me? Will it set free something deeply buried in my brain?

I find out that Robert Graf was born in 1938 in Basel, Switzerland; that would make him eighty years old. He could still be alive. If so, where does he live? I try to hunt for more facts, but nothing comes up. What happened to him?

I locate a Bertha Graf. She recently passed away at age eighty-one in a retirement home in Küsnacht, near Zurich. If she was Robert's second wife, that fountain of information has dried up.

Every new discovery intensifies my state of wild excitement, so I keep digging for more on Ursula Graf. Each time I discover even the smallest referral to her, my heart fills. There's a mention of her career and another article about her receiving an offer from a prominent US talent agency in Los Angeles. I wonder why she didn't accept it, then remember that she moved to Mexico to get married.

I scroll back to the gorgeous headshot on the cover of *Junge Mode*, a Swiss fashion magazine, and can't stop looking at the stranger who was my mother—or is my mother.

I search next for Miguel Miraldo but find nothing. I key in Miguel Graf in case he uses my mother's maiden name. Nothing pops up.

What if my mother and brother took on different identities after they abandoned me in 1992? In that case, the likelihood of me ever finding them is zero.

No! I'm not giving up. If I can't find the answers, a professional will—like a private investigator who specializes in locating people.

And just like that, another one of Zeus's lightning bolts hits me. Phil Flores, my new friend from Five Elements.

༄

A mellow harp ringtone wakes me from dreams, filled with vivid images of children playing, laughing, and spraying water at each other. Of women taking the children into their arms. Of a little boy playing with an elephant, and another boy wrapping a towel around a little girl.

When the harp doesn't stop, I open my eyes and squint into brightness; early sunrays are streaming through my great room. I realize I fell asleep sitting at my desk.

Ouch, my neck! I move my head from side to side. Through barely lifted lids I see that the screen of my Mac is dark. It, too, fell into sleep mode. I yawn and close my eyes again, ready to return to the pleasantries of the dream, but there's the harp again. I reach for my phone.

Dad says the screen.

"Hi."

"Molara, don't tell me you're still sleeping. What's wrong with you? You're supposed to stop by my house."

In my trancelike state, I recall the perplexing phone call from Amelia Rubio and my feverish internet searches. I'm about to impart this newly received information to my father when Amelia's voice resounds in my head: *Mull-ly, they lied to you.*

"You woke me up, Dad," I say. "I worked all night on a new project"—well, ain't that the truth—"and only got an hour or two of sleep." My voice is cold and brittle as ice.

"Hmm. I need you to hurry and stop by. My situation with Ava hasn't changed. You offered to help."

Before I answer, I stare at my Mac's dark screen and tap on the keyboard. The image of my mother from a modeling shoot smiles at me. I sit up straight. I fell asleep gazing at her, begging her picture to give me answers. Was she one of the women in my dream? The sensations and images from those few sleeping hours are beginning to fade already.

"Molara, what's the matter with you?"

"Okay!" I snap. "I need to shower and stop at Starbucks. You want me to bring anything?"

"Sure. Get me a cold brew with cinnamon oat milk foam."

On my thirty-minute drive from Milwaukee to Mira, I resolve to keep last night's findings locked in my mental vault. Before I make any accusations or ask for explanations from either Pops or Dad, I need to plot a whole range of maneuvers. First on my list is to find those letters Amelia mentioned—if they exist. Second, I'll have to locate whatever else is hidden from me.

I purposely drive slowly, trying to make sense of my thoughts. My first childhood memories are of our move to Mira, when I sat on the front lawn watching rows of moving trucks pull up to the two stately houses. For days, sturdy men unloaded all the stuff Pops and Dad had brought from Mexico.

I remember catching sight of crates and boxes that were placed in my father's storage area. To this day he keeps that room locked, claiming he wants nobody to disturb valuable work-related records. Are those boxes still in there? What if they contain some of the documents I'm looking for?

I shift in my seat, anxious for an opportunity to get into that space. Maybe the next time he's out of town I'll have the freedom to explore.

I also think of all the stuff Pops brought from Mexico; he needed three more moving vans than Dad. Pops insisted on bringing every single item from his hacienda to the large mansion in Mira. When he realized that not all of the ornate, often massive Mexican décor fit into the new home's large rooms and long hallways, pieces of furniture ended up in the space Pops lovingly refers to as his parlor in the sky. I once snuck up there—I think I was ten years old—and it was a terrifying experience. While I snooped around, the door swelled up and wouldn't open again. I was stuck in that unfamiliar dark attic until Pops rescued me. I haven't been up there since. But now I'm on a mission and can hardly wait for the chance to investigate.

I park my car at the end of the wide block-paved driveway that leads to my father's low-slung residence on Bayside Drive. From the street it looks more like a huge bungalow, but the structure descends to a second and third level, built into the slope, where ceiling-to-floor windows and large glass terrace doors command a view of Lake Michigan. When I was younger, the few friends I was occasionally allowed to bring home exclaimed that the house was the absolute coolest they'd ever seen. They were especially impressed by the indoor lap pool and the big outdoor negative-edge pool, both facing the lake.

During my school years I thought of it as a comfortable place because Annie, wife number three, had made it warm and welcoming. But once Annie divorced my father, he ripped out walls, overhauled the interior of the house, and redecorated every room with stark minimalism. The style was cold and cheerless, and when Ava entered the scene, she brought along her own ideas. Walls were taken down again, and new ones are in the process of being erected. Even before their wedding, Ava began spending four out of five days a week with her designers at the Merchandise Mart in Chicago. But only half of the interior has been completed, and heavy sheets of plastic still separate the livable parts from the unlivable parts. New arrivals of furniture, wrapped in protective covering, are crammed together with art objects and valuable pieces that Ava decided were okay to keep.

I step carefully, barely making my way through the clutter of furniture and other items; the noise from the drilling and hammering behind the heavy plastic sheets is offending my sleep-deprived brain.

Where the heck is he?

"Dad?" I shout and almost trip over a rolled-up area rug, sticking out from under a brand-new divan that's upholstered in a bright tangerine-and-wasabi fabric. *Shit!* Some of my coffee spills but thankfully onto the plastic cover.

I walk through the hallway and look in the other rooms, then go down the steps to the lower level. The door to their bedroom is ajar. It's the only finished room in the house, so I dare to peek in and gasp when I see the bold color scheme of yolk-yellow mixing with shiny silver, tulip pink, and candy peppermint. Yikes! Heavy blood-colored drapery covers up the expansive views of Lake Michigan. How did my father, the man who doesn't care for crazy color palettes and always prides himself on his exceptional good taste, let Ava get away with *this*?

I call out his name again. *Where in the world can he be?* I turn left, walk through another cluttered hallway, down a few more steps, and finally see him. He's sitting at the edge of the lap pool in his swim trunks, talking on the phone while his lower legs dangle in the water.

"Dad! I'm here."

He whips around and motions me to be quiet but reaches out for his cold brew with the cinnamon oat milk.

I seat myself in one of the Globo Royal hanging chairs opposite my father, sip my coffee, and read some emails. The lap pool room is long and narrow, and even though my father is speaking softly, I can hear most of what he's saying.

It's obvious who he's talking to. His deep voice is higher than normal, and his tones are singsongy, almost as if he's talking to a puppy. Correction: my father has an aversion to dogs, so it sounds like he's cooing back to a baby. Well, it must be Ava then. What the heck am I doing here if he got back together with her again? Just as I get out of the hanging chair, he disconnects the call, lifts his chin, and grins.

"Wouldn't you know," he says, "she called me." He then explains their misunderstanding. It wasn't him she got annoyed with—it was the terrible dust and noise from the construction, the total disarray of the house, et cetera. He tells me that Ava's found a lovely two-bedroom suite at the Four Seasons in Chicago and wants to live there until the house is finished.

My father is all smiles, filled with lively energy. He's obviously forgotten that only yesterday he called Ava duplicitous.

"I'm thrilled for the two of you," I say. "Can I leave now?"

He looks me up and down. "I like what you're wearing, Molara. You look trim and fit in those jeans. That spa did you good. But you're not going to work like this, are you?"

"As a matter of fact, I am." I sip the last drop from the iconic Starbucks paper cup, then throw it in the wastebasket. "Out with the old, in with the new," I say and realize my phrase has double meaning. "I plan on making a lot of changes, Dad."

"Really?" He dries his lower legs and feet. "Hope you didn't hurt yourself thinking too hard."

"Watch me," I say and walk to the stairwell.

"Wait a minute." He puts on a robe and follows me. "While I

spend more time in Chicago in the upcoming weeks, I need you to work on the zoning for our—"

"Can't do," I say. "I have too much on my own agenda. As a matter of fact, there's a brand-new project that has become extremely important to me."

He stares at me like an envelope without an address on it. "What project?"

Rummaging through your storage room. "If you intend to stay the whole time in Chicago, please give the workload to someone else or otherwise handle it yourself from your hotel suite," I say. "What else would you be doing while Ava keeps the interior designers busy? Go with her to Neiman Marcus and pick out her clothes and shoes?" I know I've hit a nerve.

"Don't be ridiculous," he scoffs.

"Why don't you have someone drive you back and forth a few times a week? After all, it's less than a two-hour drive each way." I think of my plan and quickly add, "Don't worry about your construction. The days you're in Chicago, I'll be happy to check on the progress of your house and report to you."

My father stares at me. "Hmm. As a matter of fact, they're delivering my new Porsche Taycan Turbo in a few days; I might enjoy driving it back and forth on occasion."

Before I leave the house, I turn around and see him bent over the phone, texting, smiling, looking victorious.

I close the door.

⁂

Pops lives on the same street at the end of the block in a huge lakefront Tudor home that was built in 1927 and improved with add-ons over the decades. When he purchased it in the 1990s, he meticulously updated and restored it to perfection.

This was the home where I spent most of my childhood and young adult life; I only lived with my father during the few years he was married to Annie.

When I pull into the circular driveway, Dale Daniels, the physical therapist, is loading his equipment into his trunk.

"Hey, Molly! Good to see ya. Your grandfather's doin' really well. Says he's ready to head back to work."

I chitchat with Dale for a few minutes, then let myself into the house, finding Pops in his favorite chair in the library, reading. I'm surprised how effortlessly he manages to get up when he sees me.

"Molara, mi ángel. Te extrañé mucho," he exclaims and pulls me into his arms.

"Missed you too, Pops," I answer in English, wondering if he can detect the hesitancy in my voice. Strange how last night's revelations make me look at him through different eyes. I force my mind to make a sharp U-turn, and I praise his phenomenal recovery progress. When he asks why I look tired, I don't tell him I only slept two hours last night.

We talk about how consolidation has increased across the hotel industry in the past few years due to improved conditions for mergers and acquisitions. We state our opinions on growing anxiety over the state of the hotel cycle and the importance of scale; we even touch upon politics but quickly agree to disagree. (Pops loves and admires everything about our current president. I'm of a different mindset.)

"Well," Pops says when he sees me looking at the time, "I asked Yoli to prepare carnitas today. You hungry?"

"I'm trying to stay away from meat." I raise my eyebrows. "Didn't your doctor tell you to lay off red meat as well? The dietitian gave you a vegetarian diet to follow."

"Forget it," he says. "Remember Adam and Eve's mistake in the Garden of Eden? They both bit into an apple." He laughs and winks at me. "I better not risk it."

While he's waiting for Yoli to serve him, I grab a bottle of water from the fridge, and just when I'm ready to say goodbye, he stops me.

"I forgot my meds upstairs. Before you leave, can you run and get them from my bedroom, please?"

As I grab the two bottles off his nightstand, the antique Mexican cabinet with nacre-shell inlays catches my eye and I remember how after our move to Mira—I was about eight or nine years old—I loved lying on the floor under the long, heavily beaded vintage tablecloth in the adjacent sitting room. One time, I watched Pops twist one of the bronze columns of the cabinet. To my surprise, a secret compartment opened, from which Pops removed a stack of papers.

Holding the two bottles of Pops's medicine in my hand, I stare at the four bronze columns. Are the papers still hidden in the secret compartment? Could they be the letters Amelia Rubio mentioned?

I hear Pops calling my name, but before I run down the grand staircase, I gape at the smaller stairwell that leads to the attic. Without giving it another thought, I take two steps at a time to peek. *Wow!* It's not the way I remember it from when I was locked in there as a kid. Pops has turned his parlor in the sky into a fully furnished room with a built-in skylight for natural light.

"Molara? Did you find them?"

I sprint down.

Disregarding the warning bells that go off in my head, I make a quick decision. "Hey, the door to your attic was open, so I ran up there to close it. You never mentioned the renovations. Really nice."

He looks at me. Do I detect a flicker of unease in his eyes?

"I think it's great that you found a way to display all that beautiful furniture," I add quickly. "And now that you can climb stairs again, I'm sure you'll enjoy what you have up there." I open my bottle of water, trying to hide my anxiety.

"There's nothing of interest in the attic," he grumbles.

I nod while thinking about how to lure him out of the house so I can poke around in secret compartments, cabinets, and trunks that will surely be of interest to *me*.

He puts down his fork and cocks his head. "Did I mention that I plan on coming back to the office next week?"

"That's great news!" I say, almost too enthusiastically. "Everybody is looking forward to seeing you again."

Before I leave, I blow him a kiss, then close another door.

SEVENTEEN

Mateo, November 1996
Coyoacán, Mexico

Rancor had infused every corner of his existence. The family appeared to be thoroughly discontented while ill will threatened to drown his business. Even his beloved country was suffering from a flood of steadily growing malice. But mostly Mateo could feel how rancor thrived on his own misery, fed on the wretchedness of those he believed closest to him and flourishing in the arrogance of those Mateo loathed. Never had he felt so isolated by his own pride. The abnormal and conceited unwillingness of others to listen to his warnings kept catching him off guard.

What had happened to the reality he'd so carefully tried to create, had fertilized to opulent growth, whose harvest was supposed to last forever?

The morning meeting in Grupo Miraldo's boardroom had been a disaster. Surrounded by his team from the law firm of Cortés, Correa, Enríquez, y Elias, Mateo was again forced to sit through endless discussions and negotiations while the lawyers on both sides utilized their tools of mediation to reach an agreement. As Mateo's attorneys broached many different angles of his case, they aimed to lure the opposing parties into a settlement. Mateo had faith in his legal team—after all, they had wrangled and finagled over critical points before, always producing favorable results for him and his enterprises. Because of his counselors' intelligence, skilled strategies, and aggressive craftiness, he'd won his cases time and time again.

But this round was different.

Where had Manoel dug up his crew of wily attorneys—a mix of hawks, vipers, and hyenas?

And after the unexpected new upsets of the past five hours, Mateo's team had to reassure him of the strength of his case, his chances of winning. His lawyers were confident that they could bring the mediation to a successful conclusion and award the majority of Grupo Miraldo's assets to Mateo. They strategized for the continuance of mediation the following day. Before they shook hands and went their separate ways, Mateo again reminded his legal team to aim for a settlement out of court. The lawyers agreed it was critical to keep all these matters away from prosecutors and judges. But they didn't know that Mateo was terrified of a trial where personal, highly confidential details might surface—information that could engulf him and Marco in a tsunami of indictable offenses.

His head pounded. Miserable feelings bubbled in his gut, ready to explode like shaken soda bottles. Bitter taste formed in his throat. *Bile?* He gagged and spat.

Mateo collapsed onto the ornate handcrafted sunflower bench under the old Mexican fan palm. Despite the pleasant afternoon temperature, he welcomed the shade from the fan-shaped fronds that generously sprouted from the palm's trunk; like an enormous umbrella, they formed a deep-green canopy.

"Dammit," he said out loud and dabbed cold sweat off his forehead, angry how long it took for medication to relieve his headaches.

He looked over the manicured grounds and longed for the carefree days of yesteryear. It had been right here, under this Mexican fan palm, when he'd last seen her. The image of beautiful Ula in that red gown with the dramatic red silk flower was forever imprinted in his mind; he could still see her walking away, carrying Miguel on her left hip and linking her right hand with Molara's left. Ula had said she would return to the party, but she never did.

Mateo remembered counting himself lucky in how he'd managed to outsmart the American officials and the staff at Melamed Medical Center on that dreadful day in Miami. On top of spinning falsehoods, he'd also had to keep his hapless son under control. Marco, in a psychotic frenzy, teetered on the brink of a self-afflicted abyss, terrorizing the nurses and threatening the doctors with groundless lawsuits. As always, Mateo had no other choice but to interfere. He knew how to restrain his own impulses and keep a level head to avoid more blunders.

When they wheeled Molara into surgery, he summoned his son, Benito, and León to a meeting place. So everybody would be on the same page, he drilled into them the fake but feasible story he'd constructed: The Miraldo family had planned a vacation in Florida, but when little Miguel, who suffered from a severe anxiety disorder, became uncontrollable, the parents decided it best for mother and son to return to Mexico. But Molara, inconsolable about her mother and brother leaving, tore away from her father's hand and ran into traffic.

To bypass additional complications with American authorities, Mateo arranged a private jet to return Marco and the two bodyguards to Mexico that very night. When questioned in the hospital, Mateo told the authorities and medical staff that Molara's father was needed home in Mexico, not only to be with his agitated son but also to take care of a mentally ill mother.

Mateo spent six long days and restless nights at Molara's bedside before the little girl came out of the coma. He ignored the objections of the American doctors, who believed she needed to stay under their care, claiming she might suffer lifelong complications if moved. Mateo didn't care and demanded her release, telling the physicians his granddaughter would receive better medical care in Mexico and, more importantly, would thrive in her familiar environment, surrounded by loving family.

The air ambulance jet had cost him a fortune but was well worth it. The second Mateo stepped off the plane, the American shackles fell away from his ankles. And when he inhaled the sweet

Mexican air, he again smelled freedom, tasted power, embraced his dominance.

After the horrors that had occurred in Miami receded in his mind, he became obsessed with finding Ula, inveigling her into returning with Miguel to his stately hacienda, and reuniting them with Molara—and, of course, with him. He spun fairy-tale scenarios, developments that would end all his worries and fears.

But it simply hadn't happened. Mateo fumbled in his pocket for a handkerchief and wiped his eyes. Would Ula feel sorry for him if she knew how many enemy forces were coming at him and what he was going through?

Fuck them all. He pointed at nothing. *I've always been a champion, and as soon as I am victorious again, I will find you! I will build a future with you! And if I can't have you, I'll make sure nobody else can have you either!*

He heard songbirds duetting nearby. Where were they? When he looked up, the singing stopped and he felt a sudden sensation of hopelessness.

After two additional minor surgeries in Mexico, Molara's broken bones began to heal, but the little girl continued to act disoriented. Even though the CT and MRI scans proved normal, she didn't seem to recognize anyone at the hacienda and often ran through the house and gardens as if searching for someone or something. Worse than that, the child refused to talk.

Mateo decided that Molara might benefit from the companionship of a competent female. After interviewing many applicants, he hired Adelita, a kind middle-aged woman who proved herself capable by slowly breaking through Molara's withdrawn and timid demeanor.

Because the child was eager to learn, tutors were hired. Molara had a keen sense of numbers and surprised the private educators with her early ability in math. And as soon as she learned how to read and write, several months after the accident, she started to talk again. Yet whenever someone asked her what she recalled of the recent past, she gave a blank, almost hostile stare.

Mateo expressed his concerns to the doctors and learned that if patients repressed their memories for long enough, they might be erased completely. On the other hand, a specialist said, selective memory could also be an inclination to remember only what the patient wanted to remember.

In the end, Molara's loss of memory had been to everybody's benefit. The less she remembered about her mother and twin and what took place at the Miami airport, the safer it would be for him and Marco. After all, they needed all the help they could get on that front, especially Marco, who always thought of himself as shrewd and savvy but often acted like an idiot. He'd made absurd mistakes in the wake of Ursula and Miguel's disappearance.

Mateo wiped newly formed sweat off his brow, thinking of the letters that started to arrive five months after Ula disappeared. He'd never shared the content of certain letters with Marco, the ones in which she specified why she'd felt driven to leave Mexico with the children. He'd only showed Marco the letters that spelled out precise terms and conditions to reunite her and Miguel with Molara.

It was immediately clear to Mateo that Ula hadn't composed these letters herself; she must have had help from seasoned professionals. Each one of her mailings was postmarked in Chicago, yet the return address always had a different PO box number.

Both Mateo and Marco, for their own reasons, decided not to respond to Ula's letters. Instead, the two Miraldo men hired shady detectives and sent them to Chicago. For months, despite their steep fees, those slippery characters proved unable to procure results. Apparently, information about post office boxes held by an individual, rather than a business, could only be released if the holder was served with papers. And that, of course, was out of the question, as neither Mateo nor Marco wanted to involve the forces of law and order in their already wobbly affairs.

With no legal remedy available to them, Marco came up with one ridiculous plan after another. The first began shortly after Molara learned how to write the letters of the alphabet.

"Have you lost your mind?" Mateo asked his son. "You want your daughter to write a letter to the mother she can't remember? Why would you risk stirring up memories in her?"

"What are you worried about?" Marco said. "Molara will only know what we tell her."

> You did a terrible thing when you took me and Miguel away from our home, from Papi and from abuelo. Miguel and I were happy here, but you kidnapped us! I never wanted to leave Mexico, and I hate you for what you did. Because you and Miguel left me, I was hit by a car and now have many health problems. Papi and abuelo take care of me. They would never leave me. They love me and I love them. You are not my mother anymore. Stop sending letters to me! I never want to see you again! I don't know you!
> Molara Miraldo

When no more letters from Ula arrived at the hacienda, Marco called it his victory and came up with another calamity of an idea: to declare Ula and Miguel dead.

"Are you insane?" Mateo shouted during yet another argument with his son. "I will not allow you to forge documents! What if Ula decides to return one day?"

"That bitch wouldn't dare set foot in Mexico again. She knows I'd have her arrested, not just for kidnapping but also for child abuse."

"Please give it more time," Mateo demanded, unable to reveal his own secret plans for himself and Ula. "Let me find her. When I do, you'll divorce her with proper representation and without breaking the law."

"No way, Papá! I have to go on with my life; Ula is already dead to me."

Finally, Mateo thought, feeling the headache subside. If only there were a pill that would take away his agony and let him disengage from this messy conflict. He shifted his weight around on the bench and squinted into the skies.

Ula. Ula. Ula.

Was it his longing or was it the breeze rustling through the lush plumed fronds that kept whispering her name?

Ula.

After the letters stopped arriving, Mateo wondered if something terrible had happened to Ula and Miguel. Feeling desperate about her separation from Molara, had Ula hurt herself and her son?

Well, that was precisely what Marco desired.

Mateo would never forget the day Marco burst into the office, victoriously displaying the forgery of two death certificates.

"¡Querido Dios! What have you done?" Mateo stared at the fakes from the Department of Health in Basel, Switzerland. "How did you get these? Who helped you?"

"Really, Papá? Who's been our Swiss slave? Whom have we been rewarding to do all our dirty work?"

"Graf faked his own daughter's and grandson's death certificates?"

"When did Robert Graf ever care about his daughter?" Marco laughed. "I'm on my way to have these translated and notarized." He folded the papers and placed them back in the envelope.

"You fool!" Mateo shouted. "Certificate forgery is a serious crime in every country! Aren't we in enough trouble already? What if Ula and Miguel resurface again? What if Graf decides to blackmail us?"

"Relax! Before he acquired these," Marco said, waving the envelopes, "he'd already released his own bloodhounds, not only in Switzerland but also in neighboring countries and in the States. Nothing! He concluded that either Ula doesn't want to be found or she and Miguel are actually dead." Marco clutched the envelopes against his chest and grinned. "Graf says these are ninety-nine percent authentic. Nobody in Mexico will ever question them." Before he left the room, he was all smiles. "I can't wait to tell Carla to plan our wedding."

Mateo shook his head, closed his eyes, and leaned against the backrest of the sunflower bench. Would the normalcy of yesteryear return during the upcoming festival of Las Posadas? According to the old Miraldo Christmas tradition, the entire estate would be decorated with evergreens, lilies, and poinsettias. Countless farolitos would light up the grounds for family and friends to enjoy. But given the state of prolonged hostility between his sons, he had no idea who would celebrate his favorite holiday with him.

He opened his eyes again. His manicured gardens were so rich with agave plants, towering trees, and chubby biznagas. But even the purity of this paradise failed to reduce his tension and anxiety.

A lazy lizard sunbathed safely on the wall of a fencepost cactus while a couple of red Mexican sparrows dove into the flowerbeds to kill and feed on unsuspecting bugs. *Two colliding worlds wherever I look.*

A voice broke through his reflections.

"Señor Miraldo, qué sorpresa," Adelita said. She put a picnic basket next to the bench and spread a large blanket on the grass. "Would you like to join us?"

"Where's Molara?"

Adelita pointed past the shrubs. "Picking flowers for decoration."

A smile spread over his face as he watched Molara move gracefully from flowerbed to flowerbed. What a gorgeous girl. Her sweet cherub face was framed by lustrous cocoa-brown hair; wisps of curls bounced on her forehead. A simple white pinafore dress enhanced her satiny golden skin. When was the last time he'd seen her wear something other than a white pinafore dress? She had so many of them; they were her favorite.

Molara twirled to the melody she was humming. When she saw him sitting on the bench, she looked nonplussed.

"Hola, abuelo. How did you know we're having a picnic here?"

She slowly walked towards him. From her pockets she removed a multitude of pink, purple, and yellow blossoms and sprinkled them over the blanket. "Adelita baked conchas, and I helped make the limonada," she said without looking at him.

"Wonderful," said Mateo and awkwardly lowered himself onto the blanket. "Benito told me I'd find you here." He spoke hesitantly, hoping the girl would not recall her mother's weekly outings to this very spot.

Molara lifted her head towards the canopy of the Mexican fan palm. "It's my very favorite place."

Mateo shifted when he felt the little girl's eyes on him.

"Why does no hair grow on that scar under your stubble?" She tapped her index finger on his lower right cheek, then touched his left forearm. "No hair on this scar either."

Mateo wanted to yank his arm away and roll down his sleeve; instead, he forced a laugh. "Because there are no more hair follicles in a scar."

"How did you get these scars?"

"It happened a long time ago when I lived in Portugal." Mateo faked another chuckle. "So long ago that I don't remember what happened." He crossed his arms. "Why don't you finish eating your concha?"

Throughout the meal, Mateo kept quiet. The carefree chitchat between Molara and Adelita temporarily drowned out his misery.

"I must get back to work," he said forty minutes later. He suppressed a grunt when he experienced an unfamiliar discomfort in his lower back. Slowly, he straightened and brushed a few crumbs off his pants. "It's such a lovely afternoon. Why don't you and Adelita play las escondidas in the garden and—"

"*No!*" Molara jumped onto Adelita's lap and buried her face in the soft folds of the nanny's uniform.

"Sorry, Señor Miraldo," Adelita whispered. "I don't know why . . . but she's terrified of playing hide-and-go-seek."

EIGHTEEN

Mateo, same day, early evening

Before Mateo stepped into the shower stall, he took the body brush and furiously brushed his arms, legs, torso.

There are only two possibilities, he thought. *Either the mediation will go in my favor and none of this bullshit will ever surface again, or . . .*

Mateo didn't notice the pain until his skin was beet red. He exhaled sharply. "Don't be so hard on yourself," he scolded his mirror image. "The blame lies with your son. Manoel may just be stupid enough to not accept your offers." He noticed the deep frown between his eyebrows and didn't like it. But as soon as he relaxed his face, he started grinding his teeth. Why in hell was his legal team recommending letting Manoel in on some hidden agenda? Those bloody damn fools.

"No, don't let this happen!" Mateo chided his reflection. "Never! Everything must remain concealed." He turned his back on the mirror and stepped into the steam of the shower stall, hoping the force of water would rinse off his anxiety and wash away the ghosts of the past.

He donned a lightweight pair of beige linen pants and a muted green silk shirt; the combination of these colors always reminded him of sand, sea, and carefree days in his Acapulco mansion. That, of course, was before he was forced to let go of that magnificent home, all because of Marco's egomania and his ridiculously brief marriage to Carla de La Fuente, during which the villa became a focal point for the paparazzi. The tabloids had had a field day reporting on Marco and Carla's notorious sex and drug parties.

It still enraged Mateo. The only reason Carla's badass lawyers had stipulated ownership of the Acapulco mansion was to hurt him and Marco. As if the filthy rich bitch deserved any of *his* assets after only three months of marriage to his blockhead son. Had he not given fair warning to Marco about that spoiled woman? Had he not informed his son about the deep long-standing rift between Carlos de La Fuente and himself?

The mutual hostility between the two families had started decades ago. Young and entrepreneurial, Mateo was immensely proud of his success and rapidly growing wealth. But no matter how hard he worked, the de La Fuentes would always be more powerful and influential. It wasn't jealousy. It was the unfairness Mateo resented, plain and simple. Whereas he was self-made, Carlos had been born on a mountain of old money and was able to build on it.

By pure coincidence, he'd heard of Carlos's interest in a spectacular hacienda in Coyoacán—the perfect opportunity for Mateo to injure his nemesis. Through intrigue and palm-greasing, he'd managed to finagle the elegant estate away from their owners, then invited the de La Fuentes to his first Fiesta Miraldo. Of course, Carlos and his family were a no-show.

Mateo turned off the lights to his dressing room, but before he walked into his bedroom, he stuck his head through the door to look left and right into the hallway, then stepped up to the balustrade and took a glimpse into the foyer. He heard pounding feet on the Spanish-tiled floors before he saw Elva approach the grand staircase. The old heavyset housekeeper carried a stack of neatly folded linens and towels in her arms.

"Señor Miraldo," she said, "may I bring these into your quarters now?"

"Not a good time." Mateo waved her off and listened until the sound of her steps became faint.

He pulled the bedroom door shut behind him and walked over

to his treasured antique Mexican cabinet with the nacre-shell inlays. He molded his hand around the front right bronze column and gave it a half twist. When he heard the click, he gave it another full twist. With that, a panel on the lower right side of the cabinet opened and Mateo pulled out a rectangular box; its lid had a needlework look with edelweiss and alpine flowers. He pressed his lips to Ula's keepsake box, the one she'd brought with her when she first arrived from Switzerland and where she kept her objects of interest. Though she considered it a treasured heirloom, she'd left it behind the day she disappeared with her children.

For a moment Mateo focused on the floral pattern, then walked over to the divan, sat down, and released the lid from its magnetic closure. With a sigh he removed a stack of photos; one by one he looked at the images of Ula and the twins. He let his eyes linger on a photo of himself with Ula and pressed it tightly to his chest.

"I never meant to hurt you," he whispered. "Come back to me. I'll make things right for you and the children. I promise." With closed eyes he kissed her image.

Before he placed the photos back in the box, he made sure everything was there: eleven of Ula's letters, the copy of the note Molara had been forced to write to her mother, and the two envelopes that contained copies of the fake death certificates.

Mateo closed the lid and returned the box to the cabinet's secret compartment. When he turned the knob, he heard a sound in the adjacent room. Was it a gasp? A rustle of clothes? His fingers stiffened around the knob. For a second he remained frozen, then he tiptoed across the parquet floor and peeked into the sitting room.

"Who's there?"

He stumbled through the room and looked behind furniture and curtains. Nothing. Confused, he stepped backwards and collided with a plant holder. He was able to catch the plant in time, preventing what would have been a mess on the antique hand-knotted gold-and-blue area rug. Mateo collapsed into the chair by the window. It was getting dark already. The illumination from a distant wrought-iron lamp flickered through the trees, turning their boughs and limbs into headless apparitions, like ghosts from the past. He swallowed, hoping he'd find a way out of this labyrinthine maze.

He needed to relax. A Cohiba Siglo might do the trick. He loved aromatic cigars, especially this Cohiba because it was light in taste, yet its complexity intrigued him. Before he reached for the guillotine cutter with his initials on its curved blade, he gently touched the cigar along its entire length, lightly pressing it between his thumb and forefinger. He carefully cut across the line where the cap and wrapper met. Finally, he lit a wood match and moved it in a circular motion while rotating the cigar, toasting the area of the Cohiba's foot. This slow and gentle ritual always gave him great pleasure, and as if in a trance, he tenderly drew in the first smoke and savored the rich flavors that filled his mouth. He thought he tasted coffee and creamy vanilla, maybe some leather and spices. For a delicious moment he held on to those sensations before slowly letting the smoke escape again. Relaxing back into the cushions, he watched the bluish smoke curl up in drowsy elegance.

Loud, angry sounds resonated from the foyer below. Mateo stopped breathing, holding the cigar in midair.

Heels clacked across the tiled floors, coming up the stairs. The voices got louder, sharper, before the door to the sitting room was ripped open. Both of his sons stormed in.

Manoel looked pale; his eyes were red and puffy and had deep, dark circles under them. He dashed to the other side of the room, away from Marco, before staring daggers at his father and brother. Still catching his breath, Manoel pointed at them. "You deceived me! You double-crossed me!" The accusation burst from his mouth like the cork from a shaken champagne bottle. "Because of your atrocities, I will forever have blood on my hands!"

Marco, looking unperturbed, chewed on his silver toothpick. "*You* have blood on *your* hands?" He rolled his eyes. "You don't even have the guts to swat at the mosquito that bit you."

"You tricked me!" Manoel cried out. "You took advantage of my friendship with Ramón García because he had connections to law enforcement." He steadied himself against the wall. "The two of you fabricated stories about Benito and León. You sold them out by claiming they were involved with the cartel." Choking back his emotions, he stammered, "You knew your lies would get them murdered!"

"C'mon, baby brother," Marco retorted with a sly grin, "Papá and I had nothing to do with it. It was a clash between rival gangs in the prison's maximum-security wing. León and Benito happened to be at the wrong place at the wrong time."

Manoel looked at the ceiling as if the facts were printed up there. "Less than an hour ago, I was given the proof: the information you made me pass on to Ramón was blatantly false. Your two bodyguards were blameless; they never had any connection to the cartel."

"Wrong," Marco said. "Trusted sources warned us about Benito and León's association with drug traffickers. When Papá and I asked you to pass that information on to Ramón García, it was strictly for the protection of our family."

"You lie with such ease when the truth gets in the way of your own egomaniacal agenda." Clenching his fists in exasperation, Manoel scowled at his father and brother. "You had to get rid of the bodyguards because they saw what took place four years ago in Miami. When they requested a payoff for their silence, you decided to get rid of them. Both of you planted false evidence, then used me to do your dirty work. The blood of your two bodyguards should be on your hands, but you wiped it off on mine."

Keep calm, Mateo warned himself. As gingerly as possible, he walked towards Manoel. But when he attempted to put his hand on his younger son's shoulder, Manoel stepped out of his father's reach.

"You stay away from me, Papá," he said. "It's over. I know too much. I refuse to be part of your dirty business."

"You refuse to be part of the family business that made you rich?" Marco folded both hands behind his neck. "Now that's funny."

"*Family?* You don't even understand the meaning of the word." Manoel glared at them. "I'm cutting ties. I'm terminating our business involvement, and neither of you will come near Claudia or my children again!" He took a breath. "It's over! Before I came here, I instructed my lawyers not to accept any settlement attempts from your team."

"Escúchame, hijo." Mateo tried to step towards him again, but Manoel stiffly held out his right arm, his palm facing his father.

Mateo stood rigid. "Please listen, son," he said quietly. "Every family has its differences, especially when it comes to business. But never forget that the ties of blood bind us together forever."

"You left Portugal and never saw or spoke to your father again. What happened to that forever blood tie?"

"Don't you dare compare me to him! My father was an egocentric maniac, a beast!" Mateo pointed to his right cheek and left arm. "See these scars? My father attacked me with a knife, then threw me to the dogs." He fell silent for a moment. Never had he revealed this to anyone. Involuntarily, he scratched the scar on his cheek.

"If your father was such a bastard, then why did you name me after him? Was it in retaliation, or was it to honor the old Miraldo tradition of abuse and dominance?"

"How dare you?" Mateo sensed the manic part of him coming alive. "My father was a weasel in more ways than one. Even though he treated me like a pariah, I proved him wrong! From nothing, I built my own empire." He pointed at Manoel. "Unlike my father, I created a Garden of Eden for *you*."

"Unfortunately, your Eden turned into hell for me."

Mateo stepped backwards until he sank into the chair by the window again. What had happened to his calm, gentle, easily manipulated son? Why was he so hell-bent on whatever damn mission he was on? It took a moment before he could push his face back into its customary shape again. "What is it you want?" he yelled.

Manoel pointed to the thick folder he'd thrown on the credenza earlier. "My lawyers worked on changes all afternoon, and my terms should provide enough reading material for what I assume will be a sleepless night for both of you." He looked at his watch. "My legal team finalized a new proposition, which by now should also be in the hands of your counselors." His voice was as hard and steely as the blade of a dagger.

Marco laughed. "Watching the two of you is like watching a tennis tournament played in the abode of the damned. It's entertaining." Before he stuck the silver toothpick in his mouth again, he added, "Get to the damn point, little brother."

"I want complete control of Grupo Miraldo in Mexico. In return, my shares in the US and Canada, as well as my shares in the Belize and Guatemalan operations, will be transferred to both of you. As far as Belize and Guatemala are concerned, I never asked to be associated with Marco's criminal deals in those entities to begin with."

Marco sprang to his feet. "Shut up," he yelled, his silver toothpick falling from his mouth onto the parquet floor. He glanced at it and kicked it towards his brother. "You have no idea what you're talking about, you idiot! Whatever I did had Papá's blessings. I secured a superb deal for all of us."

"Everything you did was illegal."

"Your tongue should be stapled to the roof of your mouth because you don't know what you're talking about," Marco cried out. "We needed those shell companies to launder money through. Belize and Guatemala were the ideal countries because of their lack of law enforcement, their loose regulatory structures, and their bank secrecy protection. That's why tax evasion was easy." He turned his beet-red face towards his father. "Tell him! Tell your imbecile younger son that he can't run the business like he lives in the Ice Age! Tell him to stop acting like his arrogance is a virtue." Marco plunged himself into the nearest chair and glared at the silver toothpick near his brother's feet.

"Please sit down, Manoel," Mateo said. "Let's all calm down and try to work this out in a civilized way."

Manoel shook his head and remained standing.

"Well then." Mateo lifted his chin and steepled his fingers in front of his chest. "Who built Grupo Miraldo and expanded it to other countries? Me! Who grew every damn operation? Me!" He leaned forward and, like a predatory animal about to strike, stared at Manoel through narrowed eyes. "When I asked you what you wanted, I had no idea you'd demand *my* Mexican conglomerate. The audacity—" He swallowed. "The audacity of your arrogance. What the hell gives you the right?"

Without breaking eye contact, Manoel gave a side nod to the thick folder on the credenza. "Everything is spelled out in there, but allow me to briefly provide you with a few details."

As Mateo listened to his younger son's allegations, he felt himself sinking lower and deeper into the chair. Was it possible that Manoel's accusations could remove the one necessary element that was holding his own precariously balanced pyramid together? Could it be true that the solid monument he'd built might collapse like a house of cards? How in the bloody hell did Manoel have such detailed knowledge of it all? Had he gained access to the safe behind the Diego Rivera painting where critical documents were kept, evidence that related to bank and insurance fraud, hush-money payments, and the filing of false business records?

Impossible, Mateo tried to reassure himself. He rotated the safe's combination frequently. But then, he kept a record of the combinations in the hidden compartment of the antique Mexican cabinet. Was it possible that Manoel had paid one of the servants to spy on him? Suddenly even Manoel's relative proximity increased the guilt in him.

"Now, you listen to me!" Mateo thrust himself out of the chair and walked into the middle of the room. "I've established a strong relationship with all the right people throughout the years. And those who interfere with me will suffer the consequences." He took another commanding step forward. "My business associates and friends in every country respect and welcome me with open arms. I'm held in high regard because everybody knows that whenever I put my mind to something, the results are colossal." He squared himself aggressively. "So if you're trying to manipulate me, I will make sure that you cease to exist—socially as well as financially."

Manoel returned his father's intimidating stare. "You can save your verbal acrobatics because it's over, Papá," he said in a gravelly voice. "You've tricked me long enough with your hyperbole and fearmongering. Your game has come to an end because the people you must convince from now on will learn the truth unless you agree to *my* terms." He raised his chin. "I'm sitting on an unexploded bomb. All that material"—he pointed at the pile of documents—"is *my* insurance policy."

"Ridiculous," Marco shouted from across the room. "Your bomb is nothing but a water bubble." He raised his hands and clapped them together. "Poof—gone."

Ignoring his brother, Manoel nodded towards the pile on the credenza. "Most of my information comes from people that either worked for you or from sources in upper social and political ranks—don't bother asking for names."

"How dare you! You're standing in my house, where I fed and raised you, where I tried to teach you the principles of decency. And you want to declare war on the one who made you?" Despite his unease, Mateo was furious. "You want to engage in combat? Fine! You leave me no choice but to make use of my own connections." He slammed both fists on the table in front of him. "And be forewarned: I will win the battle you started."

"Go ahead and do what you must do. But should something happen to my family or to me, my legal team will release information that leads to your demise!"

He turned and walked from the room, pausing in the doorway. "Adiós, Papá y Marco. May God help both of you."

Mateo flipped the last page of the legal documents. His head felt heavy, his body lifeless. "Unless we agree to his terms, he'll take this battle to court. Neither of us can afford to let him do that."

"I still can't believe Manoel is prepared to attack us publicly. Doesn't he know that backstabbing and name-calling might ruin his own reputation?" Marco reached for the Victorian sterling silver coffeepot to pour himself a fresh cup. He added sweet cream and stirred the mixture. "When did my flaky, insecure brother turn into such a vindictive asshole?"

"He's waging his vendetta because of jealousy and sibling rivalry," Mateo grunted, filling his own cup. Steam rose from the dark brew. Absentmindedly, he took a swig of coffee, not expecting the scalding liquid to sting his lips and tongue. As he jerked the cup away from his mouth, the burning brew spilled onto his lap. "Venom!" he cried out and hurled the white porcelain cup across the room, where it shattered into many pieces. The remains of the coffee oozed like dark blood across the floor.

"That looks painful," Marco said, watching his father dab his groin. "No matter how you see it, Manoel has always been jealous of me. He's been insecure his whole life, lacking drive and talent. He resents my confidence and courage." He dragged his chair closer to his father's. "Manoel knows you anointed me as your successor because I never shied away from taking risks. I guess I shouldn't be surprised that he's willing to take his idiotic grudge this far." Marco took one of the sweetbreads off the tray and heartily bit into it.

With his stomach already in tight knots, Mateo found it troublesome to watch his son eat. He turned his head away. "I thought I hired the best legal talent in the country, but apparently Manoel's team can't be hoodwinked." He looked upward, wringing his hands towards the ceiling. "Dios mío, why is my own flesh and blood trying to incinerate the very marrow of my bones? Where's the gratitude for the life I handed him?"

"Even if that little shit acts like a vengeful tiger, I won't let him wound you any further." Marco put his arm around his father's shoulder, leaned in to make eye contact. "Let it go, Papá. There is so much you and I can accomplish."

"Accomplish? With all of this?" Mateo pushed the thick folders away from him.

"I'm talking about a fresh, unblemished start in the United States and Canada. We already have a solid foundation there—business registration, incorporation at the state level, banking, et cetera. We'll be investing a shitload of money in the US economy and creating employment. Plus, the friendships you've established with those US senators will come in very handy with the immigration's green card through investment program."

"I know all about the EB-5 program, and it's not like the idea hasn't crossed my mind, but you don't understand how difficult it is for me to leave everything behind." Mateo made a sweeping gesture with both hands. "I love this country—the people, the food, the music, my hacienda. I built my empire in Mexico. How can I turn my back on all of this?"

"You can, Papá, because we might not have another choice."

Marco refilled his coffee cup, then bit into his second pan dulce. "We'll establish our headquarters in Wisconsin and rename the organization." He rubbed his hands together. "Wait until you hear my ideas for projects beyond commercial real estate."

Mateo stood up and walked to the large casement window. He opened it and sighed into the early morning. "You would leave your mother while she's still alive?"

"She has no idea who she is, who I am. When was the last time she recognized either me or you?" Marco joined his father by the window. Together, they gazed over the grounds of the hacienda. "Although she always smiles when she sees Manoel," Marco said flatly. "I still can't believe she left part of her estate to him and left fucking nothing to her firstborn."

"My God, why do you keep bringing this up? You did wrong! You diverted certain company funds into your pockets before they were recorded—all behind your brother's back."

"But I only took what should be my share when Mamá dies," Marco mumbled.

"And your fraud became an additional liability among all of Manoel's other charges."

Quietly, they stood side by side, each one lost in his own thoughts.

Mateo cleared his throat. "I need to show everybody that I'm a decent, caring, and trustworthy human being. Until your mother's death, I'll continue to pay the expenses of her care, no matter where in the world I end up living."

Marco whipped his head around, his eyes wide. "Are you telling me you'll consider—"

"Unless my legal team can work miracles or Manoel has a change of heart, what other choice do I have?" Mateo closed the windows. "I've crossed borders before and can do it again. I will reshape my life and build a flawless reputation in the United States—the land of plenty."

NINETEEN

Ursula, November 1996
Crans-Montana, Switzerland

During our session yesterday, you shared traumatic experiences," said Dr. Alain Féraud. "I hope the guided meditation class afterwards brought you some mental repose, perhaps helped you sleep."

Ursula nodded. "Thank you for recommending it. Meditating in the conservatory among the tropical plants and flower displays is quite soothing."

"Would you like to know why the conservatory was built down by the lake below the resort?"

"I wondered about that."

"Before this retreat was acquired from its previous owners, there were reports of residents feeling more energized. Some of them experienced relief not only from stress but also from other physical problems."

The therapist waited until Ursula had sat down in the brown tufted leather club chair before he took his own seat opposite her. "Well," he continued, "the area around the lake supposedly sits on an ancient volcano, and the previous owners claimed it was a power place due to the balance of oxygen-rich air and water. Experts were hired, and indeed, they measured high positive radiation values in the vicinity of forty thousand Bovis units." He smiled when Ursula tilted her head at him. "People with a Bovis value below sixty-five hundred usually experience low energy levels and might be more susceptible to diseases." His smile intensified. "We keep receiving favorable reports from our guests."

"In that case, I'll take advantage of the opportunity while I'm here." Ursula lowered her head, a gesture that had become increasingly automatic when she felt timid or cornered.

It had been her grandfather's plea that she seek professional help, therapy that might ease her out of a sense of constant crisis. Desperate for relief, Ursula had given in. She wanted to rid herself of the ghastly flashes that kept zigzagging through her mind—specific images, moments, voices that haunted her.

"Can you share your thoughts with me, Ursula?"

Dr. Féraud's soothing voice pulled her into the moment. "I'd like to continue where we left off yesterday," she said without looking up, "but I need to hear again that what I say will stay confidential." She sniffled and glanced at the small table next to her chair; a new Kleenex box had been put in the same spot as the days before. "Excuse me." She blew her nose.

"You are safe, Ursula."

She took another tissue and wiped her cheek. "I've never found the courage to talk about this with a professional before. But the past two days have brought some unexpected relief. For the moment, it gives me a glimmer of hope." She lifted her head to make brief eye contact with the therapist, sitting seven feet across from her.

Somehow this sympathetic-looking man didn't make her feel skeptical or anxious—feelings she'd previously experienced whenever she considered analysis. Dr. Alain Féraud's warm eyes, the color of milk chocolate, had a relaxing effect; the depth of his calm voice encouraged her to open up.

"Danke," she said and lowered her eyes again.

In her first session, she had asked the therapist if they could conduct their meetings in German, the language she'd grown up with, instead of the French spoken in this part of Switzerland.

"German is a good choice," Dr. Féraud had answered. Just like Ursula, he was multilingual.

"Yesterday, I told you about my unforgivable decision to take my children out of Mexico," she said in a low voice. "I appreciate your encouragement to share the events the way I see and feel them."

"Talking about suffering is never easy, Ursula. In the three days you've been at Panacea, you've shared much more with me than I anticipated. I realize it causes you great stress to talk about it, but you do it with the clarity of purpose that brought you here."

His deep, gentle voice and warm smile stopped her from rocking and from shrugging her shoulders to her ears, nervous tics she'd developed. Forcing herself to let go of tension, she leaned back into the chair.

"I want to talk about something else today, something very difficult to expose," she said. "I don't even know where to start." She willed herself to keep still despite the urge to start rocking again.

"Does it concern Molly?"

She looked past her knees. "It's about Molly *and* Miggy." She swallowed. "It's also about Mateo and Marco, with me in the middle." Her voice was barely audible. She placed the box of Kleenex on her lap. "Please be patient because this is very difficult for me to talk about."

Whenever Marco returned home after having been with Carla de La Fuente, Ursula endured intimidation, shaming, name-calling, isolation, and more. As painful as his behavior was, she refused to give up hope, always letting him know she loved him, would do anything for him to love her back. When she heard him sob in the middle of the night in another room, she believed he felt remorse and shame and envisioned brighter days ahead.

But his foul temper worsened, causing him to drown his misery in alcohol and drugs. The more intoxicated he was, the more sadistic he became, imposing unusual sexual fixations as well as inflicting physical and mental pain on her. The few times she tried to stand up for herself or attempted to refuse him, he screamed insults and threatened her with punishment worse than slapping.

To camouflage his sadism, he bought Ursula fancy clothes, adorned her with expensive jewelry, and showed her off in Mexican society. He consistently reminded her to be grateful for the luxuries he offered her.

Unless she was escorted by her husband or people loyal to him, she was forbidden to leave the grounds of the hacienda. Confined by walls, iron gates, and a watchtower with grim-looking bodyguards, any thought of escape from the country was pointless; Marco had taken possession of her passport.

Ursula did everything in her power to prevent a possible pregnancy. Immediately after each traumatic sexual encounter, she made sure to get up and move around the house, praying for gravity to pull his sperm away from her cervix.

She was in desperate need of a friend, a person with whom she could share her misery, an individual she could trust.

That's when Mateo entered the stage.

Ursula hoped her father-in-law could talk sense into his son and save her marriage. Aware that Marco was his favorite, she chose her words carefully whenever expressing her pain and sadness to the older Miraldo, who in return would hold her, comfort her, always promising things would change.

The more Marco's extramarital excursions took him away from the hacienda, the more Mateo came to the rescue. He escorted Ursula to the opera, to theater and dance performances at the Palacio de Bellas Artes in Mexico City. Afterwards he would wine and dine her in the city's finest establishments. They usually ran into Mexico's high society—good friends and acquaintances of the Miraldos. People often wondered why Marco wasn't by his wife's side, but Mateo had no problems excusing his son's absence with fabricated stories about business travels, important meetings, or exhaustion from too much work.

Though Ursula welcomed it when Mateo took her away from the hacienda to attend performances and introduce her to the laughter of carefree, happy people, she always wished her husband, rather than his father, was next to her.

On many occasions Mateo's attentiveness became too close for comfort—like the way he held her hand during theater performances or when he embraced her tightly for too long or when he pressed his lips close to hers.

As the embraces, the kisses, the affection intensified, Ursula dared to express her unease, but he waved it off. "My sweet, innocent Ula," Mateo said, laughing, "that's the way we do it in Mexico."

"Though I knew Mateo's affection went beyond Mexican *tradition*, I was afraid to lose the only caring alliance that was offered to me in the prison of my home." Ursula spoke softly, still looking past her knees.

"In yesterday's session you briefly talked about Mateo's estranged wife. You mentioned happiness when you met her. Can you tell me more about that friendship?"

"Mamá Marta became my surrogate mother, my guardian angel. She was loving, kind, and very talented. Because of her, I am here today." She glanced at the therapist. "I'll never understand how life can be so cruel to the most gentle and big-hearted amongst us." She lowered her eyes again. "It paralyzed me having to watch the illness take her away from the world she loved so deeply."

"Did she pass away?"

"Early onset of Alzheimer's disease sent Mamá Marta into a state of confusion soon after my babies were born." Ursula took a fresh tissue from the Kleenex box. "But for almost four years prior to that, she was my salvation. We had a unique relationship shaped by trust and love. She sensed something was terribly wrong in my marriage. She told me whenever I was ready to talk, she'd listen. I don't know if it was shame, guilt, or whatever else that kept me from telling her, but when I was ready, it already was too late." She started to rock in her chair—she needed a moment before she was able to continue. "While Mamá Marta still had the ability, she put money away so that I could be financially independent in the future. She also had a plan for my safety, but her illness pulled her into dementia, preventing her from finalizing those plans."

Overcome by emotion, she stammered, "I miss h-her. It h-hurts s-so much."

Dr. Féraud gave Ursula time to steady herself. "Your flower garden in Mexico. Did you enjoy its blossoms and growth?"

She lifted her head. "I did."

"Think of me as a gardener," the therapist said. "Everything you tell me is a seed you intend to plant. I, in return, will help you to develop your own ability to determine what seeds will sprout through hope and faith, and what seeds may need more nourishment and healing. I'm here for you. You can lean on my optimism until you're able to find your own."

Ursula hung onto every word from the therapist's lips. His calm voice sounded like a guiding spirit.

"There's a glass of water on the side table, Ursula."

She nodded and reflexively reached for the glass.

"I'm sorry," she said after a moment of quiet. "Talking about Mamá Marta is heartbreaking for me."

"Would you like to stop for today? I realize this hasn't been easy for you."

She shook her head and for the first time made unbroken eye contact with the therapist. "The worst of my shame is still to come."

"Whenever you are ready . . ."

It happened on an afternoon Marco returned to the hacienda after having been away for several days and nights. Ursula was cutting flowers in her garden when one of the servants came running, letting her know that Marco was furious because his wife wasn't in the house. She rushed home, but when she entered their quarters, he was on the phone, begging and pleading with Carla de La Fuente.

Afraid he would realize she had witnessed his vulnerability, she quietly backed out of the room.

She was arranging her fresh-cut flowers in a tall crystal vase when, visibly intoxicated, Marco stumbled into the kitchen. She tried to ignore his lecherous gaze, but he yanked her by the ponytail, whipped her around, and pressed her back against the kitchen counter.

"Why was the house empty when I returned?" he snarled. "Where the fuck were you?" He grabbed her by the shoulders and began shaking her, his face inches away from hers.

She not only detected the alcohol on his breath but also hints of Caron Poivre, Carla's signature perfume.

"Please, Marco," she said. "You just spent four days with your mistress. I'm sure you had a wonderful time. There's no need to get upset now."

"Shut your fucking mouth, you slut," he slurred. In an aggressive swoop he lifted her onto the counter, ripped her white shirt open, and leered at her exposed breasts. He grunted when he removed the belt from his pants; he laughed when he bound her wrists with it.

"Please don't do this—you're hurting me."

"You deserve it, puta. You bewitched my father; he can't get enough of you. What do you give him you don't give me?" Like a pig he made low, guttural sounds and winked at her lasciviously, calling her dirty names.

The more she struggled to get away, the more he slapped her face, her breasts, her exposed thighs.

"Stop!"

Forcefully he pushed her down again, knocking the crystal vase over. The cold water seeped against her exposed skin.

"Please . . . please stop!"

By the time he was done with her, she was bruised inside and out. Unable to move, she remained on the kitchen counter, surrounded by shards of crystal and flower petals—blossoms she'd thought would dispel some of the melancholy in her home.

Through swollen lids she watched him pull up his pants. Without giving her another glance, he said, "I'm leaving for Acapulco with Carla. Don't contact me and don't expect me back for another week."

Ursula had no idea how long she lay motionless on the counter.

Not until voices from outside the open window startled her did she become aware of her repulsive reality again. Without thinking, she grabbed her clothes, staggered upstairs, and turned on the shower.

Later, when she went into the kitchen again, everything had been cleaned up. A fresh bouquet of flowers from her garden sat beautifully arranged in a large handblown glass bowl on the counter. A note from Marisol lay next to it. *I don't dare imagine what happened. Please let me know how I can help.*

She walked into the sitting room and noticed that her hand was trembling as she put a tall glass of limonada on the side table. She let herself sink into the soft champagne-colored velvety couch. All seemed muted in this quiet space where every wall was shirred and draped in a silk fabric. With its quiet elegance, this room was Ursula's favorite space in the south wing of the hacienda. Here she found consolation.

Outside, the sky had already grown dark, and when she lit the two hanging metallic pendants, engraved with an intricate design, they cast a lovely pattern against the shirred walls.

She didn't know how long she sat in the same spot. Had she been fantasizing, thinking back to her life in Switzerland? Or had her mind simply gone blank?

"Ula?"

She froze. Had Marco come back to abuse her all over again?

Instead, Mateo walked through the door with a bouquet of gardenias.

"What happened to you?" he asked, leaning closer. "Why have you been crying? And what happened to your face?"

Filled with shame, she simply shook her head.

"Did Marco do this to you? I know he was here briefly because Marisol delivered a message that he was leaving with Carla for Acapulco." Mateo pulled Ursula into his arms. "I'm sorry, Ula, mi dulce ángel." He pressed his lips into her neck. "You deserve so much better," he whispered. "I brought you gardenias because they symbolize your purity and gentleness." He kissed the palm of her hand and from his pocket pulled a bracelet. He fastened it around her wrist. "It's Cartier's love bracelet." He covered her fingertips with tiny bird-peck kisses.

She pulled her hand away. "Mateo, this is all very wrong." She tried to unfasten the clip. "You keep making matters worse by—"

He put his index finger over her lips. "Ssssh. There's no need to question anything," he said softly, standing up. "Wait for me; I'll be right back."

She heard the clinking of crystal, the shatter of ice hitting a bucket, the pop of a bottle of wine being opened. Overcome by a feeling of confinement, she walked to the window and opened it wide. The crisp evening air brushed against her bruised cheek. She turned her head to look into the stamped metal and ebonized wood mirror, decoratively placed against the shirred fabric on the wall.

The left side of her face had turned from bright red to a deep pink; her cheek was swollen, her eyes puffy. Her damaged image forced her to confront everything that had happened on a deeper level. Had there really been a point in time when she was in love with Marco? Had she really dreamed of a fairy-tale life? She took a step back, shaking her head at her reflection. "If your life was so sweet in Switzerland, why did you search for honey in places where killer bees would sting you?"

"What did you say? You were mumbling, mi amor."

Ursula whipped around; she hadn't heard Mateo return to the sitting room. He'd poured wine into two Baccarat crystal glasses. "Montrachet Grand Cru," he said and carefully placed the bottle into the sterling silver wine cooler. "A beautiful wine for an exquisite young woman."

He handed her the glass and gazed into her eyes. "Salud, amor, y dinero. ¡Y tiempo para gastarlo."

She hesitated to put the glass to her lips. Mateo's favorite wines had made her drowsy before. She might have even passed out—she had trouble remembering. But in that moment, all she wanted was to forget what Marco had done to her. Hoping the alcohol would numb her pain, she sipped the complex and buttery drops.

"Mi dulce amor," Mateo said softly, "forget about Marco and Carla. Those imbeciles deserve each other." He leaned closer. "Drink up. This magnificent vintage will relax you, make you feel lighter and better." He looked deep into her eyes again when he took a sip from his own glass. "Delicious," he said. "It combines exquisiteness with power." He took another sip. "Smooth and sensuous, like you."

"I didn't follow my initial instincts," Ursula whispered. "Just like before, the wine made me lethargic, sleepy. I should've realized Mateo had laced my drink with something. Whatever it was, it completely impaired my judgment." She cast a desperate glance at the therapist. The look of empathy on his face alleviated some of her uncertainty, and when he nodded his encouragement, she continued.

"I remember debilitating dizziness. I think I blacked out during some of it. But in between, I heard him talk, felt him kissing me."

Without conscious thought, Ursula fastened the top three buttons of her sweater and crossed her arms tightly over her chest. "I was physically helpless when he undressed me and began fondling me. I remember having strange hallucinations. Mateo mistook my moans of despair for pleasure. I heard him say things like 'You love it, don't you?' and 'I want you to enjoy every part of me, mi amor.'" She drew in a ragged breath. "I couldn't fight him when he penetrated me," she said in hushed tones, "and when I squirmed, he thought it meant I was enjoying it."

Ursula wiped her eyes and threw the damp tissue in the already half-full wastebasket next to her chair. "I don't know how long it went on. When I woke up the next morning, he was getting dressed. I pretended to be asleep when he came to the bed again. He kissed my lips and ran his fingers over my body, saying, 'You're mine for eternity. I won't let anyone else have you, my beautiful angel.' As soon as he was gone, the room began to spin. Hours later, Marisol found me on the floor in the bathroom."

She lowered her head and stared at her knees again. "When I missed my period, I knew I was pregnant. Throughout the pregnancy, I didn't want to bring life into this cruel world. But nine months later, I gave birth to twins."

The tears came spasmodically, and she needed time to bring her emotions under control. "The moment those two tiny miracles were laid in my arms, my world began to glow," she said. "My Molly and my Miggy were like two new suns, brimming with light, warmth, and love. Giving birth to them was the closest I ever came to magic."

She dried her eyes with the last tissue from the Kleenex box and lifted her head again.

"Less than an hour after I gave birth to my twin babies, Marco informed me that he was leaving to celebrate the arrival of his son and daughter with friends; he disappeared for four days and three nights. I was alone when the physician and midwife asked for the correct spelling of everybody's names for the birth certificates. I told them Marco Miraldo was their father." Ursula rocked uneasily in her chair. "But instead," she said, barely audible, "I should have said 'father unknown.'"

TWENTY

Ursula, three weeks later

Dr. Féraud apologizes. He's running late due to an emergency." The young nurse—Colette, it said on her name tag—in a uniform as crisp and white as the fresh snow that had fallen on the canton of Valais overnight, unlocked the door to the therapist's office. Inside the pleasant, well-furnished room, Nurse Colette filled a carafe with water and placed it on the side table, together with a clean glass and a new box of tissues. "Please push this button if there's anything you need," she said, pointing to the switch next to the door. "Dr. Féraud will be with you shortly."

As she had done almost every day, Ursula sunk into the tufted leather club chair in the therapist's office—a congenial room, enhanced by a warm yellow color scheme and live plants. She wondered how many patients had sat in the same chair, hoping to relieve their pain. How many more would come. *If only these walls could talk.*

Another week and her treatments with Dr. Féraud would be over, at least for the foreseeable future. The diverse sessions and activities at the Panacea Wellness Resort had yielded hope, restored her energy level and stimulated her senses. Through daily meditation, she'd learned how to gain new perspectives on traumatic situations. She had a better sense of how to increase self-awareness and diminish torturous, upsetting emotions.

The daily sessions with Dr. Féraud had been the most beneficial part of her stay. He provided tools that helped her dreaded insomnia, reducing the flashbacks that made her hate herself. His breathing techniques also eased her anxiety whenever she condemned herself for the unforgivable decisions that had resulted in losing Molly.

To confront her miscalculations, the therapist guided Ursula to make a list of them, then showed her how to courageously face them—one by one. Grateful for Dr. Féraud's never-ending patience, she began to grasp why she kept punishing herself for events that were beyond her control. She learned to take baby steps forward and realized that the course of many events had not been her fault.

While reflecting on what she had learned, she felt strong rays of sunshine on her face. Ursula turned her head towards the large window and let her eyes feast on the spectacular scenery outside the office: snow-covered mountain peaks under wide-open blue skies.

"I'm so sorry," Dr. Féraud said when he rushed into his office. He hung up his coat and ran his fingers through tousled wavy hair. "My friend's father passed away unexpectedly, and I wanted to help the family through the initial shock of their loss." He took his seat across from Ursula, trying to pat down his thick dark-brown hair again.

Her face reddened when she caught herself observing the tall, fit-looking gentleman, whose great spirit and noble ways she'd grown to trust and admire. She shifted her gaze and diverted her thoughts to yesterday's session, when she'd talked about the difficulties involved with returning to Switzerland and her beloved grandparents. She'd expressed how much she loved this small country, so rich with natural beauty, and admitted that, when alone with nature, she was often able to forget the old skeletons she kept locked up in closets.

Dr. Féraud had told her that he also found peace of mind in natural settings, referring to himself as a solitary, outdoors kind of guy.

Against her will, Ursula glanced at the therapist again. There was no feature in particular that made Dr. Alain Féraud look so handsome, but his milk-chocolate eyes, with their intensity, honesty, and gentleness, came close. When she caught herself wondering about his life outside the office, she blushed and focused on the floral pattern in the Tibetan area rug.

"Because I'm late," he said, "I made sure we'd have extra time today." He opened his notebook. "Yesterday you expressed a need to clarify matters that still remain obscure."

"Yes, I find myself stuck in this mental cul-de-sac." She timidly looked up at him. "Perhaps you can guide me out of it?"

"Try to recall instances when you didn't feel that way. Are there moments when you don't think about what took place in Mexico and Miami?"

"Yes."

"Can you identify them? If so, try to find the connections between hope and the dynamics of life that will help you move forward."

After Molly was ripped out of their lives, Ursula, Miggy, and Marisol changed hotel rooms several times in Miami. Ursula had been afraid that the airline, alerted by their no-shows, would make a connection between the empty seats on the plane and their left-behind overnight luggage near the departure gate. The authorities who were notified might have linked them to Molly's accident outside the airport. Also, what if Mateo or Marco had told the police that Ursula had kidnapped her children? What if someone discovered they had entered the United States with fake passports? Worst of all, what if Ursula was thrown into jail, never to see her children again?

It was Bruno Rossi who took every possibility into consideration and determined that Ursula and Miggy needed new identities before they planned their next move. In due course, he came up with a novel strategy.

Bruno took his partner for the past twenty years, Joaquín Hebroni, into his confidence. The two men agreed that, for the time being, there was only one way to solve the problem: Bruno and Ursula would travel to Las Vegas and get married.

Born in Switzerland to a Mexican mother and Swiss father, Bruno had lived the first few years of his life in the canton of Ticino, Switzerland's Italian region. He was twelve when his father passed away and his mother returned with her son to Mexico. To this day, Bruno held dual citizenship and was in possession of two valid passports.

"I'm aware of the many risks we're taking, but should it become necessary, I can seek protection and aid from people in high places," he assured Ursula. By marrying her in Las Vegas, he explained, he would be able to provide her with the needed Swiss documents. As Ursula Rossi, she'd not only have authentic paperwork to travel abroad, she'd be able to take residence in Switzerland.

Bruno also obtained the needed legal instruments to adopt Miggy, making sure that all was in accordance with intercountry adoption. With Miggy's existing fake passport and identity as Michael Burgli, Bruno engineered matters so precisely that both the relevant authorities in the boy's birth country and the officials in Switzerland were satisfied.

"The woman sitting in front of you is a collection of untruths," Ursula told her therapist. "It took over a year for the needed documents to be processed. In the meantime, Bruno made arrangements for us to live with Joaquín's younger brother, Rabbi David Hebroni and his family."

Her eyes misted over when she talked about the Hebronis' generous hospitality in a suburb of Chicago. "I'll never forget how they made us feel safe and comfortable while we waited for our new identities."

Unaware that a rare smile had spread over her face, Ursula continued. "I'm sure you wondered if there was a link between my last name and Bruno's—Rossi. Well, now you know why and how that happened."

The therapist was silent for a moment. "Thank you for making everything clear."

"Bruno has been my guardian angel. What would have happened to Miggy, Marisol, and me if it hadn't been for him?" she said quietly, almost as if to herself. Again, she turned her head towards the scenery outside the window. "I wish my mind would stop being like a mirror that only reflects bad memories, constantly casting back gloom, never letting go of the cruel past." She sighed and looked at him. "Will I ever be able to wipe this mirror clean?"

"As time goes on, all mirrors become dull; they corrode and lose their shine," Dr. Féraud said. "The moment will come when you won't be able to see anything in that mirror anymore."

"I hope so." Ursula fidgeted with the buttons on her jacket. "I have trouble believing I can find the essence again, the marrow of me that was once the true Ursula."

"I believe you minimize your own strength," he said. "When you learn how to acknowledge even the smallest of your achievements, that awareness will reward you with restored hope." The therapist glanced at the notebook on his lap. "You've shared so much of your life with me during the past three weeks and often gave me the opportunity to read between the lines." He tilted his head. "You look exhausted, Ursula."

She nodded. "Thank you. I've taken too much of your time today, and my mind and body need another guided meditation in the conservatory."

TWENTY-ONE

Ursula, Panacea Wellness Resort, last day

To make sure she wasn't leaving anything behind, she checked all of the drawers in the hand-painted pine armoire again. As she zipped up her luggage, she was surprised by a wave of sentimentality.

Ursula opened the terrace doors and stepped outside. A gentle snowfall greeted her. Within minutes, it lay on her face, shoulders, and chest like a veil, almost as if it were trying to cloak her in a cocoon of memories.

The four weeks at the Panacea Wellness Resort had been a godsend. Though some of her wounds might never heal, she looked at her fate through different lenses. "Think of your life as a camera," Dr. Féraud had suggested, then he gave her card that read:

> *FOCUS* only on what is useful. *CAPTURE* the quality of each moment. When you begin to *DEVELOP*, aim to evolve from each *NEGATIVE*. If you don't like the results, take your camera, be brave, and take another *SHOT* to improve *SYMMETRY*, *VIEWPOINT*, *DEPTH*, and *COLOR*.

The alarm clock inside the room signaled it was time to head to her appointment. She went into the bathroom to dry her face and hair, brushing the remaining snowflakes off her coat jacket. She would leave her suitcase in the room until later. She took the familiar walk, ready to share more revelations in her final double session with Dr. Féraud.

—

"During the year Miggy, Marisol, and I lived with Rabbi David Hebroni and his family in the US, Bruno devised a master plan with the help of my grandparents in Switzerland." Ursula glanced at the fresh Kleenex box, hoping she wouldn't need to empty it again. "It helped that my grandparents had reached retirement age, but for crucial reasons, they immediately put their restaurant and Après-Ski Bar on the market while retaining their residence in Grindelwald."

"May I assume the sale had something to do with your arrival in Switzerland?"

She nodded. "Just as Bruno had predicted, as Ursula Rossi and Michael Rossi our passage from the United States to Switzerland didn't raise flags or cause problems; our papers were legal. Even Marisol Rodriguez, who had kept her original passport, passed the scrutiny of immigration officials. Immediately after we entered this country, we moved into Die Alphütte."

"Die Alphütte? What and where is it?"

"My grandparents' secret retreat, a small rustic chalet nestled in the mountains, high above the town of Grindelwald." Ursula turned her head to the window, thinking of the Alphütte with its overhanging eaves, standing all by itself on a sunny mountain terrace. Its infrastructure had been modernized with individualistic ideas and beautiful details inside. The old wood stove in the kitchen and the fireplace in the living room were still functional, but cozy new sitting arrangements enhanced the living areas on the ground floor. A wood spiral staircase led to three bedrooms and two updated stone bathrooms.

With a sigh, she looked at the therapist again. "It was the perfect place to hide. The nearest neighbor lived at least twenty hiking minutes below on the mountain."

"Being so secluded, did you feel safe?"

She nodded. "After we settled into the Alphütte, I began taking Miggy on hikes I remembered from my youth. Rediscovering the alpine beauty with him, I couldn't stop inhaling the sweet mountain air, wishing it would douse the fire of fear in me. At times I dreamed of a future with my twins, free of past pain. But that stretch of solace and reverie got stifled by the daily farrago of crippling premonitions, always revolving around Molly, the daughter I abandoned—sacrificed for my own freedom."

"You didn't abandon or sacrifice her," Dr. Féraud said. "You acted with the purest of intentions for your children's safety and your own." Holding her gaze, he tilted his head. "Molly is only eight years old—why do you think you've lost her forever?"

"I spoke earlier about letters I sent to Molly, to Marco, to Mateo, begging for their forgiveness. I pleaded with the Miraldo men to negotiate. Against all odds, I sought their understanding and compassion so the twins could grow up together. All my letters remained unanswered, except the one from Molly, in which she blamed me for the accident, telling me she never wanted to see me again. 'I don't know you!' was her last sentence."

Dr. Féraud raised his eyebrows. "Might there be a chance that Molly was forced to write the letter?"

"It's possible." Ursula pulled the first two tissues from the box. "There isn't a moment I don't think about the damage I caused my little girl, but more so, I have good reason to believe that Molly will never find out the truth behind everything that happened." She swallowed. "I suspect Mateo and Marco are feeding Molly nothing but lies, especially that Miggy and I are dead."

The therapist adjusted himself in his chair and crossed his legs. "How do you know that?"

"It was Bruno who first heard rumors about a serious liaison between Carla de La Fuente and Marco Miraldo. But when their glamorous wedding was all over the news, Bruno's antennae went up. How was it possible for Marco to marry Carla when officially he still was married to me?"

"What did Bruno find out?"

"Since Bruno's partner Joaquín worked in the Civil Registration Office in Mexico City, his searches led to the ghastly discovery of my and Miggy's death certificates, stamped and certified by the Health Department of Basel, Switzerland."

"Unbelievable! Forgery of death certificates is a serious crime and punishable by imprisonment, at least here in Switzerland."

Ursula nodded. "Secretly, Joaquín made copies and sent them to me. I'd never seen a death certificate and remember staring in disbelief at my own and one of my little son. *Ärztliche Todesbescheinigung*, it read and was issued by the Gesundheitsdepartement des Kantons Basel-Stadt."

"But how did Marco get ahold of such documents from Switzerland?"

"It took a while for Bruno to find out that Banco Salina Suisse had hired private detectives to monitor the activities of employee Robert Graf."

"Your father?"

Ursula nodded. "Apparently, the international financial institution had become aware of circulating rumors about my father's illegal activities in Guatemala and Belize, as well as in Liechtenstein and Switzerland. Bruno discovered unconfirmed reports claiming that he covertly worked for Grupo Miraldo and performed much of the company's dirty work."

Blinking quickly, Ursula eyed the Kleenex box but reached for the glass of water instead.

"And then Bruno connected the pieces: Marco must've given the directive, and my father, via another Swiss scoundrel, obtained the necessary documents to forge his own daughter's and grandson's death certificates." She took another sip of water. Realizing the glass was half empty, she quickly filled it up again.

"While at work at the Civil Registration Office in Mexico City, Joaquín then hit on a notarized statement, signed by Marco Miraldo, in which he said his wife had been vacationing in Switzerland with their son. Marco claimed both had drowned in a boating accident on the Rhine River during a severe thunderstorm. Of course, when Bruno and Joaquín searched for any police reports or news articles in Basel that corroborated a boating accident on that day, they found nothing."

"Why did Bruno and Joaquín decide not to report any of it to the Mexican authorities? Was it for your and your son's safety?"

"Yes. They knew dangerous people were at play. When Bruno tried to locate Francisco Cruz, the notario in Mexico City whose stamp and name appeared on the falsified documents, he discovered that the notary public had been found strangled in his home less than a week after stamping Marco's documents. Though the case was still open, there had been no follow-ups."

Dr. Féraud frowned. "There was no murder investigation?"

Ursula shook her head. "According to Bruno, solving a murder in Mexico is the exception, not the rule. Meanwhile, every single one of the fake records managed to satisfy the Mexican legal requirements."

The therapist turned a page in his notebook. "Do you know where Robert Graf might be these days?"

She shrugged. "Bruno believes he most likely is in the possession of several passports and could be anywhere—if he's alive."

"Regardless of Graf's current whereabouts, he'll be in big trouble if he's found out."

"My father never had any scruples; his world was ruled by hard cash."

"And you still think it's best to keep these criminal findings away from authorities."

Ursula nodded. "I also have done wrong, but *dead* people cannot be prosecuted for kidnapping." She lowered her eyes. "Yet here I am, very much alive and willing to share the rest of my story with only you."

She excused herself, and when she returned from a bathroom break, she found a large cup of café au lait next to her seat.

"I thought we both could use the afternoon booster." Dr. Féraud smiled.

"You read my mind. Thank you." She held the cup between both hands as she continued.

"It was interesting how quickly Miggy and Marisol were able to put down roots. My little boy, who never liked crowds or confrontation, flourished in the solitude of nature. And Marisol expressed her daily thanks in prayer for feeling safe again, surrounded by people she loved and considered her family." Ursula put the cup back onto the saucer and dabbed her lips.

"My grandparents visited weekly, bringing needed supplies up the mountain. I clearly had no intention of traveling the forty minutes' distance to Grindelwald. Even after almost two decades away, I still feared someone might recognize me. And my fear only intensified when my grandfather heard a bald, middle-aged foreigner had questioned some town folks about the Burglis, asking why their establishment was up for sale. Alarmed about the stranger, my grandfather drove to Bern and purchased two trained German shepherds to guard his family-in-hiding." A brief smile lit up her face. "Miggy instantly formed a bond with the dogs, and soon the animals followed his every step. Because they were siblings, he named them Hansel and Gretel."

Dr. Féraud cocked his head. "Any reason for those names?"

"He believed Hansel and Gretel were twins, like he and Molly." Ursula sighed. "I was amazed that he'd drawn parallels between his own life and a classic fairy tale—brother and sister trying to free themselves from a bad environment, children who are lost and must take frightening detours before they reach happiness." She began to rock back and forth. "But my story has no fairy-tale ending." She stiffly leaned back into the chair to stop herself from rocking. "Sometimes I have the urge to come out of hiding, admit to my shameful wrongdoing and face the consequences, but Miggy's optimism is a cornerstone of hope. He's convinced Molly will find her way back home to us."

"Your young son is insightful. Might this be a good time to talk more about Miggy?" Dr. Féraud gave Ursula an encouraging smile.

She nodded. "As the firstborn son, Miguel was supposed to carry on the Miraldo legacy, but Marco never showed any particular interest in him, mistaking the boy's shy and withdrawn nature as a flaw in his mental functioning. He said it was my fault. Miguel should've inherited Molara's outgoing and determined personality instead of exhibiting what he branded as girlish, bashful, insecure behavior." Ursula shook her head and sighed. "Marco never bothered to take a deeper look at Miggy, who clearly inherited Marta's fine-tuned intuition, her intelligence and creativity."

"Did Marco spend any quality time with the children?"

"No. Even as toddlers, they were afraid of their father. Though the left wing of the hacienda was extensive, I know that Marco's and my loud arguments must've echoed through the marble and stone halls. Marisol tried her best to shield the twins from hearing our quarrels or having to witness their father physically abusing me, but there were times when her efforts failed."

She stopped talking and brushed the palms of her hands over her thighs, as if to smooth invisible wrinkles from her pants. Slowly she continued to talk. "During the twins' first four years of life, the negative effects of their father's erratic behavior often disrupted their sleep and caused emotional distress. But whereas Molly at times dared to stand in front of her father, asking him to stop, Miggy ran and hid."

"Did Marco ever hurt them physically?"

Ursula shook her head. "He never laid a hand on them. When he felt they'd misbehaved, he locked the doors and forced them to stay inside, demanding that they not utter a word while he screamed at me, scolding me for being a terrible mother, incapable of raising children. In his rage, he often threw things at me and threatened to hurt me. When the children began to sob, he screamed at them to be quiet or they'd never see me again!"

"Verbal and emotional abuse is just as bad, if not worse in some cases, than physical abuse," the therapist said softly. "Did Marco ever apologize to the children?"

"After these episodes, he usually disappeared, sometimes for days," she said. "I used that time to listen to my children, hearing their innocent interpretation of what they'd been forced to witness. I always asked them simple, guarded questions, closely paying attention to their fears and worries. I never stopped reassuring my twins of my own strength, and I vowed to them that nothing and no one could separate me from them."

Chewing on her inner lip, Ursula eyed the Kleenex box. She inhaled sharply before she continued. "But I broke my promise. I betrayed their trust when Molly was torn out of our lives. And now I don't know what's happening to her—" She paused midsentence when she realized that the glowing light in Dr. Féraud's office had turned into twilight. Through the window she saw the sun dipping behind the mountains, painting boundless alpine peaks with dimming orange and purplish hues. "Whenever I find joy in witnessing my son's growth and development, I feel deep shame and guilt for failing my daughter," she whispered.

"Miggy is eight years old now, and you're homeschooling him because you fear the outside world," the therapist said. "You once dreamed of becoming a teacher; do you enjoy educating your son now?"

Ursula nodded. "To teach feels like learning twice over, especially since Miggy is a perceptive pupil. In Mexico, he and Molly grew up speaking Spanish, and because I talked to them in German, they were already fluent in both languages by the age of four. Then, during the year we lived with the rabbi's family, he had no trouble learning English, and after we arrived in Switzerland, I began teaching him some French. I also educate him in history." She felt the blood rush to her face again when Dr. Féraud complimented her. "But my lessons don't compare to those of my grandfather. Grospapi Anton not only instructs Miggy in math and science, he spends quality time outdoors with him, teaching him the relationship between natural systems and the universe. And my grandmother, Grosi Rosi, encourages the interest Miggy shows in cooking and baking."

"Your son is surrounded by love; clearly crucial to strengthen his confidence."

Ursula agreed. "But the most rewarding thing has been watching him learn to draw and paint. Mamá Marta would be so proud to see how her artistic gift has manifested itself in her grandson."

"You are doing a commendable job, Ursula—especially given what you've been through," Dr. Féraud said. "Allow yourself to be aware of your own bravery and competence. When you do, you may discover the clarity and purpose you need to take your next step."

"My next step," she said with a sigh, "is a difficult one to take, but I cannot shield Miggy forever from the outside world. I think the time has come for him to be with children his own age."

"But earlier you expressed concerns about being recognized in Grindelwald. Will you have someone else take Miggy to school and pick him up?"

"It won't be necessary because we'll be moving."

"You'll be moving?" Dr. Féraud looked surprised. "Where to?"

"My grandparents sold the business, but they'll keep their home in Grindelwald, strictly for the record. They'll tell their friends and neighbors of their desire to travel the world while they still can," Ursula said. "But in reality, all of us will be moving next month—I already bought a home just twenty walking minutes from the center of Crans-Montana."

"To our town?" The therapist smiled.

"I really like it here." She blushed and shifted in her chair. "I wonder if you know of a good school for Miggy."

"I'd recommend the École Privée Internationale; the classes are small at EPI, and the school is known for its wonderful arts program. I think Miggy will fit right in."

"Thank you. I've heard good things about EPI. I'll make an appointment with the headmaster before I leave Crans-Montana."

Dr. Féraud quickly wrote something in his notebook, then closed it. He looked at Ursula. "Since this is your last session, let's take a break before we continue."

She nodded. *My last session. I still have to tell the truth about what happened.*

TWENTY-TWO

Ursula, ninety minutes later

Thanks for allowing me to take a break; the long walk stopped my head from swimming," Ursula said, her cheeks still rosy from the crisp November air.

"Whenever you've expressed the sensation of your head swimming, you've been able to unravel some of your feelings in the session that followed." Dr. Féraud opened his notebook. "Let's go back to where we left off. You said you've purchased a home near Crans-Montana."

Did Ursula detect a faint smile on the therapist's face?

She realized he was still talking, but she hadn't heard a word.

". . . enjoy living in Crans-Montana; we're a warm, welcoming community, and EPI is an excellent choice for Miggy." He leaned forward. "Once you've settled into your new home, if you want to continue with your sessions, I'll be here for you."

Almost hesitant to blink away what felt like undeserved release, she swallowed.

"You've assisted me over many difficult hurdles and showed me how to focus on what's relevant, rather than getting lost in my erratic line of thinking, yet I continue to be so angry with myself."

"Try to let your anger pass," the therapist said. "Give it the time it needs to fade away. Envision a wide-open path ahead of you."

Ursula closed her eyes; she needed a moment to stop swaying and fidgeting. She took a deep breath and willed herself to speak.

"Even when Mamá Marta could not remember or recognize anyone around her anymore, I paid daily visits, always trying to enter my mother-in-law's uncharted world. I held her hand as we walked the grounds of the hacienda, allowing her to stop at her favorite spots, letting her touch the plants and smell the blossoms in the flower garden Marisol and I had created. Once, when we sat on the bench under the old Mexican fan palm, I wanted to cry out, confess everything to Mamá Marta, telling her about the gruesome day when I was beaten and raped by Marco and a few hours later drugged and raped by Mateo. But when shame and dismay smothered my words, I felt a squeeze from Mamá Marta's hand, as if she sensed my plight." She suddenly felt as if she was straddling a timeline. The past was tugging her in one direction and the present in another. As if from far away, she heard the therapist's voice.

"You're having another flashback, Ursula. Remind yourself that the event happened long ago. You survived it. Remember the breathing technique. Take your time."

Her hand was trembling. She closed her eyes for a few more moments, taking deep breaths. Then she nodded, encouraging herself to continue.

"As Marta's condition worsened, she often refused to move away from the easel. On those days, I stood by her side, watching chunks of color hit the canvas while tortured brushstrokes produced daunting images. No matter how painful it was to watch, I praised her creations, always embracing Mamá Marta as if it were for the last time. Sometimes she flung the brush across the room and began twirling to music that only she could hear. I cherished those few-and-far-between instances when we twirled together, wishing those hours would never end."

Realizing her hand had stopped trembling, Ursula reached for the glass of water.

"The day came too soon when Mateo and his sons decided to move Marta to a memory care facility some twenty kilometers away from the hacienda. Since I wasn't allowed to leave the grounds by myself, I had to stay behind closed gates, mourning the loss of my beloved surrogate mother. There were moments when I contemplated taking steps to end my own life. But doors to a magical, brighter world opened the second my newborn twins were placed on my chest. Studying each feature of my babies, I fell in love as never before. I promised those tiny precious beings my unconditional love and protection."

"You mentioned earlier that Marco disappeared soon after his children were born. Who other than Marisol was there for you?"

"Unlike Marco, Mateo played a large role in the twins' lives from the start, curious about their personalities and how they reacted to the world. He commented that my features had duplicated themselves in Miggy, and he gloated over how the Miraldo genes shined through in Molly. Mateo came to see them almost daily; often he arrived with expensive jewelry for me and brought rare bottles of wine. But all the precious gems in their velvety boxes ended up in a drawer under garments I never wore. Needless to say, I never touched another glass of wine he poured for me, nor did I mention my unhappiness to Mateo again. Instead, I forced myself to appear strong and in good spirits. He believed my performance, taking it as proof of my desire to be close to him. Whenever he pledged his devotion to me and the twins, I pretended to be grateful."

Barely noticeable, Dr. Féraud shook his head. "And you had to keep up this charade for how long?"

"It was during the twins' third birthday party when Mateo pulled me aside, opened a box that held an enormous sapphire ring, and whispered in my ear, 'Don't worry, mi amor, you don't have to wait much longer to wear it. Soon we'll be together forever.'"

"What did he mean by that?"

Ursula shrugged. "It didn't matter because Bruno Rossi, Marisol, and I had already started to plan our escape. I had told them what Marco and Mateo had done to me, and it was Bruno who suggested that I determine the paternity of my children before leaving Mexico."

He raised his eyebrows. "That probably wasn't easy to do, given that you were unable to leave the hacienda without a bodyguard."

"But I had Marisol. Whenever she had a day off, she met with Bruno." She crossed her legs, then uncrossed them. She fastened a button on her jacket, then unbuttoned it again.

"If talking about it still makes you anxious," the therapist said, "why not take a moment?"

"I'm okay," Ursula said in a small voice. "Marisol and I were told to collect DNA samples. To get accurate results, we needed more than one item. Marisol, who had easy access to Mateo's quarters, collected used Kleenex and dental floss from the bathroom wastebasket. She took his toothbrush and replaced it with the same brand and color, praying he wouldn't notice. She also took a dirty tequila shot glass he'd used the night before."

She fell silent, vacantly looking at the Tibetan area rug.

"I had to gather Marco's samples," she continued softly, almost as if talking to herself. "I still remember how frightened I was when I took four cigarette butts and a lump of discarded chewing gum from the crystal ashtray on his nightstand. I also replaced Marco's toothbrush. The samples seemed insufficient, but the morning Marisol was to take them to the city, luck came my way. Marco cut himself shaving, leaving sheets of bloody tissue in the wastebasket."

"What about the children's DNA?"

"That was easy. I only had to swab the inside of their cheeks." Ursula smiled vaguely at the memory. "My twins were so engrossed in the funny story I made up about noses, mouths, lips, and teeth, they didn't even ask what I was doing."

The therapist nodded. "Most labs in Switzerland have results within two to five days of the time they receive the samples. How long did you have to wait in Mexico?"

"Bruno got the results four days later, but since he couldn't call me at the hacienda, I didn't find out until Marisol had a day off again." She swallowed. "I expected to see either Marco's or Mateo's name as the father of my children, but . . ." She shook her head.

"Was there somebody else?" His voice was warm, devoid of judgment.

She smiled despite herself. "Nothing like that."

"Then . . ."

"Have you ever heard of heteropaternal superfecundation?"

Dr. Féraud sat up straight, his eyes wide. "That is extremely rare."

Ursula rubbed her forehead, then shielded her eyes with her hand. "I thought it only happened in Greek mythology. Like when Leda gave birth to two daughters: Clytemnestra, fathered by her husband, Tyndareus, and Helen, fathered by Zeus." Haltingly, she continued, "When I read the DNA results, I thought the Miraldos had found out what I was doing, that they were playing an elaborate prank."

"Understandable. Heteropaternal superfecundation rarely happens even in modern times."

She lowered her head and stared at the flowers in the carpet again.

"Miggy already wants me to tell him what he can't remember. He's curious about his and Molly's ancestry." She gnawed on her lower lip. "Of course, he's still too young to be told. But when he's older, I'm prepared to answer truthfully."

She rocked back and forth. "If she hasn't already, my Molly will have questions as well." Ursula shuddered. "But she'll keep running against a wall of deceit. I'm afraid she'll never learn the truth about her father."

TWENTY-THREE

Molly, June 2019
Mira, Wisconsin

Pops startles me when he walks unannounced into my office.

"Am I catching you at a bad time?" He strolls over to my desk and by way of habit squints at the two hand-hammered aluminum Aviator egg lounge chairs with blueberry-blue leather lining.

"Damn, I hate these uncomfortable chairs," he grumbles but sits down in one of them anyway, right across from me. "Haven't seen you all morning. What's keeping you so busy, mi amor?"

"The Vancouver title and closing documents," I reply in English, not taking my eyes off the screen.

"Why? The legal team told me yesterday that everything was good to go."

"Well"—I glance at my grandfather—"I'm reviewing and confirming all the important items related to closing. We don't want to run into a last-minute problem like the one with the Mira Resort and Casino in Vegas."

"That could've been a disaster had you not gotten to the bottom of it." Pops removes his black leather two-cigar case holder from his breast pocket, takes one out, smells it, and puts it between his lips.

Though I'm glad he gave up smoking them, I groan inwardly. I don't get his fetish of holding a Padrón in his mouth without ever *lighting* it. There are days where he goes through three of these ridiculously expensive cigars.

"Molarita, can you please stop doing what you're doing? I have some exciting news to share with you."

I push my chair a few inches away from my desk and look at him. I admit, given his age and after the medical ordeal he's been through recently, he looks fantastic. His tan face contrasts handsomely with his wavy white hair, and his more-pepper-than-salt beard is, as always, trimmed to perfection. Pops prides himself on his excellent taste in clothes and never fails to look fashionably distinguished. I remember people referring to him as the Latino Pierce Brosnan when we first moved to Mira.

"What's wrong, Molara? You're staring."

"Nothing, Pops. Just impressed by how quickly you've recovered."

"It's all about positive thinking, Molarita." He winks at me. "I think it was Pope John who once said that old men are like wine—some will turn to vinegar, but the best continue to improve with age."

I give him a limp thumbs-up, and my smile freezes when I suddenly think of Amelia Rubio's bizarre call and my subsequent internet searches. Since that night, confusion and doubt have overwhelmed me whenever I'm with Dad or Pops. I can't suppress my suspicions and am having trouble cooling the inflamed emotions.

"You're still staring. ¿Estás bien?"

A heat wave rushes to my face. "Sorry. My brain is wrapped around all of this." I gesture towards my screen.

"Well, let me take your brilliant mind off work for a moment." Pops takes the cigar from his mouth. "I have a surprise invitation for you."

I roll my eyes. "Did you forget I'm no fan of surprises?"

He grins and holds the Padrón between three fingers in midair. "Now that I feel almost better than before, I'm ready to enter the world again." He pauses and puts the cigar between his lips, as if he wants to prolong my anticipation. When he finally removes it, he holds the cigar up like a trophy. "Nelson and Rhonda Hadlow are hosting a lavish fundraising dinner for some of the biggest donors in the country, and of course"—he chews briefly on his cigar, then smacks his lips—"the Miraldos will be among them."

"I thought you turned that invitation down after you came out of rehab."

"I did, but when Nelson found out I'm back at work, he insisted we all attend." He smacks his lips again. "It'll benefit the RNC and our president's reelection campaign."

I'm not surprised. Hadlow knows Pops and Dad have no problem coming up with the frivolous maximum amount individuals are allowed to contribute.

"So," Pops says with pure pleasure painted across his face, "start packing—the fundraiser is this coming weekend and you're my plus-one."

"No way! What happened to that woman you were seeing?"

"*Circé*." He spits out the name and taps his index finger against the right side of his head. "Do I look crazy to you? That damn woman visited me once in the hospital, and as soon as she saw the shape I was in, she turned on her high heels and was out the door, ready to hunt for a new wealthy but healthy victim." He lifts his right pinky and index finger and points them downward—a gesture he adopted from the Italians to keep a jinx at bay. "That *puta* deserves her name. Just like her mythological namesake, she wants to turn men into her pigs."

Pops and his women. I've seen a lot of them come and go, most of them of a Northern European extraction; he has a thing for blondes. I shoot him a grave look. "I prefer not going to Wyoming! You're better off attending your swanky fundraiser by yourself or with another date."

"I beg your pardon?"

"Taking me to an RNC fundraiser would be like dropping a hyena into a lion's den. If your billionaire buddies hear my political points of view, it's going to be embarrassing for you and Dad."

And just as I anticipated, here comes his poker face.

"Not only do I expect you to go with me, I expect you to hold your tongue." With a tight-lipped smile, he rolls the Padrón between three fingers, then puts the wet tip of the cigar in his mouth again. He tries to stare me down.

There's a moment of dead silence. Then a bolt of inspiration shoots through me.

"Okay, Pops," I say sweetly. "You win . . . again. I loathe the whole idea, but I'll be on my best behavior."

He reaches across my desk, beaming. I take his hand, hoping my fake smile won't arouse suspicion.

"With your intelligence and charisma, you'll keep everyone spellbound." He lets go of my hand and leans back into the chair. "I just hope your father will keep his airhead wife under control; that woman only has enough mental capacity to open her mouth to drink and eat."

I grin when I recall Ava cornering one of Pops's physicians in the hospital. Dead serious, she asked if her strong immune system might be the reason she couldn't get pregnant. I force myself to stop grinning. "Okay, what time will we leave?"

"Your father ordered the company jet for noon on Friday. We'll pick you up on the way to Timmerman Field." Without giving the unlit Padrón another look, Pops drops it in the wastebasket. "By the way," he says, "the dress code for the three-day bonanza is mostly casual." He effortlessly gets out of the chair and buttons his burgundy Brunello Cucinelli sport coat. "But since the Saturday night dinner is cocktail attire, you may want to bring the Dolce & Gabbana dress you bought for MiraCo's twentieth anniversary soirée. You looked stunning in it." He slips his cigar case back in his breast pocket, lays both palms on my desk, and leans closer. "Nelson Hadlow plans on seating you next to Dudley."

I hold back a grimace. Dudley Hadlow, Nelson's only son and sole heir, is a narcissistic, power-hungry, pompous ass. *Easy, Molly. Stick to your agenda.*

"Wow!" I teasingly wag my index finger. "Are you and Nelson trying to play matchmaker?"

Pops laughs. "He's handsome, and *you*, mi dulce ángel, are beautiful. I have a feeling you guys will hit it off. You'll produce gorgeous babies and create a new American dynasty."

Obviously pleased with himself, he announces it's time for him to change clothes for a round of golf with business acquaintances. He walks around the desk to kiss the top of my head. "See you Friday, mi amor."

As he walks away, I am glad he doesn't turn around because he'd see my frozen smile melt into a defiant scowl.

Three days later, it's time to prepare for my big performance. I leave my house earlier than usual and, on the way to the offices, stop at Maxwell's apartment for the run-through of my transformation.

Yesterday, when I let him in on my plan, he grew very excited.

"But how in the world can I make everybody at MiraCo believe I'm sick?"

He laughed. "Didn't I tell you that my favorite thing in high school was doing everybody's makeup for performances? When I'm done with your makeover, I guarantee even you'll feel sorry for yourself."

While I relax on his kitchen counter, Maxwell lightly rubs green concealer over my cheeks and forehead, creates faint circles under my eyes, and finally brushes the whole thing with some whitish translucent powder. I protest when he makes my lips look dry and brittle, but he ignores me, confiscates my lip gloss, and promises he'll return it once our mission is accomplished.

"Yeeech," he says when he looks at me. "If I was a straight dude, I'd immediately queerantine myself from you." He grins mischievously and hands me the makeup mirror. "Don't you pity this poor girl?"

I laugh at my liverish likeness. I really do look like a virus has carried out a full assault of my GI tract.

"One more thing," Maxwell says. "When you walk into Mira-

Co, walk slow and take short, weak steps, like you're feeling dizzy. Watch me!"

I crack up again when he demonstrates. He pretends to be insulted but grins from ear to ear.

"Okay fine, don't walk swishy, but you get the idea, right?" He takes a few steps back, looks at me again, and shivers in mock disgust. "One last thing: *do not* be your usual captivating self. Act cranky. And during the leadership sync meeting, keep apologizing for the inconvenience you're causing everyone."

I'm nervous when I walk through the doors of MiraCo. But when I see my colleagues' pitying faces and hear comments like "Oh Molly, what's wrong with you?" and "You ought to be home in bed," I know Maxwell's artistry and coaching has worked.

Pops won't be attending our weekly leadership sync—he's playing golf with Canadian bank execs from the Floyd Banking Group. But my father almost doesn't recognize me when he enters the conference room fifteen minutes late.

"Yikes, Molara," Dad says tonelessly. "You look like Greedo in Star Wars." He backs away from me and sits at the other end of the conference table, no doubt wanting to be far away from my breeding pool of germs.

Ten minutes later I excuse myself and rush to the bathroom. Behind closed doors, I make retching noises and empty a couple of glasses of water into the toilet bowl, wondering if anyone can hear me. When I slowly reenter the conference room, I lean against the door, apologize for the inconvenience, and mutter that I need to go home. "Maxwell will take over for me," I say hoarsely. "He's been briefed on the agenda." As I limply walk from the room, Dad is bent over his phone. Hopefully he's texting Pops.

Sure enough, Pops calls me right after he finishes having drinks with his golf partners. "I heard you looked like crap, couldn't even make it through the meeting. What's wrong with you?"

"Must've eaten something yesterday that didn't agree with me,"

I say in a tiny voice. "After work I went to the shelter, then had sushi with one of the other volunteers."

"Ugh! I keep telling you to stay away from there! God only knows what diseases those people carry."

"Pops, I don't feel well. I need to run to the bathroom again."

"Wait," he shouts. "But you'll come to Montana with us tomorrow—make sure you are better!"

"I'll try," I whine. As soon as I disconnect the call, Maxwell and I burst out laughing, then continue to enjoy our dinner and bottle of wine.

―

The moment I open my eyes, I feel the effects of the second bottle of wine I should never have opened last night. I need coffee—quick.

As if he's read my mind, my buddy is already by the coffee maker. He spent the night in my apartment so he can make me look sick again if my father or grandfather come to check on me.

Maxwell hands me a steaming mug. "I'm definitely hungover," he says. "Looks like you are, too."

"You may not have to waste more of your green concealer." Unsteadily, I perch myself on one of my kitchen counter chairs and look at the time. Almost ten o'clock? I haven't slept this long in ages.

He seats himself next to me. "I'm surprised Senior or your father hasn't called you yet."

I shrug and look around me. "Comatose winos don't even know where they left their phone."

Maxwell slides off the chair and after a couple of minutes returns with it.

"Holy crapperino. Pops called four times. I'd better call him back before he breaks down my door."

"Don't forget to sound convincingly sick and frail," he whispers before I tap the speaker icon.

"Hi, Pops," I say in my best feeble voice. "I couldn't answer your calls, spent most of the night and morning in the bathroom."

Maxwell gives me a thumbs-up.

Pops's voice is gravelly. "Dammit, Molara. Didn't you take any medication for whatever is wrong with you? I counted on you feeling better by now."

"Me too," I whimper.

"This is such a disappointment!" Under his breath, he keeps muttering something in Spanish.

Maxwell feigns gagging, which causes me to giggle, but he quickly presses his hand over my mouth.

"What's that sound, Molara? Are you throwing up again?"

"No, n-ot no-ww." My bleating voice sounds like a sheep in childbirth. It's difficult to suppress my laughter.

"You just had to get sick this weekend." He sounds quite irritated. "Nelson and I will have to find a way to bring you and Dudley together this summer; I refuse to let that golden fish slip through the net." Before he disconnects the call, he says, "I hope you've learned your lesson and will stay away from that damn homeless shelter."

"With all due respect to Senior," Maxwell says, "I can't believe how he talked about this Dudley guy. Won't let this golden fish slip through the net . . . like in *net wealth*?"

Suddenly I see Pops's image bathed in an eerie light. In slow motion his handsome face contorts into a beastly shape with transparent gray skin; through his swollen purple veins I imagine blood flowing like dark water—cold, stagnant, toxic. I hear demonic laughter. Shivers run down my spine.

"What's wrong?"

I describe the horrible vision. "And I can't get that phone call from Amelia Rubio out of my head."

"It doesn't take mental gymnastics to reach that level," he says matter-of-factly and checks the time on his phone. "Hey, it's past noon. You think your folks are airborne yet?"

I call Timmerman Field and am told MiraCo's company jet

took off thirty minutes earlier than scheduled. I slide off the chair. "I don't know about you, but I'm hungry."

On our drive to Mira, we stop at Stratos, a small Greek diner reminiscent of a truck stop.

"Molly and Maxwell"—Stratos bear-hugs us—"it's about time you came to see me again." He whisks us to the last empty table in the tightly packed space. We confess our hangover to him.

"Two calamities for my friends," Stratos shouts to Sevag, the Armenian cook. "Grígora! Quick! Pronto!"

Neither Maxwell or I speak as we devour Stratos's famous omelet, loaded with homemade ground beef, Greek-style sausage, secret spices, onions, tomatoes, green peppers, and melted cheese on top of a thick slice of fried French bread. Rumor has it that years ago, when Stratos first opened his little joint, a customer watched him randomly throw ingredients and spices together. When the hefty concoction was put in front of the patron, he said the serving looked more like a calamity than an omelet, but as soon as he tasted it, the guy fell in love. Since then, the calamity omelet, along with other Stratos creations, have made him a novelty in the Milwaukee area.

"Man, I needed this," says Maxwell. "Never to taste Stratos's calamity would be like dying with unfulfilled dreams."

I grin and lay my hands on my stomach. "I can't think of a more delicious way to spend my sick day."

After promising Stratos we'll be back soon, Maxwell and I agree it's time to play Sherlock Holmes and Dr. Watson.

TWENTY-FOUR

Molly, twenty minutes later

When we pull into Bayside Drive and approach my father's house, five workmen are loading up their cars.

I tell Maxwell to drive past the house and park behind the hedge that separates the property from the adjacent lot, also owned by my father. For years he's been talking about building a guest house and caretaker's quarters on the one-acre lot on the lake—he's even had architectural plans drawn up—but to this day it remains vacant and uncared for.

Just in case any of the workmen notice Maxwell's Prius, I duck in the passenger seat while he lowers the window and pretends to enjoy the views over the lake.

"What do you know? The cat's out of the house," he says quietly, "and the workers are leaving early today."

I peek over the dashboard. "The tall, brawny guy with the red baseball cap is the foreman," I say. "He's the one who arms the alarm system from his phone."

"Yup. Looks like he just did it."

"Shit," I swear under my breath. If my father checks his phone, he'll be able to tell I disarmed it on the day I'm supposed to have my head in the toilet.

From my crouched position, I hear someone yelling. "What's going on?"

"Red-baseball-cap man said he forgot something in the house," Maxwell explains. "Looks like he's turning the alarm off again."

He gives me a blow-by-blow account of what's happening. "They're all getting into their cars now," he mutters. "But I don't know if the foreman armed the system after he came out of the house again."

I hear engines.

"They're pulling out of the driveway. Gone!"

Maxwell and I decide to leave his Prius parked behind the hedge and wait ten minutes before sneaking through the shrubs. When I unlock the massive front door, I breathe a sigh of relief: the guy forgot to arm the system.

"Yikes," Maxwell says as we make our way through the plastic coverings, stepping over tools, lumber, sintered stone, and other building materials. "What a disgusting mess."

"Ignore it." I brush dust off my shirt. "Intruders and thieves can't be fussy."

"Intruders? Thieves? Those are such strong words," he protests as he follows me down the stairs. He lets out a shriek when he peeks into my father and Ava's bedroom suite. His face twists into an expression of disgust and he waves his hand in front of his face, as if trying to shoo away a bad odor. "This interior disaster would make me impotent!"

I giggle and wave for him to follow me. "Let's hope we can figure out how to open this door," I say when we reach the end of the hallway. "This is the storage room."

Maxwell stares at the numbered buttons on the satin chrome security door lock. "Any clue what combinations he uses?"

I punch in Dad's birthday. Then mine. Then Pops's. Finally, Ava's. Zilch.

"Shit." I close my eyes, trying to think of other possibilities.

"Your father loves talking about when he negotiated luxury properties on the Gulf Coast. What's the date he took over the mega-bonanza beach and golf resort in Sarasota?"

"Maybe," I whisper, recalling the countless occasions my father has bragged about February 2, 1999. That was the day he navigated through myriad issues to close on his favorite MiraCo resort. Nervously, I press 2299. I hold my breath as I hit Enter. Maxwell and I grin when we hear the mechanized unlocking sound.

"Call me badass-sassy," he cries and flips the light switch on the left inside wall. "We did it!"

I stare into an unwelcoming square space, in which many small boxes are stacked on top of each other.

"Most of these have labels with names and dates on them," Maxwell says.

I move from box to box and look; none are sealed. I open one labeled *CDLF*. On top are Mexican court documents.

"Carla de La Fuente was my father's second wife," I explain.

We sift through photos of their wedding and newspaper clippings. We look at a torn and taped-together-again marriage certificate; a divorce decree is stapled behind it.

Maxwell is looking over my shoulder. "Must've been a very happy marriage to last only three months," he says. We both gawk at a photo of my father and first stepmother.

"Stick a cigar in her mouth, a fedora on his head, and put guns in both their hands, and these two could pass as Faye Dunaway and Warren Beatty, the hot-looking savages in *Bonnie and Clyde*," he says dryly. "Do you remember Carla?"

I shake my head. "No memories of those years, remember?"

We open another box labeled *Marta Miraldo*. It's stuffed with photos of her artwork as well as newspaper articles, singing praises of her talent. Other clippings gush about her generous contributions to charities.

Maxwell pulls out a headshot and studies it. "She looks a little like Salma Hayek. Who is she?"

"Must be my paternal grandmother. But I know very little about her, only that she was an artist. My second stepmother, Annie, told me privately that Pops never divorced Marta because of his faith, even though they didn't live together for a long time."

"Is she alive?"

"Annie said she died of Alzheimer's disease." Looking at the photo makes me sad; so much of my ancestry and early life has been kept from me.

Maxwell's phone clicks constantly as he takes pictures of everything that he deems worth being investigated—material for me to study later.

We look in boxes that contain photos and letters from other women—I have no clue who they might be. I wonder why my father feels the need to hold on to countless paramours from his past, only to let them decompose in old boxes.

I keep searching for anything that pertains to my mother, my brother, or myself, anything before or right after my accident.

Maxwell's yelp startles me. "Check out this box!"

We sift through ledgers and other financial records, and even though I don't understand accounting all that well, Maxwell notices clear patterns of improper behavior.

"Cooked books... bribery payments..." Maxwell keeps turning pages. "I can understand the numbers, but you need to translate the comments."

As I interpret from Spanish to English, he feverishly snaps photos of records and reports that correspond to illegal transactions; all of them appear to be the placement phase of money laundering.

Shiver after shiver runs up and down my spine when I unexpectedly come across the name and signature of Robert Graf on a bunch of ledgers. "Oh. My. God! He's my maternal grandfather."

"Crrraaazzzy!" Maxwell keeps turning pages. "Sorry, Molly, but that man is a total disgrace to your gene pool. He kept moving funds to personal accounts of intermediaries overseas." He surveys another page. "Look here! He withdrew funds in cash from intermediary accounts, then wired the moola back into new accounts in Mexico, Luxemburg, and Switzerland." He shakes his head. "How the heck did Graf manage to get authorization from any reputable bank without having to explain the origin of these funds? I bet none of the banks had any idea they gave legitimacy to these shady deals."

I focus on a page in another book. "Robert Graf worked for a Swiss bank. That's how he knew his way around the banking world and was able to wheel and deal with the other players."

I keep reading. "Wow! Look at this!" I point to another page and ledger. "Money laundering wasn't the only criminal activity my dad was paying this guy for."

"I can only make out fragments. Can you translate?" Maxwell hands me a letter Graf mailed to my father in September 1996. "Looks like the first and last page are missing."

I read it out loud:

happened when G, our drug trafficker, recently made a lot of cash profits from drug sales in the US. There's now too much cash out on the street. Per your instructions, G will move that cash to Belize and I will supervise him when he opens the warehouse facility (WF) in the depressed neighborhood you and I talked about. If needed, G will open another WF in an adjacent country. I am thinking Guatemala. Either of them will be for invoicing purposes only.

I currently am looking into a rare "product" whose worth the average law enforcement agent or banker won't know. I think you will like my idea for the product, but for security reasons, I must share this with you in person. What's great about it is that its price can range from a couple of cents to almost $150,000 per item (again, I will explain details in person only).

Once you agree, G will either import or export the product and safely move money into or out of the US.

G has instructions to invoice the fake WF in Belize and Guatemala for a minimal amount, e.g., "product" is worth $2,000, but it will be shipped as worth $3 million. This way it's nearly impossible for a banker or even a law enforcement officer to understand what we did.

I also suggest the next time we need money to invest in a legitimate hotel property, let's say Naples or Sarasota. We can use the same method to ship the product to Florida to fund our investment.

I'll supply invoices or letters of credit to make the transaction. I guarantee nobody will be able to understand the actual market value of the product.

Following are the latest transfers I made into your accounts in

"Too bad the pages with the banks and account numbers are missing; they could've revealed highly incriminating stuff," Maxwell says.

"Graf's letter may as well be written in Indus Valley script as far as I'm concerned, because I'm clueless as to the intricacies of money laundering." I look at him. "Can you decode any of this for me?"

"Nope! Only that your father let other people do the dirty work so he could keep his hands lily-white," he grumbles while snapping photos of the letter.

Though I'm unable to get rid of the lump in my throat, the discovery of my father's secrets electrifies my curiosity. I'm certain there'll be more skeletons to be exhumed. Furiously, I open the next box and then another and another, immersing myself in pages, ledgers, and documents.

Maxwell leans against the wall and in one long gulp finishes the water in his bottle. "I think we looked into everything except these." From the top shelf he pulls down two boxes and places them on the floor in front of me.

I stare at them. They're the only ones without a label, name, or date and they're tightly sealed with duct tape. "If we open these, we can't reseal them." I run my hand over the securely fastened flaps.

"Who wrote 'Forewarned, forearmed; to be prepared is half the victory'?"

"Miguel de Cervantes."

"Right! He's been my inspiration." Maxwell grins and pulls a knife, scissors, and a new roll of duct tape from his satchel.

I hold my breath as I watch him loosen the tape and carefully peel it off. We both inhale sharply and stare at the faded handwriting beneath it: *Molara/Miguel 1988-1992.*

"That's my twin. That's me. We were born in 1988, and in 1992 my mother disappeared with my brother." I lay my hand on the now-separated flaps, hesitant to exhume what was intended to remain buried.

"Molly, look!" Maxwell, already having removed the tape from the other box, points to one word in the same handwriting: *Ula.*

I don't know how long I sit cross-legged on the gray cement floor in this grim chamber. When one of the fluorescent lights begins to flicker, it reminds me of horror movies, when lights intermittently flare up and die down, indicating something bad is going to happen.

"Spooky." Maxwell looks at the old fluorescent tubes on the ceiling.

I blow my nose, then add the tissue to a pile of crumpled Kleenex that holds my tears, each one triggered by a strange mixture of joy, rage, confusion, and sorrow.

Joy because I can't get enough of the pictures that prove to me again and again that my beautiful blonde mother and my sweet blond brother really existed. I was with them once. I laughed and played with them. I was kissed and hugged by them. I see nothing but love and affection in my mother's eyes; the photographs clearly display the bond between a mother and her children. Could it be my mother didn't leave me behind intentionally?

Rage when I think of the deceit that clouds so many years of my life. The letter from Robert Graf details how he falsified my mother's and brother's death certificates, then invoiced my father for $20,000 for services rendered.

Confusion and sorrow because somehow I always knew how flawed my father and Pops were, yet I held nothing but love, devotion, and gratitude for them. They were the only family I knew. Two men who knowingly distorted reality and forced me to accept ugly details about my mother, believe in events that never took place.

I sniffle into another tissue when I look at a photo in which my twin and I stand hand and hand under a tall Mexican fan palm.

Our mother is kneeling on a blanket, reaching out to us. Her face reflects joy and love.

Is this the palm my uncle Manoel and I sat under not too long ago? The time when he told me how much my mother enjoyed having picnics in this spot?

Suddenly images flash through my mind. I gasp. I want to hold on to them, but they disappear as quickly as they came. Is this what a therapist calls dissociative amnesia, where the powers of recall still exist but are deeply buried in a person's mind? Is it possible for my memories to resurface after all these years?

I blink myself back into harsh reality, feeling new tears roll down my cheek. "Look at my twin brother," I say. "With his wavy blond hair and big green eyes, he's the spitting image of our mother." I sniffle and blow my nose again. "I look nothing like them; everything about me comes from the Miraldo gene pool."

"Wrong!" Maxwell says. "You and Miguel both inherited your mother's mouth." He lays several photos in a row. "The three of you have the same full, curved lips. Identical smiles, with a deep dimple in the right cheek." He stares at the photo of us under the Mexican fan palm. "I bet Renoir would've loved to paint this." Slowly, he gathers everything together. "No need to take photos of these pictures," he says determinedly and seals them in a large Ziploc bag. "You're taking these home with you."

I press the plastic bag against my chest, convincing myself my father will never miss them.

"I believe we're done here." In his usual meticulous fashion, Maxwell places everything back in the small box that reads *Molara/Miguel 1988-1992*. He tapes the flaps together again and runs his hand over the seam to smooth out any imperfection.

When I gather the fake death certificates, the marriage license, and other documents, I almost don't care if they're in the same order we found them in. "Is this everything from the Ula box?"

He nods. But when he lifts the flap, I point to a manila envelope taped to its underside. Its brownish color is similar to the box's.

"Whoa! Didn't see that one before." He peels the envelope off the flap. "It's addressed to your father."

I look at the return address. "PO Box 1033, Lincolnwood, IL

60645," I murmur. "That's a suburb of Chicago." Carefully, I remove the letter.

May 29, 2006
Marco:

For the past fourteen years, neither you nor Mateo have responded to any of my letters or to those from my professional advisors. The only reply I've ever received came from Molly when she was six years old, expressing that she never wanted to see me again. Due to the many traumatic developments that occurred before and after I took my children away from the hacienda and out of Mexico, I was forced to respect Molly's wishes, though in my heart I believe she was coerced into writing the note.

Since that terrible day in Miami, there hasn't been a moment when Miguel and I don't think of Molly. We've never given up hope of being reunited with her. We believe the moment will come when Molly decides to dig for the truth and discovers why I was forced to rescue my children from a toxic environment filled with lies, rape, and abuse.

My desire for both of my children to grow up in a happy, healthy, and safe environment was sabotaged by you and your father. To this day your actions inflict harm on the twins' innocence.

Over the years my professional advisors have discovered a multitude of your and Mateo's wrongdoings and unlawful acts, cruel offenses that also involved my father, Robert Graf, the man you and Mateo hired to be one of your fixers.

We became aware that Robert Graf acquired death certificates from the Gesundheitsdepartement des Kantons Basel-Stadt and falsified these documents by declaring my son and me dead! My counsel also learned that you filed these fake reports with the Civil Registration Office in Mexico City—another act that was punishable by law. You did these things to buy yourself a clean slate to remarry, not just once but twice.

Although we have photocopies of every document and enough evidence to cause significant trouble for you and Mateo in the Mexican courts, we are aware of your continued intent to either eliminate me or have me arrested for kidnapping Miggy. For the sake of both my children's futures, I was advised not to open Pandora's box. Instead, my counselors offered various negotiations and generous terms to you and Mateo, always hoping to find a sensible arrangement that would benefit all of us. Regrettably, we never heard back.

Over the past fourteen years, your son has asked questions. When he was old enough, he learned the truth about what took place in Mexico and the reason behind my decision to leave that country with my children. Whereas Miguel has become fully aware of the facts, I assume the reality of everything is still being withheld from Molly. I suspect that every one of my letters to her was intercepted, and I'm sure she remains unaware about what you and your father did to me in Coyoacán.

Twelve years ago, a letter was sent to Mateo, containing medical evidence about my children's paternity. In case he never shared those grim facts with you, ask him to come clean about what he did to me again and again. I hope he did not ignore that letter like all the others. It is in your interest to find out what happened on September 11, 1987, the day I was physically abused and raped—twice!

My twins will be celebrating their eighteenth birthday on June 1. They will be adults. Whereas my son knows the truth, you and Mateo have an obligation to tell Molly—she has a right to know!

Ursula

P.S. A copy of this letter will be sent to your father.

Through misty vision I see letters collide, swim into each other, and I keep hearing my mother's written words: *When Molly decides to dig for the truth . . . Lies, rape, and abuse . . . Medical evidence about the children's paternity . . .*

What happened in Mexico? *Omigod, if my mother was raped on September 11, 1987, then who is our father?*

I hand the letter to Maxwell. His granite-blue eyes grow wide and he swallows. "Your poor mother!"

My heart is heavy, my head is swimming. Just when I think I'm not brave enough to face any more pain, a rush of adrenaline catches me off guard and renewed energy flows to my brain and muscles. It's like my body wants to refuel for the final stretch. I take Maxwell's hand.

"We're not done," I say. "We have to find the other letter she sent—the one with medical evidence about our real father. It's got to be in Pops's house."

TWENTY-FIVE

Mateo, June 2006
Mira, Wisconsin

Mateo was unaware of how long he stood frozen in his home library by the fireplace. He stared at the words on the paper in his hand, his eyes glued to the graceful penmanship. Ula's handwriting was perfect, beautiful, flowery. Did he detect her faint scent on the letter? A part of him wanted to press his lips against the creamy white stationary, yet the content of the letter had sent him into a cold sweat.

Thank heavens Marco was in Florida. Mateo would try his damnedest to retrieve the original from his son's house and destroy it. He groaned when he reread the key paragraph.

> Twelve years ago, a letter was sent to Mateo, containing medical evidence about my children's paternity. In case he never shared those grim facts with you or you never bothered making your own inquiries, have your father come clean about what he did to me again and again.

What if he couldn't find the original letter—or worse, what if Marco had already read it? Mateo supposed he'd have to deny everything, including ever seeing any evidence of paternity. It wouldn't be hard to convince his son. After all, Marco loathed Ula—she had been dead to him for many years.

My twins will be celebrating their eighteenth birthday on June 1. They will be adults. Whereas my son knows the truth, you and Mateo have an obligation to tell Molly—she has a right to know!

Molara, mi dulce hija! I would love for you to know the truth. But if I told you, would you understand? Mateo shook his head. He couldn't tell Molara nor anyone else. Who had even heard of hetero-fuck-paternal-fuckundation or whatever it was called? Not until Ula's whoever-the-fuck advisors had sent him the copy of the medical findings did he educate himself on that rare occurrence. One article had said one in four hundred pairs of fraternal twins fit the description, while another ridiculous study put the figure at one in thirteen thousand cases of paternity. "Bullshit," Mateo muttered. "These medical studies are nothing but drivel!"

He leaned heavily against the mantel, thinking about the videotapes he was hiding in his parlor in the sky, the recordings he'd secretly made whenever Ula was completely *relaxed*. Those tapes were evidence of how much he loved her; they substantiated how tenderly he'd caressed her body, how passionately he'd displayed his intense feelings for her. Her moans and whimpers, her cries and howls, gave testament to her lust and desire for him.

What good will it do if Molara knows that Marco cheated on her mother, physically and mentally abused her? Even if I tell Molara how deeply I loved Ula, it will only make matters more complicated.

Mateo licked his dry lips. The complexity of it all overwhelmed him. Ula should have been his from the moment he met her—been by his side forever.

He swallowed, thinking of the few times Molara had queried him about her mother, her twin brother, and the years she had no memory of. Mateo, of course, always made sure he never varied from the old falsifications. Needless to say, he abhorred having to portray his beloved Ula as psychologically disturbed and unstable, he loathed lying about the deaths, but what other choice did he have? As much as he wanted to take the accuracy of the existing world apart and reassemble it the way he saw it, his longings remained unfulfilled dreams.

It wasn't until he heard voices coming from the hallway that his numbness dwindled.

Who was Yoli talking to? Holy shit, was that Annie's voice? What the hell was she doing back in Mira? Hastily he folded the letter, slipped it back in the envelope, and looked around for a temporary hiding place. He shoved the envelope beneath one of the box cushions of the sectional sofa, recently custom upholstered in a Luigi Bevilacqua tiger velvet. He quickly sat on that cushion, grabbed one of the books from the table, opened it, and pretended to read.

He tried to look relaxed when she walked in. "Annie? Now, that's a surprise," he said, forcing a smile. "What brought you back to Mira?"

"I came to celebrate Molly's eighteenth birthday. Didn't she tell you?"

"I don't think so." His thin smile faded. "If she did, I might have been preoccupied with more important matters." Mateo closed the book, put it back on the side table, and clasped his shaking hands.

"What's wrong? Are you okay?"

Damn. Nothing ever escaped that woman's perception.

"May I sit here?"

He nodded, instinctively running his hands against the seam between the frame of the sofa and the cushion, making sure the envelope didn't stick out.

"I hope it's not my surprise visit that makes you look so ill at ease." Annie sat at the other end of the sectional sofa and limberly folded one of her legs under her thigh.

"You look well," he said, trying to deflect the attention from himself. "What have you been up to?"

The day Marco announced his engagement to Annie MacKenna, Mateo was once again bewildered by his son's attraction to these few-and-far-between women. Carla de La Fuente had managed to keep Marco spellbound for years, but as soon as they tied the knot, their marriage became a sinkhole. In between Carla and Annie, he romanced nincompoops and nitwits Mateo barely paid attention to. He believed Annie wouldn't last long either, but she proved him wrong.

"Diamonds are a dime a dozen," Marco had told his father when he questioned his son's choice, "but red diamonds are rare and in high demand." Apparently so. Annie's temperament proved to be as intense as her hair color. With her alabaster skin, sprinkle of freckles, and heap of long, curly hair in a blend of cerise and gold, she seemed to Mateo like a red alarm button daring any guy to touch it.

"Red on the head means fire in the bed," Marco used to tell everybody. "I go nuts just thinking about having sex with her."

Mateo secretly called Annie *mujer ponderosa*, comparing her to the Celtic goddess Brigid. Why? Because Annie woke up before anyone else in the morning and never lost an ounce of energy throughout the rest of the day. When something upset her, she had no problem holding forth, freely giving people tongue-lashings. Whereas others found her mood changes beguiling and entertaining, Mateo considered them too annoying to figure out.

"Hey! Earth to Mateo." Annie snapped her fingers. "You seem far away."

He raised his eyebrows. "I was thinking how unfortunate it is that you and Marco decided to divorce," he lied. "I miss the energy you brought into our lives."

"Nice of you to say that now, Mateo." She laughed. "You seemed relieved when I moved across the country, away from the Miraldos—especially from Molly. You've always been apprehensive about my friendship with her."

Damn that redhead! How had he forgotten that she wasn't easily fooled? She had the ability to answer a question before it was asked. The woman was a damn mind reader.

"So," he said, trying to distract Annie from whatever she had her mind set on, "how do you like Idaho?"

"I finally found what I was born to do," she said. "I can't believe it took me so long to figure out what lured my ancestors to the rugged prairies under endless blue skies."

"So, what is it? What you're born to do?"

"Ranching. I'm raising breeds of cattle in a humane and ecological way." She scooted closer to Mateo, leaning towards him. "I've also been working on my long-range shooting skills and just won my first competition." She grinned. "Watch out, Annie Oakley, here comes Annie MacKenna." She threw her head back, the red and golden mane moving with her laughter.

MacKenna. Annie had firmly stood by her decision to keep her maiden name when she wed Marco; she even refused to hyphenate the two surnames. While Marco could barely control his rage, Mateo saw no problem with it; after all, he believed the union would end sooner than later. In the meantime, he very much appreciated the benefits that arrived with the MacKenna name. Born into a major real estate and restaurant family, Annie not only came from a strong hospitality heritage, she'd also spent a good decade in public relations and marketing before she hooked up with Marco. Her connections within the hospitality industry and the political arena turned out to be quite advantageous to the Miraldo name and their MiraCo brand.

As a sunbeam streamed through the window, it hit Annie's luxurious locks. The backlit mass of hair reminded Mateo of liquid flames. Querido Dios, he thought and wondered what it might feel like to run his fingers through hair like that.

"Well," he said hoarsely, "you definitely made a 180-degree turn." His nod feigned approval. "It's nice that you were able to get away to spend time with Molara. Have you seen her yet?"

"Molly and I have been together nonstop since I arrived a few days ago. Wonder why she didn't tell you."

"Eh, I've been busy, especially with Marco out of town." He felt resentment rising in his chest. How come he hadn't known about this? True, he really had been drowning in business obligations, but when was the last time he'd seen Molly? Not yesterday. The day before?

"Hey, I like the makeover you gave the MiraCo Club Resort. Very impressive. I booked one of the villas. Molly and I are having a blast."

Damn! He'd had no idea the *puta* was staying at his resort, much less with Molly. "Glad you like it."

"I'm sorry if she didn't tell you. I know she mentioned my visit to her father on the phone the day I arrived."

Her father, my ass. Mateo folded his hands in his lap and took a deep breath. "When are you leaving for Idaho again?"

"That's exactly why I came to see you today." Annie looked across the room to the bar area. "You mind if I fix a drink for us?" Without waiting for an answer, she walked to Mateo's wet bar. "Clase Azul tequila neat, right?" She winked at him. "I remember what you like. And, of course, a Kentucky bourbon for me."

The redhead always had thick skin, he thought as he watched her grimly. *She's been too nosy about Marco's life in Mexico, wanting to know everything about Ula and Carla. What if she sniffed around and found something she wasn't meant to see?*

No matter how much he and his son had tried to weaken Molly's bond with Annie, no matter what tactics they'd used, Annie's loyalty to Molly held firm. *Damn.* Without conscious thought, he ran his hand against the frame of the sofa again.

It was only midafternoon—not his preferred time for alcohol—but perhaps it would lift his spirit.

"So why exactly did you come to see me today?"

"Since Molly won't start her fall semester at Northwestern until mid-August, I invited her to spend a month on my ranch. She is very excited."

"That won't be possible," Mateo said. "Molly just started her internship at MiraCo. She's being trained to oversee various operations, making sure that all the facilities are running efficiently, and—"

"C'mon, Mateo!" Annie cut in. "She just turned eighteen! Kids her age need to enjoy their first summer after high school. My God, my friends and I had the best time traveling through Europe."

Without asking, she took their two empty glasses and strode over to the bar for a refill. "Drink up." She laughed and clinked her glass against his. "Molly needs to discover the world outside Mira." She rolled the caramel liquid around in her Glencairn glass before taking another sip. "Marco wasn't easy to convince," she said, "but a grandfather should be easier to win over." She clinked against his glass again. "What do you say?"

Mateo swallowed the burn in his throat. *Why the fuck did Marco agree to let Molara spend a whole month with the redhead? Didn't he know it would be too risky!*

"I need to talk to Molara." He pushed the half-empty glass away; he had lost his taste for it. "Where is she?"

She cocked her head. "It's Wednesday, her volunteer day at the shelter. She said she'll be back by eight."

"In that case, I have matters to attend to." He shot Annie a look. "Molly and I will discuss her options."

"Forget it, Mateo," she said forcefully. "I told you, Marco already agreed!"

"What does he care? He rarely spends time with her." He didn't like hearing his voice grow high and shrill. "You can't overrule my—" He stopped when she stood up and with long decisive steps walked towards the door.

"I'm not overruling anything! But Marco is her father, not you." Annie gave him a challenging grin. "Besides, Molly is eighteen now. She's eligible to vote, allowed to gamble—she can even get married in most states."

Without saying goodbye, the redheaded beast disappeared from his sight.

TWENTY-SIX

Ursula, September 2009
Geneva, Switzerland

Ursula had been in high spirits all day. Her mood was so elevated, she could barely concentrate on the guests and well-wishers. Usually she avoided huge events like this, but she'd made an exception for Mick's first major art exhibit at the Galerie Plateforme 18 in Geneva. Unlike her son, perpetually calm and pensive, Ursula was electrified. She imagined her brain releasing dopamine and serotonin, those magical happiness neurotransmitters that she rarely got to receive. She wondered if anyone nearby could hear her pounding heart.

Very early in the morning, they'd driven the less-than-two-hundred-kilometer distance from Crans-Montana to Geneva. After checking into the Hôtel du Lac, Mick went straight to Plateforme 18, where he and three other artists discussed last-minute details with the gallery owners for what was forecasted to be a successful La Nuit des Bains. This event, held three times a year in Geneva's Quartier des Bains, was a hugely popular affair where thousands of people looked for the opportunity to explore new art in the surrounding galleries, all within short walking distance of each other. Some visitors simply came to people watch or to socialize. Others would hop from gallery to gallery as if taking a crash course in contemporary art. But then there were those serious art enthusiasts, eager to discover new talent and invest in them.

Ursula was surprised by the distinct scent of youthful sophistication in this lively and festive atmosphere. She watched the visitors; some were sipping a glass of wine as they weaved their way in and out of the galleries.

She felt jittery, as if she had overdosed on caffeine, and looked for an area less crowded. She spotted a small alcove in Galerie Plateforme 18's atrium, quickly stepped into it, and leaned against the wall, hoping to find calm and balance again. Despite her good mood, large crowds still made her nervous. As always, she had trouble reining in her fear that someone might recognize her.

Relax! Breathe! She closed her eyes and appealed to the restorative powers she'd learned in therapy. *If I don't control my mind, it will control me*, she told herself. *I am not the frightened young Ula Miraldo who's locked up in Mexico. I am the wiser and stronger Ursula Rossi, forty-six years old, and I am free and safe in Switzerland.*

Slowly she opened her eyes, involuntarily touching her hair. Only yesterday, the stylist had chopped off her long waves, and when she looked at the chin-length bob cut and blunt bangs in a mirror, Ursula almost didn't recognize herself.

She rose to the balls of her feet and stretched her neck high, trying to find her son. She smiled when she spotted him, surrounded by yet another new group of people.

"Mom, you won't believe this," he'd said the day he received the invitation from Plateforme 18. "They want to show my paintings with other emerging artists, next to well-established ones."

From her tote she removed the extensive catalog, which listed every participating gallery and gave detailed descriptions of the featured artists. She turned to the page that presented her son. Her smile widened when she read Mick's bio for the umpteenth time.

Mick Rossi
This young Swiss artist—a recent graduate from the University of Lausanne—exploded into the public eye earlier this year when his work was displayed in a show by UNIL. Mick Rossi skillfully blurs imaginary and historical figures

together in melancholy atmospheres. While the artist allows obscure memories to expand into a dialogue between the rational and the absurd, he pushes his expressive envelope into unexpected, even baffling media without conscious reasoning. Rossi's cutting-edge work, where pleasant daydreams are juxtaposed with dark reality, clearly challenges creative and societal assumptions.

While reading and rereading the words on the page, Ursula didn't see the unhurried, steady stream of people, didn't hear their hushed voices that mixed with muffled noise filtering through the open doors from outside. She jumped when she felt a warm hand on her forearm.

"I'm sorry," Bernard Delon said, gently running his fingers up and down her arm. "I didn't mean to startle you." He handed her a bottle of Valais mineral water.

As always, his low, deep voice had a calming effect on her. She smiled and leaned her head against his shoulder, thinking of the day she'd first met him. It was the morning she registered her then eight-year-old son at the École Privée Internationale in Crans-Montana. The striking resemblance between Bernard Delon—EPI's headmaster—and Ursula's therapist was perplexing, but being new in town and feeling shy, she hadn't felt comfortable asking about it. It wasn't until months later she learned the reason: Bernard Delon and Dr. Alain Féraud were identical twins.

Growing up, Bernard and Alain had enjoyed abusing their resemblance. At school, whoever had more knowledge of one subject or another took the test as the other. Sometimes, simply for the fun of it, they changed places for their class pictures. When one got into trouble or was confronted by annoying small talk, he pretended to be his twin. During their teenage years they occasionally even dated each other's girlfriends.

Enough of these escapades! That was what Bernard and Alain's parents determined. They made sure their sons attended different universities. Then, after graduation—prior to both accepting jobs in Crans-Montana—Bernard and Alain realized they had to avoid future confusion, and Bernard legally changed his surname to Delon, his mother's maiden name.

Why Ursula, after her move to the relatively small community of Crans-Montana, secretly called EPI's headmaster "the Proxy" wasn't clear to her, but whenever she had a session with Dr. Féraud, she found it difficult to wipe his twin brother from her mind. Despite their resemblance, she noticed subtle differences between Bernard and his body double. They were both ridiculously handsome, tall, and wiry, but Bernard was slightly taller, more muscular. Dr. Féraud, with his serene, low voice and therapeutic technique, had been able to soothe Ursula's anxiety, but Bernard's even temper, his deep, gentle voice with its rise and fall and change of timbre, inspired a whole new level of calm.

It wasn't until Mick (on his thirteenth birthday he decided he was too old to be called Miggy) graduated from high school, and not until Dr. Féraud moved to Paris to open a private practice and to marry Charley (short for Charlotte), that Ursula admitted to herself that Bernard Delon, for some time already, had steadily been courting her.

She looked at him and smiled.

"I have a news flash for you," he said.

Ursula cocked her head. "News?"

"Of the eight pieces Mick had on display"—Bernard paused for effect—"every single one has been sold." His eyes, the color of milk chocolate, sparkled with excitement. "Seven of them to private art collectors who are interested in commissioning new work from him."

"That is fantastic," she said, a little too loudly. She quickly covered her mouth with the palm of her hand. "I'm so proud of him."

"And the eighth painting"—he grinned—"was acquired by the Fondation Cartier pour l'Art Contemporain."

"Really? Which one?"

"They took the largest, *Harvesting Hope*."

"I love that piece. How lucky for us that it was bought by a museum. Now we can see it whenever it's on exhibition!"

"That's not all. The Fondation Cartier offered Mick a solo show next year; apparently they've had their eyes on your son for some time."

"His talent takes my breath away," Ursula said and rested her back against the wall. "I'm really surprised how comfortable he seems, even in this large crowd."

"I think it's the art that calms him." Bernard leaned against the wall next to her. "My colleagues at EPI always commented on his peaceful composure during creative activity." He laced his fingers through hers.

It wasn't the first time Ursula had marveled at the perceptiveness of the man she'd been dating for three years. He understood Mick's and her struggle to detox from the pains of their past. He also knew how to soothe her fears and ease her guilt whenever she thought of Molly. Because of his compassion she'd finally found herself on the other side of abuse and betrayal. She squeezed his hand.

"I think the gallery will be closing its doors soon," he said softly. He took Ursula's empty bottle and handed it to one of the attendants collecting used glassware.

"Look!" She gestured in her son's direction. "There is that lady with the curly red hair again and the man with the cowboy hat." Unexpectedly she felt on edge. "Earlier I saw them talk with Mick for a long time, and then they left the gallery in a hurry." She swallowed. "Why are they back now?"

"That's the American couple; they bought two of Mick's pieces." Bernard put his arm around Ursula's shoulder. "The woman was fascinated by Mick's work. She said as soon as she saw *Dreamer*, the painting had to be hers. She also bought *Dually Destined*. She wants to surprise her stepdaughter with it."

"Did you catch their names?"

"I believe her name is Annabelle, and he introduced himself as Dwight." He looked at Ursula. "You seem worried."

"They're Americans," she muttered. "It's difficult to get my paranoia under control."

It was close to midnight when the group of eight finished their light supper in one of the small private dining rooms of the Hôtel du Lac.

"You all supported me," Mick said, his mild voice softer than usual. "Everyone here helped me become who I am today, and for that I am grateful." He looked around the table at Joaquín, Alain, Charley, and Bernard before his eyes lingered on Marisol, Bruno, and his mother. "Where would I be without you?"

Ursula swallowed. Her handsome son was growing more considerate and personable by the day. She wanted to snuggle against his velvety cheeks and kiss his fanlike green eyes, as she had done so many times when he was a little boy.

"Two people are greatly missed tonight." For a second Mick's well-defined lips and jaw quivered. "Grosi Rosi and Grospapi enriched my life in indescribable ways. Their spirits will always walk beside me, and they will forever live right here." He laid his hand over his heart.

It had been five months since Grosi Rosi unexpectedly died of an undiagnosed heart problem. Though Grospapi bravely tried to hide his grief, he was unable to cope with the loss of his beloved wife. For two months he managed to conceal his sadness, but his ninety-one-year-old body wasn't prepared to handle what colloquially was known as broken heart syndrome. Nine weeks after Grosi Rosi died, he quietly slipped away to join her.

Ursula felt a lump thicken in her throat and she lowered her head.

"At the exhibit today, someone told me I'm blessed with great genes," Mick said. "If that's true, I know where they come from."

Swallowing her emotions, Ursula returned Mick's smile. Even though she had plenty of reason to be grateful, she was powerless against the ever-recurring sadness. *My Molly!* she thought. *Where are you now?*

She looked at Bruno. Would he have some news for her? There had been no time to catch up with him since he'd arrived in

Crans-Montana the previous day to see Mick's first big exhibition. He was debating Bernard—loudly, in English—about the European debt crisis, agreeing that France and Switzerland had the most exposure to the Greek debt than any other country. The other guests at the table were engaged in lively multilingual conversations as well. Marisol and Joaquín had their heads stuck together, talking softly in Spanish; at times they quickly turned their heads as if to make sure nobody was listening. Ursula wondered what they needed to keep under wraps. Meanwhile, Alain and Mick—conversing in German, as always—were discussing the Air France flight that had crashed into the Atlantic Ocean, killing everybody on board, including one of Mick's artist friends. Ursula shuddered, remembering Mick's reaction; the crash had happened on June first, his birthday.

Her eyes lingered again on Bruno. She couldn't wait to be alone with him; she had so many questions.

Charley's voice intruded on Ursula's thoughts.

"Omigod, I'm sorry. I didn't hear anything you said."

Charley laughed. "I could tell you were far, far away, chérie. Hopefully your musings took you somewhere pleasant."

Soon after their wedding, Charley and Alain Féraud had begun visiting Crans-Montana on a regular basis, and as if drawn together by magnets, Ursula and Charley had become inseparable. Not only were they the same age, but they also shared many common interests. Depending on the season, they either hiked or skied; they enjoyed cooking together and endlessly talked about the arts, music, and literature, always discovering new topics to discuss, often late into the night.

Charley moved her chair closer to Ursula's. "Did you hear that Mick received an invite to go to the United States?"

"He what?" Ursula felt the color drain from her face.

"Yes. I was right there when this lovely couple from Idaho invited him to visit their ranch. They seemed quite eager to commission work from him."

Ursula stiffened. "Why would he need to go there for that?"

"Something to do with experiencing the place firsthand, I think. Maybe they wanted a painting of the ranch." Charley leaned closer. "Is something wrong?"

She waved her hands. "It's nothing. Just old dread surfacing again."

Charley nodded. "Don't worry about it tonight. You'll sort things out tomorrow."

Ursula shivered and pulled the Loro Piana cashmere stole over her shoulders. Why did she keep expecting the worst? She'd worked so hard on rebuilding herself, but, out of nowhere, something would trigger her and she'd be back to square one.

Charley rose from the chair and lifted her glass towards the center of the table.

"I know it's quite late, but"—she pointed to her half-full glass—"that's no reason to let a good drop of Montrachet Grand Cru go to waste before we all turn in." She smiled at Mick. "Here's another bravo to our young genius and his very promising future."

"Look at it from another perspective," said Bruno after giving Ursula an update the following morning. "Mateo and Marco literally declared you and Mick dead. If they answered one of your letters, it would be proof of their fraud."

Ursula walked over to her hotel window and looked at the golden-red and brown trees. The manicured grounds of the hotel offered a spectacle of fall colors, almost too beautiful to be true, but even nature's beauty struck her as a betrayer. She felt like putting her fist through the pane or knocking the lamp off the table but willed herself to breathe. In and out, in and out. *Bitterness and resentment are self-defeating and will shade my thoughts and actions,* she told herself. *If I allow the misery to fester, it will wreck and kill whatever hope, love, and trust I still have within me.* She felt calmer, and when she relaxed her clenched fists, the tingling in her hands and fingers disappeared.

A common raven flew very close to the window and settled on

a nearby tree branch. It opened its beak, making its calls. Who was the bird trying to reach with its repeated gurgling croaks, Ursula wondered. Would the raven's calls remain unanswered just like her letters? Would the emptiness within her emptiness ever go away? She watched the raven fly away, leaving the branch empty. She sighed, walked away from the window, and sat across from Bruno and Joaquín again.

"Molly and Mick turned twenty-one on the first of June," she said. "I cling to the possibility that Molly will grow curious and come across a document that reveals the truth, maybe even find one of my letters. But if nothing ever rouses her curiosity, then Mick and I will forever remain dead to her." Ursula's head dropped.

"You swore you'd never give up hope," Joaquín reminded her. "We know Mateo and Marco portray themselves to their associates and friends as charitable, hard-working, solid human beings. They use their charisma to weasel their way into high society. But I guarantee it won't last. The time will come when the self-centeredness, the lies, and the crimes of those two misfits are exposed to the light."

"Pride goeth before the fall," Bruno agreed.

"Until then, Mick and I live in fear," Ursula said. "Especially after finding out another one of Mateo's hounds recently questioned people in Grindelwald about my grandparents. Even after being told they had passed away, the thug hung around town and somehow heard about Die Alphütte."

"Jeez. Thank God the chalet has been sold." Joaquín gnawed on his lower lip. "What was Mick's reaction?"

"It gave him a scare; he realized the Miraldo hunt for revenge still isn't over."

"Yet whoever Mateo sent to Grindelwald learned nothing about you and your whereabouts," Bruno said. "Let's hope he realizes he's running out of leads."

Ursula shook her head. "There's still my father. What if Mateo pays him to come back to Switzerland and look for us? For the right amount of money, Robert Graf will walk through hell."

Bruno and Joaquín exchanged quick glances.

"Time to show you something." Bruno pulled two newspapers from his folder. "These issues are from 2007, but we only became aware of them a few days before we left Mexico."

Ursula tilted her head in confusion when he held *La Nueva Semana* and *La Crónica*—Mexican papers—in front of her. "What do these have to do with anything?"

"Remember how Banco Salina Suisse hired private detectives to watch Robert Graf?"

"Of course. You told me they'd learned about his illegal activities in Switzerland, Belize, and Guatemala. And didn't the bank also have unconfirmed reports that he was hired by the Miraldos to do their dirty work?"

Bruno handed the newspapers to Ursula. "Read this." He pointed to a paragraph a quarter of the way down the page. "This is where it gets interesting."

> ... and Guatemala has become one of the world's most hazardous countries. Over 6,000 murders were reported this year, more than twice Mexico's homicide rate. It is a paradise for criminals, as they have little or nothing to fear from law enforcement agencies. Even the recent restructuring of security forces did nothing but increase police corruption. High-profile assassinations and the government's inability to prevent them give rise to disabling fear and anger. Last week alone, five people, all connected to notorious money-laundering organizations, were assassinated under unusual circumstances when ...

Ursula skimmed the next lines, then sucked in her breath when she saw his name.

> Before his death, Robert Graf told acquaintances he had no doubt he was going to be assassinated. For years, the deft and dapper man had enjoyed a reputation as a financial wheeler-dealer, not only in Guatemala's criminal world but also among the higher-ups in its government. Other than

bragging about being a lady's man, he kept quiet about his roots in Switzerland, his former relationship with Banco Salina Suisse, and the ties to his shady principals in Mexico. Graf secretly spun a web of criminal activities that ranged from money laundering to drug trafficking. His web was destroyed on May 14, 2007, when Gianella Ruiz, a well-known lady of pleasure, drove Graf's BMW towards his apartment in Zone 10 from an unknown destination with Graf in the passenger seat. Right outside Zona Viva, Ruiz stopped at a red light. According to eyewitnesses, a black Mercedes SUV came to a halt behind the car, and a well-dressed man got out of the vehicle and proceeded to the BMW's passenger side as if to ask a question. The man then pointed his 9 mm pistol at Graf and fired. By the time the police arrived, Robert Graf and Gianella Ruiz were lying dead in a pool of blood. A large suitcase full of US currency, five of Graf's passports with different aliases, and two Walther PPKs were found in the trunk of his car. Rumors immediately spread that the order to kill Graf came from someone outside Guatemala, perhaps from his phantom bosses in Mexico or from disgruntled competition. Just another murder that will remain unsolved in this country of lawlessness.

The paper rustled in Ursula's shaking hands. She stared at a small photo of her father, the man she had last seen three decades ago. There he was, with thick combed salt-and-pepper hair, piercing eyes, and a Van Dyke beard that framed his time-chiseled face. His fierce expression was the same as she remembered from her teenage years when, for all intents and purposes, he'd sold her to Mateo Miraldo.

A cocktail of emotions was flowing through her; she felt dizzy. Unsteadily, she folded the newspapers and handed them back to Bruno. "I'm not sad," she whispered. "I can't even qualify Robert Graf's death as a loss. He betrayed and robbed me and his own grandchildren of a good life. He obviously did the same to many others."

"Anyone who knows what happened to you would understand." Bruno put the newspapers back in the folder. "Whatever you feel, let it all come out."

"I feel relief," she said after a while. "I'll breathe easier knowing I never have to look at or deal with that man again. At last, I have closure."

TWENTY-SEVEN

Ursula, twenty-four hours later
Crans-Montana, Switzerland

The phone rang as Ursula rinsed the remaining shampoo from her hair. Who was calling so early on her landline? But it wasn't really that early; she had stayed in bed late, losing herself in unmanageable memories again. Only when Mick poked his head through the cracked-open door, letting her know he was leaving for a long hike and taking the dogs with him, was she able to let go of the twirling thoughts, stumble out of bed, and step into the shower. But while the water pattered over her, absurd ideas continued to bombard her. Like stubborn eye floaters, mental images of the redhaired American woman and her cowboy-hat husband drifted through her head. *Why, for God's sake, can't I wipe these people from my mind?*

Ursula wrapped a towel around herself and ran into the bedroom, picking up on the fifth ring. "Oui, allo."

The line crackled. "Allo?" Was there a whisper on the other end? After her third, more commanding "Allo!" she heard the hang-up.

A puddle had formed around her feet on the ornate wood floor, and she pulled the towel more tightly around her wet body. Unsettled, she pressed the display button. *Anonyme*, it read.

She dressed and hurried downstairs. Bruno and Joaquín sat in the kitchen banquette under the large bay window, having breakfast. Their smiles faded when they saw her.

"What's wrong?"

She told them of the call. "It probably was nothing," she added quickly, waving her hands in front of her face. "My overactive imagination is like a mosquito I can't shoo away."

"You're probably still reacting to what you learned yesterday." Bruno patted the upholstered seat in the nook next to him. "Sit down, have breakfast with us."

While listening to Bruno and Joaquín's latest travel tales, Ursula sipped her coffee and nibbled on a slice of toast with Nutella; her mind was calming, her body rebalancing. As always, being in the presence of her ex-husband (they'd gotten the marriage annulled after Mick turned thirteen and once they knew their identities had been firmly established) and his actual partner gave her a sense of security. How she wished they could stay longer.

"We'd like to share some good news with you," Bruno said.

"Tell me, tell me!"

He nodded at Joaquín. "Go ahead," he said, grinning.

"Well . . ." Joaquín pushed out his chest and raised his arms in a gesture of triumph. "After forty devoted years, Bruno handed in his resignation with Banco Salina Suisse and convinced me to quit my job before I retired so the two of us can start our second act. We decided to leave Mexico and begin the next phase of our lives somewhere else."

Ursula swallowed. "I'm happy for both of you, but where will you be living?"

Bruno squeezed her hand. "We thought long and hard about it. Since Joaquín and I consider Mick and you our family"—he squeezed her hand again—"we thought we'd buy a home here in Crans-Montana."

Her eyes widened, and she pressed her face into the palms of her hand.

"Ursula? I'm sorry—"

"No, no," she cried. "These are tears of joy." She grabbed the napkin to catch the salty drops. "My heart is singing. Can't you hear it?" She hugged both men.

"We weren't sure you wanted us this close by even though the small community here understood the reason for the divorce, even accepted me." Joaquín winked at her.

"Are you kidding? I can't wait for Mick to come back from his hike." Ursula's cheeks were flushed with excitement. "He'll be thrilled."

"There's something else—something you always wanted to know but I was never at liberty to reveal before," Bruno said. "It's somewhat bittersweet." He reached for a white pocket folder with embossed initials: *CDLF*. "Carlos de La Fuente."

She knitted her brows. "Mateo's old rival?"

He opened the folder. "He and Marta were soulmates. They met during one of her exhibits, shortly after Marco was born. It was love at first sight for Carlos, though he didn't act on it since Marta was married. But he never missed an opportunity to see her at social functions or art shows.

"Meanwhile, Marta had been aware of Mateo's infidelities for a long time; she also suspected dishonest business dealings. Right after giving birth to Manoel, she asked Mateo for a divorce. He refused, using his Catholic faith as an excuse, but agreed to a separation.

"To this day Mateo remains unaware that Marta and Carlos were deeply in love and completely committed to each other." He pulled a photograph from the folder. "This is a copy of the photo Carlos had at his bedside; he wanted you to have it."

"Me?" Ursula stared at the image of her beloved Mamá Marta with a dark-haired, kind-faced gentleman. "Why?"

"Marta considered you her daughter and confided in Carlos about her suspicions of abuse. Before she lost the ability to communicate with people, Carlos promised her he'd always take care of you."

She gasped, pointing at the man in the photo. "He is the phantom? Mamá Marta's soulmate was my secret benefactor?"

Bruno nodded. "The original photograph was the only belonging Carlos asked to have placed in the coffin with him."

"Oh no! When did he die?"

"Two months ago—the day before his eightieth birthday." He removed several newspaper articles from the folder.

"Oh. My. God." She skimmed the articles. "Mateo loathed Carlos; he envied him for his old money." She stared at one of the photos. "This can't be . . . or is it?" Ursula stammered. "Marco's second wife is Carlos's daughter?"

"Indeed! Marco married Carla de La Fuente soon after he forged those death certificates." Bruno's voice was taut and thick. "Carlos tried everything to prevent that marriage from happening."

"Why?"

"He knew of Marco and Carla's codependency, how they enabled each other's fatal addictions."

"Why fatal?"

He nodded. "Because Carla went into a tailspin after she divorced Marco. She immersed herself in drugs and alcohol, always surrounding herself with people who took advantage of her wealth. She and her much younger boyfriend ended up OD'ing on methadone, chloral hydrate, and whatever other drugs they'd gotten their hands on during a trip through Southeast Asia." Bruno rubbed the nape of his neck. "For too many years, Carlos wanted to save his only child, but Carla was beyond cure." Joaquín laid his arm around Bruno, pulling him close. He looked at Ursula. "Carlos had no other family. He considered Bruno his most trusted friend, treated him like a younger brother."

Bruno sighed. "I was always by Carlos's side, throughout Marta's illness and Carla's tormented life."

Ursula raised her eyebrows. "And Mateo never found out about their relationship?"

"No!" Joaquín said. "I'm trying to convince Bruno to anonymously mail him the evidence."

"Believe me, it will give me great pleasure to hurt Mateo," Bruno said quietly. "But I'm not quite ready yet."

Ursula looked again at the candid shot of Marta and Carlos sitting on the deck of a yacht, laughing together, holding each other. "They look happy," she said. "Did Carlos's wife know about them?"

"He never married Carla's mother," Bruno said. "Carlos had a one-night stand with her after a Cinco de Mayo celebration at a friend's home. Ligia would've had an abortion after she got pregnant, but Carlos wanted a child, an heir. So they made a deal. Right after giving birth to Carla, Ligia took the money and ran off to Honduras."

"Did she ever come back for her daughter?"

He shook his head. "She got married in Tegucigalpa to a guy she'd known from childhood, the son of a food-processing tycoon. Together they had access to seemingly endless disposable funds, but since their money apparently didn't buy them happiness, they made sure it bought them a good time. They spent excessive sums on drugs and alcohol, threw exorbitant parties for friends—until the day Ligia apparently took the wrong combination of whatever."

"Dear God! She died of an overdose, and years later her daughter met the same fate? Poor Carlos. How did he deal with all of it?"

"Only Marta, before she fell ill, knew how to provide the comfort he needed; she mended his heart again."

"Did he have any family around him when he passed away?"

"Kismet." Bruno smiled. "Marta's family became Carlos's family. He considered Manoel and Claudia his son and daughter-in-law, and their four children embraced Carlos de La Fuente as a substitute grandfather."

"I remember Manoel being so gentle and caring," Ursula said. "I'm really happy for him and his family."

"There's more you need to know," he said. "When Carlos died, he bequeathed more than half of his estate to charitable causes. The rest was split between Manoel and"—he pointed to Ursula and then to himself—"you and me."

She grasped his hand. "Me? Why?"

"As I mentioned, Carlos knew how much Marta loved you, how she wanted to protect you. He couldn't stand how you were held captive by Marco and Mateo. He helped me plan your escape. When we found out what happened in Miami, he swore to rectify the Miraldos' wrongdoings in whatever ways he could." Bruno pulled a few sheets from the white folder and spread them across the kitchen table. He pointed at names and numbers.

Ursula's hand flew over her mouth. "That can't be right."

"Because of Carlos's generosity and his love and devotion for Marta," he said, "he made both of us very, very wealthy."

The quiet in the house, though soothing, suddenly struck Ursula as borderline bleak. She had hoped much of the morning's explosion of information would be smothered by the lively and uplifting conversation around the dinner table, but that hadn't been the case; the extraordinary facts Bruno had delivered earlier still twirled through her head.

She cracked the window open and waved to Bernard, Alain, and Charley, who were getting into Bernard's gray VW Golf. The start of its engine was almost disrespectful to the quiet outside. Ursula saw the taillights flash bright red before they got dimmer and dimmer as the car pulled into the expanding night.

Still staring into the dark, she heard Bruno and Joaquín's fading voices in the house, then the closing of the guest bedroom door.

Four of her dearest friends would be leaving early in the morning for the airport in Geneva. Bruno and Joaquín were heading back to Mexico City, Charley and Alain to Paris. As always, it was emotional for her to see them leave. She found it difficult to rid herself of stubborn mental images in which she became the recipient of a last hug, a last kiss, a last time.

"¿Quieres ayuda, mi chico?"

"No, thanks. I got it."

Marisol and Mick's voices snapped Ursula back to her surroundings. She turned away from the darkness behind the window and welcomed the light in the warm, cozy room. She placed herself next to Marisol on the burnt-umber leather sofa by the fireplace and linked her arm with her faithful friend's.

"There!" Mick pushed a burning log closer to the heart of the fire before adding extra wood to the healthy flames. "Beautiful!" He plopped himself onto a large, thick floor cushion and stretched his arms and legs. "Almost feels like a warm bubble bath." He snuggled his tall, muscular body deeper into the pillow. Still bronzed from long summer hikes, his skin glowed, and the reflection from the flickering flames danced in his eyes.

"How are you dealing with everything you learned today, Mama?" Mick propped himself onto his elbows. "Bruno certainly delivered a load of news, the good and the bad."

"Let's focus on only the good."

"Absolutely. I'm psyched about Bruno and Joaquín. How awesome to have them close by, especially for you when I need to travel."

Travel? The word struck Ursula like a bolt of lightning. "You never mentioned travel plans before," she said with an unnaturally thin voice. "Where will you be going? And why?"

"Well, I hope to be invited by other galleries, not necessarily just here," he said. "The reaction I got in Geneva made me think I could maybe make a go of this." He scooted off the pillow and sat on the floor, near his mother. "You've always encouraged me to overcome my social phobia. You taught me to trust myself when I was outside my comfort zone. I thought you'd be pleased that I'm finally ready for this."

She didn't like the return of her tumbling emotions. Her son, born with a cautious nature, had been exposed to countless stressful events in his early life, trauma that had caused him to be even more guarded and shy. Hadn't she—as well as her grandparents, Marisol, and his therapist—worked tirelessly to help Mick overcome his anxiety? Then why would she want to hold him back now, when he was ready to break out of his shell?

"Of course." She touched his warm cheek. "Your talent deserves to be admired wherever it takes you." It took effort to put the right amount of encouragement into her voice. "I just wasn't prepared for your sudden desire to globe-trot."

"You're worried I might want to go abroad."

Ursula swallowed. How did he know?

"I told him," Marisol said in a low, somewhat brittle voice, "about your concerns regarding the invitation."

"I was thrilled when the Dawsons said they wanted to commission work from me." Mick's eyes sparkled. "To experience the natural wonders of a completely unfamiliar setting would be fantastic—a chance to experiment with my technique and style."

"But too much is at stake for you to travel to the United States," Ursula said, barely audible. When she noticed Mick's rapid blinking, she laid her hand on his shoulder. "Remember the Miraldos used their money to make deals with law enforcement in Mexico. We can only assume they did the same in the States."

He nodded. "Bruno says there's always a chance they know more about us than we're aware of."

Aside from the occasional crackle and pop from the pine logs in the fireplace and the ticktock coming from the grandfather clock, the room was silent for a moment.

"Maybe one day in the future it'll be safe to go wherever I want," Mick said pensively. "Meanwhile, I'll focus on Europe." He scooted back onto the floor pillow and stared against the ceiling. "My instincts tell me that someday, something will change for the better."

"What do you mean?"

"For four years Molly and I spent every minute together. We shared the same fun but also the same painful experiences. She was more resilient; she knew how to cushion the blows for me," he said. "But I was the intuitive one. I often could feel what she was thinking."

Ursula smiled, remembering. "Molly sensed your pain, and you knew her thoughts."

"It's twin telepathy," Mick said. "Lately, I've imagined hearing Molly in my head again, like she's questioning everything she's been told. I don't know when, but she'll uncover what has been withheld from her."

TWENTY-EIGHT

Molly, June 2019
Milwaukee, Wisconsin

The time on my alarm clock read 2:09 when I went to bed. I must've dozed off after looking at the photograph of my mother and twin; it's now 4:58. I feel a little sluggish, but almost three hours of sleep is better than I expected. I take a quick shower, throw the terry cloth spa wrap around myself, and head for the coffee maker.

Holding the mug with both hands, I walk over to the window and take a long sip of my favorite brew, Tanzanian peaberry. I let my gaze wander to the very early dawn and see lights behind a few windows in the high-rise to my left. I wonder if the people living in those apartments are also plagued by troublesome thoughts that keep them up all night.

It's only been sixteen hours or so since I sat on the cement floor in my father's storage area. Since then, all I can think of is what I might find in Pops's antique armoire and attic. What if it gives me further proof that my father and grandfather are untrustworthy, horrible, greedy brutes? I shiver and take another long sip of the warming brew.

Is someone standing on one of the balconies to my left? I lean forward and squint. I can't make out the person's shape, but someone is smoking a cigarette or cigar; I see the glowing embers.

I have no idea how long I stand by the window—I just suddenly realize there's no more coffee left in my mug and my phone is vibrating on the kitchen counter. Maxwell's name is on the display.

"Hope I didn't wake you."

"Nope. Guess the chamomile tea and melatonin tablet didn't do the trick for either of us after you left last night."

"I couldn't wait any longer," he says. "I found another document on my phone. I just sent it to your private email."

I walk over to my desk, where three piles of printouts sit exactly the way we left them. I open the email.

"Please print it out, then delete it from your inbox. After everything we found yesterday, we need to be extra careful with emails and texts. We can't trust you-know-who."

I pull the paper from the printer. "I don't remember seeing the original in my father's storage room."

"I'm sure you did, but there's been so much. Look at the third paragraph."

"What? Shit!"

"Exactly."

For a while neither of us say a word. Then Maxwell breaks the silence. "It sounds like a wild theory, but given the circumstances—"

"The few missing pieces are at Pops's house."

～

It's six o'clock in the morning when Maxwell picks me up. "Are you sure they're not coming home earlier?" he asks for the second time on our way to Mira. "The thought of being caught by your grandfather in his house freaks me out."

"Not a chance," I say. "The Hadlows are throwing their biggest function tonight on their estate—another opportunity for Dad and Pops to promote MiraCo while mingling with tycoons. Plus, Pops texted that he heard rumors about a surprise guest from the executive branch making an impromptu appearance. He, my father, and the lovely Ava would never miss the opportunity to meet a political celebrity from the current administration."

Before Maxwell pulls the car onto Pops's driveway, I tell him to stop. "I have to disarm the alarm system from my cell before your car gets any closer."

"Why?"

"Pops recently had two cameras installed, one at the front of the house and one at the back, but they only work when the system is armed."

"Won't he know when someone disarms the system?"

I nod. "Only my father, Yoli, and I have the code, so I'm expecting I'll get a call from him."

"Shoot. What will you tell him?"

"I'll think of something."

To shield us from prying eyes, Maxwell parks his Prius next to the only other vehicle in the four-car garage, Pops's Mercedes GLS 450.

Weirdly, the door from the garage to the house is bolted from the inside. "Huh?" I look at Maxwell. "You wait here. It's best I go through the main entrance by myself, just in case."

For a moment I stand in front of the home where I lived for many more years than I did in my father's house. I stare at the massive mahogany and wrought-iron door with the Miraldo emblem carved in the middle. To this day Pops congratulates himself on adorning his Mira mansion with the Mexican hacienda entry door.

Why, after so many years of using this entrance, does it suddenly strike me as peculiar? A strange sensation rushes through me, and I wonder if it's another flash of a forgotten time. I put the key in the lock, and when I push the heavy door open, it makes an eerie grinding sound. As soon as I close it, I'm surrounded by the stale essence of transience; I sense faint echoes of unease.

"Are you okay?" Maxwell asks after I unbolt the door to the garage.

"I think I had a weird flashback when I came into the house."

His light touch on my bare arm steadies me.

"Let's go," I say. "We have work to do."

He follows me up to the first floor. I point to the door at the top of the stairwell that leads to the attic. "There's no key in the lock like the last time I was here."

"Rats."

"Pops never allows anyone to enter his 'parlor in the sky,'" I say. "Even when Yoli cleans it, he keeps an eye on her."

"Then there's got to be something up there he doesn't want anyone to find. Any idea where the key might be?"

"Maybe." I motion Maxwell to follow me into Pops's bedroom, to the antique Mexican cabinet with the nacre-shell inlays. I stand and look at it, then point to the round table with the long, heavily beaded vintage tablecloth. "When I was between eight and ten, I loved lying under that table whenever Pops was at work. It was my secret hiding place. I'd get lost in daydreaming and make-believe," I say. "One time, Pops came home unexpectedly. I was so scared he would punish me because his bedroom was off-limits. I pressed my mouth to the carpet, praying he wouldn't hear my breathing. There was a small gap between the long tablecloth and the floor, and I saw how he opened a secret compartment in the cabinet."

Maxwell steps closer to study the antiquity. "I know you can't remember anything prior to the age of eight," he says, "but your ability to recall the things you've heard, seen, or read since then is amazing. I've always envied you for that."

I stop Maxwell just before he touches the cabinet. "Did you bring gloves?" Before we came, we decided we'd cover our hands before touching anything in Pops's very private world.

"Oops!" From his backpack he removes two pairs of surgical gloves and hands a set to me. "What do you remember from that day when you were hiding under the table?"

Behind closed eyes I grab the moment when I peeked from under the heavy tablecloth and watched Pops. And just as he did, I mold my hand around the front right bronze column and give it a half twist. I stiffen when I hear the click. Like Pops did then, I give it another full twist.

"Brava! Look!" Maxwell points to a now-open panel on the lower right side of the cabinet and gently removes a rectangular box with needlepoint work. "Edelweiss and alpine flowers? Those aren't Mexican motifs," he says. "Looks like something made in Bavaria or Switzerland."

"My mother's maybe? She could've brought it with her when she came to Mexico." I close my eyes, recalling what I saw. "Pops kissed the box before he opened it."

"Well, let's see what sentimentality he's hiding in there."

My heartbeat quickens when Maxwell releases the lid from its magnetic closure and carefully removes a stack of photos. One by one he lays the pictures out in front of us. Most of them are of my mother; she's so young, so beautiful. Other photographs show her with my twin and me, but every one of them differs from those we discovered yesterday in my father's storage room.

I point to people in a slightly yellowed picture. "There we are: Pops, my father, my mother, my brother, and me. Seems like the perfect family," I mumble. "But my mother's smile looks forced, like her life at the hacienda was an illusion."

"She looks like an angel," says Maxwell. "Your father and grandfather . . . charismatic but also dark and impenetrable, as usual."

I pick up the next photo. Two young boys stand next to a priest at an altar. "That must be my father and Uncle Manoel."

He holds up a larger, even older-looking sepia photograph. "Check this one out. The one on the left has to be your grandfather, but who's the look-alike guy with the wavy salt-and-pepper hair next to him?"

I lean closer to the picture. Pops is young here, maybe in his early twenties. "That's not Spanish," I say, trying to decipher the writing on the façade behind them.

"Portuguese."

"Wow. Then that must be his father."

"The one who claimed to be the illegitimate son of Carlos I of Portugal?"

"Yup. Pops hated him, always referred to him as a demon." With a mixture of sadness and disgust, I stare at the two men.

When Maxwell is finished snapping pictures, he assembles the photos exactly the way he found them in the velvety edelweiss box, then sets them aside. I hold my breath when he removes a stack of letters, tied together with a red ribbon. He hands it to me.

The first two envelopes are addressed to Molara Miraldo, 9 Bayside Drive, Mira, Wisconsin. "My mother's letters." My throat tightens. "The ones we're looking for." Feeling lightheaded, I lean against Maxwell.

"You okay?"

"I think I need water."

"I'll get it for you."

I shake my head. "I need to get out of here for a minute." I hand the letters back to him. "When I come back, we'll read them together."

I return with Fiji water for both of us. He's sitting on the floor, holding two wrinkled envelopes in both hands. He waves them at me. "These were in the box, too. They're copies of the forged death certificates. And two keys. Could one of them be for the attic?"

"Yes! I recognize the brass one. Maybe the other is for a drawer or cabinet." I put both keys in my jeans pocket and sit next to Maxwell. My hand is shaking when I open the first letter. The fluid handwriting with perfect spaces between each word reminds me of calligraphy, but soon the decorative lettering begins to swim.

"I'd read it for you, but it's in Spanish," Maxwell says, and puts his arm around me.

I nod, wipe my eyes, and then slowly begin to translate—one letter after the other, eleven in total. Whenever I'm overcome by emotion, he comforts me until I regain my composure again.

"They told me my mother didn't want me," I say, my eyes still glued to the final sentence of the last letter. "Over and over again, they said she was a disturbed, confused, unstable person. A kidnapper who chose my twin brother over me and took him away from a loving home. My father said she deserved to be behind bars, instead of being dead." I blow my nose. "Lie after lie after lie." I wipe my cheeks and blow my nose again. "And I believed every word they told me because they were my only family. I loved Pops, I even thought I loved my father."

In complete silence I watch Maxwell take photos of the letters.

It must have been heartbreaking for my mother to write those tender, loving sentences to me, repeatedly appealing for forgiveness. Excruciating for her to keep assuring Pops and Dad that she'd keep quiet, not only about all of their felonious acts but also about the abuse she suffered, in return for letting me be reunited with her and my twin. None of those letters were ever answered except the one I supposedly wrote at the age of five or six. *Did I write it because I meant it, or was I forced to?* It's frustrating to not be able to remember anything, especially now. It's even worse to imagine the horrible things that happened to my mother, this angelic-looking young woman with her innocent smile, while the monsters who caused so much of her trauma were never held accountable; they simply went on living their splendid lives.

I want to bang my fists against my head because I can't put all the pieces together. So much is missing. How did my mother escape from the hacienda with us? Where was she when someone snatched me away in Miami? She wrote about knowing that Pops and my father had sent spies to search for her and my brother. Where were they hiding all these years? Where are they now?

Watching Maxwell stack the letters in the exact same order as he found them, I marvel at how assertive every one of my mother's letters was, even when the words between the lines revealed how much she feared the wrath of the Miraldos.

As Maxwell ties the red ribbon around the stack of letters again, I can't allow myself to stay stuck in this mental black hole. I have to be brave, climb out of it, and face whatever horror story is yet to come. This thing will never let me go until I've looked under every single stone, no matter how tiny it is.

As if from far away, I hear Maxwell's voice. "Once we're done in the attic, we'll come back here, put the keys on the bottom of the box, and lay everything on top—just the way we found it." He pulls me to my feet.

I look at my phone. Unbelievable. It's already eleven o'clock. We've spent three hours here.

"I have to call Pops," I say.

"Holy hole in a donut! Why?"

"I'd rather explain why I disarmed the system before he notices I did."

I motion for him to follow me downstairs, then open the patio doors and inhale deeply. The fresh air is a tonic for my brain.

"It feels good to get out of the murk. Time to refuel." Maxwell leans back into the glider chair and looks into the distance over Lake Michigan.

My stomach is in knots when I tap on Pops's number. He usually picks up right away, but this time it keeps ringing. I'm prepared to leave a message when he answers.

"Molara."

I hear background hubbub, wind, laughter, music.

"Hey, Pops. Can you talk?"

"Hang on."

An exchange followed by more laughter.

He's still chuckling when he gets back to me.

"Molara," he says again.

"Sounds like you're having a good time."

"Well, you're missing one heck of a weekend. We just finished breakfast and we're breaking into groups. There's golf, others go fishing, horseback riding, tennis—Nelson thought of everything. Bloody shame you got sick," he says. "If you're feeling better, you can still make it to the gala tonight. The plane is yours."

"Not a chance. I'm still under the weather." I puff out my cheeks. "I'm calling from your place."

"Why?"

"I felt like coming to Mira, get some sunshine and fresh air here."

"Why drive all that way? You have a sundeck and pool in your apartment building." Is that a snort I hear on the other end?

"On beautiful days like this, there are too many people on the sundeck. I'm still not feeling great, and I'd rather not be around anyone else."

"Are you by yourself, or did you bring a friend?"

I force myself to speak calmly. "I just told you I want to enjoy the solitude here. The sunshine and views over the lake are exactly what I need."

"Do you plan on spending the night?" His voice definitely sounds strained now.

"No, I'm heading back to Milwaukee in another hour or two." Maxwell is staring at me, wide-eyed. I grin and wink at him. "Why are you even asking? Don't you always tell me that this is my home?"

"Well," he mumbles, "never mind."

"Anyway," I say, still pretending to be offended, "enjoy the rest of your time there, and say hi to Dad and Ava."

"Wait, don't go yet. I want to tell you that Dudley is anxious to meet you. I talked him into attending Fiesta Miraldo and—" Suddenly his voice is overpowered by an announcement. "Time to head for the golf course now," he shouts. "Feel better."

I make doubly sure the call is disconnected, then plop down next to Maxwell on the glider.

"Jeez," he says. "Almost wish you hadn't put him on speaker—my heart stopped a couple of times. Is he telepathic? He definitely sounded suspicious."

"Made me nervous, too."

"But you handled yourself like a pro. Never knew you could lie like this."

I exhale my anxiety, and when I stand up, I pull Maxwell off the glider with me. "Shall we attack our final dig for the relics of a lost time?"

As I stand at the bottom of the staircase that leads to Pops's parlor in the sky, I hear my uncle Manoel's voice: *Mateo, Marco, and I signed confidentiality agreements—same as your nondisclosure agreements in the States—when we parted company.* I stare at the door above me and wonder what lies behind it.

Just as Mateo and Marco aren't allowed to reveal any of my trade secrets or manufacturing processes or my very personal reasons behind our estrangement, I am legally forbidden from disclosing information about anything that took place during those years.

Without conscious thought, I put my right foot, then my left on the first step.

Even though my father, brother, and I are forbidden from talking about the circumstances that led to the breakup, you deserve to know what was done to your mother and where you and your brother came from.

I gasp and grip the banister when a sequence of scenes flashes through my head. I see a tipped-over table under a fan palm tree. A blonde woman in a red dress is putting pants and shoes on a small boy under the table. He's crying. I see an elegantly dressed older couple; the man in the beige suit looks annoyed, and the woman in the dark-blue dress with the huge hat keeps shaking her head because a little girl is sticking her tongue out at them. The little girl—the little girl is me.

"Molly? What's wrong?"

"I think I'm remembering something from my past."

"Do you need a break?"

"Absolutely not!" I look at the closed door at the top of the stairwell and take two steps at a time. "I have to get to the bottom of this."

"What the flipping flop? Isn't this décor overkill for an attic?" Maxwell says when I unlock the door with the brass key. Almost reluctantly, he steps into Pops's parlor in the sky.

We tiptoe around a meticulously designed room, afraid to touch or disturb anything. Eight photos in identical frames sit on one of the bookshelves. One of them catches me off guard. My dear late uncle Manoel, even way back then, is standing several feet apart from his father and brother, almost as if to dissociate himself from their misdeeds. If he were alive and knew what I've discovered in the past twenty-four hours, would he be willing to fill in the gaps for me? I stare at Pops and Dad; their stone-cold faces and demanding eyes warn me to stay away from the unknown. Of course, it's not too late to stop and leave the whole thing alone. Nobody is forcing me to search further. Even Maxwell wouldn't question my decision.

Out of nowhere, I have another memory flash. A woman is dragging luggage, walking away from a car. She turns around and smiles—it's my mother. My twin is sitting next to me in the back of a car; we're both buckled in car seats. He's wailing "Mamá, Mamá" and keeps yanking on his seat buckle. "The seekers will take Mamá away."

Let's hide from everybody, Miggy, I hear myself say. I pull a light-blue blanket over both of our heads. *See, no more people. Just Molly and Miggy.* I assure him that the blanket will keep us safe, that nobody can find us, that we will be safe together.

"Miggy. Molly."

"Huh?" Maxwell says.

"Pops and Dad insisted that everybody call us Molara and Miguel, but my twin had trouble pronouncing our names. He came up with Molly and Miggy." I put my hands in front of my eyes. "Omigod, I'm afraid to trust myself. What if I can't handle remembering more of my past?" Hesitantly, I remove the silver key from my jeans pocket and hand it to Maxwell. "God knows what this will unlock."

He points to the vintage buffet with Mexican carvings below a flat-screen TV. "There are no locks on these doors. Should I open them first?"

I give a nod as my heartbeat quickens. "Let's get it over with."

We peer in and see an old VHS video system. Maxwell sticks his head deeper into the cabinet. "It's still connected to the TV."

"Are you thinking what I'm thinking?"

He nods. "There must also be cassette tapes." He pulls on the knobs of the only two drawers in the buffet. "Locked."

I stand stock-still as I watch him insert the silver key, turn it, and slowly pull the left drawer open.

"Correct. Three of them," he says. "Each one is marked with dates and names."

⁓

I don't know how long I stare right through the snowy gray screen. In a daze I watch Maxwell take the last cassette from the machine.

"Let me see all of it one more time," I plead as he puts the three cassettes back in the drawer.

"It'll take too long," he says, and turns the key in the lock. "I videoed most of it, and I'll put it on an external hard drive to get it off my phone for safety."

I just stare at the dark screen.

In the first video my mother had set up for a picnic under the fan palm. When I heard her voice and her laughter, watched her hug and kiss me, a massive dam broke, releasing a flood of memories: splashing in the fountain with my brother, picking flowers, chasing butterflies, and running through the gardens with Miggy and my cousins.

The second video showed a lot of my mother and Pops. She looked despondent, apprehensive in his presence. At one point she begged him to turn the camera off, but he ordered her to pose in the entry to the hacienda—the same massive double front door he brought to the mansion on Bayside Drive in Mira. I think of the flash I had when entering this house earlier.

"Who was the slim woman with the dark curly hair in the third video?" Maxwell is fiddling with his phone. "The one next to you and your twin?"

I feel my chest tighten and reach for a fresh Kleenex. "I remember—Marisol." I close my eyes and see a smooth light-brown face; her smiling dark eyes are the color of freshly turned earth. I can hear her lulling voice, so full of comfort and warmth. She's combing my hair while singing a song about baby chicks chirping for food and shelter and the mommy hen feeding them seeds and keeping them warm under her wings.

"Marisol? Wasn't that the name Amelia Rubio mentioned in her call to you?"

I nod.

"Holy shit!" Maxwell's eyes widen.

"What?"

"Remember the day in January when we arrived late at the shelter with the food? An older woman and a man knocked on the kitchen door."

I think for a second, then nod. "It was dark outside, but I saw a woman looking frail in her big brown down coat, with a hood trimmed in faux fur that covered most of her face. And the man wore a hooded tan parka. You apologized, letting them know they had to register in the lobby."

"Exactly! That same man came to MiraCo the following day. He asked to see you, but you were in a meeting."

"And?"

"He said his friend had an important personal message for you. I believe he said her name was Marisol."

I suck in air. "Omigod."

"I don't remember the man's name, but he wrote down a phone number."

"You never mentioned anything."

"When I got home, I looked for the piece of paper and couldn't find it." Maxwell looks crestfallen. "The next day—with everything going on—I completely forgot about it." He leans closer. "I'm so sorry! I messed up."

"After so many years, Marisol came looking for me," I whisper.

He allows me time to compose myself before he breaks the silence. "Do you want to keep going?" He points at the drawer on the right. "I'd understand if you're wiped out."

"No! Maybe there are more videos." I watch Maxwell unlock the other drawer.

"Only one VHS cassette in here." He looks at it. "Nothing is written on this side." He turns it over, squints, and holds the cassette closer to his face. "It's labeled *11 de Septiembre de 1987*," he reads out. "The rest of the writing has been scratched off."

I cock my head and point to the drawer. "Check it out. Something is stuck under there."

He looks dumbfounded. "The only thing here is this cassette."

"You can't see because you're standing but—" I crawl towards the cabinet and pull the drawer all the way out. Maxwell gets on his knees and sticks his head under it. "It's an envelope fastened with four thumbtacks." He removes his Swiss Army knife from his jeans pocket. "Don't worry, I'll be careful getting these tacks out. Later I'll put them back without making new holes." He extracts the tacks and carefully detaches the envelope.

"*DNA LABORATORIO Ciudad de México*!" he cries. "This has got to be it!"

The knots in my stomach are getting tighter; I can't tell if it's anticipation or ambivalence.

"I have a feeling that neither this cassette nor the contents of this envelope will be manna from heaven," Maxwell says dryly. "Which one first?"

I point to the cassette.

⸺

Pops's face fills the screen. Looks like he's in his late forties, maybe early fifties. "Probando, probando, probando." He's installing and testing a camera.

What follows obliterates everything I believed in.

My mother is crying, her face bruised and swollen. She confesses to Pops that my father has been sexually and physically abusing her, and that she's aware of his longtime love affair with another woman. Pops keeps hugging her, touching her as she squirms away. "Be patient, my love," he whispers. "Things will change soon." He licks his lips and stares at her lasciviously.

I choke back a scream when Pops fastens a diamond bracelet

around her wrist while ignoring her protests. He kisses her fingers, her arms, her neck and encourages her to drink more wine. My mother's head keeps falling back; she's slurring her words. It is obvious the wine was spiked with something powerful.

He kisses her, undresses her, fondles her intimately, and then—

I throw my hands against my face, inwardly begging for all of it to go away, for none of it to be true.

"Let me stop the tape."

Maxwell tries to get up, but I hold him back. "If I don't face these cold, hard facts, I won't be able to move forward."

He puts his arm around my shoulder and pulls me close. "I agree," he says softly. "Admitting your grandfather and father are morally bankrupt will be essential for you to progress."

With horror I watch how my mother becomes increasingly weaker as she tries to resist him. He ignores her struggles, continuing to interpret her confused moans and feeble movements as pleasure. My mother repeatedly cries out, "Por favor no mas," but he hoarsely replies, "You want more, mi amor? I'll give you more!" My heart cramps when she begs, "No! Don't! Stop!" He only pants, "I love when you don't want me to stop."

Helplessly, I bear witness to my grandfather ravishing a powerless young woman. His lecherous voice shatters my soul. "You love it, don't you?" he rasps. "You're mine for eternity, my beautiful angel."

<hr>

Maxwell holds me tightly in his arms. "Your grandfather is terrifying," he mutters and hands me another tissue. "I didn't think much of him before, but my God, I can't think of a single thing he possibly could've done in his life to make up for this."

I crawl deeper into his arms, and he tightens his embrace.

"You were a stranger when I met you," I whisper into his sleeve. "But *you* became my family. *They're* the strangers."

"Right back at you," he says. "Being an orphan and having to hide my attraction to other boys while going through foster homes was challenging, to say the least. I had to fight for everything on my own until I was placed in foster care with Martin and Spencer." Maxwell gives me another squeeze. "But you became the bright light at the end of the tunnel."

We hold each other in silence while the unopened envelope on the floor in front of us still calls out to me.

I point at it. "What additional horrors are in there?"

"If this letter adds more weight to your already heavy baggage, I'll help you carry it," Maxwell says, and hands me the envelope.

Someone has already ripped off the sealable flap; there's no need to be cautious about opening it. My fingers tremble as I remove the contents and unfold two pages—paternity test results from a DNA diagnostic center in Mexico. It takes me a moment to interpret the findings, but when I do, I gasp for air.

"Molly? What is it?"

"This DNA result . . ." My new reality tightens like a rope around my neck; I'm having trouble breathing. "This DNA result proves that I'm the result of a crime scene!"

Images, sounds, and feelings zoom through my head. I squeeze my eyes shut, but the horror show won't go away. My voice quivers. "Heteropaternal superfecundation," I breathe.

"Hetero . . . what?"

I hurt so much, it's like an axe is hacking into my sternum.

"Marco is Miggy's father b-but not m-my father."

I can barely get the words out.

"M-marco is my half b-brother."

I gag as scenes from the last video play in my head.

"M-my grandfather—he's my father."

TWENTY-NINE

Mateo, September 2015
Mira, Wisconsin

Our first project in Europe." Marco's eyes twinkled, and with childlike playfulness, he clapped his hands together. "Finally we're going to wrap up the acquisition and plant MiraCo's footprint on Spanish soil. Man, the timing is perfect!"

"Congratulations," Mateo said warmly. "There was a time when I had serious doubts about this venture."

"I remember," Marco chuckled. "You said a snowman has a better chance surviving on a beach in Acapulco."

"You proved me wrong." Mateo refilled both of their glasses. "The timing is perfect."

"It all makes sense. Spanish resort markets are only going to benefit from improving domestic leisure demand. Plus, Mallorca continues to be a hot spot globally."

"Exactly. Just remember not to discuss our expansion plans with anyone. We don't want the seller to know about the upside we realize exists. If they get wind of our ideas, they may second-guess the price and become cognizant of the additional value." Mateo eyed the bottle of his favorite tequila but decided against having another shot. "We've been conservative in our underwriting; any additional cost will diminish our returns negatively and may force the bank to change their terms."

"*I* did the underwriting! *I* picked the Flamingo Palace and Golf

Resort in Mallorca specifically for those reasons. Clearly, I have no intention of screwing this up. And let's not forget, I'll have Molara by my side. Nothing ever escapes her eyes and ears."

Mateo nodded. "Our girl was very smart to familiarize herself with the local business culture before drafting and negotiating the agreements as well as all of the loan docs." He glanced at the Clase Azul Tequila Ultra bottle again. "I just don't understand why she always insists on having that damn Maxwell by her side."

Marco scooted to the edge of his seat and leaned forward. "I know how you feel about him. But you can't deny he and Molara work well together."

Mateo glared at him, then waved his hand in resignation. Maxwell, with his velvety chocolate face, unmanly voice, and effeminate behavior, was one of those people who simply didn't fit in this world. If his son couldn't see that, there was no point in arguing about it again. He realized Marco was still babbling. "Come again?"

"I said Jade's accompanying me to Spain." Marco winked at his father. "She'll love Mallorca, and Mallorca will love her."

"Only last week you said you were done with her."

"Well, I changed my mind. She'll make those long Spanish nights more enjoyable." He reached for the tequila bottle and refilled both glasses. "Speaking of, what's going on with you and Lotte Jansen, Papá? I haven't seen the Dutch dame lately."

"I have no more use for her," Mateo grunted. "She got in my way."

Lotte was attractive, but she had annoyed the shit out of him. She'd snooped around his house and had an irritating habit of knocking on his bathroom door (there were six other bathrooms in the house!), asking how much longer he'd be. And every time he was on the phone, she'd made sure to be nearby while baby-talking to her yappy dog. She'd even had the nerve to complain that the rooms reeked of smoke whenever he enjoyed a cigar *in his own damn house!*

"To be honest," Marco said, "I always thought she was a bit young for you."

Coming from the baby dater? Mateo swallowed his remark. "How about lunch before you take off? I asked Yoli to prepare pipián stew."

"I want to save my appetite for the plane—we're leaving in less than two hours." Marco jumped up and clapped his hands again. "Watch out, Mallorca, here I come! Soon the Flamingo Palace and Golf Resort will fly our majestic MiraCo flag."

"¿Ha terminado de comer, Señor Miraldo?"

"Sí, gracias." Mateo pushed the plate away. "Estaba delicioso, Yoli."

"Once I'm done with the kitchen, may I leave for the afternoon? It's my sister's birthday, and I baked her favorite cake."

"Go! Have a good time," he said, looking forward to savoring complete freedom and solitude for a few hours.

Thirty minutes later—he had just lit his cigar—Yoli startled him. How many times had he asked her to knock before she entered his library?

"FedEx man delivered this." She handed him a thick legal-size envelope.

Mateo glared at the housekeeper.

"Oops." She quickly backed away. "Lo siento, Señor Miraldo."

He waved her off and scowled at the envelope. Nothing rattled in it when he shook it. What could it be? No business matters ever came to his home. He let go of the packet and watched it drop on the side table. *Later,* he told himself. *I'll open it later.* He leaned back in his favorite chair and stretched his legs across the ottoman. It wasn't even three o'clock, but he felt lethargic. Had he eaten too much of the pipián stew, or was the drowsiness due to lack of sleep? He wondered why lately every night was a repetition of the night before; he fell asleep around midnight, only to bolt up two to three hours later, drenched in perspiration and feeling haunted by the ghosts of his problematic past. To distract himself, he often read encouraging Bible verses but had trouble concentrating on the words. With the holy book lying on his chest, he remained still in his bed, usually staring at the diverse shapes of clouds that swept across the night sky. And whenever they were illuminated by bright moonlight, he imagined ghostlike features in the ever-changing formation of the clouds.

Mateo kicked the ottoman away and laid the cigar in the ashtray. He sat at the edge of the chair, bent over, and held his face between his hands. What kept unsettling him? Shouldn't his steadily expanding business, his growing wealth, and his dynamic and determined social life be antidotes to panic? Who was he afraid of? Himself?

What if God was punishing him for his lustfulness?

Mateo immediately rejected that thought. If God had designed desire to be part of nature, then his lust for Ula wouldn't be considered a sin. He relaxed into the chair again.

Without closing his eyes, he looked back in time and saw himself opening the buttons of her dress slowly, one after the other. Never had he seen skin so silky smooth. "Magnificent," he whispered as his mind's eye replayed unforgettable moments, like the setting sun dipping Ula's body in a golden light.

True, he had spiked her wine with recreational drugs—sometimes Xanax, sometimes ketamine—but that was only to help her relax and forget about Marco, her adulterous, drunk, brutal husband. Mateo's guilt melted away as soon as he recalled his tongue probing her mouth while his hand explored the wonders of her body. He licked his lips again, remembering when he'd carried her limp body to the bedroom—she'd been as light and beautiful as an Indian peacock feather.

He turned his head. Did he hear the clearing of a throat on the other side of the door? Again, he kicked the ottoman out of the way, stood up, and strode across the room to rip the door open.

"¿Qué?" he said, irritated. "What is it now?"

"I was about to knock, señor." Yoli looked offended. "I wanted to let you know that Señora Jansen stopped by to pick up her belongings."

"And? Did she ask for me?"

"Sí. But I told her you're out of town, just like you instructed."

Mateo closed the door and listened to Yoli's footsteps grow more distant. He smiled unconsciously when he heard the front door close. Yoli would be gone for hours, and Lotte Jansen was out of his life for good.

Though Lotte hadn't lived with him, she'd cleverly left personal articles behind whenever she spent a night or a weekend. The other women before her had basically done the same. All of them had dreamed of sitting on the throne next to him, hoping to be spoiled like a queen. But Mateo, whether in business or for pleasure, simply enjoyed playing the game of veni, vidi, vici; he loved getting bang for his buck. Whereas he took delight in holding on to all his business acquisitions and made huge investments to develop them, he never felt the desire to do the same with women. Though most of them had been young and attractive, none had ever given him what he needed. None would ever replace Ula.

He cracked his knuckles as he stood in front of the massive bookcase, looking for a specific book. There! He removed his favorite volume of Spanish poems and noticed the bookmark was still between previously selected pages. "Pablo Neruda. That man knew how to express the way I feel about Ula."

He inhaled and in a low voice read, "Body of a woman, white hills, white thighs, when you surrender, you stretch out like the world."

Mateo adored the intensity and beauty of the poem. "And the cups of your breasts . . ." *These words are sweeter than honey*, he thought and swallowed. "And the roses of your mound . . ."

He pressed the book against his chest, closed his eyes, and recited from memory. "I will live on through your marvelousness," he whispered. "And the fatigue is flowing, and the grief without a shore."

It's a perfect ode to a sexually submissive woman, he thought, completely clueless that the poem compared the body of a woman lying defenseless in surrender to taking control of earth and land.

He closed the book and returned it to its place next to the other hardcover volumes. Feeling uplifted, he strolled across the room, opened the patio door, and surveyed his property. Lately he had paid little attention to nature, but today he almost welcomed the whisper of wind, the innumerable bird calls. Far away, he heard an engine on the water but couldn't see a motorboat or a jet ski; only a few sailboats cruised silently in the distance. The sun was shining, the air tasted pure, and in this momentary tranquility, Mateo trusted in the safety of his secret. He inhaled the fresh aroma of a September afternoon and was contemplating a walk down to the beach—he couldn't remember the last time he had done that—when he heard the harsh, metallic ring from his landline inside the house. Who in the damn hell was calling him on a Saturday afternoon? Molara and Marco were en route to Spain, and only three others knew the number. With the aggressive ring molesting the quietude, Mateo rushed inside and looked at the caller ID. Pelón! Damn!

After Mateo moved his life and possessions from Mexico to the United States, he had trouble envisioning safety without a bodyguard. Surprisingly, Sergio, aka El Gordo, proved himself as the most dependable amongst Mateo's old Mexican guards. "Gustavo Guzman is the man you want across the border," the hulk had told Mateo years ago.

"Call me Pelón," Gustavo had said when they first met in some greasy spoon restaurant in Milwaukee.

Perfect name, Mateo thought. *With his clean-shaven shiny skull, his small round eyes, and a hoop-shaped mouth, the guy looks like a bowling ball.*

But during the next two decades Pelón proved himself an asset on many fronts, and the scope of his abilities continued to surprise Mateo. He was detail-oriented, he had technical skills, and as a bodyguard he'd developed a highly sensitive early-warning system. Now in his midfifties, Pelón still sported a glossy bald head, but dark tear bags under his round eyes gave him a washed-out look.

Some unprofessionally stitched-up lacerations on the lower half of his face hid behind scruffy facial hair.

The bodyguard, a master criminal, owned a modest ranch house in Oak Creek, mowed his lawn, and lovingly spoiled his wife and children. "My family shields my other pursuits," he matter-of-factly told Mateo. "They also give me the opportunity to enjoy an almost normal, happy existence."

Though unavoidable, Mateo regretted that Pelón had gained firsthand knowledge of his employer's twisted exploits over the years. There had been times when he thought he'd be better off without Pelón, but he'd grown too dependent on this man whom no one dared to treat with disrespect. Pelón was known for holding unreasonable grudges. He stalked his adversaries for days, until they either disappeared or swore on their mother's life never to interfere with him again. Grudgingly, Mateo himself was somewhat fearful of this crafty guy who'd gathered too much information about the Miraldos' past.

"¿Qué pasa? Espero que tengas buenas noticias."

"No good news, no bad news, just news." Pelón's laughter came harsh through the telephone wires, like an alarm clock in the middle of the night.

"Well?" Mateo snapped.

"Can I spell it out now, or do you need me to come by later?"

"Talk, but don't mention any names."

"Works for me, boss. I don't feel like driving up to Mira anyway today. I'm still jet-lagged."

"The news?"

"I followed your instructions, which got me nowhere. Then I remembered I had a few contacts in the Italian part of Switzerland. I asked those boys to stretch out their feelers and met with them in Locarno two days ago." He started to cough. "Perdón," he said between wheezing and hacking. "Fuckin' spicy Takis went down the wrong way."

Mateo rolled his eyes.

"You still there?" Pelón's voice was hoarse.

"What did you learn in Locarno?"

"I couldn't believe my luck. For a season only, one of the boys had actually worked in the old couple's restaurant in Grindelwald, right before it was sold."

Mateo held his breath.

"My Italian guy said there were rumors among some of the townsfolk, like something fishy was going on with the old couple's vacation home in the mountains. Some of these folks couldn't figure out why Grandma and Grandpa abruptly took it off the rental market with no explanation. Some locals assumed they were hiding a celebrity up there, or maybe even someone running away from the law."

Mateo pressed the receiver closer to his ear.

"There was also tittle-tattle from two farm boys. They had gone on a hike and spotted a blonde woman coming towards them on the trail, but when she saw them, she turned and quickly moved away. The brothers tried to catch up but lost sight of her. They said the only place that could've swallowed her up would've been Grandma and Grandpa's mountain house close to the trail. The hikers were intrigued, but when they approached the chalet, two fierce German shepherds chased them off." Pelón gave a subdued laugh. "Too bad I wasn't there. I know how to deal with animals."

"The hikers were locals? Did you get their names?"

"Sorry. Way back then my Italian guy had no clue that any of this might be of interest to anyone. Meanwhile, I thought you'd like to know. You told me anything connected to the old couple was critical."

Damn! Mateo ground his teeth. Had Ula been hiding in that chalet with Miguel and Marisol? His heartbeat quickened. "But the old couple died. Did you find out who bought their mountain home?"

"Of course."

"And?"

"Not the party you're searching for," Pelón said. "A year before the old folks kicked the bucket, their chalet was sold to a neurosurgeon from Zurich. I have the name of the doctor if you need it—a married guy and father of three. The family spends a lot of time in that house, and they're well-liked in the town."

Mateo dropped onto the nearest chair; the anticlimax was too much for him.

"Hola, jefe! You still there?"

"If that's all you got, your news isn't newsworthy." He lowered his voice, trying to sound official. "It barely adds anything to what I already knew." He ignored Pelón's grunt on the other end of the line. "I expected more than some ancient gossip."

"Excuse me! I'm doing my damndest! I told you that I ran into dead ends the last two times you sent me to Switzerland." Pelón cleared his throat. "Why won't you let me introduce you to my associate in Mexico? That badass has contacts everywhere—even in Europe. All you need to do is say the word."

Though tempted, Mateo dreaded hooking up with anyone in Mexico; too much was at stake. Compared to his business operations in his country of origin, his conglomerate in the United States was almost entirely legitimate. No way would he allow his past to tarnish MiraCo's reputation. "Forget it. Nobody else gets involved—in Mexico or here. There's no need to give this drama any more oxygen!"

Frustrated, he put the receiver down. *Damn this endless loop that keeps going around and around and around*, he thought. *Why in the bloody hell can't I give up?*

Brooding, Mateo was baffled when suddenly he found himself standing in the middle of the kitchen. What the hell had he come here for? A faint smell of Yoli's pipián stew still hung in the air. Vacantly, he looked at the spotless, shiny surfaces. He shrugged, then filled a large glass with water from the reverse osmosis system and took it back to his library.

Ula, Ula, Ula. As her name echoed, old questions flared up again. Who in the bloody hell financed her escape? And where on this godforsaken planet was she now? What had happened to Miguel? To Marisol? How did they all support themselves? Were they even still alive?

He drank some of the water and put the half-full glass on the table next to the legal-size envelope. *What the . . . ?* He'd completely forgotten the FedEx delivery. Mateo stared at the packet and thought of the letters he'd received years ago from Ula; they had also arrived with no return address. With reserved eagerness he opened the large envelope.

He read the anonymous typewritten letter three times, stopping periodically to glare at the five photos. He held his breath in shock and disbelief. Not until his brain screamed for oxygen did he gasp for air. Shakily, he reached for the glass of water. The muscles in his throat were frozen, and water dribbled from his mouth onto his new light-gray polo shirt. He looked at the dotted stains and gulped for air again. His breaths came shallow, and it took effort to focus on each inhale and exhale.

When he was able to get his body under control, he hurled the water glass across the room. "Engañando cabrones mentirosos," he screamed at the photograph of Marta in an embrace with Carlos de La Fuente. He spat at their happy faces, then threw the photo on the floor and stomped on it. "You two cheating, lying scumbags!"

How could he have been so clueless? How many nights had that bastard spent with Marta at Hacienda Miraldo, practically under Mateo's nose? Damn them! And damn all his employees. Had Carlos de La Fuente bribed them to keep their mouths shut? Mateo felt a wave of dry heaves coming on; the color drained from his face. He ran to the bathroom.

"I never divorced Marta!" He hissed as he flushed the toilet. He leaned over the sink to rinse his mouth. "She was *my* wife, the mother of *my* sons!" He looked at himself in the mirror and nodded as if trying to justify his own infidelities. He kicked the bathroom door closed and walked back to his library. The photo was still on the floor. He kicked it. "Damn you, woman! You knew Carlos de La Fuente was my archenemy!"

Carlos de La Fuente! Almost as if the name had found a host in

Mateo, it kept circling through his head, infecting all his thoughts. He headed for the bar liquor cabinet and grabbed the Clase Azul Tequila Ultra, poured himself a double shot, gulped it down, and waited for the anesthetizing effect.

Every sound he heard over the otherwise leaden silence that had descended on the house was unnaturally loud—the faint popping of lumber under the slate roof, a tree branch grazing against the windowpane, even his own weak breaths.

"¡Puta madre!" Mateo refilled his glass and drained it.

The letter. He looked at the two typewritten pages lying next to his chair; the words and sentences even taunted him from across the room. Fucking Carlos de La Fuente had fucked his wife. Had bought Hacienda Miraldo two decades ago and remodeled it into a luxury hotel. Had formed a close relationship with Manoel and family. "¡Qué cabrón!"

The letter! Its revelations were daggers piercing through Mateo's gut, twisting their blades with every betraying sentence.

The letter! Carlos de La Fuente had died. Carla, his heir and only daughter, was dead, too. The immense de La Fuente fortune had been distributed between various charitable foundations and a few individuals. Manoel and Claudia Miraldo and their four children were named as beneficiaries.

The letter! Like hand grenades, the words and phrases kept falling all around Mateo; the name Carlos de La Fuente was like a hydrogen bomb.

He felt dizzy and leaned against the wall. *Dear God.* Marta had loved Ula, had considered her a daughter. Had Marta, before the onset of Alzheimer's, shared her sentiments with her lover? Had it been Carlos de La Fuente who arranged Ula's escape and financed it?

Exasperated, he refilled his glass. If that was the case, no wonder he couldn't find her. With Carlos de La Fuente's wealth and worldwide connections, Ula, Miguel, and that bitch Marisol were probably living splendid lives with solid new identities God knows where on this planet. Mateo looked at his drink, then slugged it straight back.

How could he take revenge? Should he make use of Pelón's Mexican connection after all? He quickly reminded himself of the possible consequences.

"It's over. No more life support for this cancer." He crumpled the two pages, did the same to the five photos, and shoved everything back into the envelope. Then he walked into the garage, pulled the old iron wastebasket from a shelf, and dropped the packet into it. He lit a match. "Burn in hell, you lying, cheating scumbags," he hissed.

He poured water on the ashes and watched the murky muck gurgle down the drain.

No way could Mateo share any of this with Marco. God only knew how he'd react if he found out his ex-father-in-law had been his mother's paramour. Or even worse, that his younger brother had fallen into a huge pot of gold. Better to keep the contents of the letter locked up in Mateo's impenetrable brain vault.

Back in his library, he cleaned up the shards of glass. It was six o'clock, he realized, the worst time in the world to be alone. The day was over, but the long night was still ahead. He stood indecisively in the room, annoyed that his body tingled as if it were filled with carbonic acid. He left the room and walked upstairs. He stood still on the landing, undecided what to do.

Ula. Ula. Ula. There it was again. Life was so unfair. Why hadn't they been allowed to enjoy their lives together? He would never have cheated on Ula the way he did on Marta. It hadn't been his fault he'd fallen out of love with his wife. And who could blame him! Marta had betrayed him with the devil.

Mateo sensed that bad taste again, the one that got stuck in the middle of his throat. What could he do to get rid of it? He looked at the stairwell that led to his parlor in the sky. He thought of the videotapes. Watching them would fortify and rejuvenate him. With the Clase Azul tequila bottle in his hand, he walked upstairs.

THIRTY

Ursula, December 2018
Crans-Montana, Switzerland

The first heavy snowfall of the season had come during the night, and when Ursula opened the curtains, she was greeted by a winter wonderland. The skyscraping Alps looked like giant brides in romantic snowy wedding dresses. And at the feet of the mountain range, like bridesmaids in fluffy white gowns, stood countless pines, firs, and deciduous trees to celebrate nature's untouched, whimsical, fairy-tale world.

Ursula's own backyard was covered by a whiter-than-white downy duvet with thick pillows of snow lying on tree branches and shrubs.

But on this morning, the silvery world outside didn't invite her to don her Sportalm ski-wear and grab her Ripstick 96 skis. On this morning, Ursula hurriedly dressed and rushed to the hospital.

Though the Clinique Mont Louis was known as one of the best private clinics for oncology and cancer treatment, everything struck her as too white, too cold, too sterile in Room 307. The bed, walls, and doors looked bleached, Marisol's face was pale, even her silvery hair seemed like a flawless extension of the sheet that covered her body.

A lump threatened to close Ursula's throat, and for a moment, she allowed herself to be defeated by sadness. A tear ran over her cheek, finding its way into her mouth. Why had her sweet, loyal friend kept her pain a secret for so long?

Five weeks ago, Marisol had confessed she knew something was wrong, that she'd felt unwell for some time. After various tests, Dr. Sabharwal confirmed a diagnosis of pancreatic cancer. And when she was told the cancer had already spread to other parts of her body, she'd accepted her fate. "I don't want to suffer through surgery, chemotherapy, and chemoradiation," Marisol said calmly. Instead, she'd asked Dr. Sabharwal for palliative care that would relieve pain and stress. "For the short time I have left, I'd like to make the best of every day."

To avoid making noise, Ursula lifted the chair to bring it closer to the bed and saw that Marisol's talisman had fallen to the floor. She picked it up.

"My mother and my grandmother trusted in the layered symbolism of these keys," Marisol had told Ursula. "Knowledge and truth, justice and freedom, new beginnings and love are only a few of their wonderful symbols, and they've helped me through the worst of times. When I leave this life, I want my keys to aid and uphold you, too."

"But you're still here, and as long as you are, you'll hold on to these keys," Ursula whispered and laid the small silver and gold keys into Marisol's palm, gently molding her fingers over them.

Her hand twitched. "¿Dónde estoy?" she murmured without opening her eyes.

Ursula leaned closer. "You're at Clinique Mont Louis."

"I was on my way to meet the angels of God. I saw them clearly, but they sent me back." Marisol slowly lifted her lids. "What happened?"

"You developed a serious bloodstream infection and had a high fever. Doctor Sabharwal is still running a few tests." Ursula caressed her friend's arm. "But the antibiotics worked very well; in another day they'll remove the IV drip, and soon you'll come home."

"How long have I been here?"

"Almost a week. You slept most of the time."

"Que surrealista." Marisol closed her eyes again. "Is it wishful thinking, or did Molly come and see me?"

Ursula swallowed. "Mick and I took turns being by your side. Bernard, Bruno, and Joaquín visited every day. Even Charley flew in for a couple of days."

Marisol opened the palm of her hand and looked at the keys. "Now I remember," she said. "The angels told me it wasn't my time yet. I have one more task."

THIRTY-ONE

Ursula, January 2019
Paris, France

Ursula's ongoing fears that Marisol could still be on a watch list subsided when nobody at the ticket counter raised an eyebrow at her passport.

"I told you not to worry," Marisol said as they walked towards security. "There are thousands of Marisol Rodriguezes, and I clearly don't look the way I did in the early nineties."

Despite her reassurances, Ursula battled her tears when she hugged her friends to bid them farewell. She craned her neck, watching Marisol follow Joaquín through security after placing their carry-ons and coats on the belt.

Turn around and let me see your face again, Ursula thought and stepped to the left to get a better view. She saw Joaquín take their belongings off the belt. Simultaneously, they both looked in Ursula's direction, waved, and blew a kiss before they disappeared.

The moment the taxi pulled up in front of Le Meurice, the rain stopped. Cold, damp air hit Ursula when she got out. Quickly she buttoned her gray down coat and involuntarily smiled as she double-wrapped the eggplant scarf around her neck—a gift from Marisol. It was only a week ago that she had caught Marisol rummaging through one of Grosi Rosi's woven baskets to find eggplant balls of thick wool. She'd finished the scarf in an afternoon marathon session, so her knitting was a bit irregular—too tight in some places, too loose in others—but Ursula loved this scarf and had worn it every day.

"Madame Rossi." The doorman smiled, ready to escort her to the hotel entrance.

"Thank you, Jean-Luc, but I decided to go for a walk." She wrapped the scarf twice more around her neck, crossed rue de Rivoli, and headed for the Jardin des Tuileries, directly opposite the hotel.

The exercise will ease my tension, she thought. She glanced at her watch. She still had time before Bernard would return to the hotel.

There were relatively few people strolling through the Tuileries Gardens, most likely due to the earlier rain on this sunless, chilly January day. The hedges and trees were leafless, and through their barren branches, Ursula spotted one of the ponds. From a distance it looked smooth and dark like the back of a prehistoric sea monster. She passed the pond, quickened her step, and allowed herself to get lost in thought.

After the diagnosis, both Ursula and Mick had made sure to spend every available moment with Marisol. They talked, they listened, and they chose to reflect on good times only. Bernard, Bruno, and Joaquin came to the house almost daily, and together they played cards or board games, shared meals and laughter. It was after one of those cheerful evenings when Marisol asked Ursula and Mick to sit with her by the fireplace a while longer.

"Now that I've regained some strength from the infection," she said, "I hope you'll be open to my last wish."

"Of course," said Ursula.

"Anything," said Mick.

"I'd like to travel to the United States."

Everything started to blur around Ursula. Contours of past

events blended with contours of their lives in Switzerland. "I don't understand," she managed to say.

"The three of us made the best of the fate we were given," Marisol said, looking downright calm. "But before I die, there are people I have to see one more time."

Ursula and Mick exchanged a quick glance.

"You both know that during the year we lived in hiding, I formed a deep connection with Rabbi Hebroni," Marisol said. "He and I discovered spiritual similarities; often we discussed things for hours into the night." She stopped talking, as if to gaze into the past. "The rabbi's teachings convinced me I had the power to find the hidden light in everything."

"That's deep," Mick said.

"That light guided me through so many moments, but some of it remains scattered, and I have trouble putting it together. Before God calls me home, I feel the rabbi can show me how to restore the spiritual illumination. I believe his knowledge will help me repair what's still broken in me."

"Joaquín told me his brother was a longtime student of Kabbalah," Mick said. "I didn't know he had such an impact on you."

Marisol smiled. "When we lived with Rabbi Hebroni, you were a little boy. He often sat with you and his children around the dinner table, telling stories and answering your questions. Your mother and I noticed the calming effect the rabbi had on you."

"I remember always wanting to draw his stories," Mick said wistfully.

Ursula scooted closer to Marisol. "We've kept in touch with the Hebroni family via phone and FaceTime. Why travel all that distance? Wouldn't it be easier to continue your dialogue that way?"

Marisol shook her head. "Joaquín wants to escort me to Chicago. It'll also give him a chance to spend time with his brother."

"Wow," said Mick. "Are you sure you're up for this?"

"Dr. Sabharwal gave me the green light for traveling and discussed the options with Joaquín after my last appointment. He just wants to make sure you're both comfortable with it."

"I am," said Mick. He looked at his mother.

Don't let panic become your feedback now; let bravery be the only option. Ursula took a deep breath. "Absolutely."

"But there's more," Marisol said. "Since I'll be so close to Wisconsin, I'll ask the universe to guide me so I can see Molly before I die."

Like a curtain at the end of a show, Ursula's hair fell over her face as she lowered her head.

"Putain de merde!"

The sound of screeching tires, just inches away, broke Ursula's reverie. "Je suis désolée," she apologized to an angry face under a helmet, realizing she had caused a bicyclist to panic-stop.

The young man shouted a few more expletives, then hopped on his bicycle again and sped away.

Ursula looked around and realized she was in the second arrondissement. She had walked for more than an hour. She turned into rue Saint-Honoré, ready to walk back to Le Meurice.

It already was midafternoon; she hadn't eaten anything since breakfast, and dinner wasn't scheduled for at least another four hours.

Café Verlet's signage up ahead caught her eye. She licked her lips when she thought of the croque végétarien sandwich, the one with little button mushrooms, pesto, and feta. As soon as she walked through the doors, the tantalizing aroma of the rich variety of single origin coffees greeted her. She chose a small table by the window and put her coat on the empty chair across from her. As she loosened the scarf around her neck, she thought of Marisol and Joaquín again. By now they had been in the air for over two hours.

"Madame?"

She looked up to a middle-aged server in a charcoal-gray shirt and a black bistro apron over narrow dark pants.

She ordered the vegetarian sandwich, and before the server left, she added, "Et une grande tasse café au lait."

She turned her head to the window, and as she looked at the overcast sky, she twirled her fingers around the edges of Marisol's scarf.

Joaquín had assured her that all his plans were made under the safest guidelines, always suspect of the Miraldo men and their morally suspect connections. He and Marisol would not even go to the rabbi's house, instead they'd meet in a hotel in a northern suburb of Chicago where Joaquín had rented a two-bedroom suite under his name. "If anyone is curious, Marisol will be my aunt," he had said.

"I'll be very careful," Marisol reassured Ursula and Mick before leaving Switzerland.

"Remember that Molly believes Mama and I are dead," Mick said. "And the last time she saw you, she was four years old. No matter how carefully and discreetly you approach her, what if she doesn't believe you? What if she goes to Mateo or Marco, asking if they know a Marisol Rodriguez?"

"My sweet boy. I'm still giving my plans a lot of thought." Marisol laid her hand on her heart. "I'll let the universe guide me."

"Madame? Avez-vous fini?"

Ursula didn't realize she was pressing the woolly scarf against her mouth until she heard the server's voice.

She nodded. "Everything was delicious," she said and paid the check.

The attentive server took her coat off the chair and held it open for her. "Did anyone ever tell you that you resemble Catherine Deneuve? *The Last Metro* was one of my favorite movies."

"No." She blushed. "But thank you for the compliment." She lowered her head as she buttoned her coat.

The server took another step back. "Definitely a resemblance." He smiled.

When the doors of Café Verlet closed behind her, her cell phone rang. Bernard.

"Everything okay, chérie? I returned to the hotel earlier than expected."

Eager to be near him again, she quickened her pace. "I'm on my way now. See you soon."

Ursula was unusually quiet throughout the seven-course meal at Maison Jérôme.

Claudette Dubois had made the dinner invitation in honor of Mick, and the conversation revolved mostly around his art. Although Ursula delighted in the attention given to her son, she discreetly kept looking at her wristwatch. *It's almost midnight.* The Air France plane had either landed or would touch down any minute in Chicago.

Joaquín had promised to text from O'Hare. Maybe he'd done it already? Without thinking, she reached for the silenced phone in her Birkin bag. *Don't be disrespectful,* she reproached herself, but as she was about to excuse herself from the table, she felt Claudette Dubois's eyes on her.

"Les peintures de Mick sont très demandées," Claudette said. "That's why I want to show your son's work in my galleries in London, Tokyo, New York, and Hong Kong." She looked at Ursula with raised eyebrows, almost as if to seek approval.

"I never tire of hearing how in demand his paintings are," she said, "but Mick is the artist, and he makes all of his own decisions." Ursula smiled at the willowy middle-aged woman with short purple hair and matching fingernails.

Galerie Fleur Dubois in the eighteenth arrondissement was one of the most esteemed galleries in Paris. When Claudette Dubois, the founder's daughter, discovered Mick's work the previous year, she immediately offered to represent him. Since then, his paintings had stirred the insatiable curiosity of esteemed art collectors in Europe and overseas.

"Mmm." Claudette dabbed her mouth with her black napkin, then turned her attention to Mick again. "You know my goal in the contemporary art market has always been to bring rising stars to light. Your star, Mick Rossi, is rising fast." She looked around the table. "Just think: in less than four months his work will be shown at the Biennale Arte in Venice!" She paused to inspect the cork from the bottle the sommelier had put in front of her and gave her approval to decant the wine. "Many of my prominent clients and art connoisseurs hope to meet you personally. And since I plan to be in Hong Kong and Tokyo in March, the timing will be perfect for you to join me." She tilted her head. "What do you say?"

"I've never been to Asia." Mick tugged on his shirt collar. "I want to say yes"—he smoothed the napkin on his lap—"but a very close family member is gravely ill." He gave Ursula and Bernard a hurried look. "If possible, I'd like to wait another month before giving you my answer."

Claudette shrugged. "Je comprends. But the sooner, the better."

"Excusez-moi." Ursula rose from her chair and headed for the stairwell that led to the restrooms below. Two stylishly dressed women stopped talking when they passed her in the narrow hallway, then resumed their loud, carefree chitchat as they made their way upstairs.

Ursula entered the empty restroom. When she retrieved her phone, there was a new text message.

We're in limo on way to the hotel. My brother and family will meet us there. M. is doing very well. She slept five hours during the flight. Call if you're still awake.

Although Joaquin had long ago installed end-to-end encryption on everybody's phones for texts as well as audio and video calls, Ursula reminded herself not to mention names or locations when she tapped on Joaquin's number.

"Hey, you! That was fast!"

His happy-go-lucky voice brought a smile to her face. "So happy you guys made it safely," she said. "I was able to escape the dinner table for a few minutes. It's been a long, promising evening for our young artist."

"Just as we expected," Joaquin said. "Anyway, the flight was comfortable, and I already texted you that our friend slept for five hours. She looks and feels good. Here, I'll let her tell you herself."

"Me siento muy bien, mi niña," Marisol said.

Ursula couldn't stop her eyes from misting over. "It's good to hear your voice. I've been worried."

"Don't, please. I'm feeling stronger than I have in a long time."

"I don't just mean your health, I—you know."

Marisol sighed. "We've been through this, mi amiga. The universe will guide me. There's no guarantee I'll be able to connect with *her*, but I'm determined to try. If it's not to be . . . then perhaps it will be enough for me to see *our girl* from across the street."

Ursula heard fragments of Joaquín's conversation with the driver.

"We've arrived at the hotel," Marisol said. "Please don't worry about me, mi niña."

THIRTY-TWO

Molly, June 2019
Milwaukee, Wisconsin

A rumble of thunder wakes me up. Rain drums against the windowpanes. My eyelids feel leaden and when I manage to lift them, everything looks different. Why do the warm neutral walls in my cozy bedroom appear gray? Even my beautiful furniture appears lifeless, without a shadow. The whole atmosphere seems heavy and melancholy.

I press the button on the remote that opens the blackout curtains, reluctantly get out of bed, and move towards the window. They forecasted clear skies and sunshine, but rain is coming down in unbroken, slightly slanting strings.

"Raindrops are like kisses from heaven—" *Omigod! Is my mother's voice ringing in my head?* Abruptly, a memory of my childhood comes to light.

Warm and damp air greets us when Mamá opens the terrace doors. "Raindrops are like kisses from heaven; they know how to wash all your worries away," she says. We're sitting on the floor, Mamá between Miggy and me. We hold hands and watch the rain, listen to its pitter-patter.

"It sounds as if itsy-bitsy feet are moving about," I say.

"Perhaps there are tiny fairies and dwarves that live between the flowers, the palms, and the shrubs," Mamá says.

I ask her to invite the fairies and dwarves to come inside our house to dry off and wait until the sun comes out again, but Miggy is afraid the tiny imaginary beings will steal his stuffed animals and crawl into his bed. "Don't be afraid," I tell him. "The magic creatures can have my bed. I'll sleep in yours." He likes the idea.

Mamá stands between the open doors and shouts into the rain:

"Our doors are open to all of you.
You're welcome to stay till the sky turns blue.
We have cookies and lemonade during rainy hours,
And you can teach us your magical powers."

The sudden memory fades, but Mamá's singsong voice and silvery laughter is still ringing clear and pleasing in my ears when suddenly it's overpowered by a rumble of thunder, allowing yesterday's videos to penetrate my mind again. My heart cramps.

I press my forehead against the window. *Will life ever be normal again? Is there a magic trick that'll make the absence of normality normal? If my past is wrecked already, will my future be questionable?*

Maxwell believes everything might become more transparent after I confront *him*. Dear God, I don't even know what to call him from now on. Pops? Father? Mateo?

Maxwell says I should act like nothing happened, play dumb and continue to call *him* Pops for the time being. Really? How? It was the name I once used fondly, lovingly. But knowing about his crimes, how can I stay unruffled in his presence, look into his eyes?

I jump when the alarm goes off, like it does on every ordinary weekday morning at six thirty. But after these dreadful past two days nothing is ordinary anymore.

On an ordinary morning I would make coffee, take a shower, have something to eat, and read the news. Prior to this past weekend I still was interested in finding out whether Trump would reach an agreement with Mexico to avoid tariffs. I was looking up stories describing the crane that fell onto an apartment complex in

Dallas, killing two people; MiraCo was in negotiation to acquire the large property where the faulty crane had stood. Now nothing appears to be ordinary anymore.

I turn away from the window. Feeling as though I'm walking through sludge, I trudge towards my bed again but stop short when the large painting above my headboard catches my eye.

I've never considered myself an art aficionado. All the art in my apartment was chosen by interior designers, except for this painting in my bedroom. It was a gift from Annie and Dwight. They gave it to me when I turned twenty-one. I still lived on Bayside Drive with *him* in those days and was forced to hide it because he detested Annie.

Why am I staring at it now like I'm seeing it for the first time?

Maxwell loves art. The day I showed him the painting, he pointed out the unique technique the artist used to create the illusion of three dimension and went on about the work's hypnotic quality, achieved through glazing and color washes.

I stare at my painting. A slight dark-haired girl in an opaque, almost translucent pinafore dress peers down at a sheet of what I think is meant to be ice. The girl's mass of tangled curls falls over her face, her likeness indistinctly reflected in the pellucid depths below the ice. The way she stands, the way her thin arms and small hands reach down, conveys an alarming vulnerability. Below the straight line of ice is the bare backside of a boy with light hair. He stands on his toes, reaching upward; the tips of his small fingers perforate the ice barrier, touching the girl's fingers. Blurry images of their phantasmagorical faces mirror themselves on all sides of the painting, hands pierce through crystalline walls.

I've had this painting for the past nine years, and it's never impacted me like this before. Why now does it make me crumble in a Kafkaesque way I'm unprepared to deal with? Have the past weekend's revelations caused me to draw a parallel between my lost childhood and the girl and boy in the painting? My throat closes and my eyes release wounded tears. An angry wail escapes my lips.

"Oh, Molly." The gentle voice behind me immediately eases my loneliness. Only now do I remember that Maxwell spent the night in the guest room. I turn, throw my arms around him, and cling to his body as if it's the only secure sanctuary left in the world.

"What can I do for you?"

I bury my face in his T-shirt, and without looking I point to the painting. "I don't know who painted it, but that person must have felt the same way I feel now." Reluctantly I detach myself from him and apologize for sniveling into his shirt.

"Do you remember how thrilled I was the day you decided to hang this piece?" Maxwell hands me sheets of Kleenex. "After what you just unearthed, I can see how the images might affect you."

"Yeah."

"Wasn't it a gift from your stepmother? Why did she want you to have it?"

I stare at it again. "She said she saw it in an exhibit in Geneva and somehow thought of me. She and Dwight met the artist, even wanted to commission a painting from him."

"They met him? Who is he?"

I turn and walk to my dresser. In the bottom right drawer, under a vintage Loro Piana hoodie I found on eBay, is the envelope. I hand it to Maxwell. He removes the certificate of authenticity. "This artwork is a one-of-a-kind, authentic, original painting. All copyright and reproduction rights are reserved by the artist," he reads. "It's titled *Dually Destined* and was created in 2008 by Mick Rossi." He taps at the name on the certificate. "Mick?"

"So?"

"What if it's short for Miguel?" he asks with raised eyebrows.

I shake my head.

"Yesterday you suddenly remembered that your brother loved to draw. What if—"

I look at the painting again. A girl and a boy are cut off from each other, separated by unyielding barriers. They're desperately attempting to reach for each other. My heart cramps again. "Okay, fine. You win. Let's google Mick Rossi."

"This guy is doubly blessed: great talent and sooo handsome," says Maxwell as he scrolls on my Mac. "Look how he gets light to come through the paint, how he creates multiple layers of transparent colors." He clicks on another painting and enlarges it. "His work is beyond-real realism."

Even though I don't have much artistic knowledge, I understand that there's never a right or wrong way to interpret art. But when I look at Mick Rossi's paintings on the screen, I wonder if my untrained eyes detect the mind behind his art.

When Maxwell clicks on another link, a new headshot of Mick Rossi pops up. "Look, he's got full, curved lips and a dimple in his right cheek. Just like you."

My skin is tingling, but levelheadedness takes over. "Pure coincidence."

"Really? Why is there no bio for him in any search result?"

"Because he's young? Not that famous yet?"

"Still unusual," says Maxwell, still scrolling. "There's zero personal info except for one article that mentions he was raised in Switzerland."

I shrug.

"*Raised* in Switzerland, Molly. It doesn't say *born and raised* in Switzerland," he challenges. "After what your mother went through, isn't it possible that she went back to her country of origin with your brother?"

Again, I shrug. "We've searched for Ursula Rossi in Switzerland already. Only three popped up, none of them my mother."

"I'm not giving up." He puffs out his cheeks and keeps clicking and scrolling.

My phone dings, displaying a message notification. "Omigod it's *him*." I elbow Maxwell.

"What's he saying?"

I check the message. *Our flight is delayed due to weather. Call me. We need to discuss the Mira Mall and the Mira Apartment Tower in Toronto. I made a connection over the weekend that may allow us to add another parcel of land and develop it.*

"Call him back," says Maxwell. "You and I agreed to act as if nothing happened. Not until we come up with a plan."

"I don't know how I'll get through a phone call with P—with *him*," I mutter.

He scratches behind his right ear, then does what he always does when he's lost in thought: his gaze wanders slowly past me, glides up to the ceiling, then down the walls, and crawls through the air in small arcs before it finally gets stuck somewhere on the floor. "In the videos with your twin and mother you always called him abuelo. When did you start calling him Pops?"

I gasp when a new memory flashes before my eyes.

I'm sitting in a bathtub. An elderly, kind-looking woman sings to me. "Esta niña linda que nació de día—" She laughs when I splash water on her face, then continues to sing. "Quiere que la lleven a pasear en coche."

Abuelo comes into the bathroom and tells the woman she's no longer needed. He seats himself on the edge of the bathtub, rolls up his white shirtsleeves, and washes my back with a big soapy sponge.

"I'm not really your abuelo," he says.

I start crying. "Not abuelo? Who are you?"

He grins. "Wouldn't you like me to be your papa instead?" He reaches into the water and rotates the knob on top of the drain stopper. "Your other papa is hardly ever around. He never plays with you, shows no interest. I'm with you all the time." He rinses my body and hair with fresh water. "Soon we'll move to the United States, and you'll have to speak English. Perfect time to stop calling me abuelo."

I watch the water gurgle down the drain. "Why?"

"It doesn't matter, mi dulce Molarita." He wraps me in a big soft towel. "It's a good thing you can't remember anything." He rubs my body dry. "I'm your papa, your Pops. I love you so much. You are mine."

"Omigod, in Mexico he once alluded to not being my grandfather." I put my hand on my forehead as if that will rein in my thoughts. "I think I'm going to be sick. It's too much to handle."

"Be strong, Molly, like your mother."

"Right," I say quietly for want of more appropriate words to express the depth of my emotions. "You're right," I repeat tonelessly. After taking a moment to fret, I shrug my shoulders, like I'm giving myself permission to do what needs to be done.

Without another thought, I type in a reply.

You're better off staying where you are! My mood is as bad as the weather! No need to come back.

Maxwell sniggers. "Gutsy!"

"I have to be from now on," I say and forcefully hit Enter. "Sent."

He gives me a thumbs-up. "I'm going to take a shower, and then we can go back to researching Mick Rossi."

I roll my eyes. "Are you sure you don't just like looking at pictures of him? Like I said, it would be a monumental coincidence if he turned out to be my brother."

Maxwell's eyes glimmer. "There are no coincidences. You should consider your earlier reaction to his painting as a sign that you're close to discovering something big—even bigger than what you've already dug up."

"You know I don't believe in signs."

"Well, I do!"

"In that case give me a sign for what I should do next."

"You make an appointment with that guy you met at Five Elements. The PI."

"Good idea! Phil Flores!"

THIRTY-THREE

Mateo, January 2019
Mira, Wisconsin

"No! Stay where you are," Mateo said sharply. "I'll be there in fifteen minutes." He disconnected the call before the other party could say goodbye and opened the door to the conference room.

"As you can see, we will have to dig deeper before we know which areas open for us," said Lauren Maloney, the senior vice president of marketing and corporate communications. She interrupted her presentation when she saw him walk into the room. "Mr. Miraldo," she said, smiling broadly. "Perfect timing to give us your perspective."

Mateo flashed his palm at the forty-something brunette, who regularly wore too-tight sweaters and always walked provocatively straight, as if to make her breasts look like an invitation. "Something came up," he said and turned to Marco. "Take over for me."

On his way to the elevator, Mateo glanced through the glass panes into Molara's office. Watching her talk to the computer screen softened his surly expression. Most likely she was still in a Zoom meeting with the secretary of housing and urban development. Though she didn't notice him, he gave her a thumbs-up, hoping she'd get the approval they needed to finalize their enormous Sunset Springs Tower complex. As far back as the previous year, Mateo had laid the groundwork with all the right people, and in the process, the secretary of housing and urban development had become a good friend. *No problem. My girl will push this deal through.*

He took the elevator to the ground floor, stepped outside, and shivered. The sky was steel gray, and despite the gusting wind, the tree branches were motionless. Snow was falling, though none of it stuck to the ground. He used the key fob to start his SUV; whenever possible he preferred to drive the short distance between MiraCo's headquarters and his house himself. He lowered his head and rushed to the car. The thin flakes landing on his face felt like fine pinpricks. Dammit, why hadn't he parked in the heated underground garage?

He slammed the door shut. The vents blew cold air, and he shivered, recalling the unsettling news from Pelón.

"Yoli called me after noticing a sedan idling in the street for an unusual length of time," the bodyguard had said. "You may wanna to get home soon 'cause one of the two people in the car is a person of great interest."

Mateo increased his speed. *Time to install cameras around the house*, he thought.

The second he turned into Bayside Drive, a black cat shot out of nowhere, stopped in the middle of the street, arched its back, and looked straight at Mateo's vehicle. He slammed on the brakes. Only when the car screeched to a halt did the feline dart away. He cursed and thought of his Portuguese father, who regarded all black cats as companions of witches and bearers of misfortune.

Making sure the damn black cat hadn't somehow followed him, he kept his eyes on the garage door until it closed.

Pelón was in the kitchen, talking on his phone. "Entremos en mi oficina," Mateo said, signaling the bodyguard to follow him into his study. "Start from the beginning."

"I was on another *assignment* when Yoli called and interrupted a rather delicate operation." Pelón sounded more gruff than usual. When he plopped himself onto the vintage hand-carved high-backed chair, its wooden frame creaked under his weight.

"Well, I appreciate your loyalty." Mateo didn't care if his voice revealed irritation. Lately, he felt the need to distance himself from Pelón. Troubled, he eyed the bald bodyguard. He seemed bulkier. Were those dark, puffy bags under his eyes the result of extreme fatigue or a fatty liver? Maybe both. "What was so important that you had to call me away from my business?"

"As soon as I turned into Bayside Drive, I saw a blue Hyundai Accent parked in the street, right across from your house. But the second I stopped next to it, it sped away. I immediately turned my truck around, trying to chase the Hyundai, but . . ." Pelón grimaced. "The streets in this neighborhood are a fucking labyrinth," he grumbled.

"Get to the point. You mentioned a person of interest."

After he lost track of the Hyundai, Pelón reported, he'd questioned Yoli. She'd seen the blue sedan earlier in the morning, following Señor Miraldo when he left for MiraCo's headquarters. She didn't think anything of it until she spotted the car again a few hours later, sitting in the street with its engine idling and windshield wipers intermittently dusting off the flakes. Behind the wheel was a middle-aged man, and a silver-haired older woman sat in the passenger seat. After some time, they drove away again. Yoli continued to do her work, somewhat on edge, until the blue Hyundai returned an hour or so later, slowly drove around the circular driveway, and parked in the street, just as before. At that point Yoli called Pelón.

"Had your housekeeper notified me the first time she saw the car, I wouldn't have had to interrupt my other assignment," he said, shifting his bulk in the groaning chair.

"That's an heirloom," Mateo said. "I'd appreciate it if you sat over there." He pointed to the leather club chair across from him.

"Claro, jefe." Pelón repositioned himself and slapped the leather cushion. "Anyway, I was pissed that they got away from me, but I'll be a monkey's uncle—the idiots returned again."

"Stop your damn prologue and come to the point, please."

"From behind one of the kitchen windows, I clearly saw the guy; he looked like he was in his forties. The woman was older. Maybe mother and son, I thought. Anyway, I was about to head out to the street and ask them what their business was when the car pulled up the driveway and the old woman came to the front door." Pelón smacked his lips. "Excuse me, jefe, but I'm parched." He heaved himself out of the chair and without another word left the room.

"What the . . ." Dumbfounded, Mateo stared at the door as if that would make the hairless halfwit return faster.

"So, who was the woman?" he said when the bodyguard entered the study again, swinging an already half-empty large bottle of Evian in his left hand.

"Well." A tight-lipped smile formed on Pelón's lips. "Who've you been looking for since 1992?"

"¿Qué?" Disjointed thoughts zipped through Mateo's head. Was he talking about Ula? No, Ula wasn't an old woman with silver hair. He touched his forehead; his hand felt clammy. "C'mon! Stop your damn guessing games," he roared.

"The woman who came to the front door of your house was Mar-i-sol Ro-dri-guez."

Mateo leaped to his feet, almost tumbling over the ottoman. "Marisol?" He staggered towards his wet bar, took the Clase Azul bottle off the shelf, and with an unsteady hand, poured tequila into a glass. Ignoring the spillage on the shiny mahogany, he slammed back the double shot. The invigorating rush felt good. "¡Dios mío! Marisol Rodríguez?" He straightened his back. "Give me the details."

When the old woman approached the house, Pelón explained, he'd pressed himself against the wall, ready to jump into action as Yoli opened the front door.

"May I help you?"

"My name is Marisol Rodriguez. I came to see Molly. Is she at home?"

"You mean Ms. Molara Miraldo? Sorry, she's unavailable."

The old woman's voice was brittle. "When and where can I reach her?"

"You should go to MiraCo's headquarters."

"I've been there," Marisol Rodriguez said. "Please, I know this is her address. When will she be home? I can wait in the car."

"I'm sorry, but I can't help you." Yoli was about to close the massive door when Pelón pushed her out of the way. He stared down the fragile woman, wearing a thermal-reflective brown down coat that was a few sizes too big. A faux-fur-trimmed hood was pulled over her head; a few loose strands of silver hair had fallen on her sunken cheeks.

"What do you know? Marisol Rodriguez! I recognize you from the pictures." He leaned towards her, grinning mischievously. "What brings you back after so many years? What's your business with Molara?"

"My visit is personal." A rush of wind blew a new silver strand across the old woman's mouth. She didn't wipe it away, keeping both hands in her coat's pockets.

"Marisol Rodriguez!" Pelón snickered. "Please come inside."

"No, I can't do that." Visibly shaken, she stepped back too quickly and slipped on the wet slate tile. Trying to steady herself on one of the pillars, she yanked her right hand from the coat pocket, and with that, an envelope fluttered to the ground. When she bent down to retrieve it, Pelón stepped on her fingers with his heavy boot.

"My letter." The woman groaned and attempted to pull her hand and the envelope from under his foot.

"What about your letter?" He grabbed her sleeve, holding on tightly. "I know who you are; I've been looking for you way too long."

When Pelón slammed the woman against the pillar, a man jumped from the blue sedan. "You let her go this instant or the police will be on their way," he shouted, holding his cell phone in is hand.

"¡Sin policía! ¡Sin policía!" Yoli appeared in the frame of the big door, frantically waving her arms. "Don't call the police!"

Cursing loudly, Pelón released Marisol Rodriguez from his grip and pushed her away.

"You let her go?" Mateo threw his glass into the wet bar's copper sink. Ignoring the loud crunch and shards of glass flying, he walked towards Pelón. "Why?"

"Because *you* instructed us to keep the police away from your house at all costs unless there's a burglary or a life-threatening emergency." The bodyguard returned Mateo's death stare. "*You* don't want to sully your spotless reputation."

"Damn!" Mateo staggered backwards, pointing his finger at Pelón. "Damn!"

"Relax, Jefe. I got the letter!" He pulled the envelope from his pocket.

Mateo ripped it open.

My sweet Molly,
You might not remember me, but I was your and your brother's nanny in Mexico.

You and I were kidnapped at the airport in Miami in 1992; only I was able to escape.

I've tried but haven't been able to get in touch with you. I need to speak with you in person. This letter might be my last possible course of action. I pray it will get safely into your hands.

Please call me as soon as you can—I will be in this country for another two days. 1-929-718-2810.

I desperately want to see you again but more so want to tell you about your mother and twin brother.

You deserve to know what happened. The truth has been hidden from you. You have the right to know what really happened.

Your loving Marisol

"Did you call? Where is the bitch?"
"These fucking guys worked fast."
"What are you saying?"
"Of course I called that number immediately. But they either

destroyed the SIM card or microwaved their burner phone soon after they took off from here."

Mateo stared at the letter as if a secret message were encrypted in the words. "Now what?"

"I have more." Pelón opened the gallery on his phone. "Look, I was able to get a picture of the car and the license plate." Visibly pleased with himself, he added, "I already made inquiries."

"And . . ."

"I traced the license plate back to an Enterprise rental company in Skokie, Illinois." Pelón kept his eyes on the small screen while typing with his fat thumbs. "I got the renter's name, address, and phone number from the rental company."

"They just gave it to you?"

"For shit like this, I use my connections." Pelón leaned his head closer to the screen and squinted. "Joaquín Hebroni, 4131 Johnstown Road, East Dundee, Illinois. Phone number—" He glanced at Mateo. "Well, we can forget about the fucking number."

"What about the address?"

"Nonexistent. Another fake."

"And the name?"

"There are three listings for the surnames in Illinois: a Dr. Joshua Hebroni in Springfield, a Rabbi David Hebroni in Lincolnwood, and a Miriam Hebroni, listed under a Chicago investment firm." Pelón looked up. "No Joaquín Hebroni."

"The bitch says she'll be in this country for another two days." Mateo waved the letter in front of Pelón's face. "What about your contacts? Can they hack into airline manifests?"

"That's tough, but it's been done before." Pelón finished the rest of his Evian. "There's some vulnerability in the booking system used by most international airlines." He heaved himself out of the leather chair and pointed to the wet bar. "I need to fill my bottle again."

"Call your hacker right away and give him the names," Mateo yelled as his bodyguard passed him.

"That won't be easy. My guy will have to reach out to someone else with more technical knowledge." The bodyguard rubbed his right thumb over the tip of his index and middle finger and grinned. "It'll cost you."

"I don't give a damn," Mateo squawked. "This is my first chance in almost three decades to find out where they've been hiding."

"I'll get on it then," Pelón said, already texting.

Mateo stiffened when he heard the knock. He opened the door to his study just a crack.

"Your caterers are here, señor," Yoli said. "Unless you need to tell them something specific, I can handle everything."

"Do that," he said and closed the door.

Damn. Confronted with these new discoveries, Mateo had forgotten he was hosting a dinner for the governor and his wife. Other attendees included talk show host Carlson Turner, the Honorable Sean Maloney, the newly elected Senator Ella Knight, and their spouses. As for his own date, Mateo had invited Bridget von Barnheim, the attractive socialite he'd met a few weeks ago at a fundraiser in Washington, DC, when her second divorce was all over the news. Her first husband had been a bigwig in Silicon Valley, her second a media mogul. After divorce number one, Bridget had parted with an enormous amount of her ex's fortune, and it looked as if history would repeat itself. Mateo was aware of the rumors that for some time already he had been on this woman's radar. Even prior to the fundraiser in DC, she'd purchased a multi-million-dollar home on Lake Michigan, only twenty minutes away from Mateo's Bayside Drive address.

He had less than three hours before his guests arrived. With so many unresolved issues hanging in the air, would he be able to live up to his reputation as the perfect host?

First, he had to get Pelón out of his house.

"I have things to do," he said, suddenly aware of the disorder in his study. "Text me as soon as your source comes up with information."

"It's obvious you need to get rid of me." Pelón put on his heavy jacket and pulled a black knit cap over his bald head. "I snapped a picture of the old woman and the guy while they sat in the car. It's not very clear. I'm gonna text it to you."

It took some effort for Mateo to pull himself together before he walked into the prep kitchen to greet George Mitchell, Mira-Co's catering director. George and his team had been to the Bayside residence on numerous occasions, and Mateo trusted everything would run smoothly, as always. He glanced into the dining room. The table was set to perfection, and its elegant décor was enhanced by seasonal floral arrangements.

"I'm going upstairs to take care of some business," he said. "If needed, Yoli will be of assistance."

Mateo locked the door to his bedroom suite behind him, then headed for the antique Mexican cabinet, put his hand on the bronze column, and gave it a half twist. Click. Another full twist and the secret cabinet opened. He sat down, took the stack of photos from the box, and quickly sifted through the old pictures until he found one of Marisol and the children. Then he clicked on the somewhat blurry snapshot Pelón had just sent him. He enlarged the images of the two people in the car. Though older, more timeworn and sickly looking, the woman was, without a doubt, Marisol Rodriguez.

He wished he had been at home when that witch Marisol knocked on his front door. He likely would've had no control over his impulses, and Marisol's visit would've been her last act on this earth. And whoever this Joaquín Hebroni was, Pelón would've dealt with him as well.

"Those hackers better bring results soon," Mateo mumbled as he neatly stacked the photos and laid them next to the letters, tied with a red ribbon. He blinked. Ula's letters. Overcome by an unexpected urge to watch the videos, he licked his dry lips and stared into the nothingness of his surroundings. The complexity of it all overwhelmed him all at once. "Oh God," he whispered. "Only you know how deeply I love and desire her. Why did you allow fate to meet me on a road I so desperately wanted to avoid?"

THIRTY-FOUR

Ursula, January 2019
Crans-Montana, Switzerland

I had to increase Marisol's medication because her condition has worsened," said Joaquin. "She needs refills, and for obvious reasons we can't consult with a physician in the States."

Ursula's hand was pressed over her mouth as she watched Joaquin's worried face on the screen. "I should've talked her out of going on this trip," she managed to say.

"No. You know how much Marisol wanted to do this. David spent every free moment with her until—" Joaquin peered over his shoulder. "Sorry, I thought I heard something."

"Marisol? Where is she?"

"Sleeping in the next room—she was very fatigued. Though she never complains, it's obvious how much pain she's in. She's also lost more weight."

Ursula, flanked by Bernard and Bruno, looked from one to the other and then back into the FaceTime camera on her Mac. "Marisol cannot fly commercial in her condition. There are private medical jets."

Bruno nodded at the screen. "I'll arrange a transport with Air Ambulance Worldwide for tomorrow. They'll contact you directly once everything is scheduled." He put his right hand over his heart, smiling at his husband. "Can't wait to have you back here."

As Bruno excused himself to make the calls, Ursula noticed

a door slowly opening behind Joaquín's back. Dressed in a white robe, Marisol walked towards the screen and sat next to him.

"Mi Ursula, mi Bernard. Como extraño a todos."

Seeing Marisol's hollow cheeks and yellowish pallor, Ursula reached for Bernard's hand below the desk.

"Did Joaquín already tell you what happened?"

"No. He said you may want to do that."

Marisol nodded, smiling thinly. "I didn't achieve all I'd hoped for, but after more than two decades, the universe allowed me to see our beautiful Molly."

Ursula swallowed, tightly linking her fingers with Bernard's.

"When we couldn't reach Molly at MiraCo's headquarters, we drove to a palatial property on Bayside Drive—the one that's listed as Molly's home address," Marisol said. "It was already late in the afternoon, and our car was the only one parked on the street in this quiet neighborhood."

"It seemed out of place," Joaquín agreed. "I suggested we come back early the next morning when there'd be other cars belonging to workmen or staff."

Marisol nodded. "But the same moment we decided to drive away, a Prius sped up the street, pulled into the driveway, and a young dark-haired woman jumped out from the passenger side. She carried a briefcase and sprinted to the front door. We knew she'd come back because she'd left the car door open."

Ursula held her breath.

"We couldn't see who opened the front door or who the young woman handed the briefcase to, but"—Marisol's eyes lit up and her voice increased in pitch—"when the girl ran back to the car, I saw her."

Molly!

"Even after so many years, I recognized that beautiful face."

"Did—did she see you?"

Marisol shook her head. "Everything happened so fast. Whoever was driving the car was in a hurry. I rolled down the window and waved frantically, hoping to make them stop, but they either didn't notice me or didn't care."

Still holding on tightly to Bernard's hand, Ursula listened as Joaquín and Marisol took turns recounting how they'd followed the car back to the Mother Mary Shelter in Milwaukee, where Marisol called Molly's name in the parking lot.

"But she didn't hear me. Molly and the young man who drove the Prius were busy helping other people unload their cars and carry containers and boxes into the building."

Joaquín nodded. "By the time I assisted Marisol to the building, the door had been closed already. I kept knocking until someone opened—it was the same man who'd arrived with Molly. He apologized, saying he couldn't let us in and directing us to the front entry of the shelter. When we got there, two uniformed men expressed regret, letting us know we were too late for the evening meal registration."

"It was quite cold." Marisol's voice was brittle, her breaths coming shallow and irregular. "I explained we hadn't come for food or shelter but wanted to speak to Molara Miraldo."

Omigod, she looks drained of life. Ursula kept biting her lower lip.

"Marisol begged the officers to make an exception," Joaquín said. "She told them she'd traveled far and it might be her last chance to connect with Molly. However, the men stood their ground, telling us to come back in the morning when the manager was on duty."

Please, this can't be it, Ursula cried inwardly. *This simply can't be the end of it.*

"Mi dulce Ursula, forgive me," Marisol rasped, smiling weakly. "It was a long day. Joaquín will have to tell you the rest."

Ursula watched Joaquín assist Marisol into the other room. A few minutes later he returned to whatever desk or table his laptop sat on in a hotel room seven thousand miles away. She stopped biting the inside of her lip.

"I'm afraid to ask what happened next, but do tell me everything."

The following morning they'd decided to make one more trip to Bayside Drive in Mira, hoping to catch Molly on her way to work.

Around ten o'clock, a shiny black Mercedes GLS 450 emerged from the four-door garage. Because of its dark tinted windows, it was impossible to see who was in the car. So they followed the SUV to MiraCo's headquarters. When Marisol saw an elderly man emerge from the car, she gasped. "It's him. The ogre."

Since Molly hadn't been in the SUV, Joaquín decided it was time for plan B. He got out of the Hyundai, passed by the main entry, peered into the lobby, and against his better judgment, stepped inside.

"May I help you?" A security guard, impeccably dressed in a light-gray suit and burgundy shirt, stood in front of Joaquín.

"I-I'm here to see Ms. Molara Miraldo."

The guard escorted him to the reception desk. Three young ladies, identically dressed in pale burgundy suits and silver-gray blouses, were quietly talking into their Bluetooth headphones, typing on their keyboards while staring at screens. The guard waited until one of the women looked up—the tag affixed to the lapel of her suit read *Lorelei*.

The receptionist decorated her face with a broad smile. "Do you have an appointment with Ms. Miraldo?"

"Yes." Joaquín surprised himself with his brazen reply.

"Whom shall I announce?"

Joaquín swallowed, gave his name, and watched Lorelei speak softly into her wireless headphone.

"Someone will be with you shortly, Mr. Hebroni. Please wait over there." Never changing her non-Duchenne smile, Lorelei pointed to the seating areas.

Wearing blue jeans and a hooded tan parka, Joaquín felt out of place, especially when his dark-blue Matterhorn boots made a loud squeaky noise on the marble floors of MiraCo's ice palace. While waiting in this cold and formal atmosphere, everybody appeared circumspect. Trying to appear as inconspicuous as possible, he looked up at the gallery. What would he do if Mateo or Marco unexpectedly came through one of those glass doors, head towards him, ask him questions? Knowing as much as he did of the Miraldo men's past illegal activities and corrupt immoral behavior, how would he react facing them? Calculating his options, Joaquín decided to leave as quickly as possible. But the moment he headed for the exit, a voice startled him.

"Mr. Hebroni?"

Joaquín spun around, immediately recognizing the face; it was the driver of the Prius. Stunned, Joaquín nodded.

"Maxwell Walsh," the young man said and offered to shake his hand. "You have an appointment with Ms. Miraldo?"

Joaquín kept nodding.

"Your name isn't on her schedule today. May I ask what your visit is about?"

Though he'd mastered many difficult situations in his life, Joaquín couldn't remember feeling as uneasy as he did at this very moment. "Actually, I'm only the go-between," he managed to say. "There's someone else who needs to deliver a very important message to Molly—to Ms. Miraldo." He lowered his voice. "It's a delicate situation, and my friend would appreciate if she could meet with Ms. Miraldo in private—not here."

Maxwell Walsh apologized. "Unless you tell me what this is about, I can't make that happen."

Joaquín swallowed his nervousness. "My friend's name is Marisol Rodriguez. She knows Molly from Mexico and needs to see her, hopefully today." He fumbled in his parka pocket for pen and paper, quickly scribbled down a number, and handed it to the young man. "Please give this to Molly."

Why did Maxwell Walsh turn his head, as if he was looking for someone? The security guard? Joaquín's antennae, already up, suddenly stood on high alert. What if someone detained him? Dear God! Marisol was all alone in the cold car, waiting for him. "Tell Molly it's urgent," Joaquín said and hurried away.

After telling Marisol what had taken place in MiraCo's lobby, Joaquín drove to a small restaurant a few miles away.

Marisol took only a few bites of a BLT sandwich. "Molly might not remember my name and most likely was brainwashed," she said. "If she doesn't call back within the next couple of hours, I'd like to write her a note and deliver it in person today. I won't have the strength to do it tomorrow."

They were sitting in silence, watching the house on Bayside Drive and waiting for the phone to ring, when a dark van pulled up next to their Hyundai and a brutish-looking man opened the van's door.

"Drive away," Marisol cried out. "That man reminds me of the ogre's bodyguards at the hacienda."

As Joaquín sped away, he saw the van turn around and come after them, but by maneuvering the small rental car through the complicated, irregular network of streets in the area, he lost their pursuer.

Marisol sat rigid, shivering.

"I'm driving you back to the hotel," he said. "You need to rest."

She shook her head. "Molly hasn't called. I must deliver my letter to her today—I can tell my body wants to shut down."

They drove to the home on Bayside Drive again, and when they didn't see the dark van parked in the street or the driveway, Marisol insisted she take her chance.

The inside of her lip felt raw; Ursula stopped biting it. "Please go on," she managed to say.

Joaquín reported he'd kept the engine running and was ready to jump into action should anything go wrong.

A short middle-aged Latina woman answered the door, telling Marisol that Ms. Molara Miraldo wasn't available. Just when the woman attempted to close the door, a big man—the same who had confronted them in the street earlier—pushed the woman aside and in a loud, raspy voice wanted to know what was going on.

Marisol realized she was in danger, but when she tried to rush back to the car, she slipped on the tile, lost her balance, and dropped her letter. As she reached for it, the big man stepped on her hand. "I know who you are," he yelled. "I've been looking for you for a long time."

When Marisol winced, he laughed. "You're doing me a great favor, showing up here voluntarily." He snorted, grabbed her arm, and yanked her towards him. With his face close to hers, he hissed, "Molara believes her mother and brother are dead! You'll never get a chance to tell her differently." The brute slammed Marisol against the wall. "But before I kill you, you'll tell me what I need to hear. Where have you bitches been hiding with the boy?"

"I was freaking out," said Joaquín. "I jumped out of the car and from the top of my lungs yelled that he let go of Marisol. When I threatened to call 911, the Latina woman screamed, 'Sin policía! Sin policía!' That's when the guy let go of Marisol. He punched his fist into the air, yelling, 'I have the fucking letter! I know your fucking faces, and I'll be coming after you!' Then he pulled a gun. As we sped out of the driveway, he was still aiming the weapon at us."

Ursula covered her mouth and nose with both hands. "Oh no! What did Marisol write in her letter?"

"Nothing that would put any of us in harm's way. She wrote that she was Mick and Molly's nanny in Mexico. She mentioned the kidnapping in Miami in 1992 and wrote down the number we were using."

"She gave them a contact number?"

"Don't worry. After the incident, I immediately destroyed the phone."

"What if the bodyguard or the woman took down the license plate number?"

"The car rental agency has my real name, but I gave them a fake address."

"Mateo has connections everywhere. Are airline passenger lists secure?"

"It doesn't matter. Bruno canceled our flights already. Fat chance anyone will think of hacking into international air ambulances."

THIRTY-FIVE

Molly, June 2019
Milwaukee and Chicago

My mug is empty. *How long have I been sitting at the kitchen counter?* I shiver and pull up my knees to cover my feet with the pajama pants.

I look at the time. Already nine o'clock? But what is time? Now that I remember my childhood, how many breaths have I taken since I was ripped away from my mother and twin? How many hours have they been absent from my life?

I hear the faint splashing of water and realize Maxwell is taking a shower in the guest bath. I was going to do the same but was derailed by my thoughts. I'm so cold! I pull my knees closer to my chest, sitting in a fetal position.

With half-closed lids, I glance through the open balcony door and see a small bird. It's perched on top of the boxwood topiary. Another sits on the iron railing. They keep chirping, communicating with each other. The first bird flutters off the topiary to join the other on the railing. They sit close and peck beaks. Then one soars upward and the other one follows.

I am no bird; and no net ensnares me: I am a free human being with an independent will. That's how Jane Eyre responded to Mr. Rochester. Yet under her tough exterior, she longed for love and family.

I also want to be a free human being, and with an independent will, I hope to find love and family. I have to be strong.

I feel the soft touch of a hand on my shoulder. Maxwell.

"My brain won't stop playing this horror movie," I say.

"After you take a shower and get dressed, you'll feel better." He gently pulls me off the chair. "Coffee will be waiting for you, and then you need to call Phil Flores."

I wish it were that easy. When I stand in my bathroom, I feel lost, like I'm in a fog again. My reflection meets me in the mirror. *Who are you?*

I've never had a problem with the way I look. When other girls debated diets and wanted to resemble runway models or drooled over clothes they couldn't afford, I stood on the sidelines, grateful for good genes. My friends expressed jealousy because I didn't have to worry about small breasts or a too-thick waist. Even the color of my hair and my complexion became the envy of others. But here in my bathroom, I stare at my tan face and all I see is my grandfather. *No! That man is my father.* I lean closer to the mirror and stare deep into my eyes. Are they really like those of my delusional ex-grandfather, the beast who drugged and raped my mother? It gives me the creeps.

My phone alerts me to a text. I look around, needing a moment to orient myself before I realize I'm holding the stupid thing in my hand. Another ding. *Pops*, it says on the screen. Not giving it another thought, I hit Decline.

I hear the steady gush of water. When did I turn on the shower? What's happening to me? I move away from the mirror and hold my hand and arm under the spray. It's warm, inviting. I step under it, and in this very private place, I slowly escape from my troubled mind. I allow it to go blank and welcome the hypnotic warmth and gentle sounds. Before turning off the water, I adjust the temperature. The cold water wakes me up, boosts my spirit.

I dry my hair, fasten it in a simple ponytail, and finish my five-minute morning makeup routine.

I pull my favorite jeans and a sleeveless white linen tunic off the hangers, then step into comfortable ballet flats. I look in the mirror and nod. The Molly that looks back at me now is ready to amputate herself from the Miraldo curse. This Molly will not bear the burden of sins from generations before her. This Molly will only be responsible for her own actions.

⁂

"Molly! What a coincidence," Phil Flores says when I work up the nerve to call. "I've been thinking about you."

It doesn't take long for him to realize this isn't a social call and as soon as I stress the urgency of a consultation, he says, "Let me try to reschedule a meeting." Fifteen minutes later he calls me back.

"If you can be at my office by one o'clock, I'll have all afternoon for you."

Thankfully there's smooth sailing on the I-94 but the closer I get to downtown Chicago, the volume of vehicles increases. The early morning dark storms have moved east across the lake, and the sky is such a brilliant shade of blue that it hurts. I adjust my sunglasses and lower the visor. In the rearview mirror I see Maxwell. He's rechecking flash drives and reorganizing the printouts that are spread left and right of him on the back seat.

"Hey!" He doesn't hear me over his noise-canceling headphones. I wave my right hand in the air, then reach back and tap his knee until he looks up.

"Heavy traffic," I say. "It'll take longer than we thought."

"Good. I need more time anyway." His head is already bent over his tasks again.

As I close the distance to Phil Flores's address, an unexpected wave of inquisitiveness washes over me, easing my confusion and disorientation from earlier this morning. I'm ready to face what'll be. *I can do this. I can do anything.*

"Done!" says Maxwell.

I've just exited the 94 and hit a red light. "Quick, come to the front."

As he hops out the back, I notice other people in their cars twist their necks, but Maxwell never notices the attention he attracts with his good looks. He fastens the seat belt next to me and, indifferently, looks straight ahead. "Has Mateo called again?"

"Yup. He left another voice message—said they were in the air and would get here by four. He wants to meet with me at the house because he has 'exciting news' to share with me."

"And? Will you see him?"

"I'm giving myself permission to say no to anyone or anything that depletes me of morale and energy," I say and sharply turn the wheel.

Flores & Associates, it says plainly on the double-hung wood doors on the top floor of the eight-story building on West Randolph Street. A friendly middle-aged woman rises from behind the reception desk and escorts us into one of several rooms. She offers coffee, tea, or water and returns moments later with two glasses and bottles of chilled Evian.

"Mr. Flores will be with you momentarily." She smiles, softly closing the door behind her.

Maxwell spreads his folders out on the table and sets up his laptop. "Ready," he says. "Are you?"

I nod, and through the window, facing east, I see the skyline of Chicago.

"Molly."

Phil, the tall, pencil-thin, balding man with the warm brown eyes and gentle smile, walks into the room.

After a brief hug and a "good to see you again," I introduce Maxwell. Without further comment, Phil Flores seats himself across from us. "It's best if you tell me everything," he says.

And I do.

At first, I stumble over my own words. It's excruciatingly difficult to share what I've found with a third party. But whenever I lose my balance, Phil's eyes and calm voice validate my feelings. He honors my need for a break and only occasionally asks a clarifying question.

I wonder how many betrayed, depressed, and hopeless clients have sat across from Phil and unburdened their hostilities. Did they all seek revenge, expecting that Flores & Associates would render the results they came for?

While I talk, Maxwell hands Phil documents that verify my report. Amazing how much I have to say. Am I asking for too much undivided attention? When at last I think I've told all there is, I'm not only out of breath, but I feel completely empty. As if from far away, I hear Phil ask for the flash drives that contain the photos, letters, and other vital documents. But when he requests the footage Maxwell took of the third videocassette, my strength ebbs and a sense of foreboding rises inside me.

"Why don't you take a break?" Phil says. "We have a roof garden where you can unwind in the shade. Maxwell can fill me in on the rest. I know this is a lot, but we will find answers."

The friendly receptionist—Tilda is her name—leads me upstairs. She adjusts a lounge chair under the louvered-roof pergola, turns on the fan, and places a new bottle of cool mountain water on the table next to the chair. She asks if I'd like to listen to meditation music.

Perfect.

The second I lie down, my body relaxes. In the distance I see the black-aluminum Willis Tower, its bronze-tinted glass exterior thrust against the spotless blue sky.

I think of the way Phil looked at me when he suggested I come up here. Did he sense the war between love and hate that's being fought in the depths of my heart? I'd always believed Pops and Dad were my only family—unaware that this family masterfully kept me clueless about their brutal acts and malicious lies.

We will find answers. Phil's calming words ring in my ear. Through heavy eyelids I stare at the two antennae on top of the Willis Tower; their flashing strobe lights have a hypnotic effect. My eyes close.

We will find answers.

With a renewed burst of alertness after my twenty-minute nap, I rise from the lounge chair and turn off the fan and the music. I don't know why I flash a thumbs-up at the Willis Tower in the distance, but it feels right.

I enter the room two stories below the lovely roof garden with refreshed focus and concentration.

Phil looks at me, puckering his lips. "There's this proverbial saying that power corrupts, and absolute power corrupts absolutely." He drums his left index finger against the pile of files. "This is like plutonium in a nuclear reactor—ready to explode."

I lean over the table. "Even though it goes against everything I stand for, I should probably play nice with Matco before I tell them what I know. Once I do, it's going to be a shitstorm of biblical proportions."

Phil raises his right brow.

"I don't want to waste time by concentrating on their business crimes, at least not yet. That information can be used later, if needed." As if I'm reaching for help, I slide my hands across the conference table towards Phil. "My goal is to find my mother and my brother." I look at him expectantly. "Do you think there's a chance? Hope?"

Phil leans back in his chair and stretches his long legs under the table. "To move forward quickly, I'll have to involve someone else, if that's okay with you."

"Who?"

"Alex Rivas is my right-hand man; he's laser focused and laser precise. He's out of town on another assignment but returns to the office the end of this week. I'd like for all of us to meet as soon as possible."

Before we leave Flores & Associates, I ask the question that's been weighing on my mind. "My mother and brother most likely changed their names. How in the world will you even know where to begin?"

Phil smiles. "First we'll have to find the woman who called you and triggered this avalanche."

Maxwell and I look at each other and nod. "Amelia Rubio," we say simultaneously.

THIRTY-SIX

Mateo, February 2019
Mira, Wisconsin

Union City? How stupid of Pelón not to tell Mateo—or for him not to ask—which of the fourteen Union Cities in America he was talking about. Mateo'd had to make another call to find out that it was the Union City in New Jersey where Pelón had spotted Amelia Rubio at a bus stop and followed her to an apartment complex after a three-week search and surveillance.

Though Pelón kept calling it a home run, Mateo was skeptical. After twenty-seven years of costly pursuits and disappointing results, could this be another false trail?

Bridget von Barnheim groaned in her sleep, interrupting Mateo's thoughts and annoying the crap out of him.

Why had he allowed himself to fall asleep at her house? He'd already had to endure Marta's miserable catathrenia long ago, and now, decades later, he found himself next to a woman with the same godforsaken disorder.

What had he been thinking? Why had he ever entertained the idea that this relationship might last longer than any of the others?

Carefully he sat up in bed, leaned against the upholstered headboard, and stared into the room; in the dim illumination from a night-light, somewhat hidden by a modern Italian chaise, the stark contemporary furnishings in this chamber looked cheerless, strange, somber. As a matter of fact, there was nothing in this house that looked pleasing to Mateo.

So, okay, Bridget von Barnheim was an attractive woman, and he'd been proud to be seen with her at black-tie galas, political fundraisers, gallery openings, ribbon cuttings, and every event worth its salt on the social calendar in numerous cities.

"Never Too Old, Too Moneyed, Too Handsome to Be in Love" read the headline of an article describing Mateo Miraldo when he escorted Bridget von Barnheim to Milwaukee's annual Zoo Ball. Several tabloids, magazines, and online publications had named them as one of the chicest couples in society circles.

So what?

He glanced down at the pretty woman twenty-five years younger than he. Her reddish-blond hair looked tousled, the Versace silk sleep mask had shifted slightly up her forehead, and her lips formed a small O while she continued to groan. With downturned lips, Mateo looked away. It wasn't only the catathrenia that had made him decide to move on. Bridget von Barnheim had become too demanding. She wanted a commitment, kept reminding him of his age, emphasizing her willingness to be his trophy woman. "How long will it take before you admit that I'm the one you've been waiting for?" she'd asked him again, right before rolling onto her right side and pulling the sleep mask over her eyes.

"Never!" he muttered under his breath. Never would she or any other female come even close to the only woman who deserved his love. He closed his eyes, hoping to conjure Ula's beautiful face, her willowy body moving through the gardens of his hacienda.

A loud snort snatched the vision away.

As quietly as possible, he slipped out from under the luxurious fine-cotton sheets, tiptoed through her bedroom, and gathered his clothes. Pressing his pants, shirt, sweater, socks, and shoes against his chest, he noiselessly crept out of the room.

Just before he opened the front door, he slapped his forehead, remembering that the security system was armed. He didn't know the code. Now he would have to wait another hour until the housekeeper arrived.

He went into the kitchen, filled the machine with water and coffee. Every move was made quietly so as not to wake Bridget in her chamber above the kitchen. He grunted—the stupid modern house echoed more eerily than a handclap at El Castillo in Chichén Itzá.

Mateo considered how to break the breakup to her. But no matter how careful he was, Bridget von Barnheim would feel rejected and betrayed. Suddenly he found it difficult to breathe. Was his heart skipping beats? He'd recently been given medication to control high blood pressure, but he had yet to open the bottle. What for? He felt and looked good; he ate well and exercised regularly. Only a week ago, a tabloid had published an article naming him one of the "Ten Sexiest Senior Citizens in the Country." He chuckled; he certainly knew how to pleasure the other gender.

He needed space and air. Certain windows in the house weren't connected to the alarm system, and he opened the one that faced the fancy artificial water hole, the pond that housed Bridget's koi, goldfish, sturgeon, and whatever other cold-blooded species she kept there. She'd even given those slippery, limbless vertebrates names like Cutie, Chip, Pebbles, Hunky, Bubbles.

As the fresh air brushed against his face, he inhaled deeply. The mild breeze surprised him. Last week it'd been so cold, they'd closed all the schools.

He heard a rustling in the bushes under the window. Maybe a rat or a raccoon? He looked, but it was still too dark to see anything. He listened to the early February morning, heard other sounds coming nearer and then moving farther away again—a car, a barking dog, a siren. Though it would still be a while before daybreak, he heard crows emit their first caws and screeches. How many were there? He couldn't see, didn't want to see them either. His father had once told him, "If you see five crows, sickness will follow. If you see six crows, death will follow."

Mateo pulled the window shut.

He filled a mug with coffee and looked for somewhere to sit down. Neither the counter stools nor the chairs around the kitchen table looked inviting, so he walked to the adjacent room, where he settled into one of Bridget's Washington Prism lounge chairs. It wasn't comfortable either, but it would have to do until he could leave this damn house.

In the meantime, he returned to the ruminations hammering through his brain. Pelón! That oaf owed him. What in God's name had stopped him from grabbing Marisol, squeezing the information out of her, and then shutting her and that guy up for good? Yoli wouldn't have dared betray Mateo by telling anyone—she owed him, too. After all, he knew too much about her son Paco's dumbass activities. Though Paco's crimes had been relatively minor, they could've landed him in prison for a long time without parole had Mateo not paid off certain people with connections.

The hot, strong dark brew almost burned Mateo's tongue. He put the mug on the side table.

Searching for Ula had cost him a shitload of money over the years; that had never bothered him before. But when those hackers had recently demanded a small fortune for their services, Mateo lost it. Those idiots claimed they'd spent a lot of time on the task, only to come up with zilch! Nothing from the car rental agency, nothing from airline manifests. Nothing, nothing, nothing!

Damn them all! Marisol Rodriguez appears out of nowhere, and the bald-headed idiot allows her to disappear like a ghost again. Carefully, Mateo tasted the coffee. Perfect.

After the drama at the Miami airport, it had been too risky to send his bodyguards back to the United States to search for Amelia Rubio, the woman who'd given refuge to Ula, Miguel, and Marisol—and the only one who knew where they were heading next.

He stroked his chin. There had to be something he could do besides berate Pelón for letting Marisol slip through his fingers.

He straightened, almost laughed out loud as the perfect scheme came to him.

MiraCo owned a magnificent apartment in New York's Trump Tower. It had been months since Mateo was there. What better time to make that short trip again. He'd get two giggles from one tickle.

First he would ask Bridget to accompany him to the Big Apple; she had lived there with her first husband for only one year but still considered herself a member of Manhattan's high society. He'd encourage her to make social arrangements for a week, pretend to be excited, then find excuses not to go at the last minute.

Bridget would never allow herself to be blindsided and humiliated. She'd storm out of his apartment and send a service to pick up cases of cosmetics and her haute couture wardrobe. Mateo didn't care what lies she'd tell her elite friends about why *she'd* left *him*. He didn't need her A-list cronies—he had plenty of first-class friends himself.

Once he'd gotten rid of her, the real work would begin.

THIRTY-SEVEN

Mateo, two weeks later
Union City, New Jersey

Mateo had always avoided being part of what he called a *necessary intervention*, having instead rewarded others for taking care of unwanted situations or individuals. He also had never worn jeans, a cheap hooded winter jacket, or ugly boots. All these crappy items had been purchased by Pelón at some bargain store.

Reluctant, yet itching for the caper, Mateo changed into the foreign-smelling garments in an unremarkable room at an inferior motel in Union City. Everything here was so unlike him.

Pelón grinned when Mateo came out of the bathroom. "You've never looked better, jefe."

Mateo ignored the sarcastic comment, lowered the New York Knicks cap's visor on his forehead, and in grim silence followed the bodyguard outside. Despite the overcast sky, he donned off-the-rack sunglasses. "How are we going to get there?"

"We'll walk—it's less than fifteen minutes from here," said Pelón. "One of my guys rented the motel room, and there's no need for our faces to be seen by a cab driver."

"In that case, don't walk so fast! These damn boots are stiff and they're not my size." Mateo adjusted the uncomfortable, too-tight-behind-the-ears shades. Only four miles west of his upscale Midtown Manhattan neighborhood, he found himself in a foreign world, scrutinizing passersby in this section of Cuba's northernmost province.

According to Pelón and based on his two weeks of surveillance, Amelia Rubio kept the same routine almost every day. She was usually accompanied by a frail elderly man or another woman, sometimes both. The twosome or threesome would leave together, but Amelia Rubio often returned by herself to the nine-story apartment complex on Forty-Fourth Street.

The large old building had newly installed controlled access gates, but Pelón had managed to fib his way into the entrance with a crew of workmen, from whom he slyly acquired the four-digit access code. Once inside, he'd discovered that all the apartment doors and the mailboxes downstairs had only numbers on them, so the following day he'd waited inside Havana Cafeteria, a diner across the street, until he spotted Amelia Rubio carrying grocery bags from La Roca Supermarket.

"Hold the door," he'd yelled, following her inside and onto the elevator. She'd gotten off on the fifth floor and so had he. After she'd disappeared into one of the eighteen apartments on the floor, he'd made a note that she had entered 516.

"Earlier this morning, I followed our target and the other woman again," Pelón said. "The old man wasn't with them. Like every day, they went to Mi Casa, a senior citizen's community center. She should return alone around three o'clock."

"This is where she lives?" Mateo looked at the long red-brick apartment complex. He pulled the visor even lower over his face and adjusted the ill-fitting sunglasses again. "What about surveillance?"

"They've been installing new cameras every day in Union City, but so far none around here." Pelón elbowed Mateo. "Had there been cameras, I wouldn't have brought you here, jefe." With his short, fat index finger, he punched in the four-digit access code.

Mateo swallowed. The discomfort in his lower abdomen was getting worse. *Why am I here? What in the bloody hell was I think-*

ing? Still cursing under his breath, he followed Pelón onto the elevator.

"Stay near the elevator and pretend to be on the phone if someone walks by you. If they greet you, acknowledge them," Pelón said in a low voice. He unzipped his oversized parka and leaned closer to Mateo. "If things don't go according to my plan, we'll take the elevator or staircase—whatever's closer—and return to the motel."

Mateo sensed the rush of blood to his face; his ears were on fire. His breaths became shallower as he watched Pelón walk heavy-footed down the long dingy hallway. After an eerie silence, a dog barked—from the sound of it, a large dog. A baby started to cry inside one of the units, and in another apartment a man shouted something and a door slammed. Then all was quiet again.

He fumbled for his burner phone and pressed it against his ear, just in case one of the many doors opened and he was confronted by strangers.

What was Pelón doing? Mateo stretched his neck, took off the shades, and squinted down the dark hallway. The bodyguard was waving, beckoning him to come.

His legs felt leaden and his steps sounded dull as he walked the long, dead corridor with its pale white ceiling, faded blue walls, and painted red doors.

Pelón pointed to his tool belt and nodded towards the lock. "Cakewalk," he whispered with a toothy smile. "Now we wait inside."

Mateo stepped behind the bodyguard and into a small, dim foyer, just big enough for a sideboard with coat hooks to the left and an oval mirror to the right. Already in a state of nerves, he didn't see the umbrella stand that caught his foot. Reflexively he seized the thing and stood motionless for a second. As if in slow motion, he turned his head towards Pelón, who stood in the middle of a compact kitchen. There was a sink unit with a small countertop. Several metal shelves, loaded with kitchen utensils, hung on the walls. The stove and refrigerator looked like they had come from a different era. Diffused daylight shone through the closed curtain, and under a window stood a narrow table covered with a crocheted ivory cloth. Two chairs were equally angled opposite the table. Despite its Lilliputian size, everything looked organized and spotless.

Pelón motioned him to move on. The area rug under both men's rubber-soled shoes swallowed their steps. Straight ahead was a closed door. The bodyguard leaned his ear against it. "No sound," he whispered, gently pressed down on the handle, and opened the door to a small living room with a brown velvet sofa and a coffee table flanked by two easy chairs. Just like in the kitchen, nothing took up much space except for a large bookcase packed with books. More books were piled in a neat arrangement under the coffee table. Pelón pulled the door closed again and pointed to one more room to the right. Again, he leaned his ear against the door.

Mateo cringed when he heard the squeak of the hinge. Two twin beds stood on either side of the wall, in one of them lay a fragile old man with messy white hair. The Einstein look-alike lifted his head off the pillow. "¿Quién está ahí?" His thin right arm reached forward. "Amelia? Maria?"

In shock and unable to move, Mateo had melted into the doorframe. A black cat stood at the foot of the bed, its back arched, fur erect. The animal hissed at him. For seconds their eyes locked, staring each other down in hatred and fear.

"¿Quién está ahí?" The old man had sunk back into his pillow.

Pelón glanced at Mateo and held his index finger over his lips. He took a step forward and bent over the bed.

"Relájate, amigo."

The old man stiffened. "Who are you? What do you want?"

"I came to see Amelia Rubio. I'm an old friend of hers."

"I-I don't know anybody by that name," groaned the old man. He scrambled his bony knees up into a pointed triangle under the bedcover.

Mateo kept his gaze fixed on the wrinkled face; the skin was mottled and stretched thin like tissue paper over tendons, crisscrossed with a net of bluish veins.

"Hey," Pelón purred, "my name is Oscar." With a grin, he winked at Mateo. "Why don't you tell me yours?"

"Luis."

"Okay, Luis. Is it okay if I sit on the other bed while I wait for Amelia?"

"I told you I don't know anyone by that name," said Luis in a strained voice.

"¡Cabrón! Don't lie to me." Pelón's voice got louder. "You called out her name, and I've seen you with her."

"I am old, I get confused." Luis's lips quivered, and his cloudy eyes stared straight into nowhere. Slowly, he straightened his legs under the blanket.

Mateo, still fused to the doorframe, couldn't stop himself from inhaling sharply when he felt a painful leg cramp setting in. As soon as he shifted his weight, the black cat let out a shrill wailing noise and leaped off the bed towards him. He hissed, ready to kick the animal, but it had already darted past him into the small foyer.

"Who else is here?" Luis gasped.

"No one." Pelón shot an irritated look at Mateo. "Your cat got spooked."

"No! I can tell." Luis's pajama-clad torso shot up, and in quick, jittery movements his hand searched for something between the wall and the bed.

Pelón grabbed the old man's arm. When he yanked it up, some sort of a remote device fell out of his hand. "What is this?" he yelled.

Luis fell back into the pillow and cried out in pain. "I pushed the button. Help is on the way."

That was all Mateo needed to hear. Without waiting for Pelón to give him a sign, he turned and ran out of the apartment. The stairwell was closer than the elevator. He opened the door and listened. Quiet. He had no idea why, but instead of racing downstairs he climbed the narrow, winding staircase one flight up. Breathing heavily, he peeked into the corridor. Energetic Cuban rumba music came from inside one of the apartments. Further down, two people with grocery bags were entering another unit. With no one else in sight, Mateo hastened towards the elevator. His heart was pounding, he had trouble breathing, and his hand shook when he pressed the button.

"Hey," a young man said when he stepped into the elevator.

Mateo gave a quick nod, then lowered his head, pretending to read something on his burner phone.

The elevator stopped on the fifth floor. As soon as the door opened, three teenage girls shrieked at the sight of the young man. They hugged and in rapid Spanish talked about a concert they planned to attend; none of them seemed to be paying attention to Mateo.

It was snowing outside and the temperature had dropped. Mateo, reluctantly grateful for the ugly cheap jacket, pulled his hood over the New York Knicks cap, put his hands in his pockets, and walked away quickly.

What was Pelón doing right now? Had the old man really sent an alert? Pelón would know how to deal with whoever, making sure nobody could identify him. Or had he left the apartment to wait outside for Amelia Rubio? What would he do with her? Damn! Damn! Damn! Maybe this godforsaken plan had been jinxed from the get-go.

Mateo was exhausted. He stopped and looked around. Was he even walking in the right direction? When he came to the next crossing, he looked right and left. *Ah! Carlitos!* He remembered seeing the colorful signage of that restaurant shortly after they'd left the motel earlier. He crossed the street and turned left at the next corner. "Thank you, dear God," he whispered when he spotted the flickering motel sign down the block.

Still surprised that his brain had evidently led him in the right direction, he saw Pelón's rental car. The bodyguard had intentionally parked it a few doors down from the room he'd rented.

Mateo pulled the door closed behind him, secured the door chain, and tried to catch his breath. When he'd convinced himself he was safe, the drab, stale-smelling room suddenly felt like a welcoming oasis. The curtains were still drawn, and he dared to turn on the light. His clothes were hanging where he'd left them, and his shoes were waiting for him on the floor. Quickly he changed and stuffed the cheap garments and boots back into two shopping bags. From the inside pocket of his dark-brown cashmere coat, he pulled out his phone and checked for messages. Five texts from Marco, one from Molara, and numerous others from friends and close business associates. He would answer them later. Among the missed calls, six were from Bridget; she'd left two voice messages. He felt no need to listen to them.

He looked at his burner phone. What should he do with it? Calling Pelón was out of the question and so was waiting for him in this room. Mateo buttoned his coat, grabbed the two shopping bags, and turned off the light.

He had to be careful walking; his Gucci ankle boots had a leather sole. Obviously, he could not afford to slip, twist an ankle, or break a bone. What kind of explanation would he give an EMT or a paramedic? They'd surely ask him what he was doing in this neighborhood.

The shopping bags presented another problem; he needed to get rid of them. He'd heard of clothes depots for the homeless but had no idea where to look for them. Still contemplating what to do, he spotted a construction dumpster in an alley. Finally, a tiny stroke of luck. Making sure his actions went unnoticed, he hurled the two bags over the edge and into the container.

As if absolved, Mateo stopped at the next busy street and hailed a taxi. "Drop me off at Tiffany's on Fifth Avenue," he told the driver. Not that he wanted to buy anything, but in case the driver noticed, he planned to go inside the flagship store, look around for a few minutes, leave, and quickly head to his home in Trump Tower, adjacent to Tiffany's.

After what he'd been through, his New York apartment had never looked better.

⁂

Mateo's pounding heart woke him with a steadily increasing pumping. What was that confusing pile of dreams he'd just labored through? The frenzied jumble of words, the sounds and images? When he rubbed his eyes, the memory dissolved like a dense fog at dawn, yet the chaos of the past hours hung heavily in his head. Through hazy eyes, he looked at the clock. It wasn't even midnight. He still wore the same clothes. Earlier, all he'd been able to think of was showering and changing into fresh garments, but he had done neither after his inevitable confrontation with Bridget von Barnheim.

"Where *were* you?" She'd stood straight as a candle in the foyer, beautifully coiffed and dressed to kill.

"I had business to attend" was the only response that came to Mateo's mind at that moment.

"From the way you look, I can only imagine what kind of business *that* was," she wailed. "Why did you even ask me to come to New York with you? I had to attend three events by myself, throw away expensive tickets, and make lousy excuses for you." Her jaw was clenched. "Nobody," she hissed, "nobody does this to Bridget von Barnheim, especially not an old man like you." She tossed her head back and forced a laugh. She opened the coatroom, threw her haute couture faux-fur leopard-print poncho over her shoulders, and grabbed her Chanel bag. "Have your housekeeper pack my belongings," she said without looking at him. "A service will pick everything up in the morning."

Well, Mateo thought, *at least one of my plans didn't fail.* Of course, getting rid of Bridget hadn't required great skill, while the more vital matter remained unresolved.

A shudder ran through his body when he looked at the burner phone. No calls from Pelón, and Mateo had been told not to contact him. If Pelón got arrested, would he talk? Feeling lifeless, he slumped into the cushions.

That might be the answer. He'd just sit here and not move. Perfect way for time to pass him by when he no longer had to swim or kick against it. He closed his eyes and wondered what it would be like if they never opened again.

The disposable phone rang.

"Listen carefully, jefe, and don't interrupt me." Pelón's voice was grave. "I never got to our target because of the old guy. I did what needed to be done." He noisily cleared his throat. "Don't call me. I'll get in touch with you when the time is right." Another pause. "I just texted you a number. Write it down and keep it safe. His name is Ignacio, but he goes by Nacho." He paused again. "Did you get it?"

"Yes."

"Call him if you don't hear from me again."

"But why—"

"No questions! Just listen. If you need to call Nacho, do not mention my name! Instead you will say, 'My brother can't fix my laptop. I was told you could help me.'"

"I don't understand."

"You don't need to understand! Nacho will. Did you write it down?"

"Yes."

"Now destroy the phone you're on! Do it *right away!*"

The line went dead.

THIRTY-EIGHT

Ursula, February 2019
Crans-Montana, Switzerland

It was around six o'clock—maybe another thirty minutes before the first appearance of the morning light. Still relishing the warmth of her bed, Ursula listened and the absence of all sound announced the arrival of snow. *It must have snowed all night*, she thought, a whisper of happiness flowing through her. Although she believed it to be only her imagination, even the air in the room smelled different, clean and melancholic.

For weeks, every person in the canton of Valais had been waiting for snow. Instead, the winter sun—though lower than in summer—shone brightly in clear blue skies. Even yesterday there had been no clouds or a change of wind to hint at a change in weather.

"It snowed," Ursula said softly when she felt Bernard's lips on her shoulder.

"Marisol's wish came true; she's been hoping to see it one last time."

Facing each other, they did not need to speak. They knew what the other was thinking.

She inhaled his warm breath. "Did I ever tell you my favorite quote by Marcus Aurelius?"

"Tell me again."

"'Accept the things to which fate binds you, and love the people with whom fate brings you together, but do so with all your heart.'"

"Meeting you may have been fate," Bernard said, his face close to hers, "but falling in love with you surpassed all my control."

Twenty minutes later, Ursula opened the curtains. Large crystal flakes floated silently from the sky, adding more fluff to already-thick white blankets that overnight had spread across the snowy grounds. "So beautiful," she whispered.

After showering, she slipped into soft yoga pants and donned her favorite sweatshirt. "It's still early. Go back to sleep." She kissed Bernard's forehead.

For a second she stopped behind the door to the living room and listened. Then, as she'd done for the past three weeks, she quietly opened the door, half fearing the worst and half expecting the miracle she knew was hardly possible.

Nurse Juliette was readjusting Marisol's position in the hospital bed that Ursula had rented even before Joaquin and Marisol returned from the United States. She had placed it in the alcove, surrounded by bay windows.

Ursula tiptoed closer and whispered, "How is she doing?"

"She had difficulty breathing during the night, but as always, the medicine gave her the comfort she needed."

"Is she sleeping?"

Juliette nodded. "Before she fell asleep, she told me she was waiting for the angel to take her home." The nurse smiled when she looked at Marisol. "She said her soul was ready."

Although Ursula had prepared herself for this moment, the nurse's words catapulted her into a state of mental blankness.

"What's wrong? Are you okay?"

"It's nothing. I'm good." She noticed for the first time how small the nurse was, almost as if she'd shrunk overnight. "It's just that I can't imagine my life without Marisol."

Juliette nodded. "I understand. She's a remarkable woman."

"You look exhausted. Why don't you go to the guest room and rest. I'd like alone time with her before Bernard and Mick get here."

Sitting next to the bed, Ursula couldn't take her eyes off the woman who'd been like a mother and sister, most definitely a confidante and very best friend. Marisol's hair looked as if it had been finger-combed onto the pillow, white on white in blended harmony. Her once heart-shaped face with its rounded cheeks had shrunk over the course of her illness, and during the past few days those cheeks had sunk in further, her soft brown skin tones growing darker. Ursula looked past those changes. Marisol's true beauty prevailed even over the ravage of cancer.

Some spittle had formed at the corner of her mouth, and when Ursula dabbed it away, she opened her eyes.

"Mi amor. Look outside. It snowed all night. I couldn't wait to show you."

A lopsided smile formed on Marisol's lips. "The magic of the first snowfall, so serene." Her eyes opened wider; her smile intensified. "My soul will travel above this peaceful white world when it makes its journey home."

Ursula swallowed and softly laid her hand on Marisol's. She wasn't surprised her friend seemed more alert and sounded more energetic. Both the nurse and the doctor had said some people showed a brief surge of vitality in the days or hours before death.

Marisol looked at her. "Will you lie here?" There was a glowing expectation in her warm brown eyes. For a tiny moment Ursula believed she could see the old sparkle again.

Lying side by side, gazing at the pristine serenity on the other side of the big bay window, they reflected on their past together. Ursula had no idea how long they held hands and talked before Marisol's energy began to fade.

"Should I get Nurse Juliette? It's been a while since your last dose."

"Not yet. I want to be awake when Mick gets here."

Ursula glanced at the time. It was just after eight o'clock. "He should be here any moment; he took the earliest flight out of Barcelona."

"Tell me about the opening of his new exhibit."

"The headline of one review read, 'Mick Rossi, the Pulse of the City.'"

"Mi Mick." Though weak, Marisol's voice still hinted at remnants of its silvery beauty.

Ursula so badly wanted to squeeze her cold hand, rub it warm again, but her fingers felt as thin and light as dry twigs.

"There are three recipes I need to share with you before I leave." Puzzled, Ursula turned her head.

"Rabbi Hebroni helped me search for the ingredients." Marisol's breaths became shallow, and she closed her eyes for a moment.

"The first recipe: Confront your fear and doubts. If you do, new portals to surprising dimensions will open." She stopped again, her breaths coming more labored.

"The second recipe: Never let go of hope. If today looks like Sodom and tomorrow looks like Gomorrah, you will find joy ahead by seeking spiritual maturity." With difficulty she pulled her other hand from under the blanket to take Ursula's in both of hers. "To become what no one else is becoming, you have to do what no one is doing." She twisted her mouth into a smile.

"The final recipe: Justify trust and it will generate love. Nurture love and it will deliver trust." Depleted of energy, Marisol closed her eyes.

Ursula tried but failed to suppress a sob. "Sorry," she murmured.

"Tears are healing agents. They bathe your soul." Her voice was barely audible.

There was a soft knock at the door.

"Mick?" Marisol looked up expectantly.

"Yes." Ursula kissed her friend's cheek and noticed her cold skin had become more mottled, more blotchy. "I'll give Mick some time alone with you."

Joaquín had prepared a simple tray with croissants, fresh berries, yogurt, and buttered, salted toast with radishes for everyone, but Ursula had no appetite. Quietly she sat at the table with Bernard, Bruno, and Joaquín.

"Excusez-moi." Nurse Juliette had noiselessly entered the breakfast room. "It's time for Marisol's next dose."

Mick's eyes were puffy when he returned to the table. With a weary sigh, he stirred his spoon in his cup and stared at the swirling liquid. At last, he dropped the spoon on the saucer. "She had difficulty speaking, but there was this brief moment when the sun peeked through the clouds and the brightest of rays streamed into the room and bathed her in this intense light." He looked at the wintery scene outside. "She put her right hand on her heart and laughed like a little kid. She said an angel was standing right next to me." He pressed his index fingers against his eyes to wipe the wet pink rims. "She said the angel wants me to know that Molly will find us, and when she does, she'll bring along someone very special for me."

Ursula held her breath, hoping her hard-won inner calm would sponge up new tears.

"There's something else," Mick said. "Marisol kept muttering Amelia's name."

"Oh no," Joaquín interjected. "I forgot."

"Forgot what?"

"When Marisol and I were in the States, we hoped Amelia would take a train or bus to Chicago since she still refuses to fly."

"Did she come?"

Joaquín shook his head. "Marisol left message after message. When none of her calls were returned, she remembered the old gentleman Amelia took care of. She called him, but his line was out of service. Marisol was worried something had happened to Amelia, and I promised to follow up, but with all that's been going on, I completely forgot."

Bruno leaned towards his husband. "You had your hands full. I'll find out what happened to her."

Nurse Juliette cleared her throat. Nobody had heard her come into the room.

"Marisol is asking for all of you," she said softly. "Before you go in, don't be surprised if she tells you about things that only she can see. Being a hospice caregiver, I've been privileged to be with patients in their last moments who've experienced visions. It's called terminal lucidity."

The nurse had put five chairs around Marisol's bedside and waited until everybody was sitting. "It's been a great honor to take care of you, Marisol. You've brightened my life, and I thank you." She leaned over the hospital bed and gently touched Marisol's cheek then quietly stepped away.

"Mira!" Marisol said, her eyes half open. "Mi mamá y papá lindos." A smile lit up her face. "Santiago, my handsome brother." She laughed and opened her eyes wider. "You all came for me." For a second she stopped breathing, then gasped. "Un ángel en luz brillante," she rasped. "More angels. Such magnificent light."

"They're here for you." For the first time, Ursula didn't choke on her words; she felt surrounded by an oasis of serenity. "Go with them, my sweet friend."

"Love and light. It's everywhere," Marisol said, barely audible.

Bruno and Joaquín leaned over the bed and whispered their farewell in Spanish.

Bernard touched Marisol's cheeks. In hushed tones he said, "Thank you, Marisol. Knowing you enriched my life."

Ursula and Mick each held one of Marisol's hands.

"I love you so much," said Mick.

"Until we see each other again someday, somewhere," Ursula said, feeling Marisol's last breath on her face.

Three days later, Charley and Alain arrived from Paris, and the group of seven took the Les Rousses-Le Bâté ski lift to Lac de Tseuzier. While Mick and Ursula scattered Marisol's ashes according to her wishes, Joaquín read the spiritual verses his younger brother Rabbi David Hebroni had chosen for Marisol.

Throughout the meaningful casting ceremony, a mild breeze swirled the ashes above the untainted Valais winter wonderland and into the heart of the Alps.

Letting go of Marisol's last cremains, Ursula murmured,

"Your spirit will never be far away

You'll walk beside us every day
Unseen, unheard but always near
Always loved, always missed, and always dear."

※

Ursula removed the latest volume of her diaries from the drawer and sat down, looking forward to some undisturbed time. She had just written *March 1, 2019* when the phone rang.

"I need to see you. Can I come over now?" Bruno's voice sounded strained.

She ran into the garage, hoping to intercept Mick and Bernard before they left for Mick's studio to oversee the packing procedure of two new pieces to be shipped to the Galerie Fleur Dubois in Paris.

"Don't go!"

Mick lowered the window.

"Bruno is on his way over here. I think something happened."

Ten minutes later Bruno came through the front door and held his phone in front of Ursula's face. She stared at the headshot of a gray-haired older man. Below the photo in bold letters it read, "Luis Rivas found murdered in his bed. Police is asking for any . . ."

"What is this?"

"An article in *El Nuevo Heraldo*—Union City's community newsletter."

Mick scratched his temple. "Doesn't Amelia live in Union City?"

Bruno nodded, looking haunted. "And Luis Rivas was the old gentleman she took care of."

"What happened?"

"Ever since Marisol's passing, I've been trying to reach Amelia. Thirty minutes ago, my phone rang—I almost didn't answer because I didn't recognize the number. Strangely enough, I had a feeling it might be her." He dropped onto the couch. "You won't believe what she told me . . ."

Luis Rivas, Bruno explained, was the brother of Amelia's former neighbors in Miami's Little Havana. Luis had no spouse or children and had worked most of his life as the groundskeeper and custodian at Mi Casa, a senior citizen community center. When his macular degeneration got to the point where he was unable to see faces, read, or drive, he retired and depended on friends to assist him. Amelia was one of them. Her late aunt's stepsisters had long passed away, but she kept their apartment, adjacent to Luis's. On most days, Amelia escorted him to Mi Casa, where he partook in programs for the visually impaired.

As Luis became more fragile, the engineer of their apartment building installed an alert device by his bedside in case he needed help. Less than a month ago, emergency responders rushed to the apartment and found him gagged and strangled.

In a tight Hispanic community, where many people knew and respected Luis, everybody offered their help to track down the murderer. A young man and three teenage girls reported riding the elevator with an older man with his head bent over his phone, someone they'd never seen before—just around Luis's estimated time of death.

They said the old man on the elevator was almost six feet tall with salt-and-pepper hair sticking out from a New York Knicks cap. One of the girls saw a small oval birthmark on the corner of his right lip and a scar under his stubble. Another girl noted that he wore a blue-and-black Freeze Defense winter jacket. She recognized the jacket because her father had bought one at Walmart just a week before, when it went on sale. She also said she smelled an expensive kind of men's cologne on the stranger.

Ursula held her hand over her mouth. "Mateo has a birthmark on his right lip and a scar on his cheek. He wasn't happy that even his beard couldn't hide the scar."

"Amelia is convinced Mateo and one of his thugs were trying to find her." Bruno pressed his lips together, narrowed his eyes.

"The beast in Mateo will never give up, not until he gets what he wants. Unbelievable that after all these years, we're still not safe from him."

"But now there's been a murder," said Bruno. "If someone can identify him, he'll be arrested."

Mick jumped off his chair. "He's like a tumor! A stinking, festering boil that needs to burst," he exclaimed. "What else did Amelia say?"

"There were a few other witnesses," Bruno said, "like the waitstaff and some of the regulars from the Havana Cafeteria across the street. They noticed a burly bald man who kept returning for a couple of weeks before Luis's murder. The stranger always ordered a large black coffee to go, then sat at a table by the window and kept an eye on the building across the street. Also, a busboy recalled seeing Amelia pass by the restaurant one afternoon. The bald guy slammed money on the table, ran after her, and followed her into the building."

"But Amelia is okay, right?"

He nodded. "She said she'd always kept quiet about what happened in 1992, not only to protect herself but to keep you safe. When the police interrogated her about her connection to Luis, she saw no need to tell them she'd lived next to Luis's brother in Little Havana all those years ago. But she contacted Luis's nephew, a former policeman, now a private investigator. She said she trusts him completely; he'll advise her on what to do and what not to do."

"What if Mateo sends another one of his goons to look for her?"

Bruno shook his head and pointed to the article on his smartphone. "I seriously doubt he'll be that stupid. By now, he has to have heard that the police are following eyewitness leads." A smile spread over his face. "Pardon the expression, but I'm sure Mateo Miraldo is shitting his pants right now."

THIRTY-NINE

Molly, June 2019
Milwaukee, Wisconsin

All morning I argue with my weaker self, the part of me that urges me to confront *him* about the atrocities that torment my soul. But the voice of reason is stronger and demands I wait.

Sitting in my car in MiraCo's parking lot, I blink into the sun and vacillate between the options. It's not even ten o'clock, and *he* doesn't expect me until eleven. The weather is picture-perfect, and I have a pair of sneakers in my car. And just like that, I know what to do.

I drive the short distance to the clubhouse, where everybody is surprised to see me. No wonder—I haven't golfed since early last summer. I hop on a cart and steer it to the driving range. A full bucket of balls is waiting for me.

Before putting my phone on DND, I call Maxwell.

"Hey you," I say. "I'm at the driving range."

There's a pause. "The driving range? Did you change your mind about your meeting?"

"Nope, but before I face *him*, I just feel like whacking a ton of balls into kingdom come."

Although I'm a lot more resolute one hour later, I have to stop for a moment to gaze at MiraCo's headquarters. It's arguably an architecturally impressive structure, but *his* promises of one day owning MiraCo never made me excited about the prospect of taking over. Actually, the mere thought of it now gives me the creeps. Standing in bright sunlight, I peer at the glass entry; the people inside look like puppets in a shadow play.

My heart is pounding as I walk by the same reception area, climb the same steps, and greet the same employees I have for more than eight years. Everything feels ridiculous and fateful at the same time.

I inhale sharply, take three more steps, and open Mateo Miraldo's office doors.

"Molara," he says with a smile that stays frozen on his face.

In this elegantly furnished office, a huge window front unveils sweeping views of the golf course, and like a striking painting, it fills the room with a certain spirit. *He* sits behind his Parnian spiral desk and makes a sweeping gesture, inviting me to sit down.

As always, his thick, wavy white hair is perfectly styled and complements his tanned complexion. His salt-and-pepper stubble is well-maintained, and his groomed hands, with the shiny buffed fingernails, rest on the almost empty surface of his desk. His dark eyes briefly pierce mine, shift away, then dare to find mine again.

How did I love him all these years when deep within me I now realize what love is not? I fake a smile, but all I can think of is what this defective man hides under his flawless persona. This rogue who raped my mother. This monster who scared her and my brother into hiding after seizing me and holding me like a security deposit. My smile fades.

The best course of action is to keep Mateo engaged in conversations that have nothing to do with what he's been keeping from you, Phil told me. *Instead of doing what's expected of you, as you've done in the past, throw both Mateo and Marco off balance by disagreeing with them on business or personal matters. But don't give anything away that might alert them to your discoveries.*

"Molara," Mateo says again, "why haven't you been answering my calls? Your text last night about wanting to see me was the first I've heard from you since I got back." He briefly breaks eye contact to reach for his expensive cigars. Before he puts a Cohiba between his lips, he squints and tilts his head. "You seem off," he says, tapping his middle finger against the cigar. "What's going on with you?"

"Well, while you were in Wyoming, I had a lot of time to think." I speak slowly, enunciating every word. "Recently, you and Dad"—I almost choke on the word—"asked me to investigate licensing the Mira name for your new projects in Panama and Canada." I lean back and cross my legs, hoping to look at ease and confident. "After scrutinizing the small print, I don't like it! I also don't like the way you count on me to structure everything."

His expression changes to one of complete incomprehension, which gives me a weird, unexpected sensation of power. He takes the Cohiba from his mouth, but before he has a chance to say anything, I hold up the palm of my hand.

"I don't understand why MiraCo chose second-rate developers and why we demand they pay significant amounts of money up front." I shoot him a baffled look. "And since when do we ask for an unusually high share of profits just for our name brand? It's dishonest and doesn't make sense."

Mateo's bewilderment seems genuine. "What are you saying?"

"Please don't tell me you and my *father*"—I spit out the word—"had no idea that the partners, banks, and whoever else you chose to involve yourselves with this time have a record of not doing due diligence." The adrenaline is coursing through my veins. "I'm out! There are too many potential risks. I'll never put my name on transactions I can't support."

He's trying to interrupt, but I keep talking, elaborating on a variety of schemes that border on fraud. I surprise myself with how the sentences keep pealing from my mouth, almost as if I had rehearsed them for a final audition.

When I'm done, I expect an explosion, but he appears to be frozen. Neither of us moves; it feels as if one of us has pressed the pause button on the remote control.

Mateo's Wyoming suntan has taken on a grayish undertone. When he finally breaks through his paralysis, he mumbles, "Complete damn madness," and slams his palm on the shiny desktop.

I don't attempt to say anything, nor do I storm out of the room, although I feel like it. He leans forward and, as if remotely controlled, slams his palm on the desk three more times. "You of all people should know that I'm a very honest man. I *never, ever* engage in crooked deals." With an angular movement, he puts the Cohiba between his lips and tries to stare me down, letting the cigar wander from one corner of his mouth to the other.

We both glare at each other in silence. Finally, he jumps out of his chair and throws the cigar into the wastebasket. "Whatever virus infected your gut this past weekend obviously messed with your head as well. If you can't be trusted with our credible plans for Panama and Canada, I have plenty of lawyers, advisors, and controllers who'll leap at the opportunity to structure these ventures."

"How lucky for you—" I almost add *Pops* but gulp it down in time. "I'll finalize the projects I've been working on and then take time off."

He sits down again. "You'll what?"

It might not be what Phil Flores had in mind, but now is the perfect time for me to say it. "I've worked my butt off for Mira-Co, never missed a day, and always did what was asked of me. There was a time when it felt good to be the go-getter, but I've reached cruising altitude here and can't climb higher. I can't even enjoy cruising because MiraCo's gravitational pull is dragging me down and holding me back from more important matters." The chair screeches loudly when I stand up.

He stares at me through narrowed eyes and chews on his lip as if it were a lemon rind. "You'd better backpedal fast on all your nonsense," he grumbles. "If you follow your delusions, you'll never reach your destination."

"Wrong," I say. "I believe there is a whole world waiting for me, and I am determined to find it."

As expected, Marco storms into my office an hour later. "I can't believe what I just heard," he yells. "How dare you say that the . . ."

Wide-eyed, I let him talk. Like a waterfall, he babbles on and on, claims I'm incapable of handling Panama and Canada and accuses me of being two-faced, ill-mannered, ungrateful.

"Have you ever seen your grandfather and me be anything less than honest and responsible?" His voice is shrill.

I swallow the painful urge to answer with the truth and listen to the rest of his aimless ramblings. Nothing he says makes sense; his drivel sounds clumsy, like that of a simple child.

"Well." He points his finger at me when he finally runs out of steam. "You'd better have something to say in your defense."

"Ouch!"

My one-word response is not because his ridiculous accusations hurt me, but for the first time, I realize how painfully bruised and insecure my half brother Marco is.

The silence that follows rings loudly in my ears.

"Oh," he mutters, then turns and leaves.

―❦―

For the next two days I work until late in the evening to finalize the projects I've committed to and am proud of.

Mateo purposely avoids me, and I know why: he expects me to crawl back to him and apologize. Twice I hear him talk or laugh louder than usual—always near my office when my door is open. I'm sure his intention is to demonstrate how unbothered he is.

Meanwhile, I force myself to keep a cool head and behave as if everything were normal. Clearly, some of my coworkers sense the tension. At times I notice their puzzled looks, and I imagine they put their heads together once I'm out of sight.

Maxwell texts he overheard Betsy—one of Mateo's assistants—saying she can't wait for the week to be over because she needs relief from the rising temperature around Mateo.

Just like Betsy, I'm ready to be done with this week. Thank God it's Friday!

My phone rings. *Ava*, says the display. That's weird. I don't remember the last time she called me.

"Molara! Hi! It's me!"

"This is a surprise."

"I know, right? Can I see you? I have something extremely important to share with you." She giggles.

"Um, when?"

"Well, it's almost five o'clock." Her voice rises by an octave. "Can you meet me at the club for champagne and a little nibble?"

"I'm still at work, and I've got plans after. Maybe another day? I'm sure your husband will be happy to spend the evening with you."

"What? Don't you guys talk? Marco and Mateo hopped on the plane an hour ago—they're on their way to Panama." She giggles again. "Please, drop everything. I have to tell you something even Marco doesn't know yet."

Now I am curious. I text Maxwell, informing him of the change in plans and promising to report as soon as I'm on my way home.

―

"Hi!" Ava jumps up when she sees me and throws her tanned arms around me. She looks like she just came off the runway, in an unmistakable Versace microfloral-pattern minidress and greenish ankle-strap sandals with dangerously high heels. She looks me up and down. "It's not fair to look so pretty without makeup. And how do you stay so thin?"

I shrug and compliment her stylish outfit.

"Thanks. I ordered a bunch of Donatella's collection after the show in Milan." She strikes a pose. "But I don't know how *you* do it. I could never look as cool and elegant in the kind of simple, plain clothes you wear."

Was that a compliment or an insult? I bite my tongue.

"So, what's up?" I seat myself across from her.

"Have some Cristal Brut." She points to the bottle in the cooler next to her, then motions the steward to come to our table.

"Nice to see you again, Ms. Molly," Horace says when he fills my glass and refills Ava's. "It's been a while. How have you been?"

"Very well, Horace." I return his smile. *If only he knew . . .*

Ava snaps her fingers. "Ten minutes ago, I ordered Beluga caviar and blinis. Can you see to it, please?" Then she bats her fake eyelashes at the steward. "Oh, and while you're at it, bring us some of the French premium foie gras. I've had a *craving* for it all day."

She pulls her chair closer to the table, looks left and right as if to make sure nobody is listening, and leans towards me. "Did you know that Marco and I have been seeing a fertility specialist for the past few months?"

I shake my head.

"I. Am. Pregnant," she whispers. "When I found out today, Marco had left already. I'm gonna wait till he gets back to give him the news." She pats her toned, flat stomach. "I have a perfect idea for how to surprise him." She giggles again.

Not wanting to say the wrong thing, I clap my hands together. "Congratulations! How far along are you?"

"I missed my period like two weeks ago and ran to the doctor. He confirmed it today." She looks at her belly and raises her glass. "Here's to a new Miraldo heir."

"Should you be drinking?"

She shrugs. "I wouldn't even know I'm pregnant if I hadn't gone to the doctor today. I'll start behaving myself right after I tell Marco." She leans forward again. "Can you believe you're going to have a baby brother or baby sister?"

Wrong! I refrain from telling her I'll be the baby's aunt. "Fantastic!"

"I'm sure it's gonna be a boy," Ava says in between bites of her caviar-laden blini. "Marco will be so overjoyed—his other son died so tragically."

Dear God. I push a strand of my hair out of my face, trying to keep my expression neutral.

"I love that I gotta eat for two now," she says, and slices a thick piece off the foie gras. "Don't worry, I'll make sure the baby spends a lot of time with his older sister." She tilts her head and looks at me. "Hopefully he'll inherit those fabulous Miraldo genes. Nobody in my family looks as beautiful as you or as handsome as Mateo and Marco. And nobody on my side is as smart."

She keeps babbling on about how much fun it will be. She already has ideas about the nursery and plans on contacting Nanny Poppinz, the nanny agency that celebrities use. "But you know what? Since Marco is already sixty, I always think of how . . . ehm . . . you know, that I will outlive him." With the mother-of-pearl spoon, she scoops up the last of the caviar, rolling up her eyes as if she's thinking. "Good thing my baby will ensure my financial future."

Is it a lump in my throat, or did the cracker with foie gras get stuck? I drink some water to rid myself of the lump. I drink more water to douse the firework of thoughts exploding in my head. Poor woman, she's so clueless about everything. How will she deal with Marco's rage when the other shoe drops? I've never paid much attention to Ava before but now feel bad about what's ahead for her and her unborn child.

"Sorry, but I have to go; I have plans with Maxwell."

"Maxwell? Is he that cute gay guy?" She grins. "That's so funny. I'm meeting my two gay friends too, my interior designers. Whenever Marco is out of town, I let them spend a night at the house. We always have so much fun together—they're a hoot." She stands up and looks at her tummy. "Wow! Look, Molara! I think I'm beginning to show already."

"I don't think that's possible so soon," I say, suppressing a pitying smile. "Anyway, Ava, thanks for sharing your news with me."

"Isn't it funny that you're my daughter and I'm only three years older than you?" She laughs and hugs me. "Stepdaughter, I mean." She scrambles into her silver Bugatti Chiron, and before she closes the door, she shouts, "This was so much fun. We have to do this again really soon!"

After a full Saturday of hanging out together at the Lake Shore Country Club with a couple of Maxwell's friends, Maxwell spends the night at my apartment so we can get an early Sunday morning start for our drive up to Kohler. We've booked tee time at Whistling Straits golf course, supposedly the most difficult course in the United States.

"Should we check our phones, just in case?" Maxwell twists his mouth into a teasing smile. "I know we both agreed to turn them off for the weekend."

I laugh. "Admit it, you're a phone junkie. Do what you must."

He raises his right eyebrow. I envy his ability to do this. I've tried it many times in front of the mirror but have never managed to achieve anything more than a weird forehead contortion.

"How do you do it?"

"Do what?"

"That thing with your eyebrow?"

He does it again and shrugs. "Well, are we going to check our phones before we leave?"

"You're the addict," I say and bite into my buttered bagel.

After hunching over his screen for a few minutes, he exhales and leans back. "Jeez," he says. "You'd better power up your phone."

"Why?"

"I have several missed calls from Phil, and he texted both of us to call him as soon as possible."

"On a weekend?" I drop the remains of my bagel on the plate. "I'll call him from my landline and put him on speakerphone; it's a clearer reception."

"Molly? I hope everything is okay. I got worried when I didn't hear back from you."

I apologize and quickly inform him of our weekend social media cleanse. "It was Maxwell who caved," I say, grinning. "By the way, he's sitting next to me."

"Good," says Phil. "I won't mention names, but after my right-hand man came back from his assignment, I brought him up-to-date on your case." I hear rustling on the other end. "Well, some unexpected, rather mind-blowing connections came to light. Can you come to my office?"

Neither Maxwell nor I speak. My stomach gurgles loudly.

Weirdly, the Keurig machine on the kitchen counter responds with a fizz.

"Molly? Maxwell?"

"We're here," says Maxwell. "We're just taken aback."

"Phil, can you give us a clue?"

"Not over the phone. Let me just say, we have a breakthrough—a *very* good one."

"When can we come?"

"The sooner the better. If possible, today."

"It's Sunday. You're working?"

"Absolutely. I'm dying to tell you what we learned."

FORTY

Mateo, June 2019
En route to Panama

Soon after they finished eating, Carmen, the flight attendant, removed the dishes from the table that separated the four oversized cream-colored leather seats.

"May I serve or assist with anything else?"

"Not now," said Marco.

Mateo listened to the deep white sound coming from his new Gulfstream's engines. He wished the ceaseless hum would lull him into easy sleep. Instead his heartbeat was like thunder in his chest. He hoped his racing heart was due to the double espresso and not a medical problem.

He glanced at his son.

Marco was looking out the wide oval window. Without turning his head, he said, "We both did our best for Molara. We offered her a great job and a brilliant future. Too fucking bad she can't see it. You and I certainly can't walk her to the finish line."

"But what made her go off all of a sudden?" Mateo rubbed his stubble. He hated the lack of clearness, the absence of distinctness. "I can't shake the feeling that she discovered something while we were gone. She certainly had time to snoop around."

Marco rolled his eyes. "You overthink everything. I'm the only one who knows the combination to my storage room. But if it makes you feel better, I'll make sure nobody went in there and messed with the old records."

"Right," Mateo said too quickly, not about to mention what he kept hidden in the secret compartments of his own house. "Right."

"You know, there's really no reason to keep all that old stuff anymore. What the devil for?"

"Maybe it's time to get rid of it. Can you burn it all?"

Marco clapped his hands together. "Remember I told you Ava had me build a workroom for her pottery in the basement? Next time she's with her designer boys in Chicago, I'll give her new kiln a nice workout." He grinned. "It'll be such a relief to get rid of all that old shit."

Mateo rubbed his stubble again. "What if Molara got in touch with Manoel before he passed away? What if she talked to Claudia and the kids?"

Marco snorted. "Forget it! She has no memory of them. And even if she did, your imbecile younger son signed the same documents as we did." He shook his head. "I bet he never even discussed any of it with Claudia or his kids. He was always too embarrassed about our more adventurous business dealings."

Forgotten emotions hit Mateo like a thunderbolt. He clenched his fists. "May his soul rest in peace."

"At any rate, I made sure Robert Graf was the only person named on *delicate* documents. I also resolved the minor maneuvers we made in the States—the ones that may not have been completely legal." Marco's grin melted. "Why are you looking at me like that?"

"What minor maneuvers? What are you talking about?" Marco had a habit of giving a cosmetic facelift to ugly truths, failing to mention undesired wrinkles. What had his son not been telling him? Had he *really* resolved questionable operations, or had he stashed the evidence away in the storage room, together with all the old incriminating stuff?

More hair-raising possibilities sped through Mateo's mind.

Until Marco checked the storage room, he wouldn't rule out Molara rummaging through those boxes. And why had she really been in his house while he was in Wyoming?

His pounding heart started to scare him. *Please God*, he begged, *not another damn stroke.*

Trying to calm down, he inhaled deeply and looked at Marco as if he were seeing his son for the first time: a carefree and condescending man with a spoiled smile playing around his lips. *Dear God, don't do this*, he pleaded silently. *You already alienated Manoel from me many years ago—please don't drive a wedge between me and Marco.*

Mateo's mouth was dry, leaving him with a bitter taste. He pressed the call button and told Paul, the second flight attendant, to bring them water and a bottle of Clase Azul Día de Muertos.

When they were alone again, Marco leaned towards his father. "Relax! Whoever says money and power doesn't tilt the scales of justice is a bloody fool," he said, still grinning. "The laws for the wealthy have been and always will be different." He downed the tequila, refilled his glass, and lifted it towards his father. "Being a risk-taker is nothing to sneer at. I inherited this gift from you, Papá. You taught me how to turn a bad situation to an advantage."

For the next twenty minutes, Marco rambled on about his ingenuity. Over and over, he referred to himself as a respected entrepreneur to whom cunning came as second nature. Mateo didn't interrupt, even felt a sense of satisfaction for having passed on valuable traits, but he also felt guilt-ridden when confronted with Marco's condescending smugness. But when he started slurring his words, Mateo removed the half-empty bottle from his son's hand.

"Enough," he said, realizing the word had a double meaning. *Those who talk a lot about themselves usually have little to say*, he thought.

He motioned Carmen to remove the glasses and bottle from the table, then she pushed the button that turned Marco's chair into a chaise; he had already fallen asleep.

Mateo was jealous. He so badly wished for even a quick power nap to restore himself. Knowing that wouldn't happen, he slowly stood up. He groaned; his whole body ached. He walked stiffly to the lavatory.

The luxurious bathroom, with its large oval window, was bright and airy. Fully equipped with the finest fixtures and latest technologies, it even had a shower for long-range flights.

Mateo locked the door, stared out of the window into the endless blue. When he turned to the mirror, he was taken aback by the image of an old man greeting him.

"What happened to you?" he asked his reflection. Just yesterday he'd played eighteen holes and still had energy to attend the dinner soirée in the governor's mansion. Hadn't he surprised everybody with his vitality and appetite for life in Wyoming? Even women twenty, thirty years his junior had flirted with him.

So why couldn't he recognize this alien in the mirror?

Suddenly his hands were on fire. Damn! He had forgotten to shut off the hot water. He grabbed the cream-colored hand towel with its bold gold *M* in the middle. Carefully he dried his still-burning hands, then wiped the steamed-up mirror.

"You're on your own," he told his reflection. "But who can you trust or rely on?"

He thought of Pelón. Mateo hadn't heard from him since that fateful day in February. The guy had made many enemies throughout his career. Perhaps he'd finally gotten arrested. Or perhaps he'd just dropped dead of natural causes from being so damn overweight.

Then there was Molara, with her sudden distant behavior and frosty indifference. A chill ran down Mateo's spine. She'd always been highly perceptive, and she had a photographic memory. Dear God, had she started to remember fragments of her past? He had to find out what she was up to. But who could he trust to spy on her? Sure, he could hire a private detective, but there would be too many questions. Mateo had no intention of sharing the answers with a stranger.

He remembered the number Pelón had given him at the end of their last phone conversation. He had tucked it away with the rest of his secrets in the armoire. What was the guy's name? Didn't it have something to do with food? Of course—Nacho.

Even though Pelón had vouched for Nacho's dependability, Mateo hated the idea of having to acquaint himself with a new shady character. But what other choice did he have? He made a mental note to call this Nacho as soon as possible.

He noticed sweat on his forehead and questioned why everything seemed like madness in a world already full of complications and cruelty. A world that until yesterday had seemed far away. A world Mateo neither understood nor wanted to live in. Why did everything suddenly seem wrong? What had triggered it? Who was the cause behind it all?

He staggered back when the conniving eyes in the mirror revealed recognition. "No!" Pointing at the reflection, he hissed, "You did *not* do anything wrong! You always did your best to make things right again."

FORTY-ONE

Ursula, May 2019
Hamburg, Germany

Hope you enjoyed your stay with us, Mrs. Rossi," the receptionist said, handing Ursula itemized statements for two suites.

She glanced at the man's name tag. "Thank you, Marcus. The Fontenay is a lovely hotel. We really appreciated the pretty views over the park and Lake Alster."

"Well, we hope to welcome you again."

"I hope so," Ursula said, smiling broadly.

She and Bernard had flown to Hamburg for Edge of Today, the biggest exposition in Germany. Mick was one of only three young artists who'd been selected by an international jury. After four event-packed days, they'd all be flying back to Switzerland this afternoon.

"Was it your first visit to Hamburg?"

"I came here once before, but that was many years ago. Since then, Hamburg has grown and improved in many ways."

"Wouldn't it be nice if that was true for everything?" Marcus grinned widely. "I woke up one morning to discover that I had been replaced with a much older version of me. Not fair, because old Hamburg keeps getting better and younger."

"Nein! Ist das möglich? Ursula Graf? Can it be possible?"

Ursula's carefree laughter got caught in her throat, replaced by the almost-forgotten fear of being found. Alarmed, she turned her head towards the voice. Who was this tall, attractive woman?

"Unbelievable! It really is you."

She took a step back.

The woman's smile faded. "Don't tell me the years have aged *me* beyond recognition." But immediately the twinkle in her eyes returned and she stretched out her arms. "It's Elke Schott," she cried out. Without another word, she hugged Ursula.

Stunned, she tried to relax into the embrace of the woman who'd been her closest friend during her modeling career.

"Please tell me you have a moment to catch up," Elke said, pulling Ursula away from the front desk.

They found a shaded table on the terrace with views across the lake.

"What in the flipping heck happened to you?" Elke said after she ordered two cappuccinos. "The last time I saw you was at that fabulous engagement party for you and your handsome Mexican prince at the Grand Hotel in Zurich. And then I never heard from you again."

Ursula swallowed. She'd written to Elke many times; apparently none of her letters had made it out of the gilded cage that imprisoned her. "It's a long and complicated story."

"I had no idea how to reach you. Even your despicable father was nowhere to be found. I went to your old house to inquire about your whereabouts, but your stepmother slammed the door in my face."

Feverishly thinking about any plausible explanation, Ursula gestured her friend to continue.

"Over the years I kept googling you, but you had zero online presence. It was like the earth had gobbled you up. I imagined the worst." Elke shook her head. "Never mind, you're here." She leaned closer. "But where were you all these years?"

Weighing her response, Ursula settled for half-truths, blaming herself for her inability to adapt to life in Mexico and maintain the passion she'd once felt for her husband. She didn't say anything about the mental and physical abuse she'd endured, nor did she talk about her ongoing fear of Mateo and Marco Miraldo.

"Mmmm." Elke tilted her head to the left. "You know, when that handsome devil carried you off to Mexico, I thought you were the luckiest girl on earth. What went wrong?"

"Forgive me, but there are things I'm unable to talk about right now." Ursula lowered her voice. "I needed a lot of therapy; it was the only way to move forward and raise my son safely. I'm still trying to rectify my mistakes."

"I was under the impression that you had no more use for me. That the wealth you married into had gone to your head."

A strained smile formed on Ursula's lips. "Just the opposite. Circumstances changed to the point where I had to keep my circle of friends tight," she said. "Maybe you can tell that I'm not the vivacious, carefree girl you once knew."

"The past is irrelevant," Elke cried out, waving both her hands as if to rid herself of unpleasantries. "Let me share my mantra with you: the nicest thing about the future is that it always starts tomorrow."

Ursula heard persistent pings coming out of her orange Kelly bag. "I am sorry, I need to take this." She walked over to the balustrade to check her phone. There were three messages from Bruno. He and Joaquín were with Rabbi Hebroni on a study tour in Israel. There were also three texts from Mick. She quickly texted back, then returned to the table.

"Is everything okay?"

Ursula nodded and put the phone next to her coffee cup. "My son will let me know when he'll pick me up." She looked at Elke. "Meanwhile, let me hear your life story. You look so happy."

"Well." She grinned. "I ended up making good money with my modeling career and got used to a *very* nice lifestyle." Finger-combing her thick auburn hair, she winked. "But knowing that all models have a shelf life, I didn't hesitate to accept Julian Brower's marriage proposal while I was still in the springtime of my life."

"Julian Brower, the actor?"

"None other! For five years I strutted with Julian through glitz and glamour, but that all fell apart when he went to New Zealand. His role in *Aboriginal Secrets* won him an Oscar, but he also collected another trophy: his eighteen-year-old costar Alinta Adams." Elke leaned across the table. "Do you remember how you always teased me about my shrewdness? Well, my practical knowledge won me a juicy *mega*-million-dollar alimony suit that allowed me to keep moving through all the elite circles of Europe—and boy did I have fun!" Elke pointed to the nine-carat blue sapphire ring on her left hand. "This was my engagement ring from Luther Adlon."

"The Adlon Cosmetic mogul?"

"Yup," she said, motioning the server to bring two more cappuccinos. "Although my Luther was a bit older than I, we were a match made in heaven and enjoyed every second we had with each other. Every morning he sang 'Nessun Dorma' to me, the most romantic aria in opera. He meant everything to me, but when he passed away, his two sons from a previous marriage claimed their father had been in an unfit condition to manage his estate. They accused me of taking advantage of my husband's fortune." She dismissively waved her hand. "Not to bore you with details of the three-year dogfight, but the judges ended up ruling in my favor." She tilted her head again. "I'm surprised you're unaware of all this. It was all over the news."

Ursula blushed. "After leaving Mexico, it was in my best interest to stay away from news. My own issues caused enough stress and anxiety. The ills of the world made it even harder for me to trust people."

"I get it. It's nerve-wracking to read the daily op-eds and watch all those talking heads carry on about the crisis du jour. Sometimes I wish I could quit the daily grind and say adiós to the rat race."

"Why can't you?"

Elke shrugged. "Since I have no children, my work makes me feel like I have a place in the world."

"You started to work again?"

"After settling with Luther's sons, I changed my name back to

Schott and opened ESP, short for Elke Schott Production—my rather successful talent agency. Call it ego or the need to be the big kahuna, I adore being in charge."

Grateful that Elke was talking about her own life rather than asking Ursula more questions about hers, she listened with great interest, admiring her friend for never having lost her famous joie de vivre from bygone days.

"Remember all the crazy things that happened to us during Fashion Week in Paris?" Elke suppressed a laugh and discreetly nodded towards an elderly lady who had walked onto the terrace with an austere expression, holding two poodles on a rhinestone-adorned double leash. The dogs' limbs were hairless, with just pom-poms around their front and back paws. Even the poodles' tails were rounded off; only their chests, stomachs, and heads had been left with hair.

Ursula almost choked on her sip of coffee. She held her hand in front of her mouth to keep from laughing. "Like Gaultier's prêt-à-porter, when I could barely walk in that tight leather ensemble while trying to control two pink poodles on a leash?"

"Yes!" Elke guffawed at the memory. "Remember how they piled your hair up in a pompom to match the dogs? I don't know how you kept a straight face while pirouetting around that pink poodle after it squatted on the runway and peed."

"Omigod, I was mortified." Ursula pointed at her friend. "But what about the time when your heel got caught and broke off during the Yves Saint Laurent show? People didn't even realize you fell because you nonchalantly took off the other shoe and, without losing a step, dropped both shoes onto the lap of a young man sitting in the front row. The reviews the next day were all about 'ubermodel Elke's precise acrobatic timing.'"

"Don't you remember who the young man was?"

"No. Who was he?"

"None other than Julian Brower. He called me a few days later, claiming that my gold stiletto had left a permanent mark on his magic wand." Elke threw her head back and laughed. "Within a year, we were married. I wanted to tell you, but by then you were in Mexico already."

While relishing memorable moments, Ursula fought the intrusion of her troubled mind. She had a burning desire to tell her old friend the truth, shed a bad conscience.

Elke looked at her thoughtfully. "What are you thinking?"

"There are things I'd like to tell you but can't. All I can say today is that my son and I have been forced to live in hiding." Without thinking, she looked around. "I'd appreciate it if you didn't mention running into me to anyone."

Visibly touched, Elke said, "Can you give any details at all? I'm connected to a lot of important people who might be able to help you."

"I appreciate your offer, but I have trusted friends who've managed to conceal my identity and my son's. Keeping today's encounter secret is all I ask of you, please."

"Of course. I promise."

A ping alerted Ursula to a new message.

"It's time to go." As soon as she rose from the table, she became aware of the absurdity of her situation. She'd just allowed herself to reconnect with the past. Perhaps her complicated life was ready to release one link of the fateful chain at a time.

"Wait, wait." Elke held her arm. "I just found you, and I'm not letting you disappear again. How can I reach you?"

Ursula handed her phone to Elke. "Put in your number, and I promise to keep in touch."

Throughout the return flight to Geneva, Ursula let the memories from her youth wash over her, memories that for too long had lurked around the edges of her subconscious. So many ugly scenes, things she hadn't even understood at the time, suddenly made sense.

Ursula had been only sixteen years old when she invited Elke to visit her. She'd noticed her father ogling her friend from the moment she set foot in the door.

She remembered kicking Elke's leg under the table, mouthing apologies to her friend. She'd been embarrassed by her father and stepmother's disgusting table manners. They'd slurped their drinks, chewed with their mouths open, and never hesitated to burp loudly. Faces sweating, they kept dipping big, crusty chunks of bread into the steaming pot of cheese while drinking too much Brächere Brönnts, a caramelly sweet schnapps. Although Ursula and Elke liked cheese fondue, Robert Graf wagged his finger each time they dipped even the smallest piece of bread into the pot.

"Girls, watch your calories," he kept saying. "Too much dairy and too many carbohydrates will ruin your figures." With glassy eyes he ogled Elke's chest. "But there's a rule in the Graf house: if the bread falls off the fork and into the pot, you have to kiss your neighbor."

Though Ursula made sure not to lose as much as a morsel in the fondue pot, her drunk stepmother, sitting next to her, kept losing one after the other, giggling foolishly whenever she stuck her greasy lips on Ursula's cheek. Her father had placed himself next to Elke, and each time he dipped a chunk of bread and his fork came up empty, his laughter grew louder.

Immediately after dinner, Ursula pulled her friend into her room, again apologizing for her father's disgusting behavior. They stayed up until late into the night, giggling as they shared their secrets and dreams.

When Ursula woke to rustling sounds, she realized her father had sneaked into her room. He had covered Elke's mouth with his large hand and was whispering vile things while he grabbed her between the legs. Forgetting how much she feared him, Ursula jumped from her bed. Screaming, she pounded her fists on his back. When she managed to drag him off her best friend, she tore his favorite checkered shirt. Robert Graf whipped around, slapped his daughter hard across the face, threw her against the bedposts, watched her fall down and kicked her in the stomach.

"You breathe one word to anyone about this and you will suffer the consequences," he said to both girls before he backed out of the room.

Early the following morning, Elke packed her bag. "I'll always be grateful how you saved me from your despicable father," she said. "That man is a disgusting pig, and his bitter wife a greedy enabler. You must get away from these two monsters—the sooner the better."

Days later, during a terrible argument between Robert and Bertha, Ursula became aware of a concealed peephole from an adjacent room into hers. Her father had always been listening and watching.

She shuddered when the plane touched down at Sion Airport. It was raining, and thick drops pearled down the other side of the glass as Ursula rested her forehead against the window. She wondered where she would be and who she would have become, had she taken Elke's advice after that terrible night and run away from the malignant Graf home. Of course, it had been impossible. Robert Graf had known his daughter was well on her way to being one of the most sought-after models in Europe, and with his insatiable appetite for money, he'd kept his icy clutches on her. He'd only released his prize possession the day he sold her, delivering her into the iron grip of Mateo Miraldo.

Robert Graf was dead and couldn't hurt anyone anymore. But Mateo, though an old man now, had remained monstrous and violent. If Bruno was correct, then he had been behind the murder of Amelia Rubio's friend.

FORTY-TWO

Molly, June 2019
Chicago, Illinois

Even though it's been clear to me from the beginning that our unexpected early Sunday morning meeting with Phil will be anything but ordinary, I can't seem to pull everything together.

Phil is already waiting for us in the small lobby of Flores & Associates. His face is unreadable. "With temperatures in the low eighties and a steady breeze off Lake Michigan, sitting indoors would be a waste of a Sunday. Hope you guys don't mind doing this on the roof terrace."

We follow him under the louvered-roof pergola. On the round table are manila envelopes and folders, meticulously laid out. There are two open laptops and four chairs for three of us.

Other than having exchanged greetings downstairs, I haven't said a word, but I can't take it any longer. "Please don't keep me in suspense. I feel like the cat on a hot tin roof." Remembering my surroundings, I add, "No pun intended."

"Ah! Here he comes." Phil hurries towards the sliding door and opens it for a tall dark-haired man who's balancing a tray with glasses and bottles of water. As soon as he puts the tray on a side table, the man—I guess him to be around my age—turns to me.

"Alex Rivas." His voice is sonorous, his handshake firm. He

holds on to my hand when he says, "You may not remember, but we've met before."

More than a foot taller than me, this ruggedly handsome stranger reminds me of a young Javier Bardem. A wobbling weakness takes root in my knees when I notice his violet-blue eyes. Without warning, a memory seeps through the tight filigree mesh my brain has woven.

I lie in a small bed, cocooned in my mother's arms. I tell her how much fun I had playing with new friends, especially the boy who has eyes like flowers. "Yes, Alejandro's eyes are violet, like the petals on the jacaranda trees," *my mother whispers and kisses my forehead.*

Holy f—! I stare at the tall man as another flash pierces through.

Miggy and I are in a small fenced-in yard, laughing, shrieking, and running away from Alejandro, the older brother of Maritsa and Joel. Alejandro is holding a water hose, chasing us with the cold spray. The grass is wet—I slip and fall. I shriek when the spray hits my back. Alejandro drops the hose and helps me get up again.

"Did you hurt yourself?" *he asks.*

"No!" *I laugh and run away from him.* "Bet you can't catch me now."

Alex's violet-blue eyes smile into mine. "My siblings and I played with you and your twin brother—I was eight, four years older than you."

I find it difficult to master my wobbling knees. "Where was that?"

"In Amelia Rubio's backyard—she was our neighbor in Miami's Little Havana."

I hold on to the edge of the table to steady myself. "Wait. What? You know her?"

Alex pulls out a chair for me. "Let me fill you in."

While he talks, both of my hands are steepled over my mouth and nose. Only when he finishes do my hands, like heavy dumbbells, fall into my lap.

"Whoa! I felt something extraordinary was going to happen," Maxwell says, wide-eyed. "First came the call from Amelia Rubio, then you met Phil Flores at the spa in Lake Geneva, and now Phil introduces you to Alex Rivas, who knows Amelia Rubio. They all connect."

My heart feels like it wants to gallop away. I'm on pins and needles, waiting for the next revelation.

"When Phil briefed me on this case, the name Miraldo sounded familiar," Alex says. "Then I remembered that three decades ago my siblings and I were told not to mention Amelia Rubio's name to anyone, and we should forget having met Ursula Miraldo and her kids. I overheard my parents talking about Amelia Rubio having to sell her house because she was afraid of a Mateo Miraldo."

I climb into a blue car; I'm crying. I don't want to leave Amelia's Smurf-like house with the red roof and the green door. I tell Mamà I want to stay here and have fun with my new friends. "Like Miggy, I don't want to play the hide-and-go-seek game anymore."

"Please be patient," she says. "I promise the game will be over soon."

Alejandro, Maritsa, Joel, and their parents stand by the curb. I wave to them until I can't see them anymore.

"Back then, Little Havana was one of the hottest zones of the Miami drug wars." As if from far away, Alex's voice draws me back into the now. "My family, our friends, and our neighbors had to be careful about who they trusted. Some thugs kept coming to our house, threatening my parents, wanting to know about Amelia's whereabouts. Shortly after that, we also moved away."

I stare at Alex's lips. Every new sentence brings me closer to why I'm here.

He rubs his chin. "I'd forgotten about what happened in 1992. Not until a few days ago, when Phil told me about your case and showed me the files, did a bell go off in my head. The second I looked at your old photos, everything came together. I recognized your faces. I remembered your names—Molly and Miggy, the kids we'd played with in Amelia Rubio's backyard." A frown line forms between his brows. "I was only eight years old then, but I remember that your mother seemed afraid; she looked exhausted. Today I know why." He points to the documents and videocassettes. "I read and watched all of it."

After another moment of silence, Alex removes envelopes and photos from one of his folders. He lays them out in front of me. "Take a look." His deep voice is gentle. "These were taken in Amelia's backyard in June of 1992. Maybe they'll help you remember."

I don't know how long I stay hunched over the table on Phil's rooftop terrace with my gaze fixed on the photos.

"Molly."

My eyes wander to the two antennae on top of the Willis Tower in the distance. Just as they did when I lay on the lounge on this very terrace, they beckon me again. But this time, their flashing strobe lights do the opposite of hypnotizing me.

"Molly."

I turn towards his voice.

"I do remember," I say. "It's all coming back." As much as I try not to take this chaotic ride so emotionally, I pull the Kleenex box towards me. The two demanding, indifferent men who raised me said that crying was a weakness. "If you have a problem, find a way to fix it," Mateo always demanded. "Don't make me feel ashamed of you," Marco would yell and walk away. But since rediscovering my past in storage rooms, attics, and secret compartments, my floodgates haven't been able to hold back the accumulated pressure.

I excuse myself and walk away from the table. Standing by the railing, I let the sun dry my cheeks. When I gain control of my emotions, I seat myself next to Alex again. "Please go on."

I hear the scraping of furniture. With his long legs, Phil is pushing the ottoman away from his chair. He puffs out his cheeks. "It still blows my mind what Alex is about to tell you."

Alex removes a photo from another envelope. "This is my father's older brother, Luis, who lived in New Jersey. We were his only family, and he often visited us in Tampa to escape the harsh winters. Later, he developed macular degeneration and couldn't work or travel anymore. Due to other health issues, he became frail and depended on friends and neighbors to take care of him. His favorite caretaker was none other than Amelia."

My hands are steepled over my nose and mouth again; I'm holding my breath.

"A few months ago, Uncle Luis was found murdered in his apartment. The police are still looking for the suspects." Alex opens another folder. "These are copies of the police reports." He flicks through some pages until he finds what he's looking for. "Witnesses reported seeing two people around the time of the murder. One was a gruff, burly guy. The other was an older man with salt-and-pepper hair, a scar, and a small birthmark distinctive enough to be seen through his stubble on the right side of his face." He lays the pages in front of me.

I try to connect what I'm seeing. Is it because I feel numb that nothing seems particularly significant to me? I look at the pages so intently that I'm unaware of how close I am to Alex's face. When I turn my head, I feel his breath on my skin.

"I'm sorry about your uncle. But what does that have to do with . . ."

The corners of his mouth turn up. "Since the police investigation is at a standstill, my father asked me to do some probing of my own."

As the midday sun glints in his eyes, there's a flash of exhilaration.

"Are you hinting that this"—I wave my hand over his files—"is the tip of the iceberg?"

He nods. "I asked Bob, our forensic sketch artist, to come with me to New Jersey to interview three teenage girls and a young man who'd been on the elevator with an older man—someone they'd never noticed in the building or in the neighborhood." He points to one of the paragraphs. "The kids described the older man as about six feet tall and in good physical shape."

Alex's overview turns into moving images that run like a feature film before my mind's eye.

"Forensic artists are trained to ask all the right questions, and Bob is one of the best. These are the sketches he made." He pulls three pages from the file and lays them in front of Maxwell and me.

My brain shuts down, as if it refuses to accept what I'm seeing. Maxwell leans his head over the drawings and lets loose a long, low whistle.

In these pencil sketches is the face of an older man with salt-and-pepper hair under a New York Knicks cap.

I'm shaking my head, pushing so hard against the pain of disbelief that I feel dizzy.

"Molly?"

"It can't be."

"It is! Just look at the shape of the nose, the eyes, the birthmark," Maxwell says. "This is Mateo."

"But no. He would never wear clothes like this. And he would never risk getting caught. He's always had people do his dirty work for him."

Maxwell mutters something.

"What?"

"'He who fights with monsters should look to it that he himself does not become a monster,'" he quotes, stone-faced.

"Seems as if everybody underestimated Mateo Miraldo's capacity for self-delusion." Phil remains calm, unruffled, but his brown eyes radiate eagerness. "Let's not forget the reports that describe another man leaving the building around the time the medical examiner established Luis's time of death."

Alex pulls two other pencil sketches from the folder and lays them in front of us.

I shake my head again.

Maxwell agrees. "Never seen this guy."

"Some folks in the diner across the street said they saw both these men enter the building." Alex frowns. "We have no proof yet, but from what we've learned, we can assume the burly one was hired to do the dirty work for Mateo."

"We've already sent the sketches to our competent contacts

around the country, asking them to be on the lookout." Phil's soothing voice is encouraging. "From all the documentation you guys brought in, from everything you told me, and after seeing these sketches, I think Mateo came to New Jersey to confront Amelia Rubio himself. Most likely he was still ticked off about missing his opportunity to deal with Marisol when she came to his house looking for Molly." He points to Mateo's face. "No doubt he remembered Amelia and Marisol's relationship, and since Marisol had slipped through his fingers, he wanted to lead the hunt."

"Exactly," Alex chimes in. "For decades, Mateo searched for your mother and brother. He probably knew this would be his last chance." He cocks his head. "The question is, if they were after Amelia, why did they kill my uncle?"

"Oh no! That means she's still in danger."

"She's a tough old lady," Alex says. "She laid low for a short while and stayed with a friend a few blocks away. But she's back in her apartment now, doing what she likes best: taking care of people."

My heartbeat quickens as my mind moves some puzzle pieces together. Alex has been in touch with Amelia. Did she tell him what happened to my mother and brother? Is this the reason why Phil called us in today, on a Sunday? I open my mouth, then close it again, afraid of hearing what I want to hear.

"I know you're on the edge of your seat, Molly," says Phil. "But we thought the long prologue was needed to understand the epilogue." He gestures to Alex.

Is it my imagination, or do his violet eyes sparkle when I look at him?

"I told Amelia that you and I were meeting today." His smile is so genuine, it changes the landscape of his face, like a flower garden coming alive. "She wants to tell you herself what she knows."

"Amelia is here?"

"Unfortunately not," he says, still smiling. "But she agreed to meet with a colleague of ours in New Jersey for tech support, and we arranged—" The alarm on his phone stops him midsentence.

"Here we go." He wakes up the two laptops, clicks on Zoom links, and places one MacBook in front of Maxwell and Phil, the other in front of me. He pulls his chair close to mine.

I hear voices, then see a middle-aged, balding man with dark bushy eyebrows. He wears an earring, and on his burgundy T-shirt is a white imprint that says, "It is what it is, unless it isn't."

"Hi, everybody," the man says hurriedly. "Give me another second, please." He disappears from the screen.

"That's Sam Silver, our colleague," whispers Alex.

I hear the shuffling and scraping of chairs, then see a woman's plump upper body. She's wearing a white scoop-neck shirt, and a gold cross necklace rests on her brown skin. In Spanish she asks Sam what to do. He tells her to sit next to him and look straight at the screen.

My heartbeat is in gallop mode again. The woman has a round, brown face; her wavy, dark hair with silver streaks is combed out of her face and falls loose behind her ears. She leans away from the screen, looking uncertain. "Necesito mis lentes."

"Remember to speak in English," Sam whispers, handing her dark-rimmed spectacles.

She puts on her glasses. "Querido Dios." Her voice chokes with emotion. "Mull-ly! Is this really you?"

Miggy sits on Marisol's lap, pressing Julio and his blue blanket tightly to his chest. He looks tired, but he's laughing at Amelia. "Try to say Molly." He giggles, then repeats my name slowly, "Mahhhly."

"That's what I've been saying." Amelia shrugs. "Mull-ly, right?"

"No." Miggy chuckles and snuggles into Marisol's arms. He's yawning.

"Please, Amelia, can you play Chocolate one more time with me?" I hold out my hands. She agrees and together we singsong, "Choco-choco-la-la, Choco-choco-te-te, Choco-la-Choco-te-Choco-la-te." We sing and clap our hands together, faster and faster, until Amelia mixes up her words and hand movements.

"You win again." She kisses the top of my head, laughing. *"You're too fast for me. After playing all day outside, you must be tired, too."* She gives me a hug. *"Buenas noches, mi querida Mull-ly."*

Looking at me through the screen, the same round cocoa-colored eyes have deep smile lines around them.

"Amelia," I breathe.

"Mull-ly, you recognize me after all these years?" Her Cuban accent is heavy. "Alex told me you had trouble remembering much of your childhood years, but that your memory is coming back now." She takes off her glasses and wipes her eyes with the back of her hand.

"You taught me how to play Cho-co-la-te," I say. The just-recaptured memory is still lingering.

"You were a little girl, but you learned that game so fast."

"You drove us to the airport in a blue car. Were you there when the accident happened?"

"No. I didn't know until later, when Marisol got in touch with me to warn me about Mateo and Marco." Amelia wipes her eyes again. "After that, I only heard from her sporadically—she always reminded me to be careful of the Miraldo men. I knew she was safe somewhere with your mother and brother, but I never knew where." She sighs. "Do you know that Marisol tried to find you in Mira earlier this year? Unfortunately, that didn't happen."

Seconds pass, and I wait for Amelia to continue, but she doesn't.

"Did Marisol ask you to call me?"

She nods. "She had so much to tell you, but more so, she wanted to see you one more time before she died."

My mouth falls open, but no words come out. Absentmindedly I gather my hair in both hands, loop it a couple of times, and tie it in a knot on top of my head. When I get my thoughts in a logical order again, I push away the pencil sketches; I don't want to see *their* faces. "Marisol died?"

"She had terminal cancer, Mull-ly. When she passed, your mother and brother were with her."

My heart hammers against my throat. "Where are they?" I don't recognize my voice—so tense, so frayed. "Please tell me where I can find my family."

For the next ten minutes I don't interrupt Amelia. Every word produces vivid scenes in my mind. When she stops talking, complete silence envelops us on Phil's rooftop garden. I don't even hear the city noises eight stories below on West Randolph Street. Only when an airplane drones overhead towards O'Hare do I look at Phil. His face has lost all color, and he looks ill. I know he's older, but does he have a health problem? A weak heart? Is he a diabetic? I can tell he's struggling to keep his composure, and though I'm overwhelmed by what I've just heard, I now worry he is going to collapse. "Are you okay?"

He nods, puffs out his cheeks, then ever so slowly blows out the air. "This now links *me* to the whole chain of events." Through pursed lips he blows out more air. "The Salina Group, an international private bank, hired the PI firm I worked for in 1992. My boss at the time chose me to assist a senior executive of the bank in a private matter. The case was rather sensitive, and I signed an NDA." Phil looks at me, then turns to Alex and Maxwell before addressing Amelia on-screen again. "For more than a year I assisted a gentleman whose name you just mentioned—Bruno Rossi."

I need to quickly rewind the movie in my head. Amelia told us that my mother, in an attempt to change her identity, got married to a Bruno Rossi, who then adopted my brother. I hesitantly ask Phil, "What makes you think it's the same person?"

"When I visited a former colleague in Mexico recently, we chatted about old acquaintances and clients. I learned that Bruno took retirement in Crans-Montana, Switzerland."

"Molly! I told you!" Maxwell jumps up, sits down, then bounces up again. "The painting in your bedroom!" He grabs my shoulders. "Didn't I tell you there might be a connection?"

"Omigod!" The movie in my head is moving fast. So fast it's setting my brain on fire even as goosebumps form on my skin. I'm shivering.

Warm fingertips brush against my arm.

"Molly."

His voice suspends the movie. I turn my head, and Alex's violet-blue eyes smile into mine.

"I believe you've found what you've been searching for," he says.

FORTY-THREE

Mateo, July 2019
Mira, Wisconsin

He barely slept that night, and when he did, he fell into unilluminated dreams that roused him, frightened him. His eyes searched the dark, expecting someone sitting next to his bed, waiting to take him away.

When the morning finally dawned with its hazy transient light, he was so relieved that he almost gleefully jumped out of bed, but his limbs were heavy, forcing him to rise slowly. He groaned and damned the unfairness of it all.

A hot shower reduced some of the pain, and after meticulously picking out his clothes, he dressed in eerie silence. Buttoning his blue Brioni shirt, he longed for nothing more than hearing the clatter from the kitchen below, wouldn't even mind hearing Yoli's perpetual humming—a sound that normally pissed him off.

Yoli, never in a bad mood, smiled when he entered the kitchen. She'd already set the table for him. He was used to the single place setting—as a matter of fact, he preferred it—but never had he felt as alone as he did this morning. Though hungry, he couldn't manage more than a few bites from the chorizo and avocado omelet. He didn't really care for his beloved café con leche this morning either.

Looking past his plate, across the spotless table and into a murky void, he was unaware of his fork stabbing the avocado slices.

"¿Algo anda mal, señor?"

He almost jabbed the fork into the plump brown arm of Yoli, who stood irritatingly close. Again, she asked if something was wrong with the food or if he wasn't feeling well. He managed a half-smile.

His longtime housekeeper, who most likely knew him better than he did himself, smiled back.

"I'm saving my appetite for the US4KIDS fundraiser luncheon in less than two hours. I'm the designated speaker," he explained, trying to sound nonchalant. Halfway out of the kitchen, he stopped. "By the way, did Molara come by recently when I wasn't at home?"

"No, Señor Miraldo," she said. "I haven't seen her in some time, been wondering myself." When she pushed the chair under the table, it made a screeching sound. "Has there been a problem?"

"Of course not!"

At MiraCo, he tried to walk briskly through the labyrinthine glass-lined corridors. He felt like a trapped rat in a maze when he made all the familiar turns—right, right, left, and right again. Not until he pulled the door to his office shut behind him did he feel unobserved, undetectable.

For more than a quarter of an hour he sat idly behind his desk, still struggling to figure out Molara's bizarre behavior. She'd been distancing herself, more every day, and every day with fewer excuses. And each time he tried to confront her, she kept him at arm's length.

Her sidekick—the pretty boy with his pink shirts and slim-fitting suits—had also become more reserved, less visible.

Never having been let down by his keen intuition, Mateo couldn't shake the sinking feeling that Molara had acquired knowledge of something hidden and forbidden, perhaps even shared it with that damn Maxwell Walsh.

The last time he'd brought up her odd conduct with Marco, his son had shrugged, changing the subject to his wife's pregnancy and the importance of a new heir stepping into the Miraldo empire. "Ava did say she recently had a lovely dinner with Molara," he'd mused. "Apparently, she was thrilled to learn about our baby."

With his stomach already in knots, a new cramp surged from Mateo's guts to his brain. Was it possible Molara had gotten wind of the DNA test?

Mierda, mierda, mierda!

He pinched the bridge of his nose, digging his fingernails into the thin skin. How would Marco react if he found out Molara was his half sister?

Ignoring the morning hour, he popped open the cabinet and poured himself a double shot of tequila. Due to his empty stomach, the desired effect came fast, allowing him to let his mind go blank. Only when he heard the knock at the door did he snap out of his daze.

"Would you like to go over your speech—I have it right here." Brandi Bowman, Mateo's executive assistant, held the pages in her hand.

"No. It's perfect the way it is."

"Indeed, it's excellent, Mr. Miraldo. Really, really excellent." She put the pages on the side of his desk.

Before Brandi left the room, he called out to her.

"Sir?"

"Did my granddaughter come in today?"

"I heard she was in her office before the crack of dawn, but she'd already left by the time I arrived."

"Where is Walsh?"

"I was told he left with Ms. Miraldo."

Damn! He looked at Molara's photo on his desk. *What gives her the right to avoid me? She owes me an explanation.* He'd call and text her again after the fundraiser. And if she didn't answer, he would track her down until he stood face-to-face with her.

He contemplated the dialogue, then dictated distinct questions into his phone, preparing answers in case Molara bombarded him with accusations.

"How can you forget all I've done for you?" he asked the photo in the frame. "Didn't I give you everything you desired? And must I remind you of the golden future I've laid out for you?"

The blinking light on his business phone reminded him of his schedule. He pressed the speaker button. "Yes?"

"Your driver is waiting downstairs, Mr. Miraldo. Traffic is light; you should arrive at the Tripoli Center in less than forty-five minutes."

Sven Salvesson, US4KIDS committee chair, gave Mateo a lengthy introduction, in which he commended MiraCo's long-standing generosity, praising his success and thanking him for his steadfast commitment and dependability.

Though used to accolades, Mateo never tired of hearing them. Slowly he managed to shelve his earlier distress. When it was time for him to speak, he rose effortlessly and stood tall behind the lectern.

He delivered his address with confidence and passion. Presenting himself as an expert on the topic of children in need, he laced his delivery with personal stories—much of it embellished, other parts completely false. He kept every detail of his presentation short and to the point to make room for the applause, the cheers, and the laughter that would occasionally interrupt his delivery. He ended with an effective, carefully constructed closing point and inhaled the crowd's standing ovation in the filled to-capacity ballroom.

But as soon as he stepped off the stage to join the other illustrious guests at his table, reality smacked him so hard in the face that he barely made it through the rest of the hour. He was in no mood to cope with the yakety-yak of fellow attendees, bothering him with unpleasant questions.

"Take me to my granddaughter's address," Mateo told Norman, one of MiraCo's full-time chauffeurs. He looked at his phone again. There had been no reply to his two text messages or his short voicemail.

The drive from the Tripoli Center to Molara's apartment building in Milwaukee took twenty minutes, giving him a chance to silently rehearse his confrontation.

"Wait down here," he told Norman. "I don't know how long I'll be."

Mateo remembered the doorman; he had seen him before. "Is my granddaughter at home?"

"Sorry, sir. I just started my shift."

While on the elevator, he fumbled for the key in his coat jacket. For a second, he thought he had forgotten to take it. When he finally held it between his fingers, he blew air through his lips, sounding like a tire slowly losing air.

He knocked softly, then harder. He leaned his ear against the door. He heard nothing. He inserted the key into the lock; it didn't turn. He looked at the key, tried again, then checked to see if it was bent. He spat on it twice and tried a third time.

Staring at the key, he realized what was wrong: Molara had changed the locks.

"¡Tonto del culo!" He flung the key against her door, where it bounced off and landed at his feet. He didn't bother to pick it up. One way or the other, Molara would know he'd been there—the doorman surely would tell her.

"Where to next, Mr. Miraldo?" asked Norman.

"Home!" he barked.

Mateo's misery only intensified when he saw three landscaping trucks blocking his driveway on Bayside Drive. He stormed into the house. "What's going on? The noise out there is deafening," he yelled.

"But Señor Miraldo," Yoli said, "you asked me to call the landscaper to get rid of the overgrowth and dead shrubs. The landscapers came right after you left this morning. I didn't expect you back until later tonight."

Dammit, he'd forgotten. He'd wanted the bluff cleared before his Independence Day celebrations. "I'm going upstairs and don't want to be disturbed!"

Where was his burner phone? He remembered hiding it in the

armoire. Mateo twisted the knob, waited for the click, and opened one of the secret drawers. There it was. He powered it on. Nothing. No text messages, no missed phone calls. ¡Qué cabrón! What was wrong with this guy? He should have had some information by now.

Mateo hadn't heard a word from Pelón since the disastrous setback in early January. The stress of that day, compounded by radio silence, had probably caused his damn stroke. As much as he had tried to get past it all, Molara's sudden change in behavior had catapulted everything to the foreground again. That's why, five days after the trip to Panama, he decided to reach out to Ignacio or Nacho—whatever Pelón had said the guy called himself.

Mateo looked at the four disposable phones he'd recently purchased and decided to use one of the Alcatel TracFones first. With mixed feelings, he dialed the number.

"How can I be of assistance?" The man's voice was squeaky, as if he'd inhaled helium.

Following Pelón's instructions, Mateo muttered, "My brother can't fix my laptop. He said you could help me."

"Damn right I can." The squeaky voice got an octave higher. "Where and when can I meet you to look at it?"

Mateo made some quick calculations. Obviously, he wouldn't let this shady stranger into his house. "How about this afternoon at Starbucks in Whitefish Bay?"

"It's out of the way for me, but I assume you want your laptop to work as soon as possible, correct?"

He gulped. "Uh, yes."

"How about five this afternoon?"

"Okay."

"I'll need a deposit."

Mateo arrived twenty minutes early and decided to wait in his car across the street. At this hour, relatively few people were walking in and out. At 4:55, he entered the coffee shop and ordered a tall Iced White Chocolate Mocha.

Only three other customers were inside. Two young girls sat

across from each other at a table, and a middle-aged woman stood by the window counter. All three were bent over their phones.

While Mateo waited for his order, a short, sturdy man with a buzz cut and lazy stubble came rushing through the door. He looked to be in his early to midforties and was dressed in loose-fitting jeans and a no-tuck blue-and-white striped shirt.

"I'll have a venti Iced Peach Green Tea Lemonade." The man's voice was loud, squeaky.

Mateo swallowed.

"No, cancel that." The squat man fiercely waved his hands. "Make that a trenta Iced Guava White Tea Lemonade instead."

Then, like a clairvoyant, he turned, made eye contact with Mateo, and in quick, small steps walked towards him. Not even five feet tall, the man raised his chin to look up at him.

"Let's talk about your laptop in my car."

For the next fifty minutes they sat in Nacho's Kia Sorento behind closed windows. The engine was running, the air conditioning hissing.

"So," Nacho said after he took down the requested information, "for now, this is all I need. Give me a few days to get back to you." He scribbled something on a piece of paper and showed it to Mateo. "My retainer fees. Cash only."

Though appalled by the amount, Mateo didn't blink. Having learned from his dealings with Pelón, he had come prepared.

Watching Nacho stash the plastic envelope with the money under the floormat, he said, "Since you're not a professional private investigator, I assume your methods are illegal. That's why I must insist you—"

"Hey!" As he had in the coffee shop, Nacho aggressively waved his hands. "Do not micromanage my work. I'm good; I know what I'm doing. Pelón knows I'm the *best*! That's why he told you to contact *me*." He tilted his head back to slurp the last of whatever was left in the thirty-one-ounce cup. He belched discreetly behind his hand. Twice. "Let me assure you again: I will get you results!" From the door's side pocket, he retrieved a Hefty bag and threw his empty cup into it, then held the bag open so Mateo could discard his cup as well. He tied the bag and put it on Mateo's lap. "I don't allow trash in my vehicle. On the way to your car, toss it in a garbage bin."

Not used to being given orders, Mateo choked back his reply. At once, he felt confined in the claustrophobic interior of the vehicle. Before he opened the door, he turned to Nacho. "What happened to Pelón?"

Looking almost dwarfish behind the wheel, Nacho donned his sunglasses. "He had some business to take care of in Mexico."

That had been five days ago, and Mateo still hadn't heard back from Nacho. Meanwhile, the Fourth of July weekend was coming up, and as he did every year, Mateo was to host his annual "Brave Hearts, Bright Stars in Mira," a three-day mega-celebration, reminiscent of his Fiesta Miraldo in Coyoacán. Guests were expected from all over the country, including a few celebrities from the political sector as well as from the entertainment industry. All of the Mira Hotel rooms and suites had been blocked out, golf tournaments had been scheduled, a traditional New England clambake on the beach had been arranged, and Marco had chartered a large yacht for a dinner cruise on Lake Michigan on July 3.

The planning for this mammoth undertaking had started while Mateo was still recovering from his stroke, and Marco had taken on most of the responsibilities. Even Molara had pitched in. But judging by her recent behavior, Mateo questioned if she'd even attend.

How was he going to explain her absence to the Hadlows *again*? He'd invited Nelson and Rhonda, and their son Dudley was cutting short his vacation in Dubai, anxious to make the long-overdue connection with Molara.

While he steamed over his misfortune, the TracFone's shrill ringtone pierced his ears like an annoying child's high-pitched scream.

"Yes?"

"I have information for you."

The squeaky voice sounded like music to Mateo. "When and where can we meet?"

"There's a park a half mile south of the Starbucks in Whitefish Bay; you can't miss it. Can you be there in one hour?"

Damn. Mateo was supposed to meet the event director, the head of catering, and the hotel manager to go over some last-minute details. Now he'd have to postpone the meeting to tomorrow. He'd have no other choice, unless the—

"Hey! What's going on with you? You still there?"

"Okay, okay," Mateo snapped. "In one hour."

"Don't forget to bring the outstanding big ones."

***

Mateo listened to Nacho's report, only interrupting when he wondered if he'd heard correctly. As if frozen, he sat on the park bench, looking vacantly at dogs of all breeds and sizes chasing each other. Occasional laughter drifted over from their owners; they stood in small clusters, watching their four-legged friends.

His worst fears had come true. Molara had somehow gotten ahold of skeletons he'd hoped would never surface again.

Had she found a way to break into Marco's secured storage room? Had she figured out the secret compartments in his own armoire? Whatever she'd done, she'd apparently had help from that damn Maxwell as well as from Flores & Associates, a highly rated PI firm.

Mateo stared at a Doberman pinscher, snarling at a mutt. As if from far away he heard Nacho's squeaky voice.

"I couldn't get past the doorman in Molara's building, but I found a way to break into Maxwell's apartment. I wanted to hack into his desktop computer, but the guy only has a laptop that he takes with him wherever he goes." He stopped and elbowed Mateo. "Hey, you still with me? You look like a deer in the headlights."

"Jesus! Yes. Go on!"

"Anyway, I planted a couple of listening devices in Maxwell's apartment. So far, only two conversations took place there. I found out that Molara and Maxwell, together with Alex Rivas—he's a Flores & Associate employee—booked a trip to New York on the Fourth of July. They plan on spending one night there before continuing to Geneva, Switzerland."

"Switzerland?" Mateo's jaw dropped. "Why the stop in New York?"

"They talked about meeting someone by the name of Amelia Rubio."

Holy mother of God! Mateo stood up and walked the distance between the fence and the bench before he was able to sit down again. He felt as if he were caught in a tsunami.

Nacho elbowed him again. "Hey!"

Mateo blinked.

"I took photos yesterday in Chicago with my long-range camera." Nacho pointed at a skinny older man. "That's Phil Flores, the principal of Flores & Associates. Next to him is Alex Rivas, and you know the other two."

"Where were these taken?"

"At NoMI, the restaurant in the Park Hyatt."

"Why there?"

"Maxwell and Molara stayed there for one night."

"When did they check out?"

"Earlier today, around two o'clock. I followed them back to Maxwell's digs in Milwaukee."

"And? Did you get any clues?" Mateo rubbed his temples. His head hurt.

Though he wasn't smiling, Nacho chuckled. "Here," he said, then from his pocket he pulled out AirPods. "Listen for yourself."

Mateo heard indistinct chatter, doors closing, shoes scraping along the floor, and finally Maxwell's fast-talking, effeminate voice.

Maxwell: I have Alex and Phil's guidelines on my laptop. Shall we go over them again?

Molara: No, let's just hang. I need a minute to detox.

Maxwell: Okay. Go lie down on the couch. I still have lemonade in the fridge. Want some?

(Footsteps moving away, clatter of dishes, the sound of pouring liquid, footsteps coming closer.)

Molara: Thanks. I forgot how good your lemonade is.

Maxwell: So, what's your next plan of action?

Molara: Mateo's been texting and calling. He even tried to get into my apartment. As much as I don't want to confront him face-to-face, I will have to jump over my own shadow, tell him what I've learned and what my decision is.

Maxwell: I'm coming with you.

Molara: Of course. I need a witness—though I doubt he'll have the guts to hurt me.

Maxwell: You can't rule anything out.

Molara: No, but I'll tell him that Flores & Associates has copies of our findings. He needs to know that if anything happens to us, the police will be notified.

Maxwell: When and where?

Molara: Hopefully he'll agree to meet me tonight. Either at the Mira Hotel or the clubhouse—it's got to be where someone can see us arrive and leave again. If he wants to meet tomorrow morning, then it has to be in my office. (Yawning.) Before we head into battle, I think we both need a power nap.

Mateo's heart clanged in his chest. He was sweating; Nacho's smartphone almost slipped from his clammy hands. Everything and everybody in the park suddenly tilted, like in a scene of a Hitchcock thriller. *Please don't let me get sick.* He opened his mouth, only to close it again. Whatever had exploded inside him seemed completely jammed up by muscle spasticity. He gulped in air and removed the AirPods. Trying to sound above it all, he said, "Well, since you heard it, what do you think will happen?"

"You're asking me? I may have big balls, but neither of them is crystal."

Mateo jumped off the bench and walked over to the fence, where he stood for a moment. "Fucking-goddamn-shit!"

He returned and plunked back down onto the hard cedar slats. "When I came to meet you today, I knew you wouldn't hand me a winning lottery ticket, but I *never* expected any of this." He didn't like the grin on Nacho's face. "Why are you looking at me like that?"

"Hey! I'm just sitting here, waiting for you to tell me what to do next."

Mateo ran a hand through his hair. "I want you to follow them to New York and then to Switzerland. I don't care what it costs."

"That might be a problem."

"Why?"

"First, I need a passport with a different identity. Second, it's the Fourth of July weekend. I seriously doubt my contact can help me on such quick notice."

"You're kidding, right? Nothing is impossible for the right amount of money." Angrily, Mateo slapped his thighs with both hands. "I think that's enough for today." He turned his head in all directions, making sure nobody was watching before he handed Nacho a fat envelope. "I expect you to make this work."

"Must I repeat myself? I know what I'm doing. There's nobody better than me." Nacho got off the bench and squared himself in front of Mateo, looking down at him. "Because I'm the best, I'm going to destroy this phone. Next time you hear from me will be from a different number." Without another word, he turned on his heel and with surprisingly quick strides walked away.

What the fuck? Mateo still had questions for the tiny man with the huge ego. But instead of running after Nacho, he remained rigid. He squinted into the deep orange sun, already low over the horizon. *That damn fireball never stops setting and rising*, he thought and slowly stood up. *Damn all the odds. I can't allow this to be the sunset of my life! Tomorrow I'll see a new sunrise and for damn sure will see many more after that.*

FORTY-FOUR

Ursula, July 2019
Crans-Montana, Switzerland

"What's so funny?" said Alain when he and Bernard caught up with Ursula and Charley at the spot where they'd started their hike.

"We thought you couldn't hear—you were so far behind us." Ursula started to giggle again.

"Your laughter is infectious. It made us laugh without knowing why." Grinning, Alain waved his finger at his wife. "Which of your stories did you tell?"

Charley tittered. "None you know."

With that, Ursula bent over laughing again.

The two women were still chuckling when they reached the small parking lot where Bernard had parked his Range Rover. Except Alain, everybody had left their phones in the vehicle earlier; they'd wanted uninterrupted time during the three-mile hike around Lac de Tseuzier, a lake framed by majestic cliffs and waterfalls.

"For not being an outdoorsman, I enjoyed this," Alain admitted on their short drive back to Crans-Montana. "Especially with no emergency calls from my patients."

"I don't know about you guys, but I'm famished." Charley tapped Bernard on the shoulder. "You're the one with clout in this town—can you get us into La Toque Blanche? I'm dying for their bouillabaisse."

"My phone is still powered off."

"I'll do it." Ursula reached for her phone and waited until it lit up. "So many messages. Missed calls, too." She looked closer. "They're from Bruno. I'm calling him back," she said.

"Hi! Our phones were turned off. You're on speaker. Is everything okay?"

"Yes! Yes! I have mind-blowing news to share with you."

"About Mick? Did he win the—"

"Please come to our house as soon as possible. I can only tell you in person."

Just as Bernard pulled his SUV into the driveway of Bruno and Joaquín's chalet, Mick arrived on his BMW Motorrad. Unfastening his helmet, he asked, "What's going on? I was in my studio when Bruno told me to drop everything and head over here."

The group was ushered into the open space living area, where Bruno put his hands on Ursula's shoulders, gently pushing her onto one of the white couches. "Amelia called." His smile illuminated his whole person.

"And?"

He waved his hands in bewilderment. "It's simply mind-boggling how it all connects."

"What is? I don't understand."

"I don't either, at least not yet." He took a deep breath. "Amelia tried to fill me in on everything, but she talked so fast I had trouble following her. What I do know is that Molly discovered you and Mick are alive. She knows why you needed to escape from Mexico; she also came across the fake death certificates. She found all the letters you wrote to her—letters she never knew existed." Bruno's eyes welled up. "She knows about the abuse you suffered from Marco. She has the evidence of what Mateo did to you."

"Omigod!" Ursula's voice was frayed. "Do Mateo and Marco know? They wouldn't think twice about destroying whoever obtained that information."

He shrugged. "That I don't know." He held on to her shaking hands.

"Mama."

As if in a trance, she turned her head towards her son. "Molly knows."

"It's really happening, Mama." Mick's voice quavered. "The truth has finally surfaced."

"Wait, there's more," Bruno said. "Remember the Rivas family that lived next to Amelia when you stayed with her in Little Havana? You and Molly played with their children."

Mick nodded.

"Of course," said Ursula.

"I forgot to mention that Molly hired a private investigator firm, and one of the PI's is Alejandro Rivas." Bruno wiped his forehead. "Alex is the nephew of Luis Rivas."

Mick scooted closer. "Wait. What?"

"We need to head to our library," Bruno said. "Joaquín has set up his computer for the Zoom call."

⁓

A balding man with dark bushy eyebrows came into focus on the screen. His canary-yellow T-shirt displayed the words "I have no Hair and I don't Care."

"Hey, I'm Sam Silver, a coworker of Alex Rivas. I've been assisting Amelia with these Zoom calls." He motioned for her to sit in front of the screen.

"Aren't they supposed to be here already?" Unease spread over Amelia's round face; she nervously pulled on a silver streak of her hair. Instead of looking into the camera, she was looking at Sam Silver. "Where are they? Mull-ly's plane arrived over an hour ago." Her right hand held on to the gold cross of her necklace.

"Don't worry, they're on their way. Traffic from the airport is a bitch at this hour." Sam reminded Amelia to look into the camera and speak English. "I'll be nearby for technical assistance if anyone needs me," he said, then disappeared.

While everybody else in the room had endless questions for

Amelia, Ursula sat rigid, feverishly trying to wrap her mind around what only an hour ago had seemed an impossibility.

In 1992 Marisol led us to her sister-in-law, Amelia Rubio, in Little Havana. Sergio Rivas and his family were Amelia's neighbors. Luis Rivas was Sergio's brother, and when Amelia had to escape Little Havana, she became Luis's caretaker in New Jersey. Luis's nephew was Alex Rivas, the little boy Molly played with in the days before Mateo's goons kidnapped her . . .

Ursula felt her chair being pushed directly in front of Joaquín's computer. *Marisol, Amelia, Sergio, Luis, Alex, Molly . . .* Still dazed by what she had just learned, she kept nodding at the wide-eyed Amelia on the screen.

"The doorbell just rang." Amelia was clutching her cross. "It's happening, Ursula! Your Mull-ly is here."

Why did her heart cry out over past pain when, at the same time, it celebrated the present? Why were her vocal cords paralyzed? Why did everything seem unreal?

"Mama!"

Not until Ursula had wiped away the salty mist did the face of a young woman come into focus.

"Mama!"

As if time stood still, Ursula saw four-year-old Molly: the sparkling hazel eyes, framed by long dark lashes; the finely shaped nose and full lips; the defined cheekbones; the chin with its distinctive dimple; the wavy dark hair that yielded a kaleidoscope of caramel honey and golden tones; the ringlets that fell over her forehead.

As Ursula had done so many times in the past, she instinctively reached out, wanting to brush back one of the delicate curls. But the instant her fingers touched the screen, she snapped out of her trance.

"My Molly." Her voice was little more than a murmur. "In a crowd of thousands, I would recognize you."

FORTY-FIVE

Molly, sixteen hours earlier
Mira, Wisconsin

Mr. Miraldo already arrived ten minutes ago," says Becky Baker, the assistant manager at the Mira Golf Resort and Spa. "He's waiting for you in the Badger Meeting Room."

I elbow Maxwell as we follow Becky down the long hallway. "How suitable—he chose the *Badger* Room." My voice, together with our footsteps, is swallowed up by the thick carpet with its three-dimensional layering effect.

"The badger is omnivorous and nocturnal," Maxwell whispers. "An aggressive predator within the *weasel* family."

Even after Becky exits and closes the door, Mateo doesn't turn around. Like a statue he remains standing in the middle of the open terrace door, facing the vista of the golf course in semidarkness. Strategically positioned tree-canopy lights shine down on the eighteenth hole.

Without taking my eyes off Mateo's back, I step forward and motion Maxwell to follow me. We stop at the end of the rectangular walnut conference table with an epoxy riverscape motif running from one end to the other. Because its length will provide a tolerable barrier between us, I hope Mateo will place himself at the opposite end of the table.

Meanwhile, he hasn't moved. Is he trying to throw me off balance, or does he need more time to regain his own equilibrium?

As if in slow motion, he turns. His eyes are like tar, his lips pressed together.

I can hear him grind his teeth.

"What is *he* doing here?" His gruff voice injures the stillness of the room. "Leave!" He points at Maxwell, then at the door.

My emotions threaten to overwhelm me again, but I find the strength to control them. "Maxwell will stay," I say. "He knows everything."

"Knows what?" Mateo thunders and moves towards the opposite side of the conference table. He stops abruptly, stands rigid, and grabs the back of the chair.

I've seen this pose countless times in meetings when he needs to establish or wants to reinforce his position of power.

Like opposing fighters, he and I stare each other down. I recognize the flare in his eyes. He might think it's an effective tool for dominance, but his body language is off.

"After avoiding me for over a week," he bellows, "why the need for a meeting tonight?"

There's an irregular rhythm to his voice.

"You may want to sit down."

"Don't be absurd!" He remains standing. "Explain yourself, *Molara Miraldo!*" My name hangs distortedly on his lips.

Despite his pomposity and obvious attempt to rattle me, I feel surprisingly relaxed. This is *my* moment!

"For as long as I can remember, you've warned me never to trust anyone other than you and Marco," I say, speaking slow and resolutely. "I was forced to believe every falsehood you hammered into my head. For twenty-six years you took advantage of the memory loss I suffered due to trauma. You fed me barefaced lies about my mother and brother."

I stand upright, feeling taller, stronger. "But my memory came back, and now I know that, as a young child, I told you and Marco on several occasions that I believed remembering real events, but both of you convinced me otherwise. You gaslighted me by sowing self-doubt and confusion in my mind. You undermined my judgment and intuition by distorting my reality. Over and over, you drummed into me that my past was pointless—that it made no sense to get stuck in it."

"I advised you wisely," he scoffs. "Had I allowed you to believe in ghosts, then your past would still be haunting you."

"But you failed. The older I got, the more I became convinced the past I needed to remember did exist." I maintain eye contact. "It existed and it's part of me. Yesterday, today, and tomorrow are connected in a circle."

"Spare me your damn psychobabble!"

I ignore his outburst. "You can deny the truth, but you can't erase it."

"The truth?" He titters and folds his arms tightly over his chest. "Is this going to be another lecture about MiraCo's conduct not meeting your rigorous standards? Well, let me—"

"Not where I was going, but sure, let's start there. I know the truth about the fraud you committed in Mexico, Guatemala, and Belize."

Mateo inhales sharply.

"I know the truth about your money laundering in Central America, as well as in Europe. The truth about your involvement with Robert Graf. The truth about you having him do all your dirty work so your name remains unblemished."

"Bullshit!" His flared nostrils are caving in.

"The truth about innocent people being killed because you and Marco gave the orders. The truth about why you had to abandon your Mexican enterprises."

"Complete nonsense," he roars, furiously shaking his head.

"I saw the evidence, buried in Marco's storage room. I read the ledgers and letters."

When I lean ever so slightly forward, Mateo tilts back, staring blankly at me.

"You don't know what you're talking about! You have no idea how business was done in Mexico," he howls. "In those days, we had to use any means available to accomplish anything at all. Everybody did it!" He bangs his fists on the table. "Don't you ever speak to me of things you'll never understand. And shame on you for breaking into private areas in your father's house whe—"

"*My father?*"

"What?" He cocks his head and slumps into the chair.

I can tell his mind is racing while he fumbles for something in his jacket pocket. He removes his cigar case and opens it. "Whatever business dealings we had ages ago in Mexico have zero impact on what I've established in this country during the past three decades." He jerks his chin up. "You of all people should know that *my* MiraCo is a squeaky-clean, highly respected organization." He leans back and crosses his legs, looking like his usual unflappable self, but when he pulls a cigar from the case, his hand is shaking. "Whatever you're accusing me of is nothing but dried-up bullshit. Stop wasting my time with your nonsense." He dismissively waves his hand, then gets out of the chair, as if ready to walk away.

"You may want to hear another truth: the main reason why I asked you to see me tonight."

His head snaps in my direction.

"I found letters addressed to Molara Miraldo, letters from my mother that you kept from me. Letters that prove she and my twin are alive, while you and Marco made me believe they were dead."

Mateo's arms fall to his side, hanging limp like dog tails on either side of his torso. The angry red blush disappears as his face drains of color. He removes the unlit cigar from his mouth and crunches it with his fingers. "You broke into *my* house?" He blinks rapidly. "I have security cameras. I can have you arrested for illegal entry."

"For entering the home I grew up in? The home that's still listed as my residence? The home that's in trust in both of our names? The home I have the keys and alarm codes to?" I must force myself to speak calmly. "If you want to call the authorities, please go ahead. Unlike you and Marco, I have nothing to hide."

"Why are you doing this, Molara?" His voice is hoarse. "Who's turned you against me?" He shoots an angry glare at Maxwell.

"I finally understand why my mother had to get away from you and Marco, why she feared for herself and her children. I know about Miami. And I know you still haven't given up on finding her."

His titter turns into a broken, evil-sounding laugh.

"In June of 1992 you hired thugs to find us, bring us back to Mexico. Your cruel mission failed, but you won by tearing three lives apart."

"¡Querido Dios!" He looks at the ceiling and raises his arms upward, as if begging for help. "¡Ayúdame! ¡Esta loca!" Then, through narrowed eyes, he looks at me and scoffs. "How in the hell did you get everything so damn wrong?"

My brain's messaging system is working on overdrive, threatening to overwhelm my tear ducts. *Don't you dare*, I warn my limbic system, *this is not the time for a full-on cry fest.* I swallow. "For the first time, I got everything right," I say. "Finding the truth restored my memory."

"Your memory? You have no idea! Let me explain the actual meaning behind it all."

"I went into your attic."

Mateo's mouth sags. He grabs the back of the chair in front of him, pulls it out, and collapses back into it. With palms on the table, he turns his head as if he's looking for one of his lackeys to back him up.

"You are possessed," he yelps. "You allowed the devil to play tricks on you and your damn memory! Let me, eh, I can prove that—"

"I found the DNA results," I say. "I watched the videos. I saw and heard what you and Marco did to my mother again and again." I resist the urge to charge at him, bang my fists against him. "I bore witness to the unimaginable things *you* did."

He tugs on his earlobes, rubs his eyes, and puts his hand over his mouth, like the three monkeys molded into one—*hear no evil, see no evil, speak no evil.*

"Throughout their marriage, Marco emotionally and sexually abused my mother. *You* did the same and worse. You drugged her, kept assaulting her."

"Nooo," he howls. "It was Marco who abused her. I *loved* Ula! Let me explain how it—"

"You spiked my mother's drinks. You forced yourself on her. I know because you *videoed* yourself doing it."

"No-no-no!"

"I know that you and Marco raped my mother on the very same day. I know she requested DNA testing. I know you're aware of the results."

Malice is written all over his face. He looks like a dormant killer virus, ready to attack.

It takes all my strength to stay calm. "When will you share your secret with Marco? When will you tell him that *you* are my father and that *he* is my very-much-older half brother?"

Mateo's face is metamorphosing from demonic to completely void of expression. He looks like a shadow of the man he once was, a timeworn sculpture about to crumble. There's no life in his cold eyes. He lets out a croak, then rasps, "You simply don't understand the—"

Again, I interrupt. "Your gaslighting has come to an end. Your house of cards has collapsed."

I nudge my knee against Maxwell's but he—on the same wavelength, as always—has already selected the video clip. With an outstretched arm, he points the screen of his phone at Mateo.

I close my eyes.

My mother cries out. I don't have to see the video. My mind's eye replays her bruised and swollen face as she confesses to Mateo that Marco has been abusing her and that he loves another woman. She drinks more of the wine, begs him to stop.

Mateo sits frozen, staring at Maxwell's screen until it goes silent and dark. His head drops, and he clenches his fists. When he looks up again, his expression morphs from confusion to fury, and gradually into haughtiness.

"You've got it all wrong! Your mother loved me as much as I loved her." His baritone voice rises to a tenor. "Marco abused her! She came to me for comfort. I showered her with gifts of love, took her to operas and plays, introduced her to society. We planned a future together."

His selective amnesia is nauseating. "I'm finished with you, with Marco, with MiraCo," I say. "I'm leaving!"

"Impossible." He grabs the edge of the table to push himself into a half-upright position. "Where do you think you can go without me?" he hisses through curled lips. "You belong here. With me."

As if rehearsed, Maxwell and I step away from the table and walk in lockstep towards the door.

Mateo shoots past us like a dart. He spreads his arms, attempts to block the wide door. "Don't you dare," he snarls. "I am your father!"

"But I am not Molara, the gullible child, anymore." My sharp voice sounds like a double-blade guillotine cutter. "I am Molly, the adult who found her memory again." I push him aside. "Stay out of my way."

"If you leave, you'll end up nowhere—with nothing!"

I bite my lip, shake my head.

"I'll forgive you for your behavior and insults! This is your chance to turn around! Come back!"

I quicken my step.

"I know what you're up to, Molara," he screams. "Wherever you go, I will find you!" His hysterical laughter echoes behind me, then fades away.

FORTY-SIX

Mateo, twelve hours later
Mira, Wisconsin

More than six hours of uninterrupted sleep? Mateo couldn't believe his eyes when he looked at the time. It was ten minutes to seven o'clock. Next to his cherished retro alarm clock—its face was the Mexican flag—stood the Xanax bottle. Never having taken the drug before, he marveled at how quickly the little white rectangular tablet had calmed his brain and central nervous system after the unfortunate clash with his daughter.

But he didn't want to dwell on last night. He pressed the remote control, and the blackout curtains opened noiselessly, giving way to the morning sun and blue skies. A new day with new beginnings.

The book on the nightstand caught his eye, and he remembered the notes he'd jotted down before he fell asleep. Like a bookmark, he'd put the sheet of paper between the pages of *The Capitalist Comeback*. He glanced over his notes, nodded, and resolved to proceed with the tasks in the exact sequence he'd indicated.

Filled with renewed zest, he swung his legs over the edge of the mattress.

After a reinvigorating shower, he carefully selected his attire. He examined himself in the full-length mirror and liked what he saw. Having chosen his short-sleeve mesh-knit navy polo shirt, khaki-colored chinos, and tan suede ankle boots, he felt rather dapper. From his watch collection, he picked the Omega Seamaster, then tucked a pair of black Barton Perreira sunglasses into the breast pocket of his shirt. Before he walked out of the room-sized closet, he glanced once more into the mirror. He was ready to greet his VIP and celebrity guests, soon to arrive for his annual "Brave Hearts and Bright Stars in Mira."

Midmorning, Marco walked into Mateo's office and plopped himself into one of the chairs across from his desk.

"What's wrong?" Mateo asked when he noticed Marco's flustered face. "There'd better not be any last-minute complications with the festivities."

"Things are going according to plan as far as that's concerned, but Ava was nauseous most of the night, and when she finally fell asleep around three o'clock, Molara had the audacity to wake her up at six."

Mateo stiffened. "She called Ava? Why?"

"Well, the call was for me, but I was in the pool, doing my laps. Anyway, Ava was so drowsy, she's not sure she even heard correctly. Sort of made no sense, what she told me."

"What did she say?"

"That Molara was telling me goodbye?" Marco shrugged. "That I should ask you about the meeting she had with you last night—something about her *true relationship* to us?"

Damn! This was not the way Mateo had intended to broach the subject. When he shifted his weight around in the leather executive desk chair, it squeaked and made a flatulent sound. He cleared his throat. "Molara tricked us."

"What do you mean?"

Not willing to be cornered, he relied on his lifelong ability to spin a crafty reply. "If you really think about it, she has outwitted us for some time already."

"What? Like when? How?"

"Remember when she didn't go with us to the Hadlows' in Wyoming? She only pretended to be sick, wanted us out of the way so she could break into our homes."

"Break in? She's got keys to both houses; she knows the security codes."

"I meant to say she wanted to break into *your* storage room."

"Not possible. Nobody knows the combination to its security lock. Not even Ava."

"Believe me, Molara and her damn friend figured it out. They opened every box. They took pictures of ledgers, documents . . . They have copies of it all."

Marco slapped his forehead. "I was going to get rid of that old shit. Guess I wasn't fast enough."

Mateo stared at his son. "You don't seem the least bit bothered by what she did."

"Why should I? That old stuff can't be of interest to anyone." Marco waved his hand dismissively. "What was she looking for anyway? So much in those boxes is from before she was born. What's she going to do with it in this country?"

"She also claims to remember everything."

"What are you saying?"

Choosing his words carefully, Mateo wove a brand-new web of lies and half-truths. The longer he talked, the easier it got.

At first, he suggested that Molara had only bamboozled everybody into believing she'd lost her memory to get attention and sympathy. He then insinuated that she most likely had been in touch with Marisol Rodriguez and Amelia Rubio all along—that they'd told Molara her mother and Miguel were alive. But if they really were in cahoots, was it for extortion? Blackmail? A play for absolute power at MiraCo?

The more Mateo exaggerated and catastrophized, the better he trusted his make-believe monologue to reshape reality. When he was done with his delivery, he tried his best to look forlorn.

Marco just sat there, frowning. "What the devil is she up to?"

Mateo shrugged. "Judging from her behavior last night, she's lost it. She blames both of us for her misery, even said she wants nothing more to do with us or MiraCo."

"That doesn't make any sense." Marco's voice was hard and flat. "After working her ass off, she wants to walk away now?" He furrowed his brows, waving his index finger. "Something doesn't smell right. I suggest you immediately put our legal teams on high alert."

Mateo gulped; he needed to calculate quickly. "Let me be clear . . ." He shifted his weight again. "Remember how I made changes in my estate planning even before that damn stroke I had earlier this year? Well, I made Molara the trustee of her trusts. I believed it was a wise decision."

"I tried to talk you out of it, but in hindsight, maybe it was a good idea. Those trusts guarantee her a very comfortable life. She's also made a shitload of money working for MiraCo." Marco leaned forward and narrowed his eyes. "But she'd better not come after MiraCo—she'd better not threaten us with any bullshit." Leaning back into his chair, he gave Mateo a cool, quizzical look. "Papá, it's no secret that my relationship with Molara has always been fragile. I doubt I'll even miss her. But you were the one who raised her. You were more like her father than her grandfather."

Mateo gulped back his unease. "Why are you looking at me like that?"

"Because Molara said something about our true relationship. What could she possibly mean?"

Mateo interlocked his fingers to stop his trembling hands. "I have no idea." He willed his right leg not to shake. "Whoever cast a spell over Molara is dragging her in the wrong direction." He spoke slowly, intending to sound calm. "I hope she'll realize where her home is." He pushed himself out of his chair. "I have a feeling she'll be back."

"I wish I could say that, but I don't give a damn," Marco sneered. "The whole thing is weird, though. Something smells fishy, and I don't like it." He grabbed the framed photo of Molara on Mateo's desk, looked at it for a second, and slammed it face down. Then he stood up and brushed over his white linen shirt. "Let's count our blessings that she won't be around this weekend to ruin things. We need to focus on *our* lives and what's important." He patted Mateo's shoulder and donned his sunglasses. "Come on, Papá, it's time to greet our distinguished guests."

~

Normally Mateo disliked hosting big events in and around his private mansion, but the happy faces, loud laughter, and nonstop expressions of gratitude at his hotel earlier had put him in too good a mood to be annoyed by the hustle and bustle on Bayside Drive. After he exchanged a few words with the event planner, he went upstairs to find some quiet in his bedroom suite. But his brief solitude was interrupted by a knock on the door.

Yoli! That damn woman had an uncanny skill for intrusion. "¿Qué quieres?"

"Lo siento, señor." She only opened the door a quarter. "This came special delivery." Her voice sounded muffled through the narrow opening; her hand waved an envelope.

"Okay! ¡No más molestias, por favor!"

No return sender, just his name and address. Instantly the fun of the past few hours was replaced by foreboding. He ripped the seal open and unfolded a small sheet of paper.

> I've been trying to get ahold of you.
> Call me ASAP from the number I recognize.

Mateo's chest tightened. No name. Could it be Pelón? No, Pelón had demanded that he get rid of the phone he'd used back in February. It had to be Nacho.

He looked for the TracFone. Where had he put the damn thing? Since it wasn't in the armoire, it had to be in the attic. Even though the entire second floor was off-limits to the event planner and his crew, Mateo stuck his head through the door and looked left and right before he hastened up the flight of stairs. Out of breath, he unlocked his parlor in the sky and retrieved the burner phone from one of the secured drawers.

There were four missed calls from Nacho. He stared at the

phone, oscillating between calling back and waiting. On one hand, he didn't want to ruin the euphoria of a perfect afternoon. On the other hand, he needed to know why Nacho had placed four calls. Hopefully the guy had gotten a fake passport and was in New York already. Perhaps he also wanted to tell Mateo he was ready to follow Molara and that nitwit Maxwell to Switzerland.

He leaned against the wall and closed his eyes. If Molara uncovered Ula's hiding place in Switzerland, would he finally get a chance to see his beloved Ula again? He would apologize, tell her that his mistakes had been made from a place of pure love. She would understand; she would forgive him.

But what if Molara turned her mother against him? Mateo's smile faded quickly.

After the third ring, Nacho's high-pitched voice pierced through. "What took you so long, old man? Another ten minutes and this number would've been history."

"I told you I had a busy weekend coming up," Mateo said, annoyed. "I assume you're in New York by now." He held his breath. Was that laughter on the other end?

"I'm out!"

"What?"

"I really don't even have to let you know that I'm done with you, but I happen to be a nice guy and respect your old age."

"What the fuck are you talking about?"

"Okay, listen! I did contact the guy for the passport."

"And?"

"Turns out he knows Pelón."

"Good. Did he say what happened to him?"

"I'm not at liberty to tell you, but I suggest you hire yourself a couple of experienced security guards."

"Excuse me?" Feeling lightheaded, Mateo leaned against the wall again.

"Do the names Benito and León ring a bell? Weren't they your loyal guards before you ordered them to be slaughtered in a maximum-security prison?"

"Ridiculous rumors! I had nothing to do with that," Mateo shouted. "How do you even know of them?"

"Because I'm the best at what I do. And guess what else I found out?" Nacho chuckled. "I bet Pelón never told you he knocked up Ramona, his older brother's fiancée. Well, when the shit hit the family fan, bullets came flying, and Pelón fled across the border with Ramona to make an honest woman of her."

Mateo raised a sardonic eyebrow. "Riveting story."

"Wait! There's more." Nacho's voice got an octave higher. "Although his family in Mexico considered Pelón a leper, he never gave up trying to get into their good graces again. His wish finally got granted last month when he visited his hometown. He also found out that his brother and cousin had been whacked years ago. He vowed to his family he'd avenge their murders."

Mateo reached for the arm of the sofa, then sunk onto it. "But what does any of this have do with—"

"Well, Pelón was informed that you and your son needed your ex-bodyguards to disappear because they knew too much about your crimes."

"Utter bullshit! Rumors only!"

"Hey, don't you yell at me, old man. Be grateful I'm letting you know that Pelón is on a revenge mission."

"You tell him it's nothing but damn hearsay and—"

"I really don't give a shit what you did way back in the Ice Age," Nacho cut in. "But I sure as fuck don't want to be connected in any way when Pelón comes after you and your son."

Silence.

"Hello? Nacho? Hello?"

For a minute Mateo stared at the TracFone in his hand. When he tried to reconnect the call, he realized the burner on the other end had probably already found its way into a shredder.

He made his way back down the stairs. As if frozen, he stood in the middle of his bedroom. What should he do? He was in no mood to play host to a mob of happy people. He almost felt like running away from his life, his mansion, MiraCo—suddenly it all felt suffocating.

Music drifted up from down below. The band was going through their sound check on the elaborate stage that had been built on the beach for one night only.

Mateo blinked, remembering Ava's excitement after he'd hired the Bayou Busters, a sought-after New Orleans group that played music ranging from fifties rock and doo-wop to blues and zydeco. He walked to the window. Although it was still light outside, lanterns and torch lights around the perimeter of the grounds had already been lit. High cocktail tables, covered with black and white Spandex skirts to match the color scheme of the evening, were interspersed around the patina bronze grandeur fountain in the middle of the manicured lawn. The catering crew, dressed in white Bermuda shorts and black polo shirts, stood around the catering director, most likely getting final instructions to guarantee a flawless event.

Under different circumstances, Mateo would've enjoyed seeing the spectacular setup on his grounds, would've been excited to play host to the crème de la crème of society. Instead he felt desperately lonely. But it wasn't just loneliness, it was fear. He'd never been without at least one person to do his dirty work for him and protect him. Now his fixers were accusing him of butchery.

Thoughts of Molara, which he'd managed to push out of his mind, rushed back unbidden. She'd said she loved him. Why did she now believe him guilty of kinky perversions?

Overcome by a wave of nausea, Mateo felt like spitting out his misery. Was that a lump in his throat? He'd felt it there before whenever he believed it was the end of something. However, his life had always gone on, and the lump had always disappeared. But now the thing in his throat seemed bigger. What if it was a tumor? Would it eventually suffocate him? Gagging, he staggered into his bathroom, barely making it in time.

His private phone rang. Dear God, it was Dudley Hadlow—the young man Mateo had hoped would become Molara's husband. He cleared his throat, forcing joy into his voice. "Dudley! We missed you and your folks during the welcoming event earlier. When did you arrive?"

"Sorry, but my parents and I can't make it." Dudley's voice was toneless. "My mother fell and broke her femur; she's in surgery right now. My father asked me to let you know."

Mateo perked up slightly. At least he wouldn't have to make excuses to the Hadlows for Molara's absence. "I'm terribly sorry, Dudley. Please tell your father I'll be in touch with him tomorrow and—"

"Okay." Dudley disconnected the call.

He stared at the silent phone. *What time am I living in? When has everybody become so damn discourteous?*

A quick shower resuscitated him. He chose a pair of comfortable slim-fitting black trousers and a black T-shirt. Normally, Mateo liked himself in all-black Armani gear—it contrasted nicely with his tanned face and white hair—but this evening, he felt like he was going to his own funeral. He took a deep breath before he descended the wide flight of stairs.

Yoli stood at the bottom, talking to a tall, brawny man wearing white Bermuda shorts and a black polo shirt—obviously a guy from the catering crew.

"Señor Miraldo." Yoli's face lit up. "Do you remember my son, Paco?"

The last time Mateo had seen Paco, he was a gangly, awkward-looking teenager who had gotten himself into serious trouble with the law. Now the guy looked like a heavyweight champion—definitely had bulked up since the day Yoli came to Mateo, begging him to save her son from the law. "I thought you had moved to Alaska?"

"Things didn't work out for me there." Paco's voice was low and rough. He stuck out his big hand to shake Mateo's.

"Your caterers needed extra help tonight, and Paco happened to be free." Yoli chuckled. "Plus, he could use the money."

Paco nodded. "I know this isn't a good time to ask, Mr. Miraldo, but I'm looking for work." He leaned closer and lowered his voice. "I'll never forget what you did for me seven years ago. I'm strong and reliable and can do *anything*—no matter what."

Was it possible the universe had sensed Mateo's torment and sent him a new fixer? He inhaled sharply, then looked Paco straight in the eye. "Let me think about it. Your mother will tell you when and where to meet me after this weekend," he said with an air of indifference. "Now excuse me, I must greet my guests."

Mateo put a spring into his step. Once again, his luck had changed from bad to good. Before he opened the terrace doors, he turned around to take another glimpse at Paco.

FORTY-SEVEN

Ursula, July 2019
Crans-Montana, Switzerland

On this Wednesday afternoon she would see her again and never forget it was a Wednesday for the rest of her life. It had been her favorite day ever since her twins were born on that very day of the week.

She stood outside her house and waited. Dusk would approach in another hour or so. Everywhere, edges had already softened in the muted golden light of this summer afternoon, and in its delicate, pastel light, Ursula experienced the feeling of becoming one with her shadow. She was glad therapy had taught her to embrace her shadow self rather than reject it. A more balanced life had been the reward

Earlier she'd clipped a fully-in-bloom flower, and while she waited, she inhaled the light fragrance of the white Tranquility rose and pressed the almost-thornless stem to her chest.

A silence hung over the area—a stillness so huge and complete it had a sound of its own. Even the birds had stopped chirping, as if their song would be an insult or a provocation.

Ursula marveled at the wide grassy meadow in front of her, rich and radiant, as if carved from an emerald. In the background rose the Valais Alps. The contour of the northeast ridge of Bella Lui rose and fell invariably, reminding her of low-frequency wavelength illustrations, except for the pure white peaks that poked against a cerulean sky.

As always at this late hour of the afternoon, when rays of light cut through the atmosphere at an oblique angle, the massif appeared to be close enough to touch, yet it was as unreachable as the stars.

Breathing in nature's solitude, Ursula remained still, awaiting her twins' arrival.

During yesterday's unforgettable two-hour Zoom, everyone had agreed that Mick should pick up Molly and Maxwell at the Geneva airport. Holding her daughter for the first time in twenty-six years would be a transcendent experience, something Ursula was not willing to share with hundreds of strangers in the hustle and bustle of an airport. She wanted that long-awaited encounter, for which she had no vocabulary to describe, to take place on the pure soil where she and Mick had created their unspoiled dwelling.

Standing still, she held the rose close to her heart. Waiting.

Mick's two Labradors, Belle and Beau, were lying next to her feet. Suddenly they stood up and pricked their ears, their tails moving back and forth like a broom.

Before she saw the car, Ursula heard the gentle crunch of pebbles under car tires, and the soft hum of an engine resonated with the wind. The sounds enveloped her like music; they carried her from twilight to dawn, where dreams and reality merged.

As they had thirty years ago on a Wednesday afternoon, Molly and Mick would arrive together.

Molly, three hours earlier

It feels like I'm split in two. For the umpteenth time I type and delete. My head is filled with sentences that run through my brain like a news ticker. I know exactly what to text Mateo and Marco, but it's making me deeply uneasy, and I erase all of it again.

I lower the iPhone to my lap and look out the window. Is that crescent shape Lac Léman? I've seen it in maps and pictures while familiarizing myself with Switzerland.

I stand up and lean over the partition that separates the suite seats on our Swiss Air flight. Maxwell is taking photos through the window.

"Hey! We're coming up on Geneva."

He turns around. "If I'm on pins and needles, I can't even begin to imagine what you must feel."

"Like my body is on fire."

Throughout the passport control formalities and the wait for our luggage, Maxwell leaves me to my own thoughts. Occasionally I feel his hand on my back as if to let me know he's still there.

"This is it," I say when we walk through the doors to the arrival area.

I see him immediately. My twin.

As soon as he and I lock eyes, twenty-six years of stored-up confusion is replaced with certainty. The bond between us feels like a stretched rubber band, a magnetic connection that pulls us into each other's arms.

"Tears of joy," Mick murmurs. "Mine started long before I saw you come through the arrival gate."

I have no control over my own floodgates; all I can do is nod into my twin's neck.

I don't know how long we stay entwined in each other's arms, turning back the clock, reviving the bond that was formed in our mother's womb. When we manage to release one another, it feels as if the broken pieces inside me are put together again.

As if he's read my mind, Mick says, "The part of me that was missing all these years is whole again."

When we clasp hands, the rhythm of our pulse is like a harmonic melody.

"You're the link to my past, the bridge to my future," I manage to say.

"Do you remember how shy and scared I was when we lived at the hacienda?"

I nod.

"You were my strength then, the voice in my head," Mick says. "Even after we were cut off from each other, I imagined hearing you."

"I've found where I belong," I whisper.

As if from far away, I hear Maxwell. "No thanks. We can handle it."

In unison, Mick and I turn around.

He looks embarrassed. "Sorry, this guy keeps asking if we need help with our luggage." He waves a young man away. "So sorry to interrupt your reunion."

"Maxwell! How nice to meet you." Mick reaches out.

"Same! I mean, we met yesterday on Zoom but—"

"Nothing compares to face-to-face." A shy smile forms on Mick's lips.

Am I imagining it, or is Maxwell blushing? Yes, there is definitely a pinkish flush on his golden-brown cheeks.

"So you're the one with the sixth sense." Mick's smile intensifies.

"I, ehm, I never know how to define these intuitions. But when I saw the artist's name on Molly's painting, I just had a feeling."

"Maxwell believes that whenever you have concerns, the universe will give you hints and signs in unexpected ways. It's his way of explaining the unexplainable," I say. "So weird that the painting was a gift from Annie—"

"The woman who came to my art exhibit in Geneva." Mick finishes my sentence.

"Serendipity," Maxwell says quietly.

Mick nods. Still holding me tight, he pulls Maxwell into his arms next to me.

Cocooned between my twin and my best friend, the world stops moving. In this soundless purity, my loneliness, fear, and anger ebb away.

I have come home.

FORTY-EIGHT

Molly, March 2020
Crans-Montana, Switzerland

For more than two decades I feared being misunderstood. Why? Because my individuality and sincerity had been extinguished by two men who were indifferent to right and wrong, to good and bad.

Hope had fallen into a deep sleep in my subconscious and, like Sleeping Beauty in the fairy tale, waited to be revived by love and trust.

I didn't connect with my innermost self until I physically reconnected with my mother and twin. I still can't find words special enough to describe the security and comfort that emanates from them. Every new sunrise makes my soul blossom; every sunset attests to belonging and truth.

Eight months have passed since fate led me home and united me with Mama and Mick. Thirty-four weeks, and I can't stop looking at their beautiful faces. Two hundred and forty-three days, and I never tire of hearing their voices. Three hundred and fifty thousand minutes I've feasted on love, the most powerful sustenance on earth, which had never weakened with the passing of time.

I found out that Mama and Mick had held a weekly picnic during the months of summer. She would bake Basler Brunsli cookies and he'd make lemonade, and together they would spread out a blanket on the lawn, share good memories, and always express hope. And during the winter months, they would set the table with an extra glass of lemonade and a plate with cookies for me. Every year on our birthday, Mama baked Bünder Nusstorte, our favorite pastry, filled with nuts and caramel.

It blew me away when Mama handed me her diaries—twenty-six books in total, one for every year we were separated. I've read them again and again and again, amazed by the way she transposed her fears and guilt into verse. After she allowed me to see it, she offered the same opportunity to Mick, Bernard, Bruno, and Joaquín—even to Maxwell, whom Mama instantly embraced as a family member.

Sometimes she agrees to narrate one or more of her stories; most of them are written in short stanzas. A few days ago, after she recited the poem in her final entry, nobody spoke. The pure and heroic spiritualism in her world of thought gave all of us plenty to think about. As her friend Elke Schott put it once, "Life forced Ursula onto a tightrope, but she refused to fall off."

And then there's Mick!

The day the veil on my memory began lifting, I remembered a shy, quiet little boy who was wary of noise, movements, and most people. Astounding how Mick learned to transcend his anxiety during the years of trauma and loss that followed the escape from Mexico.

"Had it not been for Mama, things would have turned out differently," he said. "She was the one who encouraged me to draw and paint. Her eyes detected the deeper meaning in my art. She knew that stress and trauma had left me painfully pessimistic about humanity. When I sought comfort in depicting imaginary scenes, she helped me realize that most of my work was based on reality."

One of Mick's earlier paintings, *Descents and Ascents*, shows the magnitude of his feelings—nude children and adults with empty, indifferent expressions climb and tumble from impossible constructions.

He said, "When I finished the painting, Mama instantly realized I'd depicted my awareness of other people's difficulties to see and understand each other."

Another one of his earlier paintings, *Unbroken Bond*, has me spellbound: In the black void of space float two colorful strands of a double helix. Hidden in that twisted ladder are two indistinct faces; only two features are prominent, but while their lips look identical, one set of eyes is green, the other hazel.

"What do you see, Molly?" asked Mick.

"I see a bond, an infinite union," I said. "You painted us."

"Uncanny," he said gently. "That's almost verbatim what Mama said when she first saw it."

Mick's love and appreciation for Mama is profound. He and I often sit on the floor of his studio as he recalls the past. Motionless, I listen to the tangled and complex circumstances Mama bravely battled through. How she truthfully explained her most difficult decisions, how she guided her young son past enormous obstacles.

Side by side, we sit quietly and look at Mick's work in progress. "Molly," he says, "do you have any idea what you did for Mama?"

"Me? What did I do?"

"You restored her sense of humor. She can laugh at herself now."

I put the pen down. My fingers have cramped from all the writing, and my brain needs a rest.

Sitting in the sunny alcove in Mama's kitchen, I relax into the back cushion and look at the majestic mountains in the distance—alpine ranges that have been here for many millions of years.

I lay my hand on the journal I started at Five Elements in Lake Geneva more than ten months ago. Given that nature has never been in a hurry to create all of its wonders, and given that it took Mama twenty-six years to finish her diaries, I guess it's okay to take my time with mine.

FORTY-NINE

Molly, September 2019
Crans-Montana, Switzerland

Two months ago, Marosanto's doors opened wide, welcoming me to fresh beginnings, to things that have never been.

Marosanto! Mama named her magnificent chalet after Marta and Rosi and Anton. The more I'm told about them, the more I want to hear. And while I listen to the stories about Marta and my great-grandparents, their faces smile at me from photographs.

Every new day is like a miracle. I never believed this kind of happiness, fulfillment, and love existed. In Mama and Mick's presence I can set aside all my anxieties about the future, leave behind the memories of a dark past, and delight in the now.

Nothing compels me to return to Mira. But since there are matters that have to be reviewed, I hired a new team of advisors and lawyers in the States. They, together with my consultants and attorneys here in Switzerland, now take care of my trusts, the transfer of my investments, and the sale of my properties.

Maxwell decided to return to Wisconsin last month to straighten out his own affairs. Although well prepared for a possible face-off with Mateo and Marco, he dodged the guillotine. The day he went to clear out his office, Mateo had been invited to speak at a real estate conference in Las Vegas, and Marco was in Panama, hoping to calm down investors who'd accused the Mira Hotel Group of mismanagement and financial misconduct.

When Maxwell returned to Crans-Montana, he brought detailed reports about drastic changes in the Kingdom of Mira. One night, after dinner at Bruno and Joaquin's house, we listened to his tell-all.

"Mateo definitely is not ready to give up power. He's more relentless and aggressive than ever before, and he can't accept opposition in any shape or form. Meanwhile, Marco is ready to oust his father and doesn't hide his ambition to be numero uno." He said the Miraldo empire reminded him of a dysfunctional monarchy, with its ongoing battles between the old king and the crown prince. Apparently many of the power players at MiraCo are on edge, unsure of how this game of chicken will end. And due to the bitter battle between son and father for control and autonomy, an exodus within MiraCo's upper ranks has already taken place. Several top guys, once Mateo's strongest allies, have quit; others were fired.

"The best part," Maxwell said, "is both Mateo and Marco decided to issue statements, explaining Molly's absence when employees started to second-guess the reason she left. But the bulletin from Mateo was at complete odds with the announcement from Marco. Wild rumors and absurd speculations have spread like a virus throughout the entire organization.

"Because everybody knows Molly and I are close, they kept bombarding me with questions. I played dumb and made up a story." Maxwell winked at me. "I said I had an offer from Amnesty International and planned to relocate to Thailand."

October 2019

In the past I often likened my life to a ten-thousand-piece jigsaw puzzle, too complicated to put together. But after the eye-opening discoveries in June that subsequently led me to Phil and Alex and then to my family in Crans-Montana, all the pieces are beginning to fit perfectly, even the difficult ones have suddenly fallen into place on their own.

The day Maxwell's application for a Swiss long-stay visa was approved, his puzzle piece promptly connected with that of my twin. I still am awed by how the universe linked my brother and my best friend together. It took me awhile to sense the connection between them, but Mama noticed it in a nanosecond. "From the way they looked at each other when Maxwell wiped a tiny smear of paint from Mick's cheek, I saw their future," she said.

I rarely think about my future because my present is filled with too much joy. But regardless of what my mind ignores during the day, dreams become the window into my unconscious at night. When I wake up, I wonder why my eyes can see everything so clearly during sleep but never get a glimpse of it when awake.

My unconscious mind's higher awareness started revealing itself after Maxwell returned from settling his affairs in the States, when he told me of his visit to Phil Flores. Though Phil was doing remarkably well after his knee-replacement surgery, he hinted that it might be best to leave him to his recovery for the time being. "If Molly wants to talk or Zoom," Phil told him, "Alex is waiting for her call."

Maxwell, of course, interpreted it as a sign. "I saw that spark between Alex and you the first time we met him at the roof garden," he said. "The way you guys looked at each other during every meeting that followed—something was obviously there. So, Molly, what are you waiting for?"

It's not that I'm waiting, I just don't know how to interpret my feelings. What does falling in love feel like? Either it's been so long that I've forgotten, or I've never really been in love. There's no checklist to let me know that what I'm feeling is the real deal.

Since I left the States, I've only Zoomed three times with Alex. At the end of our last video chat, he cleared his throat and said, "I feel like you need more time to adjust to your new life, but I want you to know I'll always be here when you're ready to talk again."

That was almost two months ago.

Since then, I keep seeing Alex in my dreams.

I'm no expert when it comes to romantic relationships and am hesitant to share my sentiments with someone else, especially when I can't make sense of my turbulent feelings. I can't stop thinking of Alejandro, the boy I met when I was four years old—the boy I didn't want to leave so many years ago. Has it really been fate that brought us together again twenty-six years later?

I was raised by two men who gaslighted and cheated on women, men who knew how to twist any situation to suit their needs. It was their behavior that made me hesitant to get involved with the opposite sex.

I keep reminding myself that Mama, Mick, and Maxwell were able to overcome the hurdles of a brutal past. The affection between Mama and Bernard is a treasure to behold, as is the connection between Maxwell and Mick.

If their lives turned on a dime, may I dare and dream?

December 2019

Being able to put every detail of what's happening onto these white pages is fantastic.

What I only believed possible in dreams two months ago I now experience in my waking state. At times I pinch myself to make sure I'm actually awake.

After my journal entry in October, I couldn't deal with the conflict between my brain and heart any longer. As soon as I confided in Mama, I chided myself for not having done it earlier. She suggested that if I'd subconsciously allowed fate to decide my course all along, then what was preventing me from accepting what fate was trying to bind me to now?

"Look at your journey as one of a thousand miles," Mama said. "It may look like an endless odyssey, but by taking a single step today, you'll get closer to where you want to be tomorrow."

I never believed in telepathy, but it must exist because the day I decided to take that single step forward and call Alex, he was already a step ahead.

"I couldn't wait a moment longer," he said the second his face came into view on the screen from seven thousand miles away. Throughout our two-hour conversation, Alex turned my sunny world even more brilliant. "I realize you have no desire to return to the US," he said, "but if you're willing to let me visit . . ."

"It was written in the stars," said Maxwell.

"Karma, kismet—it's all magic," Mick agreed.

Alex arrived a week after and has since made that round trip twice more. It's amazing seeing how every part of my life keeps falling into place after watching things fall apart for far too long.

―

During Alex's first trip, we had a few surprisingly mild October days, and I introduced him to the beauty of the Alps. Never having hiked like that before, he couldn't get enough of the sights, always wanting to conquer another height. And as we climbed and talked, we not only discovered that we have similar life goals, but too often surprised ourselves by reading each other's mind.

"Do you believe in soulmates?" I asked Alex.

He smiled. "On the day we met, our souls recognized each other."

And when I told Alex that my mind's ten-thousand-piece jigsaw puzzle was almost complete, he said, "I'll help you find the final pieces."

FIFTY

Molly, April 2020
Crans-Montana, Switzerland

Two months ago, Switzerland reported its first coronavirus case in the canton Ticino, and by now COVID-19 has spread and this country already has a relatively high infection rate. Our neighbor Italy is in a national lockdown, and Mick's art exhibits in Milan and Rome, as well as in Berlin and Amsterdam, have been postponed indefinitely.

While the pandemic has turned life into an unrelenting grind for many people, Alex and I have taken advantage of those fortuitous hours. Falling in love was inevitable. When I leaf through some of my recent journal entries, our love story reads like a romance in a dystopian novel.

Our small group of eight here in Crans-Montana decided to stay sealed within our bubble. When we need anything from stores we can't order online, Mick and Maxwell volunteer to venture out. And though we admire them for the way they meticulously sterilize not only themselves but also the products after they return home, watching them in action is hilarious.

Life with the outside world continues strictly via Zoom. At least every other day, Mania chats with Charley in Paris and Elke in Hamburg; once a week we all partake in an across-the-ocean Zoom-fest that includes the Hebronis, Amelia, Phil, and now the Rivas family as well.

Despite the imposed lockdown and shutdown throughout most of the world, for the first time in my life, I have the feeling everything I touch is perfect and everything I attempt to do turns out well. Regardless of whatever challenges I previously overcame, I never expected this kind of happiness.

~

Typically, when I make my journal entries, the world around me seems to hush and I'm neither aware nor concerned about what's happening around me. But now I feel his nearness, and when I lift my head, I look into violet-blue eyes. His face is less than an inch away from mine. He kisses me, and a surge of electricity jump-starts my heart.

"Sorry for interrupting your thoughts," he says. "I came to let you know our bubble-buddies are having cocktails downstairs. Dinner will be served soon."

Mick clinks a spoon against his glass. "Maybe you know already, but this morning I read there'll be a referendum later this year to legalize not only civil marriage but also same-sex adoption." When he lays his hand on Maxwell's shoulder, they both beam from ear to ear. "We decided to be the first ones in line when it goes through."

"What great news!" Mama jumps up to hug them. "Let's plan an engagement party to brighten up this tedious covid situation." Her laughter is infectious.

"Would you object to a Mexican theme?" Waiting for Mama's reaction, Mick looks uncertain.

"Why should I object?" Reflexively, she lays both hands over her heart. "This will be the first time I get to truly enjoy a Mexican fiesta."

Alex, who's proven himself a top chef, volunteers to present us with a special culinary Mexican experience.

"Hey, what's the secret?" I say when Joaquín and Bruno keep whispering to each other.

Joaquín grins. "The party has to be at our house. Bruno and I have the perfect décor for the event."

"When we moved here, for whatever sentimental reason, we brought quite a bit of memorabilia from Mexico, including piñatas from Acolman," says Bruno. "Now we have a reason to unpack the boxes."

I don't know how they did it, but when I walk into Bruno and Joaquín's house two weeks later, it feels like I'm entering a foreign world.

Mariachi music is being piped through their state-of-the-art entertainment system. A chorus of violins, guitar, harp, and vihuela greets us with "Cielito Lindo."

"Where in the world did you acquire all the décor?"

Bruno proudly explains when, where, and why he purchased the many artifacts. "I'd honestly given up on the idea of ever taking these things out of the boxes again." He walks us over to the eye-catching extended dining table, and we take our seats. "We wanted to reflect the colors that are typical of Mexico. Red represents the earth and sunsets, green symbolizes lush nature, and yellow is for the sun and fruit."

We admire the spicy tones of the striped tablecloth and the handmade centerpieces, all interspersed with fresh pineapples, mango, papaya, and a bounty of candles, succulents, and cacti. Wherever I look, the house seems to have transported itself to a different atmosphere in a different time. Unpleasant images from a long-ago past enter my mind, but this time there's no sentiment attached. I blink those images away; they don't matter anymore.

I feel Mama's eyes on me and pin a smile on my face. I owe it to both of us.

"Did everybody take a look at these?" I point to the printed menu cards on top of each place setting. "Alex, how did you manage to get the ingredients for all these courses?"

"Maxwell and Mick dug up what I needed. I don't know how."

For starters, Alex surprises us with a Jerusalem artichoke tamale with pine nuts and spinach pipián sauce, followed by a crab tostada with lime and radish under a habanero chili sauce.

"Fantastic!"

"Delicious!"

"Out of this world!"

"Beyond tasty..."

I've never seen Alex blush before, but it's adorable watching him try to cope with the compliments.

Open-mouthed, we look at the plated entrée: roasted eggplant in a black garlic mojo with macadamia nuts, basil, and a hoja sauce.

"With culinary skills like yours, what possessed you to become a private investigator?" Bruno puts his fork and knife on the plate and leans back into his chair.

Alex laughs. "When my father told me cooking wouldn't make me rich, I went with my instincts."

"And? Did PI work pay off?"

"Let's just say no knife was needed to cut my own checks."

※

After Joaquín hangs the third of the piñatas in the hallway, we take turns getting blindfolded. Like children, we let ourselves get spun around and disoriented, and we try to whack the colorful star-shaped container with the piñata buster. Mama and I fail miserably, and Bernard and Maxwell aren't much better, but the competition between Bruno, Alex, Mick, and Joaquín is fierce. Finally, Alex delivers a blunt blow and is unanimously declared the winner.

I'm not the only one whose belly hurts from laughing, especially when all of us end up on our knees, cleaning up a wide hallway floor blanketed with wrapped candy and silly little toys.

Maxwell lifts his head. "Whose phone won't stop ringing?"

I look at Alex. "That's your ringtone."

He returns a few minutes later with a strange expression on his face. Whenever Alex furrows his brow and presses his lips together, it signals bad news. "That was Phil," he says.

"Is he okay?"

"He needs to Zoom with us as soon as possible."

FIFTY-ONE

Molly, thirty minutes later

"Hey, y'all." Phil looks somber. "Sorry to interrupt your festivities but, um . . . you'd all better sit down."

When we get settled, he clears his throat. "I just got a call from the Milwaukee Police Department." He clears his throat again. "Marco Miraldo was murdered."

"Wait! What?"

Alex's hand clasps mine.

Mama covers her mouth.

Mick's eyes are wide open, his brows pulled up high.

Maxwell's mouth is shaped like the letter O.

"Who did— What has the police— Why was . . ." I stutter, not knowing where to start.

"The police contacted me when they found a note with Flores & Associates' phone number in Marco's car," Phil explains. "It happened right outside Mira. Apparently Marco was on his way home when a van shot out of nowhere and blocked his car. A man jumped out, fired shots through the window, and shouted, 'This is for killing my brother Benito and cousin León! Burn in hell, you fucker! Your rotten father is next on my list!'"

"A revenge killing." Bruno's voice cuts the silence.

"Benito and León?" Mama whispers. "I remember them from the hacienda. They were at the Miami airport with the man who kidnapped Molly."

Phil gazes into an invisible distance. "Due to the pandemic, streets everywhere have been relatively empty, especially in the secluded areas around Mira. A teenage girl was sitting in her backyard on her tree swing, making phone calls. Though she was shielded from the street by shrubs and arborvitae, she could see a dark van nearby and noticed its engine was running the entire time she was on the phone with her friends. Just when she was about to go back into her house, she heard the van's engine rev up, followed by screeching tires. When the girl saw a man jump from the van with an assault weapon, she videoed the whole scene." Phil's voice has gone monotone. "Because of her excellent video footage, the police were able to trace the vehicle and apprehend the killer." He rummages for something on his desk, then holds up a mugshot of a bald man. "His name is Gustavo Guzman, better known as Pelón."

Alex, Maxwell, and I stare at the mugshot on the screen.

"No shit!"

"Are you seeing what I'm seeing?"

"Omigod!"

Phil nods. "I knew you'd recognize him."

"He's the guy they've been looking for in the murder of my uncle Luis," Alex says. "Unbelievable how the composite drawing matches the mugshot."

"Yup."

"Did he confess?"

"Not quite. Guzman claims an alternate personality committed the crimes." Phil rolls his eyes. "Meanwhile, fingerprints in various police databases link him to other murders; some appear to be mob connected and made to look like suicide or death by natural causes. The FBI is already involved with the local and state law enforcement agencies."

"Will fingerprints be enough to convict him?"

"Probably, but they began comparing Guzman's DNA to evidence from other crime scenes." He briefly averts his eyes. "Let me screen share the first news report in The Daily about Marco's murder. I'll give you a moment to read it."

We all stare at the screen.

Milwaukee, April 25

Milwaukee police confirmed that the man shot dead on Central Street earlier today was billionaire Marco Miraldo, co-owner of MiraCo, an international real estate conglomerate. Due to video footage taken by an eyewitness, a suspect was apprehended and is in custody. "We understand this is a high-profile story, however, we urge everyone not to speculate as to the motive, as our homicide investigators will be following the evidence," Milwaukee police sergeant Marsha Brine said at a news conference.

Mama, so pale, looks at Mick and me with wide eyes. "I'm struggling to comprehend that this violent man who had us living in fear has been reduced to a battered body on a slab in a morgue," she says quietly. "The brutal circumstances of his death might make some people pity him but—I can't." Her eyes smile when Bernard hands her his handkerchief.

Mick sits up straight. "I lost Molly and a lot of my childhood because of him. Getting away from him was the best thing that could've happened to me."

I admire my twin; his eyes are so clear, his words so resolved. Meanwhile, I need a moment to sort out my jumbled mess of conflicting sentiments and memories.

Alex's palm is still pressed against mine, and sensing his pulse gives me encouragement.

I hear myself murmur, "Strange as it may be, I don't feel bad about feeling good."

Bruno leans forward. "Phil, you said Guzman shouted something about Marco's father being next. Did anything happen to Mateo?"

"Something did happen, but not because Guzman got to him. Mateo Miraldo was hospitalized last week with a severe case of covid. Only hours after they intubated him, he suffered a hemorrhagic stroke and went into a coma." Phil puffs out his cheeks, then slowly releases the air through pursed lips. "Before he died, Marco, who had complete financial and medical power of attorney, went to the hospital. But he didn't intend to see his father, even if they'd allowed the visit—he only went to sign the authorization to take Mateo off all life-support systems. Marco was on his way home from the hospital when Guzman killed him."

"When bad karma lands, it lands hard," says Maxwell.

Mick nods. "Uncanny how they both died on the same day." He turns to Mama and me. "They'll never look for us again. Can you believe it's all over?"

"Well, not quite," Phil says. "I hate to put more burden on you, Molly, but the authorities need to speak with you."

I want to object but realize it is useless.

"I'll help you with the police and FBI, but you'll know best how to deal with all of the legal matters."

Pensively I look to the people in the room, then back at Phil. "How naive of me to believe I had freed myself from everything."

Alex lays his arm around my shoulder. "The best way to get rid of problems is to solve them."

Phil nods. "From what I understand, the estate belongs to you now, Molly. You're the new sole owner of MiraCo."

"Wait! What?" I put my face between my hands. "Please, no!" I wish I could simply forget everything I just heard. How nice would it be to give my brain a rest. But instead, an epiphany hits me. I remove my hands from my face. "I'll need time to discuss this with everyone here. I also want to run it by my legal advisors in Switzerland and my attorneys in the US."

"Understood. I'll keep everybody at bay in the meantime."

Alex pulls me closer. "You look exhausted," he whispers.

"Sorry, but there's something else," says Phil. "It's Marco's wife."

"Omigod, I forgot about Ava," I say, immediately feeling guilty. "How is *she* dealing with everything?"

"Surprisingly calm, especially since Guzman was apprehended. After the murder, she was afraid that both she and Maya were also in danger."

"Maya?"

"Her two-month-old daughter."

"Of course." I bite my lip. It had been so easy to wipe Marco from my mind, but shouldn't I have remembered Ava and her pregnancy? "Why did you need to get in touch with her? Did the police ask you?"

"No, she kept calling my office herself. Left message after message begging me to meet her alone."

I sit rooted to my chair. "And?"

"I met her in the backyard of her house in Mira. Although she tried to convince me 'the whole covid scare was a hoax,' she finally agreed to sit outside despite the damp April day." Phil suppresses a smile. "She talked about a yelling contest between Marco and Mateo. Apparently, Marco had been on a mission to clean out his storage room when he decided to open a bunch of letters from Ursula he'd previously ignored. One of them had the paternity results."

Mama moans softly, drops her lids.

Mick's eyebrows are pulled together, and the corner of his lips have narrowed. I can't hear what he's mumbling.

Maxwell keeps shaking his head.

"A lot of the argument was in Spanish, but Marco and Mateo spoke enough English for Ava to get an earful," Phil says. "Marco kept screaming about finding evidence that Mateo had repeatedly raped Ursula and that Molara was his half sister.

"They viciously accused each other of crime after crime. At one point Mateo yelled, 'You idiot, you were supposed to get rid of everything in your storage room! Because of your goddamn carelessness, Molara and Maxwell got access to it, made copies of incriminating evidence, and took everything to goddamn private investigators! Now one of my fixers needs to break into Flores & Associates and eliminate the evidence.'"

"So that's how Ava learned Molly was a client of ours," Alex mumbles. "But how did Mateo find out?"

"He'd hired Ignacio Ibarra—better known as Nacho—to follow Molly and Maxwell. So far, this tough little guy has only been under investigation with no grounds to charge him yet, but he's been singing like a canary." Phil takes a sip of water. "By the way, Ava mentioned that soon after the argument, her husband tried to burn the contents of the boxes in a kiln, but it apparently became too tedious for him. So he asked his construction workers to dig a hole in the adjacent lot and had them throw all the boxes in there. He himself poured fuel over everything and set fire to it."

The eight of us sit very still. I look past the monitor, into Bruno and Joaquín's house. What was colorful and spirited just an hour ago now feels shrouded in a shadowy world.

I think of Ava and how some women attract a certain type of man and vice versa. I think of Maya—an innocent baby girl.

I think of Mateo and Marco, how they lived miserable, lonely lives and died brutal, lonely deaths.

"Phil?" Alex says. "Why do I feel you have more to say?"

"Molly, you need to know the reason why Ava got in touch with me."

"Okay."

"I realize this whole thing is no laughing matter, but when Ava contacted me, she told me to *investigate* Marco's and Mateo's wills and trusts. She said she can't be a businesswoman since nobody taught her how to run a big enterprise like MiraCo. She said all she's interested in is for Flores & Associates to *investigate* how much money Marco left her and her daughter." Phil suppresses a grin. "It took some time to explain what a private investigator actually does. But when I advised her to get in touch with her late husband's estate lawyers, Ava outright refused. She said the lawyers were disrespectful and treated her like a child because she didn't understand their legal jargon, that they asked her questions she couldn't answer. She said she only trusts you, Molly." He clears his throat and takes another sip of water. "When I told her my clients' contact information was confidential, Ava said I was as disrespectful as Marco's lawyers."

Throughout the conversation, my body has been completely tense, almost as if I've been fighting my emotions with all my might. But as soon as I relax, the answer comes to me.

"I do have an idea. I know what needs to be done."

EPILOGUE

August 2023
Crans-Montana, Switzerland

I am sitting on the terrace of my Shangri-la, my nirvana, my dreamworld. I lay the pen down. Judging from the golden light in the sky, it must be midafternoon. I realize I have been writing for hours. A warm late-summer wind sweeps over me, and petals of alpine geraniums flutter down, landing on the last page of my journal.

I lean back into my chair and look up to the long balcony, where cascades of foliage and flowers in vibrant colors trail and tumble happily over the sides of hanging baskets. Like Mama, I adore flowers and believe their fragrance not only brings happiness but also attracts all good and decent things.

Another quick rush of wind grabs more colorful petals, and like snowflakes, they swirl down. Smiling, I stretch out my arms and hold open my palms to catch them. It feels like nature is laughing with me. I am so happy.

When I brush the colorful corollas off the page, they make a little rainbow-like mound next to my journal.

I take the pen and continue writing.

Ever since I started journaling in April of 2019, I've tried to depict the story of my life as accurately as possible. I've detailed stormy sequences of unplanned and extraordinary changes. I've narrated the fights to be fought and the games to be played. I've chronicled the problems to be solved. But most importantly, I've written about my visions and how they came to fruition.

By now my story has filled three volumes, and I often think it reads more like a fable with imaginary events and characters than a biography. But according to Hans Christian Andersen, life itself is the most wonderful fairy tale.

Speaking of fairy tales—

Last year, when same-sex marriage became legal in Switzerland, Mick and Maxwell wholeheartedly said "I do" to each other. They were the first two men in Crans-Montana to walk out of the civil registry as husband and husband. Before their wedding, they had already been fostering two Kurdish refugee children whose mother sadly passed away soon after she and her children were given asylum in Switzerland. Less than two weeks ago, Maxwell and Mick's determined efforts paid off when they were granted permission to legally adopt Ariya, a lively five-year-old girl, and her precocious brother, Jorin, who just celebrated his third birthday.

More merrymaking took place the day Mama happily agreed to become Ursula Delon and when Bernard at last moved into Marosanto. Touched to tears, the newlyweds watched Mick hang his newest creation, *Symbolism of Love in Color*, above the mantel in their living room. As for the engraving on the brass plaque on its frame, Mick chose a saying by Aristotle: "Love is composed of a single soul inhabiting two bodies."

When Joaquín and Bruno returned home from a five-month cruise around the world, we celebrated Bruno's eighty-fifth birthday. After the festivities, he and Joaquín announced they were done with traveling and planned to enjoy the rest of their life with "family" in Crans-Montana.

And as for me—

Well, before I end my long narrative, I'd better explain some of the things that have happened during the past couple of years.

Since I had no desire to take a penny from wealth that was acquired by Miraldo misdeeds, I followed my idea to turn the bad and ugly into something good and beautiful. First, I found an investor who has specialized in taking private companies public. The long transaction was a task of mammoth proportion, but after completion, all of my advisors applauded my strength of will. MiraCo ceased to exist; instead HH Futurum is being managed by an unrelated party whose success or failure will not matter to me anymore.

The all-cash transaction made international headlines, especially when it became known that the entire megabillion fortune would go to philanthropy. In collaboration with my family and advisors, a specially designed trust was created, and the *Revival of Hope Foundation*, a nonprofit organization, sprang to life. Though still in its infancy, *ROH* is growing fast and already has over two hundred employees. Our global goals are to provide hope and resources for those without life's essentials. We're committed to our motto: "live to give."

Ava at first flipped out when she was informed of the transaction but apparently did not understand any of the proceedings. Eventually she just threw her arms up in resignation, telling her advisors to make sure she and her daughter would be well taken care of.

That whole chain of events took place during the height of covid restrictions, none of which Ava took seriously. "The government is using this dumb coronavirus to play games with us —I don't believe any of it is true," she said in one of her calls to me. She was furious when I refused to meet her and her own team of lawyers in person. It took months before she realized that what I'd negotiated with her advisors had left her a very wealthy woman. I'm still not convinced she fully understands the value of the gifts in trusts set up for her and her daughter.

We haven't heard from Ava in months, but my legal team was informed she'd moved to Texas, married a rising country singer, and changed Maya's name to Willow.

Considering that all this took place in a relatively short period of time, I want to believe the generational Miraldo curse has finally been broken.

As I sit on the terrace of my Shangri-la, our own recently finished first home in Crans-Montana, I feel the time has come to bring closure to what no longer exists. I close that dark chapter and open the door for a bright future to come in.

———

"Mommy!"

I turn around. My handsome husband, carrying our precious daughter, is walking towards me.

"Mommy, look." Marisol is waving a white Tranquility rose in her tiny hand. "For you."

"How beautiful. Thank you. I bet you found this rose in Omi's garden." She nods and giggles when I tickle her chin.

As always, I feel a sense of awe when I look at my almost three-year-old daughter. Her clear eyes sparkle like sapphires. I press my lips into her soft light-blonde hair. "I love you so much," I say, and kiss her plump caramel-colored cheeks.

"Hey," Alex protests, "I want some of that." He pulls Marisol and me onto his lap.

Nestled between us, Marisol turns her sweet face towards the afternoon sun; her lids are half closed already, and she's sucking her thumb.

For the briefest of moments, I let myself be transported back to a time and a feeling that I believed was lost: the lightness of childhood, with no expectation of a future and no burden of a past.

"A penny for your thoughts." Alex pulls me closer.

I look into his violet-blue eyes. "Guess what? I filled the last pages of my journal."

"Does that mean you're ready for your next step?"

I feel myself blush. "With so much material, I'd like to write a memoir."

Alex nods. "Bringing everything to the light, including all the secrets, will be a symbolic severing of ties." He hugs me more tightly. "I can't wait to read it."

"There's no need; you know the story of my life already."

"Not quite," he says, and kisses my lips. "Every story has a title. I don't know the name of yours."

Never wanting to lose what I feel in this moment, I snuggle deeper into his arms.

"Molly's Milestone."

Made in the USA
Columbia, SC
16 May 2024

ff4feb32-e960-48b5-a121-68234f4b0efaR01